The Moonlight Brigade

Also by Sarah Jane Stratford

The Midnight Guardian

The Moonlight Brigade

A Millennial Novel

SARAH JANE STRATFORD

St. Martin's Griffin ✠ New York

This is a work of fiction. All of the characters, organizations, and events portrayed in this novel are either products of the author's imagination or are used fictitiously.

THE MOONLIGHT BRIGADE. Copyright © 2011 by Sarah Jane Stratford. All rights reserved. Printed in the United States of America. For information, address St. Martin's Press, 175 Fifth Avenue, New York, N.Y. 10010.

www.stmartins.com

Library of Congress Cataloging-in-Publication Data

Stratford, Sarah Jane.
   The moonlight brigade : a millennial novel / Sarah Jane Stratford.—1st ed.
      p. cm.
   ISBN 978-0-312-56014-0
   1. Vampires—Fiction.   I. Title.
   PS3619.T7425M66 2011
   813'.6—dc22

                                                                    2011020411

First Edition: August 2011

10 9 8 7 6 5 4 3 2 1

For Stephen: Fake brother. Real friend.

The Moonlight Brigade

Prologue

Rome. Summer 1941.

I always thought it was easy to outwit fools.

She had long since given up on the idea of anything being easy, but she couldn't help hoping. Hope was all she had, besides determination. And in these grim times, neither was likely to take her very far.

She slipped through the alleys and side streets with a grace that all her former dancing partners would never have recognized. Her black coat and thick-soled boots were meant to make her nearly invisible and inaudible. But of course, to those looking and listening, it was as though she wore cats' bells.

They came upon her as she neared the Via Sacra. They stood before her, nudging each other and smiling, little boys playing a game. She recognized one of them. He'd lived on her street. He had been a fat child, laughed at and left out of games. He used to follow the adolescent girls around in worship, and they laughed at him as well. She never had; she had always politely ignored him. But here he was, taller now and fat still, wearing a black shirt and smirking with delight at his prey.

"It's her, it's her, didn't I tell you?" he crowed to his companion, almost spitting with pleasure.

The thinner, more discerning one studied her.

"A find, indeed, Sandro, if this is who you say."

Giulia gave them a bland smile.

"I'm sure I don't know what you mean. I'm on my way to visit my grandmother. She's been very ill."

Sandro snorted.

"I know you, Giulia Merlino," he said, drawling out the surname with scorn. "I know who and what you are. I remember you before you decided you were too good for us and went to England for education. I know that both your grandmothers are long dead, probably from broken hearts."

"You know nothing of the sort."

Sandro's compatriot broke in.

"Your education was of little use to you, if you thought you would do well to leave England and come home to organize against Il Duce. It is a shame you could not have put your supposed brains to some better use. However, you will be no great loss. A woman as unattractive as you should not be giving the great new empire children. If you still could."

He sneered, hoping to see her blanch or blush, but she paid him no mind.

"Please, gentlemen, let me pass."

"No, I don't think so. Sandro, go and alert the office. Tell them to rouse the best interrogators. One of our most wanted is found."

Sandro was chagrined.

"But, but I was the one who told . . . We will be bringing her in together, won't we?"

"Are you disobeying an order?"

Sandro looked from one to the other, as if for all the world he expected that Giulia might intercede on his behalf. Despite the circumstances, she felt a laugh rise in her abdomen.

The other Blackshirt cleared his throat, and Sandro bowed his head and stumped away.

Giulia slipped her hand inside her pocket, closing her fingers around the smooth little switchblade she'd been so pleased to secure. A pistol would have been better, but they were trickier to come by. She decided that as soon as she was out of this mess, it was a trick she was going to master.

The man smiled at her as he produced a pair of handcuffs, which he twirled with exaggerated insouciance.

"Why do you not try to run, Giulia? Are you too proud to die from a shot in the back?"

She did not answer but simply willed him closer. Something about the turn of his smile, the swagger in his stance, told her that whatever disparaging remarks he might make about her looks, he had it in mind to enjoy her while she was still whole. She was, after all, a find. He moved closer; she could smell the cilantro on his breath.

"Perhaps, even though they say you are so clever, you are a fool after all. Don't you know the streets are not safe for traitors?"

"Yes," she answered, and lashed out with the knife. Her instinct was sure, but she had underestimated his ability, and he caught her wrist, so that she only grazed his shoulder instead of slashing his throat. She cried out then, more in fury than fear, and kicked at him. He dodged her and laughed.

"So, the little rebel likes to play rough, does she? A shame she doesn't know what she's doing. We will be more than happy to teach you."

Then Giulia heard a whisper, a man's voice telling her to "move aside." A voice that burrowed deep inside her and lit a candle. She knew exactly in which direction to move, and she was strangely unsurprised when Sandro's heavy body dropped on her assailant like a bomb, crushing him against the cobblestones.

Sandro's face was frozen in utter terror. He looked like a gruesome mockery of a mask from the Commedia dell'Arte, except for the five puncture wounds that encircled his face. The thin Blackshirt struggled feebly, but most of his bones had been shattered.

"Help. Help me," he begged, through the blood that poured out of his mouth.

Giulia bent to the pile of men, curious. She examined Sandro's neck. There were deep puncture wounds there as well, but no blood poured from them.

"Please," gasped the dying Blackshirt.

Giulia contemplated slashing his throat after all, to put him out of his misery, but decided it wasn't worth cleaning her knife afterward. He would be gone soon enough.

She stood and scanned the roof from which Sandro had been tossed. Nothing. She felt her own blood course with increasing urgency. She replaced the knife in her pocket and, although she wasn't sure why, started to run.

Chapter One

Berlin. April 20, 1941.

The Nazis prided themselves on being boisterous singers, and the show they made of gathering around tables set with the bounty of a Christmas feast, all to sing songs praising their Führer on his birthday, was laughable to anyone who dared to laugh.

The figure of a man lounging outside the house, just out of range of the candlelight, did not laugh, but rather yawned. Every well-appointed house in Berlin was hosting an eerily similar party. The candles in a wooden ring, as if they were at a child's party, the table as heavily laden as rationing would permit, with rabbit, bratwurst, rice porridge, and a plum cake that must have used up a month's sugar ration—it all transcended ridiculous and was instead boring. The toasts, the songs, even the jokes were the same, as though everyone were acting in the same play.

"One that could not be more dull if it were called *Puritans on Parade*," the figure muttered, nudging his brushed wool fedora farther up his forehead to study the faces inside. To a casual passerby, it might be assumed he was a vagrant—until one noticed that his fine tweed overcoat was of a quality rarely seen, even in peacetime. Under the coat, he exuded a strength and swagger that most found intimidating, and others, intriguing. Of the latter, these often ended up finding out more than they wanted to know—and always too late.

Another song honoring Hitler commenced. The unseen watcher rolled his eyes and turned from the window, focusing on his hand. He curled and uncurled his fingers several times, then held them straight and outspread, popping out long, sharp talons from under the nails. They snapped back in place, then shot out again. Several more times they sang out and back, lethal cuckoos in a clock, and their owner smiled down at them with fondness. He might have been a young boy playing with a switchblade, but of course, Mors was no boy. Nor was he young, except at heart. Rather, he was older than anything in Berlin except the dirt. And what he could do with these talons was something few wanted to see.

The song finished, and Mors yawned again, the unnecessary action one of his few sources of amusement. If anything, Germany under the Nazis was even more egotistical and vicious than he had found it when he first arrived in 1938. He and four other British millennial vampires had hoped to bring down the Nazis and thus prevent the war that was now devastating so much of Europe. Berlin, a chilly place in 1938, was now downright icy, even in spring.

The Nazis confounded him, which was a rare feat. He had thought he had seen the basest of humanity before. He'd romped happily through the reigns of Caligula and Nero, after all, and had seized the opportunity to have a drink with Attila the Hun.

Brutal warrior. Wonderful drinking songs, though. Very clever rhymes.

The British vampires had seen ghastly things all throughout their own land, and in their travels had seen even more. Chaos fed the demon inside, but most vampires—especially as they grew older—preferred humans when they were at peace and harmony, pursuing art and invention. Such things fed the human soul and thus sweetened the blood of even the lowest criminal. So it was a blow, after such a lively interval as the 1920s and much of the 1930s, to see the world descend into hell again. And what a hell! The Jews had known plenty of grief, but having survived in Europe through the Middle Ages and to be so seemingly integrated now, well, it was no wonder they little expected such disaster in the age of radio, telephone, film, and short skirts.

"And it's only getting worse. For all except those who deserve it," Mors grumbled, his eyes tinged with red as he glared at the celebrants.

He knew it only too well. He had spent several months scouring Europe, searching for his missing friend Cleland and engaging in any military conflict he could in the hopes of turning the tide. His own successes had been disturbingly few, thanks to the persistence of battles being waged mostly during the day. The Allies' low success rate upset him far more.

Convinced at least that Cleland had not gone back to England or anywhere else on the Continent, Mors had returned to Berlin, full of horrible certainty. He would prefer the novelty of uncertainty. Since he could not allow himself even to contemplate the idea that Cleland was dead, Mors was now almost sure that his friend had been captured and was still being held. He would have to be found. Soon.

Certainty. They had been so full of certainty. When the British vampires arrived soon after Kristallnacht, they were sure they'd be home in a few months at most. After all, they were millennials, more than one thousand years old and thus possessed of immense power. It took special skill and weaponry to kill a millennial. The five of them—Brigit, Cleland, Swefred, Meaghan, and Mors—had the strongest confidence in their intelligence and abilities. Which hadn't been enough against the strength of human will. But time quickly became a gushing wound, spilling out and out and out, and their accomplishments were absorbed in the pool and as good as unnoticed, undone.

Until the end.

They had disabled a hangar of planes and destroyed a bomb-making factory, along with, it was hoped, most of the Nachtspeere, Hitler's special team of vampire hunters. But it did not go as planned. Swefred and Meaghan had sacrificed themselves in an explosion that decimated the Nachtspeere. But that explosion had also separated Cleland from the others. Mors had assured Brigit that Cleland was not dead. Brigit. He had held her, stroked her hair, wiped her eyes. And knew she needed to leave him. Or rather, he needed her to leave him. They were best friends, as close as brother and sister, but his real love for her had burned inside him for centuries. If they were alone together, really alone, it would be too unbearable. Something would break. She needed to go back to England to her partner, Eamon, and Mors needed to search for Cleland alone. He had spent plenty of time alone and had no fear of it.

He feared for Brigit, though, however irrational that was. He was a double millennial, far more powerful even than she. Otonia, older yet and the leader of the British vampire tribunal, had once told him she thought vampires could gift each other some strength under extraordinary circumstances. With nothing else to give Brigit, Mors had kissed her and felt a measure of himself slip out of his body and into hers. It was a little thing, he assured her, and he as good as ordered her to go home, where she would be safe while he carried on the war effort in his own way, heading to Russia. He wondered if she'd believed him, any of it. She knew he was a storyteller, after all.

It had taken more than he could have imagined to leave her sobbing behind him in that dark tunnel while he walked off whistling. Whistling! He wondered if she hated him in that moment.

She might have forgiven him if she'd known the pain he was in, far beyond the love he'd finally confessed. That gift was more costly than anything in Harrods. He'd struggled his way to neutral Sweden to recover himself, which took much, much too long by his standards.

Since he was already bathing in the novelty of guilt, he decided to compound it by confirming her safety, as well as asking if Cleland had come home. He had sent a telegram to Eamon, feeling sure of the moment when Eamon was near the machine Otonia had stolen. He had not been surprised to feel that certainty. Brigit had a powerful connection to Eamon that extended over the waters. Mors had given her something of himself. It was only right that there be some small part of her inside him.

Eamon, he knew, valued his honor. If Mors swore him to secrecy about his true business, he would keep that secret, even if it troubled him. The telegram Mors soon received was terse indeed, the younger vampire's rage showing through the purple lettering. But it told Mors what he needed to know: Brigit was safe, there was no word of Cleland, and Eamon would say nothing to anyone, not even Cleland's beloved partner, Padraic. So there it was.

And here he was, back in the palm of the iron fist that was strangling so much of Europe. The war was going well for Germany, despite not having subdued Britain. The few snatches of Goebbels's birthday speech Mors had managed to hear the night before only confirmed the worst. A revolting speech, adulating Hitler as though he were a god. Mors had seen many Roman emperors proclaimed gods in their day. It rarely went well.

The one piece of grim luck Mors had been allotted since returning to comb Berlin for Cleland was the sight of Nachtspeere. Despite the millennials having incinerated so many of their numbers that August dawn, they were gradually being replenished. Which meant someone, somewhere, thought that vampire hunters were still needed. That was all to the good, even as the thought made his eyes glow that much more red.

Evening parties were still a place where guard was let down, faculties distorted by drink, and hearts swollen with warmth and good feeling. The opportunity was offered to interrogate someone on their way home. So Mors waited, and watched. And at this, the seventh party spied upon this evening, there was a member of the Nachtspeere present.

The Nachtspeere had white-blond hair and the sort of square chin that would shoo him straight into matinee-idol status were his nose not so small. That didn't dissuade one of the young girls from showering him with familiar smiles and overly tinkling laughs and all manner of flirtations so as to make herself look foolish. At last, the hosts, weary of the diversion, suggested to the Nachtspeere that he ought to see the girl home, as she was looking peaked.

"And we're open for business." Mors gloated, cracking his knuckles.

The hosts found the Nachtspeere and girl's coats and hats and wrapped the pair up with a studied efficiency. Mors shook his head. One would have thought every man and woman in Germany had endured efficiency training.

The average wheel cog is not so well oiled.

The tipsy Nachtspeere didn't seem sorry to be leaving and tossed an arm over his sudden companion's shoulder, allowing his hand to brush her breast. The girl giggled nervously.

"Dieter, you embarrass me."

"Shame on you, Dieter, stop embarrassing the young lady," Mors scolded, dropping heavy arms around the couple, who jumped and shrieked. Mors laughed his booming, singsong laugh that kept them from realizing they were being propelled into shadows.

"Were . . . were you at the party?" the girl ventured timorously, although of course she would have noticed him. Although he appeared to be in his early forties, his effortless magnetism—to say nothing of his obvious wealth—would have rendered him the object of all that glad-eyeing, not Dieter.

"Oh, my dear, I have been to all the parties," Mors informed her. "But here's the bastard of the matter. There's one particular guest I'm always trying to find, and he always eludes me, slippery little devil. Then I saw you, Dieter, and I knew you were a fellow who might be able to help. You seem the sort who has access to classified information, if you get me."

A wave of gratification washed over Dieter. The man's voice was so warm, melodious, his accent so educated. It, more than his elegant clothes, bespoke him as the very finest in German society, perhaps the descendant of a titled family. Dieter would be more than happy to tell this man anything, and he desperately hoped he had some useful information. The parade of rewards he would receive in return goose-stepped across his mind.

"I believe you are in the truly secret police, am I right? The branch so special one dares not speak its name?" Mors asked, eyebrow raised.

"Gestapo?" the girl piped up, not wholly willing to be ignored. "That's rather exciting! Have you arrested any Jew dogs?"

Dieter didn't hear a word of her prattle, he was staring at Mors.

"How . . . how did you know?"

Mors raised an eyebrow, then darted his eyes to the all-but-invisible insignia on Dieter's shoulder, nearly buried in the seam. The sign of a fang, with a red slash run through.

"What do you know of him, Dieter? I promise there is much reward for information."

"Which 'him,' sir? There is more than one animal we seek."

The delighted astonishment that rushed through Mors stayed well under the surface of his skin. "Seek!" Then Cleland was indeed at liberty, and he and Mors must have gone in circles searching for each other. The other "animal" could only be Mors himself. He pressed his advantage. The silly lad obviously thought he was a rich man on a private enterprise—the sort who pays bounties for vampires and displays relics of them like bearskins. Mors played it up.

"I am interested in all animals; you must see that."

Dieter grinned and leaned in confidentially.

"There is a Dutch rat, hoarding more rats, attempting to shuffle them out."

Mors kept his eyebrows firmly in place.

"Dutch? You're quite certain?"

"Oh, yes," Dieter gloated. "Thanks to our good work, he's heard of the August Incident—"

Oh, now, really—"the August Incident"? Must they be so prosaic?

"—and we think he's coming to Berlin. If more rats follow, then straight into the cage they go."

Mors was bewildered. A Dutch vampire? Could that perhaps be Cleland in disguise? It was a touch bizarre, but delectable. Cleland must have some plan.

The girl giggled, intruding inappropriately on the important talk of men.

" 'Cage'—you mean Dachau? Why don't you just say so? Serves the stupid Jews right, if they think they can come back in here."

Dieter glared at the girl.

"I think it's time you went home, Maria," he announced in glacial tones.

Maria began to argue, and Mors, irritated, stepped in to silence them. But Maria, having drunk far too much, lashed out at Dieter and knocked Mors's hat off, revealing the whole of his memorable face, including his famously bald head. Dieter exhaled long and low, and Mors could feel the man's skin tingle with chilly anticipation. The new Nachtspeere were taught by the Irish hunters whose skill was renown through the vampire world, and had been made to study history. Few vampires were bigger history than Mors.

Dieter's thought process was far too slow. Mors took hold of the man's right hand as it reached inside his jacket, and instead lifted the stake from its holder himself.

"There is no need for such action, and besides, you must know this little stick is ineffective against the likes of me," Mors scolded, rubbing the stake to dust in his hand. His eyes still on Dieter, he stuck out a foot to trip Maria as she started to run away. She smacked the ground hard; even Dieter could hear her nose break as it hit the stone alley.

"Stop your yowling, you horrid girl," Mors told her, pressing his foot into the back of her neck. She was promptly silent. "Women do tend to overreact, haven't you noticed?" Mors inquired.

"Help, Hegarty!" Dieter screamed. "Nachtspeere, someone, it's—!"

Mors clamped a hand over Dieter's mouth and sat him down, nearly folding the man under him.

"This doesn't have to hurt. I might even let you go—I'm a sweetie like that. Just tell me what I want to know."

Dieter tried to lunge at Mors, growling, *"Blutsauger!"*

"Yes, technically, I am a bloodsucker," Mors agreed. "Although there's rather more to it than that. Oh well, if you won't help . . ."

Dieter squealed and clutched at Mors.

"Wait, wait, no! I can tell you he's nearly here, the Dutch one. We think he'll be searching the tunnels, perhaps near the Stammstrecke route of the U-Bahn. Hegarty and Malone are setting the trap even now. They'll be expecting me!"

That last was a lie, of course, but Mors thought the rest of it well worth investigating. He very much wanted to know who this "Dutch one" was. Mors patted Dieter on the shoulder and stood, knowing full well the Nachtspeere was going to lunge at his neck with a dagger.

"Oh, Dieter, really!" Mors sighed. "Not the quickest study, are you?"

He forced Dieter's hand to drop the dagger and then reach for his pistol, putting a bullet into the prone Maria.

"Very ungentlemanly of you," Mors said, turning the pistol back on Dieter's own head and pulling the trigger. "Some men simply can't take rejection."

Wiping his hands on Dieter's handkerchief, he cataloged the information, his mind already ticking toward the next port of call. A mysterious Dutch vampire, who he hoped was not in fact so mysterious, possibly walking into a trap tonight. A gift for the Führer, indeed.

He had to hurry without appearing to hurry. If a hunter called Hegarty was nearby, caution must be used. Mors was exceedingly fond of the element of surprise.

Mors tossed the handkerchief into a rubbish bin and made his way toward the Stammstrecke line. His fingers were tingling. The smell of impending death was already in the air.

Chapter Two

Berlin. April 20, 1941.

The streets were swollen with drunken revelers making their way home. Mors slipped through the empty spaces in the crowds, impervious to their various noxious odors. They were all so happy, so full of good food and drink, stuffed to bursting with cheer and song and goodwill. Were they other people, in another place, Mors would be tantalized. As it was, German blood had long since ceased to tempt, much less nourish.

The long-memorized map of Berlin unfolded before him, allowing him to concentrate his focus on the clash to come. He hoped he was being followed—he wanted someone to see him in action. He was hungry for a real battle.

Hungry. The hunger inside Mors was a living thing, almost like the demon itself. He had risen from the grave with it, and it was one of several characteristics that had marked him, made him something unique even among the world of the undead from the very start, long before his name and face began to be known. It had taken different directions over the centuries and occasionally seemed to exist quite separately of him. These last months, it had been steadily refining itself, a weapon forging in Hell's own fire. Mors had chosen not to give it a name but allowed it to help him like one of his enhanced senses. It was a friend, helping him regenerate his strength and search for Cleland. A search that, once completed successfully, would result in a new weapon, one that no longer adhered to rules. He wanted a great victory. He was going to have one.

He reached a station on the Stammstrecke line and entered, slithering unnoticed off the platform and burrowing down to the tunnels that ran beside the tracks. His immediate sense was one of disappointment. There was no one, nothing, certainly not Cleland. Mors inhaled to clear his head. He trusted his senses. Something was coming.

He was soon rewarded with a shout, the scuffling sounds of ambushed, confused feet, changing direction and running hard. The tunnel reverberated with the howls and whoops of excited men, thrilling to the chase.

As Mors galloped to catch up to the pursuers, the unexpected sound of crisp little heels, undeniably a lady's, trotting well ahead, swam into his senses and disappeared. A lady's heels, running with a particular, inhuman force. Something was deeply amiss there, but he had now come upon the hunt. He was in time to see a man fling a spiky mace at his prey, which the pursued caught and whirled back at those chasing him. It was only fine reflexes that kept the hunter from losing an eye. The second hunter took advantage of the vampire's pause, putting on a burst of speed, slamming his victim against a wall, and pressing a large brass cross to his bare neck. The vampire thrashed about, his howls echoing up and down the tunnel, which filled with the smell of burning flesh.

"Now, Malone, now!" The hunter demanded.

Malone made no move to assist him. His companion turned and saw Malone's mouth open . . . and blood pour out of it. Malone's body dropped to the floor, and behind him, a flashing grin exploded under the shadow of a fedora. Mors nudged the hat back to the crown of his head so that the hunter could see him wink.

"You!" the man gasped, his eyes brightening. He snatched the cross out of the vampire's smoldering flesh and held it before Mors. The agonized vampire, whom Mors had mechanically registered was indeed not Cleland, collapsed in a heap with a small cry. Mors regarded the bright, bloody cross with some amused disgust.

"Now Hegarty—it is Hegarty, isn't it?"—the man was too stunned to check his affirmative nod—"you must know that's not going to incapacitate me."

"I wouldn't be so sure," Hegarty snarled with a menace Mors found charming. The man knew his stuff, too. A large cross like this, wielded with both faith and menace by a hunter whose calling this was, could hurt even a pre-Christian millennial like Mors. Hurt, but not, as Mors had warned, incapacitate. In no mood to demonstrate as much, Mors seized Hegarty's wrist and twisted his arm aloft so that they could speak face-to-face, despite the man's resistance.

"I will admit, I'm a bit affronted that you would think I could be killed at all, much less by accident, but we'll let that drop. What I particularly want to know is—"

"I'm damned if I'll tell you anything, Mors!" Hegarty cried. Mors adroitly dodged the spit that was hurled at him and contemplated the livid hunter. He had the rich, tangy scent so distinctive to Irish hunters. It aroused Mors's appetite, making him almost dizzy. If the man wouldn't be of use one way, it did not mean he was worthless. Mors's fangs slid out, and he lashed with the speed of an adder, taking a long drink.

"Hm," he remarked, pulling back and rolling the blood around his tongue. "Did you have rabbit for lunch?"

The hunter redoubled his vain attempts to free himself, blood gushing down his neck, soaking the brown shirt that marked him as important, treasured by the Reich, even if he came from elsewhere to do a different sort of job. Mors continued, blithe and unruffled.

"You had it with a Guinness though, didn't you? More than one, I'd warrant. Not wise. It goes much better with a Burgundy, I believe. Ah well."

Not wanting to waste more decent food, he clamped his mouth across the wound and drank deeply. Hegarty's blood tasted vaguely of the power-grabbing drive of the Nazis, but there was no denying he was less revolting and more satisfying than any of them.

Finished, Mors dropped the body and squatted beside the new vampire, who had recovered enough to scrutinize the tunnel floor, as though he had dropped something. The skin where the cross had burned him was blistered and oozing. The sort of wound that would hurt for hours before it began to heal.

"We'll have to get some water on that, and ointment if we can find any. They can help," Mors said by way of greeting. "Here, let me—"

"Where are they?" the vampire demanded in a croak.

"Dead, naturally. I always do these jobs to completion," Mors informed him.

"All . . . everyone?" the vampire seemed disbelieving, his eyes wild, raking the dark tunnel. He put a hand to his injured flesh and snatched it away with a sharp cry. Mors took charge.

"We must get you somewhere more comfortable. Can you stand?"

"Yes, of course. There's nothing wrong with my legs," the vampire grunted, struggling to his feet. Mors could see the effort had cost something and that the vampire was attempting not to sway. He instantly liked this unexpected companion.

"You are of course the Dutch vampire they were tracking. A pleasure to meet you. I am Mors."

The vampire's dark blue eyes focused at last and went round. He was lanky and almost absurdly Aryan with a shock of blond hair and chiseled features. By a human standard, he was perhaps not quite nineteen. Mors suspected he was not particularly old for a vampire, either. Maybe only twice that. But there was a force in him that glowed through his eyes and made Mors smile. The vampire smiled back, pleased despite his pain, revealing blindingly white teeth.

"Mors! Of the British tribunal. The millennial Mors!" he cried in perfect English. "I don't believe it."

"Few do," Mors agreed. "I'm in a state of disbelief myself. The European refugees told us that any vampire who hadn't fallen prey to the Nachtspeere had emigrated. And yet, here are you, deep in enemy territory. I suppose truth is truth to the end of reckoning, hm? Except when it isn't. Not that they lied, of course. There's the news you hear and the news you feel. If only vampires had a proper communications system, hm? Now, come along, let's get to a shelter. I know a decent enough spot quite near here."

The young vampire looked dazed, the usual expression of anyone who had never before heard Mors talk. He followed with no further argument.

They wended their way through the tunnels, Mors quietly hoping there would be no more trouble. He kept up a steady stream of chat as they went, which he would have done in any case. While he was bitterly disappointed to find that the Dutch vampire was not Cleland, he had to admit he was unsurprised. After so many months, he could not really expect to find his friend again so easily. It didn't stop him from being elated to find another vampire.

"Marvelous, of course, that some of you eluded the bastards and survived," Mors continued, relishing this opportunity to speak without riddle for the first time in months. "But a damned shame the Nachtspeere know it. I must say, their breadth of knowledge rather irks me. And their capacity. I suppose that's what comes of roping in Irish to train recruits. Those two went down quickly, though, so perhaps they haven't sent the best and brightest. Ah, here we are!" He led the vampire through a hidden door and into a spare but cozy hideout someone had built off a wine cellar.

"Dug by a connoisseur, I imagine, don't you think? Do sit down."

The vampire sank into a chair, managing a grin.

"I must say, Mors, thus far the stories about you do not exaggerate."

"That's a shame. I want to outsell the Greek myths someday. You'll have to regale me at length, in any case, but before we get any further, you must of course tell me your name."

The vampire grinned again, a habit of a grin, from one who knew he was about to get a response. "My name is Rembrandt."

Mors cocked his eyebrow.

"Fancy yourself a Dutch master, do you?"

"The name existed before the painter; he just made it famous." Rembrandt smiled slyly. "You named yourself for one god, I for another."

Mors laughed. It had been a long while since he had been genuinely amused. He had almost forgotten how good it felt.

"A very good name, indeed. And you wear it well."

He brought Rembrandt a bowl of water and a cloth to dab on his wounds.

"I'll see if there's any blood. This place is a bit lacking."

Mors had made it a point in the last few months not to make anything for himself that might be construed as a home. Instead, he shifted around from nook to nook, tending to his sleeping and grooming needs with the barest of attention before returning to his business. He was not interested in being comfortable.

Neither was he interested in going anywhere near the lair where he and the other British millennials had lived while they tried to carry out their mission against the Nazis. He had not even returned for his own things, but simply gathered new clothes as he needed them. Now that he was back in Berlin, there were plenty of poky underground niches to stow things for a night or two. A vampire moving about on his own had no end of flexibility.

Mors was pleased to find some tea and brewed a pot, wishing he'd thought to save some of Hegarty's blood. At least the tea, though second rate, provided its own comforts.

He handed Rembrandt a white cup festooned with bluebirds and sat down opposite him. The politeness, the ritual, it was all such a dichotomy under the circumstances. A relic from another era. They might have been two gentlemen in one of the more exclusive clubs.

Which, in a way, we are.

A curious silence fell as they regarded each other. At last, Rembrandt burst out, "Is it true, what they say? That an army of millennials came and blew up a thousand Nachtspeere?"

The words were boyish, but the tone was of a creature who knew his own hunger and could channel it. Rembrandt's expression was bright yet serious. He wanted to know the truth.

"How did you hear that?" Mors asked.

"Oh, the occupiers, speaking of a particular pestilence," Rembrandt spoke hastily, uninterested in such details. "'Inhuman rats causing real damage'—you know the sort of talk. It was when they spoke of a great general's unreported assassination and the explosion of a train that I knew it must mean something truly great. The best sort of vampires. I wanted to come here, to be of service if I could."

"Great, yes, but no army. We were merely five millennials. Of course, me being one of them made it more like six, or perhaps ten or twenty," Mors smiled. "It had to be millennial strength against the Nazis, we knew that. We uncovered quite a bit of information to pass to human militaries, who would have done well to use it, and created a certain amount of chaos. Perhaps you heard of two hundred men slaughtered in a theater? And the incineration of the Nachtspeere, yes, that was us. After we had disabled about fifty Luftwaffe planes. We lost . . . two of our number there, though."

He stopped abruptly, but Rembrandt gazed openmouthed, as though Mors were a god.

"How is it you survived?" Mors asked. "We understand the Nacht-speere were busy in Europe some time before official occupation."

Rembrandt's face clouded.

"Yes. Although they were kept from the Netherlands until we fell. Then some of those filthy collaborators decided to work with them. I was already running an underground railroad; I'd helped others escaping Germany and Austria who didn't want to stay in Holland. Now the Dutch vampires were trying to get out as well, and it was harder. There weren't enough boats going to England, or anywhere safe. I tried. I hadn't realized just how effective hunters could be when . . . well, anyway, it got more difficult. I had to help anyone who came to me, of course, but even keeping my strength up was a challenge. One had to be mindful of whom one ate."

Mors nodded, knowing the problem well. That form of resistance was more difficult in the occupied countries than Berlin. With fewer Nazis to choose from, any deaths were immediately noticed, and retribution was harsh. One wanted to avoid eating human resistance fighters or people targeted for persecution. Any patriot wanted to do his or her part to help a nation under siege. But although vampires enjoyed a challenge, the curfews, hunters, and discretion, along with the heavy atmosphere of dread, drained too much joy out of life.

"I was soon the only one left," Rembrandt told him. "It was time to get out, but then I heard about you, so I changed course. I suppose I am too late."

"No. You are not too late," Mors murmured, almost surprising himself. "I think we can work together very well."

As soon as he said it, he remembered that Rembrandt was being tracked by the Nachtspeere. The fact that three of them were dead would not improve matters. But Rembrandt knew the dangers. He was here anyway. If he was not a millennial, he was still a vampire. He could help.

Another brilliant smile tore across Rembrandt's face.

"Consider me your lieutenant in this war. At least until we find your captured friend."

White and blue shards flew through the room and bounced off the walls. Blood-drenched tea dripped from Mors's fist, and larger chunks of china pierced the pale flesh where the cup had sat in his palm. His eyes swelled red, and a vein popped in his forehead.

"Say that again," he barked.

Although stunned and cowed, Rembrandt had presence of mind to know that he was not the target of such fury. He had not expected to be the bearer of news.

"The . . . I heard there was a missing millennial. That is, that female, Apolline, she called herself, from Paris, she told me. It sounded absurd, but if he was injured, then perhaps—"

"What did she . . . Where is she now?" Mors was standing over Rembrandt, fighting to control himself.

Rembrandt's eyes widened.

"You said they were all dead!"

"I beg your pardon?" Mors was baffled.

"In the tunnel, you . . . she and I were running; she's much older and so much faster. It seemed incredible, but you said they were all dead."

Mors realized what Rembrandt had meant, and remembered the sound of heels running ahead of Rembrandt and the hunters. Another vampire. Forgotten in the swirl of events. It said a great deal about her that she had run on rather than try to help Rembrandt. But her character was her own concern. Mors had to speak to her. At once.

She can't have gotten far.

As they retraced their steps in an attempt to pick up the scent, Mors turned the information over in his mind. Much though he was elated to have his theory confirmed—that Cleland had been captured rather than killed—it still made no sense. Not in the human scheme of things, and not by the laws that bound vampires and hunters. But wartime always changed rules. It was a more prolific playwright than Lope de Vega. And the Nazis were their own extraordinary selves, reinventing human laws and twisting them into knots. Mors no longer bothered questioning their behavior, much less presuming it to be anything recognizably human. So Cleland had been badly injured, and they had somehow captured him and continued to hold him. Now he knew.

This is a scenario that can't but end in tears. And a few well-placed rips, too.

The vampires were busy concentrating and spoke little. Mors could feel the discomfort emanating from Rembrandt, as well as a fierce anxiety. He obviously needed to eat and rest but would just as obviously make short work of anyone who suggested as much. Mors's fondness for him grew.

Although Mors did not want to distract either of them, he was curious about Rembrandt. It was, however, considered gravely impolite to ask new vampire acquaintances about their origins. They might offer their tale, or invite you to ask, but these were stories just for the maker and the made and only to be shared should the inclination arise. That Rembrandt operated alone and seemed to have done so for at least a few years suggested that he, like Mors, remained unattached for whatever reason, and certainly separated from his maker. Of course, that was likely where the similarities between them ended. When it came to makers, Mors was wholly unique. A story that was not freely told.

Hours later, they were still searching, and even Mors was exhausted. He was cross at not having gotten a stronger grasp on her scent, and Rembrandt was cross that his own sensors were not yet possessed of the vigor and delicacy required to pick up such a wisp of a trail. It was impossible that nothing should be lingering, that the tunnel should have absorbed it all, but Mors knew only too well that Berlin was the home of the impossible. Hot fury bubbled inside him, and he wanted another cup to smash.

Rembrandt sat down suddenly, startling them both.

"I'm sorry," he stammered. "I guess I'm a bit tired."

Mild guilt swept through Mors, and he nodded. He supposed Fate was having a laugh at him for pushing them both so relentlessly, because as it happened, they were now only a few yards away from the very place he had sworn not to reenter. But it was there, it was safe, and it was comfortable. His body allowed itself a sigh, and he helped Rembrandt up, propping an arm around him.

"Come on, there's a perfect lair right along here. I think there might even be some blood in the icebox."

Turning the corner to the tunnel that led to the millennials' Berlin base made Mors's heart burn. Each step reminded him of the many predawns he'd returned here, hoping that the night's work had been a breakthrough, discovering later that it had not. It was full of memories he had no interest in revisiting. For the barest second, it was this that he thought made his hackles begin to rise. Then he came to the slab that served as the lair's guard. It was ajar.

Not so much that a human eye would notice. Nonetheless, something smelled rotten.

Rembrandt looked uneasy, too, although he was nearly asleep on his feet and no longer able to concentrate. Mors wanted to leave him there to rest a moment, but the younger vampire shook his head and padded after him.

The lair was cold, dark, and musty. The sudden smell of a Nachtspeere flew up Mors's nostrils and made his stomach turn. His talons popped out, and he touched the tip of his tongue to his elongating fangs. More blood was about to be shed, and he hoped it would be in Cleland's bedroom.

Which smelled of nothing but emptiness. Mors walked more silently than a cat toward the smell . . . in his own former room.

He flung the door off its hinges and turned up the oil lamp propped on the wall. Nothing. Then a figure in the bed rolled over and grinned at him lazily. She spoke in a breathy, musical purr.

"Well. You certainly took your time coming to find me."

Chapter Three

It was said of General Vitus Vipsanius that the moment he was born, a thunderstorm commenced—Jupiter himself, celebrating the arrival of the extraordinary man. It was also said that he was born with a fierce glint in his eye and the first sound he emitted was not a cry—but a laugh.

Vitus was the only man who ever laughed when this story was told. Those who knew him were sure it was true.

Though brilliant in the schoolroom, it was Vitus's early prowess with a wooden sword on the training field that began to make him famous among the wealthy and powerful in the republic. He was obviously meant to be a leader of men, on the battlefield and off. Many of the republic's senators, jealous and concerned, prodded their sons to strive harder. But Vitus seemed kissed not only by Jupiter but by Apollo. He was the sun on earth, outshining all who stood near him. Undoubtedly he was destined to be a consul, and perhaps the youngest ever seen. There were those who whispered what a relief it was that Rome had sensibly abolished kings, because if ever a supreme and permanent leader was born, it was Vitus. He could be even greater than a king because he had attributes that were almost more than human.

Even as a youth, however, Vitus extolled the principles of the republic, was a proud republican through and through and determined to be its most loyal defender. He was a high-ranking citizen landowner, yes, but also a rare career soldier. Rather than consul, he became the youngest general the republic had ever known, and not many years passed before he commanded the most elite of the legions. They never lost a battle.

Most generals gave up the hands-on business of fighting, believing that they ought to command from on high. Vitus was of a different mind. He knew he was more valuable in the heart of combat, giving orders while eviscerating the enemy almost single-handedly.

Though impressive, Vitus was not a man deemed strictly handsome. His was instead a face of immense character, although the longer anyone, male or female, looked into his green eyes, the more attractive he became. On the battlefield, however, there was no question of his beauty. He could do things with a sword or a pair of swords that no one had ever seen. They seemed simply to be outgrowths of his hands and flew about in a dizzying, blinding dance. In fact, this was how Vitus thought of them. His weapons were part of himself, so of course they could never be dropped. Neither could he be touched. However thick the fray, Vitus could always see the pockets of space between the bodies and the flying weapons. He slipped into those spaces with the fluidity of a cat, or, as his enemies would have it, a weasel, his very bones seeming to compress. Thus did nothing touch him, nor his horse, which flew like Pegasus under his light touch.

His enemies, though they swore they would stop at nothing to kill him, could not but admire him. It was well known that any man who came near him in battle was a risk taker indeed. Challengers lasted only so long as Vitus wanted the fight to continue. Like any feline playing with prey, he enjoyed the game, but when he was ready to move on, he did just that.

The general did, however, have his own way of acknowledging a valiant foe. There were those men who put up a strong fight, perhaps even almost getting the better of Vitus. In the end, they were always slain, though Vitus made sure to use his quickest, most merciful cut so as to wholly free the soul. He then did something even his own men found disconcerting: He took up the body and dipped his fingers into the man's blood, which he then tasted. No one ever dared ask him about it. The secret truth was that Vitus believed this taste of a vanquished adversary's blood gave him some of the man's strength and further inured him against harm. Later, when the battle was won and all that was left was for the bodies to be collected and funerals held, Vitus always made sure to find this man's body again and leave one of his own coins beside it. The fallen's fellows could place it in his mouth and send him to the ferryman, who would regard his passenger with that much more respect.

Long after a man of his stature and ability would have been expected to at least augment his military career with one in politics, Vitus still commanded his legion and it was still undefeated. At more than forty years of age, he could easily spend most of his time in Rome, reaping riches and gaining power. Vitus deemed such a life dull. As he was stronger and fitter than many of the men half his age and constantly developing new tricks with his sword, he saw no reason to put down his weapons and bid his men good-bye. His beloved family had died of fever, and so his soldiers were his blood. Besides, to his shame and sorrow, the republic was falling plague to civil wars. The very fabric of the society he loved so much was in danger of irreparable damage. He was needed.

Each man in the legion loved him like a father. Indeed, to some, he was the closest thing to a father they had ever known. And they all had a son's fond, foolish wish that he might marry again so that he might be as happy as he so richly deserved. A few remembered his wife, Valeria, and related the stories of how she had ridden beside him on every campaign, her back as straight as any man. She had been mother to the camp, and nurse, tending any soldier who was injured or ill. She had been a kind of older sister to Felicia, daughter of Quintus, the general's trusted aide-de-camp. In the end, it had been Vitus who nursed Valeria, and he had not looked at another woman since her death. There were those who noted that he had chosen to bury her body rather than cremate it, as was the custom. A burial was an old-fashioned rite, something foreigners still did, but Vitus always went his own way. It was seen as a measure of his devotion to her that he did not like the idea of her body being destroyed by fire, turned to ashes. Better to set it gently, lovingly in the earth, let nature tend to it, let Valeria's perfection nourish the flowers that would grow above her. Or so they opined, because Vitus never spoke a word about it.

A woman to match Valeria would be hard to find, but it was a source of some frustration to the men that Vitus did not even bother to try. Nor did he seem at all fussed about it. It was said he never even frequented a brothel or enjoyed the favors of a slave. It wasn't right. And yet, his prowess as a fighter only grew, raining his own unique form of justice down upon the enemy.

An enemy that was increasingly a former ally. The republic was fracturing.

"I cannot understand it, Quintus," Vitus remarked to his aide-de-camp as they oversaw the watering of the horses. "What do these people want, a return to monarchy?"

"Gods forbid," was the fervent answer. Quintus was younger but had a grizzled, careworn appearance that made him seem far older than his leader.

"I hope so," Vitus agreed. "Rome's buildings might be plain, but she is a city that shines from the inside."

"Rome is certainly better to its women than Greece ever was." The men turned, not having heard Felicia approach. She smiled her big, ready smile. "Rome educates its girls, and its matrons enjoy liberty. Would that we were allowed in the Senate—well, that would indeed be something. But perhaps you think I'm being foolish."

This was punctuated by a mischievous grin, as the entire legion knew how clever Felicia was. Army life allowed her even more liberty than a life in Rome would, and this was one of the many reasons she insisted on remaining with her father and the only world she really knew. Vitus returned her grin with interest.

"The first chance I get, Felicia Quintanilla, I shall stand before the Senate and insist they open their ranks to women. And that you be the first female senator. I have some pity for those who come after you, though, as they will have quite a bit to live up to."

"As it ought to be," she rejoined. "It's important to have something for which to strive. Besides, nothing worthwhile is, or ought to be, easily gained."

"Ha!" laughed her father. "Don't say such things to the general, my girl. A man who wins battles with such ease does not want to have to think they may not be worthwhile."

Vitus laughed as well, and the three went on with the business of the fort, but Vitus found his mind turning toward Felicia in a manner wholly unexpected.

Quintus loved his daughter and knew his heart would break were she to leave him, but for her own sake, he fervently wished she would marry and enjoy a quiet life with a man who loved her. He often expressed as much. Felicia always laughed.

"But I have a marvelous, lively life with four thousand men who love me, and you most of all. Why would I ever wish to change it?"

She did not plague her father by adding, "And besides, what man would want to marry me?" She knew he thought her beautiful, and she had no wish to argue.

It was only those who didn't know her who considered the girl ugly. She had a prominent nose and a jagged pink scar on her cheek, thanks to a mule that had spooked and thrown her when she was a child. She was tall and gangly, and despite the tightness of her braids and the liberal application of oil, her wiry hair refused to stay in place. But she had an easy laugh, played and sang beautifully, and was a skilled nurse. Vitus sometimes wondered why none of his men sought to marry her, and he expected they felt awkward, what with her father always present. He said as much to Quintus.

"What man wants his father-in-law always within shouting distance?"

"A man who is worthy of my daughter would have no fear of my proximity," Quintus rejoined.

"Too right!" Vitus laughed. He clapped Quintus on the back and strolled away.

Some weeks after this exchange, the legion was engaged in a brutal battle in Gaul. No one had forgotten its sack of Rome some centuries previous, and Rome was still determined to call this land its own. Vitus found the tribesmen of the country tiresome, though the land was lush. They adored fighting but had no organization, no leadership. Rome was right to try to tame this place and its peoples, but Vitus privately thought the Senate had better plan to base a legion or two there permanently, once that was achieved. The natives were the sort who would always want independence.

The battle was quickly decided, but not without consequence. Vitus went to speak with one injured soldier whose wound was threatening to become gangrenous.

"Bear up, Justus," he told the suffering fellow. "The doctor and Felicia here are taking the finest care of you, and so are your household gods. You're not done spreading the glory of Rome through the barbarian world."

"I know, General. Thank you," the man replied in a gasp, managing a smile.

Vitus gripped his hand and swept from the tent. Felicia followed him, on her way to fetch more water.

"If I may, General, the men always do seem to heal remarkably after you speak with them. It is singular."

"What are you suggesting, Felicia, that I have magical powers? Perhaps I am Apollo in disguise? If that is the case, I really ought to get myself a better chariot."

The girl smiled but refused to laugh.

"Perhaps I only mean that you are a unique leader. And man."

He looked straight into her black eyes. They were dancing. There was something saucy in her smile, and he was so stunned, he couldn't even bring himself to smile back. She was slightly taller than he, but he was too big a man to be bothered by such a trifle. The only thing troubling him was that he'd never noticed those eyes before.

That night, he prayed to Apollo, Hecate, and his own Lares. Valeria was more than ten years dead, but she had been a rare woman whom he loved with all his soul. Was it right, was it dishonorable of him even to consider taking another wife?

He pressed the green head of Hecate, which had been the gift of his mother, against his heart and felt it grow warm under his palm. He looked down at it and swore, just for a moment, that it winked.

Vitus was a man who knew his mind and, although he was meticulous with battle plans, was not one to hesitate when he was sure he was right, which was virtually all of the time. So the next day, as the legion was packing to head back toward Rome, he took Felicia aside.

"It's come to my attention, Felicia, that your father would like to see you married."

Felicia turned white.

"What . . . what do you mean, General?"

"Marriage. You know, the joining of two people and their families and properties. Of course, sometimes there are other benefits."

She managed a wan smile.

"Of course, if my father gave me a direct order for the good of our family name . . ."

"Felicia Quintanilla, bite your tongue! Who in this company gives orders besides me?"

She gaped at him now, perplexed. He grinned.

"But I am aware that there are times when orders are inappropriate. There are favors that must be asked, and one cannot expect a favorable answer, although, of course, one might hope."

Her brows were marching up her forehead, but she said nothing.

"The fact is, Felicia, that I've come, a bit belatedly, to realize that you are a rather remarkable young woman. A bit too young, of course, perhaps young enough to be my daughter, Hecate help me, but if you don't find me wholly repulsive and aged, well, I wonder if you might consider becoming my wife?"

The words and tone were cheerful, casual, confident. But the eyes, his clear green eyes, told a deeper truth. Heart and soul were in those eyes, and a promise that both those things were quite ready to be hers.

She didn't need to tell him that she had fallen in love with him several years ago and thought she would live a life of exquisite pain, being always so close and so far. And she wasn't a woman to try to coax more loving words from him or tease out the courtship so as to capture his heart more fully. She could see what was and had nothing more to wish for. Her own heart was too full to allow her to speak, but she held out a trembling hand. He took it, and each felt that their entire world was suddenly complete.

Left to their own devices, Vitus and Felicia would have held their wedding in the camp, but Quintus and the entire legion, bursting with joy and pride, wanted a proper wedding for their general, and that meant being in Rome. Which they were anxious to reach in any case, because the Senate seemed in dire need of their general's sensible advice. The political situation was becoming more fraught.

"Caesar has formed a triumvirate. It seems they intend to rule like three kings. Even worse, there are apparently those who wish to give him a lifetime dictatorship. What on earth are they thinking?" Vitus glumly reported to Quintus.

"It's the internecine rumblings, sir. They see him as a man who could prevent rebellion and war."

"The Senate need only stand strong and everyone obey the Constitution to achieve the same."

"He's a general and a politician, sir, and people are tense. They feel they need a powerful man at the helm."

"Yes. But surely they know that to cede some values in times of crisis risks the chance they might be gone forever?"

"This is, perhaps, something you might bring before the Senate."

Vitus nodded, turning the argument over in his mind, considering how he would speak. His legion's record stood on its own—more impressive than Caesar's. But that other man came from a better family and had better political connections. Whereas among Vitus's soldiers it was stoutly pronounced that neither attribute made Caesar a better man, it was also understood that may not stand for much in a Rome increasingly fractious. There were other, quieter concerns as well, which Quintus had to whisper to Vitus when he was sure they could not be overheard; it was something he did not want even Felicia to know, although undoubtedly she already did.

"There are rumors, sir, of a sort of witchcraft."

"Witch—!" To Vitus's shock, Quintus slammed his palm over the general's mouth to contain the outburst. Vitus wanted to fling his subordinate from him but controlled himself and acquiesced to whisper, absurd though he found the conversation.

"Since when do modern Romans believe such nonsense?"

"There is proof. Things . . . seen." Quintus's voice dropped to a mortified mutter.

"This is no time for circumspection," Vitus scolded.

"Vampires, sir. They speak of vampires."

Vitus could not contain his laugh.

"Vampires! Those are villains in stories to frighten the children into going to bed without complaint! What rot. I'd sooner believe in succubi. Seems much of men's souls are getting sucked into the ether these days."

"People say the bodies display the signs."

"Then it is a very clever murderer, or a group of assassins. Conspirators, perhaps—now that makes sense. More fear, you see? As I said, clever."

Quintus tried to look convinced. Vitus laid his hand on the younger man's neck and pulled him into a quick embrace, then pushed him back to look into his eyes.

"I have no doubt the gods are testing us, my friend, and I do worry that we are proving ourselves a disappointment. But that only means we must fight harder rather than give in to fear and weakness. And if indeed the gods have sent monsters disguised as humans to walk among us, well, it's said there are those specially trained to hunt and destroy such creatures. Faith. Faith and fortitude—that's all we need. We may fail the gods, but they do not fail us. And we may fail Rome, but it will not fail us."

He fitted his helmet more tightly to his head and returned to the waiting horses. As he mounted—still virtually leaping up onto the animal's back in a manner many younger men had tried and failed to imitate—he turned back to Quintus with a promise in his eye.

"And we will not fail Rome. Not on my watch."

Vitus had stopped many enemies cold, but even he could not stop rumors. The stories were flying in from every direction, each one more fantastical and horrific than the last. Soon each man was assuring the other that entire legions had been eaten by vampires, that Rome was in a state of siege, that the whole world was on the verge of collapse. They began to squabble among themselves as to what to do, where to go. Surely, to continue on this path toward Rome was asking for a violent death.

Exasperated and infuriated with the ceaseless reports brought to him by ever more uneasy officers, Vitus finally spurred his horse up a hill and turned to glare down at his men. The sun formed a great fiery ring around him, and he appeared nearly twice his usual size. Despite the light behind him, they could still see the temper in his eyes.

"Soldiers of Rome! I charge you, all of you, to remember that you are not little children but grown men who have fought hordes of enemies and been victorious, each and every time. Rome needs you now and needs your strength. There is talk, I know, of vampires. My brothers, I do not fear vampires. Rather, I fear the foolishness and weakness of men. It is this that destroys civilizations. The great Roman republic is beginning to crumble, not because of legendary beasts but because of the weakness of men. Rome, which laughed at kings and improved upon the democracy of Athens, could bow again to a king. Is this what you wish to see?"

"No!" came the resounding cry, although the men at the edges of the gathering kept one eye over their shoulders.

"And further, let me ask you this: Have I yet to guide you wrong?"

"No!" The cry was more assured this time.

"Have I ever failed to protect you?"

"No!"

"Do you continue to trust me?"

"Yes!"

"My legion, each of you has been as brother and son to me. Until the day I die . . ."

"May you live forever, General!" came more than a few hearty cries. Vitus laughed and shook his head.

". . . I will serve you as you have served me, and together, we all serve Rome. My legion, put aside childish fears. Think not of bloodsucking creatures of myth, but rather of what comprises your blood. Good, true, Roman stock. The greatest blood the world has ever known. It is powerful, it is hot, and it makes you who you are. Treasure it and use its strength for Rome."

The men cheered, each of them renewing their love for their great general and privately hoping that, should the Senate decide it needed a single man at the helm permanently, they would alight upon him, not that overrated Julius Caesar.

That night, the camp was restless, but the men tried to behave as normal, being determined to make their general proud. Felicia was restless, too, but for different reasons. She had wanted to run to Vitus, throw herself on him, from the moment he turned and looked down on the legion from the hill. She didn't care that they were not yet married. She could not wait another minute.

Quintus saw her slip from her tent and pick her way across to Vitus's tent. He smiled.

"Good for them. Perhaps we'll see some real joy of this night, nine months hence."

Vitus was pacing, trying to calm himself to sleep, calm the hunger for Felicia that had somehow stirred up as he was tamping down fears. The only thing that had stopped him from marching to her tent and seizing her was concern for Quintus's fatherly feelings. It was right that a woman should be a virgin on her wedding day, and Quintus had wanted his daughter's marriage for so long that to strip it of any perfection would be to create a wound that wouldn't heal. No, Vitus loved his loyal aide-de-camp more than he wanted to sate his desire. They would be in Rome soon, he and she would wed, and she would be all the sweeter then.

Yet suddenly, here she was, slipping into his tent. Behaving like a minx but looking like a woman consumed by love. For once, Vitus was without words. They fell on each other in a mad passion, kissing until both their mouths were swollen. They pulled at each other's clothes, heedless of the odd rip, the broach whose pin bent and went flying into a corner. She gasped and groaned at the feel of his calloused hands running up and down her body, stroking her expertly, teasing more warmth from her. She could hardly believe the variety of sensations running through her, the sweet pain and painful sweetness of it all. She climaxed with a guttural cry that made her feel like a beast and only inflamed both of them further. It was already late, yet they continued to make love for hours, unable to bear the separation of their bodies.

They didn't even realize they had collapsed, more unconscious than asleep. Her hair was strewn across the sheets, half in his mouth. His leg was wound around hers, his hand still clutched her breast. Her hand lightly brushed his neck.

It was those fingers, giving one quick squeeze in his flesh, which made him stir again. It was still dark, the lamp beside the bed nearly burned out. He paused. No, it was not the squeeze. It was something else that had awoken him, something speaking to the soldier, calling on his ability to rouse instantly when something was amiss.

Quickly, silently, he reached for the lamp and held it over Felicia.

In the dim light, he could see a figure of a man, bent over her, kissing her neck, a hand covering her face. The man looked up with a smile. His eyes were bright red, and Felicia's warm, wet blood dripped from his fangs.

Chapter Four

Berlin. Early spring 1941.

As Mors and Rembrandt exchanged a glance, the female vampire yawned and stretched, pushing her hair back from her face.

The sort of hair that could frighten the children.

Her hair fell in old-fashioned ringlets that rested on her shoulders and was dyed a platinum blonde that even Jean Harlow would have found too bright. Copper and silver streaks wound through the mass of white gold, creating an effect that almost shimmered. After a few blinks, Mors could see what he was sure many men had seen—it had a curious appeal that gradually became attractive. If it was perhaps a touch too distinctive to keep a vampire completely safe, well, it showed that she enjoyed teasing the boundaries of safety. Mors understood that. He wondered how old she was, and how she had managed to elude the French hunters.

"I must of course get dressed before we speak in earnest," she announced, smiling, her eyes fixed on Mors. She stood up, letting the eiderdown slide off her, utterly unconcerned that she was completely naked. Rembrandt choked and looked away, but Mors's eyes did not even flicker from her pretty, languid face. She had no way of knowing that Mors had other senses capable of assessing her decidedly luscious body. Nor could she know that it would take much more than bare flesh to rattle him or gain an equal, much less upper, hand.

Undaunted, she lazily wrapped the eiderdown around herself like an afterthought. "There is wine in the kitchen and some of your British tea, which I've not touched. But of course, you are both free to remain as you are, if you like."

"No, no," Mors said with grave politeness. "Do please take your time."

Her light laugh followed them into the main room. Mors found himself smiling. He appreciated a professional vixen. He even had to respect her cunning, much though he didn't want to. There was no question but that she had expected they would eventually find her, with no exertion necessary on her part. She had made herself comfortable while waiting for them, not knowing if Rembrandt had survived his ordeal, and found the most perfect spot for such comfort. The millennials hadn't lived there in months, but a frisson of their essence clung to the walls and environs.

It was that essence that was creeping over Mors's skin—ants methodically eating the flesh of a man dipped in honey. Meaghan, Swefred, Cleland, Brigit—he could clutch each of them in his fists, bring them to his mouth, swallow them whole and keep them . . . but they were still gone. He was enveloped in a raw itch. He must move forward.

Action is eloquence. And joy's soul lies in the doing. I will have the whole of joy's soul if I have none of my own. I will have it, and then I will have the full measure of joy as well.

He had been pacing and nearly forgotten Rembrandt, who was hissing at him softly so as not to be overheard. Rembrandt was now fully awake and on edge, ice tingeing his blue eyes.

"Are you all right?" Mors asked.

"Her . . . you need to know . . . she—"

The French vampire sashayed into the room, and Rembrandt's mouth snapped shut. She took the measure of them both before settling herself into a chair. To Mors's satisfaction, she selected the seat that had always been the favorite of Swefred's. Any other, and he might have had to ask her to move.

She twirled a long finger through a ringlet and grinned at the two males. There was such an ease and cheerful impudence about her, Mors felt himself not unpleasantly drawn. Her clothes, like her hair, had the flashiness of a showgirl, and it was plain she wore a corset. He could hardly blame her, as the corset went a long way to putting her ample bosom at its best advantage, and creating a marvelous curve down her torso—just begging to be cupped. Her mouth was wide and sensuous, her huge eyes inviting. Mors saw it without seeming to give her a glance, taking quiet amusement in knowing how much this must pique her. But games were for later; now was the time for work.

"Let's not bother with silly little pleasantries, shall we?" Mors began. "None of us has the time. I am Mors, a millennial of the British tribunal, which I suspect you know something of, and if you have any information about my friend Cleland, please, tell me all of it now so I can better find him."

The vampire blinked, and her lower lip curled in an uncalculated pout, but she recovered with admirable grace.

"Do you always begin acquaintances like this, without even asking a name?"

He could have shouted. It was only the accent under her accent that stopped him. She obviously wanted to command the situation, but Mors knew a weapon when he smelled one and could discern the vague hint of Irish under the Gallic-inflected English. A secret she no doubt intended to keep. If need be, he could yank it out from underneath her.

"My friend Rembrandt tells me your name is Apolline, but I suppose I could have confirmed as much. Unless perhaps he's wrong and you have another name? Something a bit less Continental, maybe?"

Her eyes twitched at the edges. She forced them wider and smiled.

"Apolline is correct. Of course, Rembrandt would have told you everything."

Her blazing smile turned to Rembrandt, who had her fixed in a stony stare.

"Yes." Mors leaned forward, forcing her to turn back to him. "Now then, about my friend?"

His expression wiped the smile off her face, and she answered him plainly.

"I overheard some Nachtspeere speaking of a great undesirable they'd captured. One that could do for them what no one ever expected. And wasn't it funny, that it was he who had hoped to cripple them?"

"And that was all?"

"I was curious, of course, but trying to be careful. We're not all millennials."

Despite the candor in her mien, Mors knew there was something she wasn't telling him. He raised an eyebrow, waiting for her to continue.

"You got closer than that, you—" Rembrandt began, and Apolline barreled on, attempting to drown him out.

"What I told Rembrandt was that they had the vampire here in Berlin and I was trying to get more information. After all, there aren't any other vampires left in Europe, or so I thought, and me being me, I thought perhaps I could, well, shall we say, burrow my way in? Help my fellow creature?"

Mors turned from her would-be winning smile to Rembrandt's flared nostrils and narrowed eyes.

"Help your fellow creature," Rembrandt sneered. "Letting a Nachtspeere—"

"How dare you!" She cried, jumping to her feet. Her skin started to contract as the demon rose. Mors put a hand on her arm, his eyes still on Rembrandt, waiting for more.

The younger vampire hesitated, eyeing her up. The pause allowed her to collect herself. She turned back to Mors, the demon back in place.

"It's not one's favorite solution, of course, but it was the only reason I thought a lone vampire like myself could have even half a chance. So, yes, I played the part of a human prostitute and allowed a Nachtspeere to have his way with me. Under such circumstances, men always say more than they might otherwise."

She tossed her ringlets and treated her audience to a saucy wink. Mors found the performance silly but was entranced with the possibilities. Able to convince a Nachtspeere she was human, willing to sleep with him, using the man's passion against him—she could go far. She could be the key to a locked door.

"He likes you, this Nachtspeere?"

"Traugott? Yes, I think he does, the silly beast," she answered with a sly smile. Mors noticed the Irish accent was coming through more strongly. He suspected she hadn't spoken so much English in a long time, and some old habits died very hard indeed.

"Did he tell you anything else?"

"Only that I was phenomenal." She cut her eyes at Rembrandt as he sputtered, then went on. "And that I was a smart French girl to come to Berlin. Here I would get to witness wonders like nothing seen on this earth, if I cared to become his friend."

"There are certainly more things in heaven and earth than are dreamt of in the Nazi philosophy." Mors snorted. His mind was spinning ahead. He would have to make sure of her first. She was not a vampire who inspired confidence, even without Rembrandt's animosity. If it was true, however, that this Nachtspeere was entranced by her, then she might be able to coerce him into spilling more secrets. The trick was earning her loyalty. Unlike Rembrandt, who he knew without question was a fine partner in this battle, this gorgeous vampire seemed too selfish, as well as thrilled by the danger of consorting with the enemy, to be wholly reliable. She would require some effort on his part.

"You are indeed a clever and lucky beauty to have secured such a friend." Mors complimented her in his most lilting tones. "And I need hardly tell you the sort of friend I could be, were you willing to accept my friendship."

Were she human, she would have caught her breath. As it was, her lips parted and her fingers clutched at her skirts. Mors could feel her body warming to him. The prospect of being his partner—and much more—was an apple ripe for sinking teeth.

"I would be honored to be your friend, Mors, and do all that is in my power to assist in this war. After all, I want to see my Paris belong to the French again!"

She held out her hand and he took it.

"Of course you do," he said with a smile, giving her hand a squeeze. A sort of chirp escaped her before she could control it, and Mors was pleased Rembrandt didn't laugh.

"Well," she said, recovering herself. "This has been a stimulating conversation. You gentlemen won't mind if I retire to the bath, will you?"

It was an invitation, not a question. Her attempt to see him cede some control. A game. Mors only winked at her.

"Yes, dear, you go and get yourself nice and clean. You'll sleep better."

She hesitated, then nodded at them both and wafted off to the bathroom. In a few moments, they heard running water. Rembrandt leaned forward and spoke to Mors in a harsh whisper.

"It wasn't like that! I met her near Potsdam, she was fraught, said she'd heard of me, was looking for me, knew the Nachtspeere were closing in and was desperate to escape. Well, she was convincing and I was glad to have the company of a stronger vampire, truth be told. We bunked for the day, and when I woke up, she was gone. I'm not so good with individual scents yet, or maybe there's something odd about hers. But after two nights of not finding her, I thought I'd better just get on. Then I got to Berlin and came upon her. . . . She was with that Nachtspeere, and they didn't see me, but Mors, she was playing no game, I swear. She was enjoying it! His face was buried in her neck, and she was in ecstasy. She may have been playing a whore but not a prostitute."

"I see your concern," Mors said, also seeing the picture of the ecstasy. "And that explains why there's a stink of Nachtspeere in here. But you can't have been too troubled, or you wouldn't have been trying to help her when I found you."

Rembrandt's mouth dropped open.

"Help her? Help her! I was chasing her! I'd waited till long after they were done and he was gone and then I confronted her, and she started playing that game she tried with you and then she laughed and said, 'Good luck finding out more,' and took off running, and I went after her. And then those Irish hunters started chasing me and I yelled but she screamed and ran faster. And then you know the rest."

Mors opened a bottle of wine and took a long drink. Apolline had asked Rembrandt for help, offered help of her own, then left him to his fate. An act bereft of honor and one that she had yet to even acknowledge, much less issue an apology for. However, she had to be brought under his leadership before he could upbraid her.

"Yes. I do see," he told Rembrandt at last. "But this is war. We can't choose all our allies. We must make compromises. Let me help her remember her true loyalties, discover if she is at heart trustworthy, although cowardly. You need not forgive her, of course, but she can help me tremendously, and I must have that help. Now, don't fret." He held up a hand, seeing Rembrandt about to argue. "I'm hardly going to set her loose to do as she will without keeping an eye on her. Not that she'll know, of course."

Rembrandt looked somewhat mollified, though still displeased. "Won't she smell you, if you're spying on her?"

"When you get to be my age, you have ways of controlling your scent." Mors grinned. "It's not easy but it can be done."

"You're joking," Rembrandt accused, though he couldn't hide his fascination.

"Often, but not now. It's quite complex. In any case, she's not more than a centennial, and her own abilities are only just refining—"

They heard the whoosh of bathwater as the drain was pulled. Mors imagined her patting herself dry. Some of her abilities were highly refined indeed. For the first time in months, he felt a twinge of desire, something so different from how he felt about Brigit. That was its own animal. But this, this could be something else again. He wanted to be purely cynical and businesslike, thinking of it as a means of binding her to him, discovering via her passions where her truest loyalties lay. He knew there was more to it than that.

"We ought to get some sleep," he told Rembrandt. "There is more ahead than even we know."

That day, he slept alone, in Cleland's bedroom. Until he was sure of her, he would not allow himself such pleasure. Not in proximity to beds last slept in by Meaghan, Swefred, and Cleland.

The first order of business was to find a new lair. That accomplished, Rembrandt went off to hunt, Apolline to find her Nachtspeere, and Mors, after a short interval, tailed Apolline.

The Nachtspeere was found near Tiergarten. On seeing her, his face lit up so it was almost as bright as her hair. He spoke a quick word to the men he was with and hurried to meet her, leaving the men nudging one another and winking.

"*Ma cherie* Apolline!" he cried, embracing her. "How did you know to find me here, clever girl?"

The man's French was flawless. He was far more handsome and urbane than Mors expected, with a breezy confidence and a careless, crooked smile that, if he didn't know better, Mors would swear had been copied from his own self.

Except that mine isn't an affectation.

"It wasn't easy, Traugott." Apolline teased him. "I have been searching far too long and am quite exhausted."

"What a shame. We shall have to get you a drink and perhaps a bit of a lie-down?"

A girlish giggle rewarded this suggestion, and the two strolled off arm in arm, Mors at a short distance behind. For all his charms and the high rank denoted by his uniform, Traugott could not rate much as a Nachtspeere, not if he believed the female on his arm was a woman—nor if he failed to sense a millennial vampire following him and memorizing him down to the last hair on his head.

At a modest apartment block, Traugott invited Apolline inside. Mors scampered up the wall. It took all his concentration to sense where they might be. He willed Traugott to crack open the window, it being a warm night, and the Nachtspeere unknowingly obliged. Through the slats of the shutters, Mors could see that Traugott had removed his pistol and was opening a bottle of whiskey.

"Mm, you do treat me well," Apolline said, sipping her drink.

"I'm only just beginning," Traugott promised.

"And this is you when you're distracted by the war," she praised him.

"Why distracted? The war is going very, very well. Perhaps a few minor annoyances here and there, but nothing worth a fuss." He had pulled off her dress and was slowly unlacing her corset.

"Does that mean that secret plan you mentioned is working?"

His hands, stroking her breasts, paused.

"Now darling, I told you, it's very naughty to keep asking me about that."

"Well, I'm afraid I can be naughty. Perhaps you'll have to punish me," she told him with a roguish chuckle.

"Mm, perhaps I shall," Traugott murmured, nibbling her thigh.

She helped him off with his undershirt and ran a finger down his chest.

"Just tell me this, at least. Does it involve power?"

He slid off her chemise and rolled on top of her.

"My girl, I am part of an alliance that will give me—us—power like no man has ever known. But it's delicate. Just like you."

"But darling—"

"Ah, no. No more talking."

And there was no more talking. Or not the sort Mors had any interest in hearing. He worked his way down the wall, satisfied at least that Apolline was doing as she'd been asked. She certainly didn't seem to mind, either. Mors was amused, and approved.

This was the way of war. One should be prudent, yes, but not a puritan. Not if it interfered with progress.

She did not return to the lair until late the next night. Mors couldn't blame her, as the place they had found was hardly suited to modern living, even for a vampire. It felt like an ancient encampment, down to the dirt floor. This pleased Mors. It reminded him of his days as a general.

The blast of war is blowing in my ears, and battles must be planned.

He was sketching a map of Berlin in the dirt, considering all the likely places for bunkers. It would be one of these, something richly fortified, where they would be holding Cleland. The "alliance" Traugott had spoken of, if it was real, must be with someone in the inner echelons of the party. Mors theorized they were trying to brainwash Cleland and thus use him as a weapon of their own. He grimaced as he made his tracings. They would have their work cut out for them there.

On hearing her light tread, Mors automatically wiped the floor clean with his foot and laid his hands behind his head, as though he had been resting after a busy night.

"Good evening," she murmured in that voice that was so oddly breathy for one who didn't need to breathe.

"Welcome back," Mors answered with a warm smile. "Were you able to discover anything?"

"Only that he says there's some sort of alliance and it's a great secret but will give him and all involved a lot of power. At first, I thought he was the leader, but now it sounds as though there is at least one above him, perhaps more than that. It is difficult to say, what with getting only bits at a time."

She looked frustrated and exhausted. Mors stood up so she could have the chair, and he sat on the bed.

"You stayed the whole day, too. How did you manage?"

"I didn't realize how late it was; I had to play it very carefully, staying. The great good luck is that his flat is his own, so there was no one to come in. We made a game of it, playing house. He had sausages in the larder, so I made him a lovely meal. Then I spent the rest of the day alone in the bath. I suppose I ought to be hungry myself, but really I'm just tired."

Mors believed her, even before she turned large, almost sorrowful eyes up to him. Her old Irish accent was coming through ever more strongly and sounded something close to sweet. She was tired but could wake up quickly. He grasped her plump hand and pulled her to him.

If her mouth was not as perfect as Brigit's, she was still delicious, and Mors allowed himself to fall down this particular rabbit hole with all the delight he'd anticipated. It had been a long, long time. His mind wanted to pretend she was Brigit; his body didn't care. She was such an odd creature, clinging to her *fin de siècle* hairstyle, engaging in nonvampiric ways.

"I was a nude in the Folies Bergère," she whispered as her chemise fell to the floor, "until just a few weeks ago." Mors was not surprised. A mad thing, to insert herself so prominently in the human world, but of course she had done it. Whether she was wild, foolhardy, or a child run amok, she was something to enjoy. Not love, perhaps, but a sweet bath just the same.

Her body was extraordinary. Her curves were the sort seen only in the comic books not easily bought. Her skin was tangy under his palm, his tongue, and was the funny lukewarm of a vampire that could, when expertly handled, grow hotter. And as Apolline came to discover to her absolute delight, Mors was quite the expert.

Somewhere along the journey, he whispered into her hair: "Tell me your Irish name."

With a mind so deranged by pleasure, a body so possessed, she murmured back without hesitation: "Deirdre."

Deirdre. Yes. The daughter of sorrows. A vampire name worth keeping.

He ran a finger under her lower lip.

"It's perfect. Will you let me call you that, my dear?"

This was complex territory. A vampire's name was a sacred thing, not to be questioned. Mors didn't know why he suddenly felt so strongly on the subject. He knew, however, that he was right. The room was dark, so he could only vaguely see her eyes seem to unfocus before they smiled at him. She pulled him closer and kissed him—a kiss that was full of true affection, not desire. Now he understood. He had defined her to herself for the first time in decades. She may not have liked having come from Ireland, but she liked the name itself. It was nice to hear it again, spoken by one who had the tricks to tease it out of her and thus earn the right to use it.

No, she was not Brigit. But she had her own charms, and he availed himself of them for hours more.

Despite their new understanding, Mors spied on several more of Deirdre's meetings with Traugott. He thought if he heard the man's words and tone himself, he might get something more from them. Everything that she reported was, however, proving accurate, and so Mors began to use what threads there were to search likely places for Cleland's prison.

"If Cleland's a millennial, though, how can they hold him?" Rembrandt asked. He had taken apart a wireless and was rebuilding it to his own specifications as Mors made a list of the places he had examined.

"My assumption is that he was terribly injured, and it's possible to maintain such an injury. I have seen it done before," Mors spoke with flat bitterness. "And the Nachtspeere have been well advised."

"I don't understand. I thought they were supposed to be top-notch, but this Traugott, he must know Deirdre's a vampire, how can he not? That hair alone!"

Mors had not intended for Rembrandt to start calling her Deirdre, but as soon as Rembrandt had heard Mors do so, he seized on it. Like Mors, it was a name he felt suited her far more than Apolline. Unlike Mors, he was delighted at an opportunity to provoke her. Mors knew he ought to at least suggest Rembrandt desist, but since Deirdre seemed determined not to let her ruffles show and Rembrandt had by no means forgiven her for leaving him to his fate with the Irish hunters, Mors kept his counsel. He was too old to moderate squabbles and had other things on his mind.

"Traugott knows she was a French showgirl. Exoticism is to be expected. She dazzles him. Besides, how much do human men ever know of women's beauty secrets?"

Rembrandt made a sound very like a snort and shook his head. Then his face lit up.

"There we are!"

The clipped tones of a BBC reporter came through over the wireless, just as clear as Cleland or Swefred had ever been able to tune them.

"Rembrandt! Aren't you a genius?" Mors congratulated him. Rembrandt ducked his head and grinned. They listened to the rest of the broadcast in silence. Some news brought nods and smiles, like British bombardments in Germany and a strong counteroffensive in Egypt. Other news brought mashed lips and shaking heads—more bombing of London and sinking of British ships.

Too soon there was nothing more to report, and other home news was discussed. Rembrandt started to turn the dial, but Mors stopped him, wanting to hear more British voices. Wanting more than that. Possessed of teammates again, he now wanted something like an army. The vision of himself driving a tank straight through the Reich Chancellery burst into his brain. The tank would be attacked long before he got there, of course, blown up, and he with it, but it was a gorgeous thought.

If I could soften up the city first, or had enough auxiliary forces . . . There is a way. There is always a way. I was a leader of men before, so why couldn't I be so again?

Mors patted the wireless approvingly then put on his hat and jacket, gesturing to Rembrandt not to join him. He knew Rembrandt wanted to continue scanning the waves, to see if perhaps the Dutch partisans were able to broadcast any news.

Crowds were spilling out of a nearby cinema, with cliques of young girls chattering happily, but Mors was still hearing the pleasing tones of his own British in his head. He made his way to the Wilhelmstrasse and strolled it methodically, all his senses working overtime to feel whatever there was to be felt. Most of the government was housed here; this was the heart of power. It was the most reasonable place for the Nachtspeere to hold Cleland.

Or so Mors had thought, but once again, he walked all the way up to the Brandenburg Gate and felt nothing. He absentmindedly turned onto the Unter den Linden and joined those promenading the grand street. The wartime blackout did not faze them, and in fact, they hardly seemed to notice it. They were far more happily engaged in flaunting their joy in being the wealthiest and most powerful Germans, who would soon rule the world.

Not if I have anything to do with it.

The thought had no sooner finished when a scent struck him—a punch in the solar plexus. It was faint, but it was a scent he'd know anywhere. Cleland.

A cry escaped him and he began to run, but the scent was gone as quickly as it had appeared. He spun on the spot, his eyes raking everything, everyone, searching. He ran several steps in each direction, but there was nothing. It was as though it hadn't existed.

Fury contorted Mors's features, the demon inside overcoming his control for the first time in decades. Worse, Mors's first instinct was not to fight it but rather to let it run free, terrorizing the crowd. He was just master enough of himself to pull his hat low, stagger blindly to a bench, and collapse on it, burying his vampiric face in his hands.

There was a couple on the bench, and their chat instantly silenced as Mors flung himself beside them. He could feel them looking at him, the woman especially. At last she asked, her voice full of warm concern, "Are you all right, sir?"

Mors kept his eyes screwed shut, lest any red glow between his fingers.

His fangs dug into the flesh behind his lip. "Yes, thank you," he answered, not trusting himself to say more. She smelled sweet.

He knew her hand was reaching for his arm and was relieved when the man with her grunted, took hold of her elbow, and propelled her off. Mors took a breath through his warm palms, the otherwise unneeded oxygen serving to clear his head, and his complete mastery returned. The demon slipped back down inside. He took his handkerchief, wiped his face, and then leaned back on the bench, assuming the air of a man enjoying the night while his thoughts galloped madly.

Cleland! After so many months, even the hint of him was a joy and a relief—but how was it that the scent had appeared and then vanished without trace? Mors remembered what he had told Rembrandt, that there were ways of controlling one's scent, but Mors was certain it could not be turned on and off like a switch. Or if it could, did that mean his horrible hypothesis was right, and that Cleland had been brainwashed and was now being used to draw Mors into a similar trap? That was possible, which meant Mors would have to tread carefully in order to circumvent danger and help Cleland. Faint though the odor had been, however, Mors was doubtful he would not have at least seen his friend. The science of vampire odor was complex indeed, but under such circumstances, and without the full force of his feelers, he should not have gotten a scent without also getting a sight.

There was another possibility, one that he was steadfastly ignoring even as it tapped at his conscience with merciless rhythm. It spoke in Cleland's own voice, saying what Cleland had told him so many, many years ago. That there were indeed such things as phantom scents, and that Cleland had often smelled his dead partner, Raleigh, for many years after that vampire was murdered by Irish hunters.

By the time Mors had settled his thoughts enough so he was able to move, the street was empty. He hadn't even noticed. He was hungry but did not want to search for a meal—not tonight. He could take care of that tomorrow, along with a great many other things.

The next night's meal was perfunctory and forgettable, a replenishment solely to maximize his powers. He made his way to the nearest dark corner from the spot where he had smelled Cleland, and closed his eyes.

All vampires found whatever they might seek via scent, but each had their own unique method. Some were innate, some were learned. Mors's own abilities, honed, expanded, and refined over the centuries, were marvelously potent. He had an array of senses that existed almost separately of himself and the demon. Smell and touch collided and wound together, but there was also a deep intuition that sang through them. Under his bidding, they became individual creatures and wafted out away from him, seeking prey, yes, but they could look for so much more. They knew the openness of his mind, the expanse of his curiosity. They knew he liked anything interesting—anything that furthered his knowledge or experience. They were always eager to please.

The seconds ticked by remorselessly, but Mors was not worried. He knew there was something to find. Whether it was a phantom, a lure, or truth, it would be found and followed.

It struck. His senses lassoed the scent and pulled Mors along, almost in a trance. Down the Unter den Linden, slipping in and out between people, on and on till he turned onto the Bebelplatz. He crossed the square and stopped, right in front of Saint Hedwig's Cathedral.

As Mors collected himself, he realized that the scent, which had been getting stronger, had vanished again. Or perhaps morphed. There was definitely something here he was supposed to know. He scanned the parishioners leaving the church after evening mass. Then he pivoted and focused, as though looking down the barrel of a gun, straight at a man. A bishop.

The bishop's voice was rather too loud and ebullient as he talked to the provost, who did a masterful job of hiding his distaste. The bishop kept calling the priest "Lichtenberg," a familiarity—and insult—that even Mors found appalling. He could feel hostility oozing from under the man's cheerful façade, marking him as an enemy. An enemy not only to Mors but also to the clergy of Saint Hedwig's, and perhaps more. Why that should be so, Mors could not fathom, but it was clear that Father Lichtenberg regarded the buoyant man with suspicion. At last, the provost said, "Forgive me, Bishop Oster, but I must speak to Herr Kappel about his wish to establish a family pew." And he bowed himself away.

Oster did not look the least put out. Instead, he folded his hands and contemplated the lovely old cathedral before him with a benign smile. Mors edged closer, studying the man. Then he noticed Father Lichtenberg talking to a young curate whose mistrustful glance kept falling on the bishop. Mors's eyes met the curate's, who paled and turned away. Mors warmed to the curate, marking him as someone he should get to know, after he had spoken to the bishop.

"Good evening, Your Grace," Mors greeted him politely.

"Good evening." Oster smiled, taking in Mors's impressive appearance. "I do hope you're one of our congregants."

"I dare say I ought to be, but I'm afraid I'm one of those who prefers the sight of a church from the outside." Mors laughed deprecatingly. Oster joined him, his hearty laugh managing to sound more reproachful than an actual reprimand.

The bishop was a tall man with a barrel chest that might once have been impressive. His magnificent vestments could not conceal a plump, sagging belly, though Mors sensed Oster was vain enough to wear some sort of girdle to try to improve his physique. His doughy face was overly smooth and clear, with a pink complexion, large round chin, and droopy eyes. The face of a childlike clown. Mors longed to paint a red oval around the generous lips. From under his miter, tufts of gray-gold hair poked out, free from the oil that failed to slick them down and only enhancing the clown-like effect. Mors knew better, however, than to consider the man any sort of joke. The Roman Catholics were a minority in Germany, yet this man oozed power and ambition. Even if Mors hadn't marked him as dangerous, the loathing emanating from the curate even while chatting with parishioners told him nearly all he needed to know.

Nearly.

Although it was a subject to which Mors had paid scant attention, he'd heard enough to know that the Catholic Church—indeed, all the Christian churches—were on uneasy ground in Germany. The Nazis liked them for their organizing ability but had ordered them to speak nothing of politics, unless they spoke in the party's favor. There was trouble otherwise. Mors had a feeling he knew just what kind of trouble that was.

Oster, however, was a man completely at ease and oppressively confident.

"You are just the sort of citizen I was hoping to know better when I came to Berlin," Oster gushed on merrily. "And of course, please know you are always welcome to come and call upon me. No need to be intimidated by all of this," he finished, with a grand gesture at his impeccable vestments.

"Thank you," Mors answered. The man's unctuous smile was starting to make him feel ill.

"And do please join us for services. You needn't worry about the mass being overly traditional, or not when I say it, that is. Which is not as often as I'd like, as I was just explaining to dear Lichtenberg, who works far, far too hard. I'm a rather modern man, sir, very forward-thinking in my views and philosophies."

Mors did not need his sense or his senses to tell him that there was something deeply sinister about the bishop's meaning. Over the bishop's shoulder, he saw the curate glaring at Oster's back. Mors met the curate's eyes again. The curate flushed and ducked back inside the cathedral. Mors raised his hat to Oster and bade him a good night.

He felt the man's probing smile follow him all the way back across the square.

No need to memorize me, he wanted to assure Oster. *You'll see me again* very *soon.*

Chapter Five

Vitus swept his sword from under his pillow and made to slice off the vampire's head in one stroke, but the creature was too swift for him. It cackled, seized the barely conscious Felicia, and ran straight through the tent's canvas wall, leaving a hole edged in blood. Vitus snatched his tunic and tore after them, even though the vampire's speed was so much greater than his own. Fury drove him, pushing him past his own capacity. He knew from the stories that the vampire would have to stop if it wanted to continue feeding, and that's when he would vanquish it. He shut his mind to every other possibility.

They were sprawled under an elm tree, the creature lying on top of Felicia, his hips moving rhythmically against hers as though he were ravishing as well as destroying her.

"Get off her!" Vitus bellowed, the sound echoing off the surrounding trees and rocks. He plunged at the vampire, even in his horror and despair having the skill to avoid striking Felicia. He aimed for the flank, wanting to look this bit of the underworld in the eyes before he sent it back to where it belonged. Blood flowed from the wound, but not much. The vampire growled and looked up at Vitus. In the moonlight, the creature's glowing red eyes and distorted features were hypnotic in their repulsiveness, and Vitus thought he might vomit.

"Get up and fight, you coward!" Vitus ordered. "Or do you only attack helpless women while they sleep? Certainly, no woman awake would be seduced by the likes of you."

The vampire coolly rose and assessed Vitus. Its face slid silently, effortlessly, back into human form. Despite himself, Vitus was fascinated. There was no sign of the monster that lay below the smooth, olive-toned skin and placid brown eyes. The hair fell in boyish golden brown curls over a high brow. A smile spread across the face, gentle and shy. The vampire was suddenly a Greek youth, and an attractive one as well. Knowing that the pretend youth had used that smile to seduce and kill hundreds or perhaps thousands of women, Vitus was filled with even more venom. He swung the sword again, using a stroke that had never failed, but the vampire ducked it with ease.

"If you think Xenon can be killed by the likes of you, even of you, General Vitus Vipsanius, you are a great fool," the vampire taunted, his features growing monstrous again.

"So you know me?"

"Your name is famous. Not as much as Julius Caesar, but then, he is a better general."

The vampire clearly intended to goad Vitus, but he had misread the man.

"That would be the rumor, yes. Now, you have a choice, beast. Fight me or run away and never return."

Xenon let forth a high-pitched giggle, and Vitus swung again, this time managing to slice through the creature's bicep almost to the bone before the vampire swirled away from him. Its disgusting giggle morphed into a groan of pain that Vitus found intensely satisfying. Xenon leaped for him, and Vitus danced away, parrying with his innate grace and long-honed skill. He needed this to be quick—he did not for a second forget that Felicia was in desperate need of help—but he knew the vampire would not readily relinquish his prey. It must be killed; there was no other option.

The injury did not stop Xenon from attacking Vitus with the force of twenty men, and the one small pleasure Vitus could achieve in what swiftly became a brutalizing fight was the unmistakable sign that Xenon was shocked at the strength and ability of his antagonist. This was a man who remained standing and fighting many minutes after he should have been dead. It was enough to make even a vampire wonder if some of the most fantastical stories about the general were true.

"Getting tired, vampire?" Vitus taunted, dancing furiously. In the years of battle, he had learned to control his breathing, letting it work for him so that he did not succumb to panting. He knew it was baffling and infuriating the vampire, and he wanted more of it.

Xenon lunged at Vitus, all ten claws outstretched. They were like the claws of a lion and difficult to avoid. They slashed Vitus's chest, and a hissing sting went through him. He kept his composure only by the most arduous effort. For a moment, he futilely longed for a second sword or even a dagger. That one extra blade would be such a blessing. The wish was gone as quickly as it had arisen. He had weapons the vampire did not.

"The stories say vampires move with the speed of light, that no human can withstand them," Vitus observed. "I think we're proving that's quite a lot of rubbish, aren't we? Or are you the shame of your brethren? The runt of the litter? They usually drown runts, you know, but perhaps someone was disposed to be kind toward you. Or just wanted a good laugh."

It was working. Xenon grew more incensed, and his fighting became less focused and more flailing. Vitus stabbed and Xenon moved just enough to avoid the blade's piercing his heart. It did, however, run through a rib, and the vampire wailed.

"Never fought a true Roman before, have you, vampire?" Vitus inquired savagely, twisting the sword as he pulled it from Xenon's chest, loving the feel of more bone and flesh being sliced and splintered. "Perhaps you want a bit of what I've got? Who could blame you? But it's something one must be born with, and you, foul thing, were clearly born to a deformed rat."

Vitus was having a difficult time hiding his exhaustion. Xenon, his face etched in rage and a peculiar shame, saw the sudden advantage and leaped, sinking his fangs into the general's jugular. The man did not even scream. Xenon sucked harder, the richness of the blood making him loosen his hold so that Vitus could force his sword in and up. It went straight through the long-useless kidney and out Xenon's back.

Xenon pulled himself off Vitus with a howl that made leaves fall off their branches. He stumbled, fell backward, and curled into a ball, pressing his tunic against the congealing blood.

Ignoring the blood gushing down his neck, Vitus crawled over to the vampire. The death he knew was coming fast would not prevent him from claiming victory. He dug his fingers into the still-open wound in the moaning vampire's back and scooped out a dollop of the creature's cool blood, which he then swallowed.

The vampire, feeling Vitus behind him, turned over and slammed the general into the dirt. He had recovered enough to smile.

"You may have fought well, Vitus Vipsanius, but I still got the best of you in the end. I always do."

"No," Vitus corrected the vampire. "You've killed me, but that doesn't mean you've got the best of me. Not even close."

Men's shouts were heard in the distance. Xenon glanced in their direction. Then his gaze fell upon the general's bloody fingers. The expression of worried bafflement that spread across his monstrous face made Vitus laugh weakly.

Xenon hardly seemed to notice.

"What . . . did you . . . ?"

More shouts, gaining ground. The vampire hesitated, then gave Vitus a hard kick, shattering several ribs, and tore off into the night.

Even had the men been closer, it was still too late, and Vitus knew it. Each movement cost him effort he hadn't known possible as he crawled over to Felicia, pulling himself over her so that he could look into her eyes. There was still a minute glimmer of light in them, though her face was ghostly white.

"Felicia, my own girl, I am so, so sorry. Forgive me."

She could no longer speak, but her hand, tucked in his, squeezed very slightly, telling him it was not his fault and there was nothing to forgive.

He couldn't hold his head up anymore. It dropped of its own accord beside her, fortuitously allowing him to whisper that she might hear it.

"I love you."

Again, the infinitesimal squeeze.

Even the gods did not know which of them died first.

The bodies were just starting to cool when Quintus and the small band of officers found them at last. Quintus fell to his knees by the bodies and wept. The other officers said nothing, merely removed their helmets and used them to do as they knew their beloved general would have wished— dig a grave big enough for two.

They finished as the sky was turning purple. Quintus placed a coin in each mouth and directed that the bodies be laid to rest exactly as they had been found, for this was how they were meant to go forward into the Fields, bound to each other.

"Wait," he implored as the men began to shovel dirt over the two people he loved more than any others on earth. He just wanted to look one more time. Finally, he turned away; he knew that if he looked any longer he would never be able to allow them to be covered.

It wasn't until the ad hoc funeral was finished that the men were at last able to talk about the nature of the deaths. There was no mistaking the wounds in the neck of each lover, and only a fool would suggest it was the work of a known animal. Their general, who had been wrong about nothing, was at the last fatally wrong about one thing. Vampires did indeed stroll among them and were hungry for good blood.

"How on earth could the beast have gotten in the tent, though?" wondered Caius Dominito, the camp prefect. "They have to be invited."

Quintus sighed.

"The general always said his tent was a public space, welcome to any who wished to visit him."

A long dispute then followed as to what to report to the legion. Caius Dominito thought it wisest to say the deaths were the work of assassins sent from Gaul or Germany, something the men would believe and help them to focus their anger more healthfully. Quintus argued that Vitus would have railed against such slander, that the truth was the only option. Another officer suggested that the truth would stoke more fear, and another wondered if they should blame Caesar, whose rise Vitus had wished to see thwarted.

They were still unresolved when they returned to the camp, but the legion was in such disarray, it hardly mattered. Rumors had spread like plague, and everyone already believed their own version of the calamity. It was a day of horror, lamentation, and unheard-of infighting. All exhortations that they should at least be on the move, get away from this cursed spot, could not be heard in the din, even though every last man was indeed determined to escape, to save his own skin if nothing else. Yet no one was able to stir.

With each passing hour, Quintus grew more uneasy. There was something else in the air, something besides the despair and his overwhelming sorrow. There had been a moment, before the bodies were buried, when he touched Vitus's face and thought it felt like something more than a death mask. As if there were something hot growing under the cold skin, something indefinable. He was sure he had imagined it. Vitus had been possessed of an indomitable life force that seemed impossible to annihilate, so of course it must still be there, somewhere. And yet, even as Quintus tried to reason and remonstrate with the men, he found his mind wandering to the fingers that had touched that skin. They tingled in a manner that disquieted him.

As the sun began to set, the squalls only grew louder. Vitus would have been aghast to see the legion he had nurtured with such care reduced to this. Quintus wondered if the unrest wasn't due to something beyond them. They all understood the trickeries and treacheries of men and could stand against them with honor. But when the enemy was something far less certain, something unknown, they collapsed within themselves. Confronted with what their erstwhile leader had called a children's horror story, they became children. It didn't matter that they had not been told the truth. They were convinced of it anyway. Watching this dissolution, Quintus realized that Vitus would not have stood a chance with the Senate. Fear, at its most base and irrational, was a greater power than reason. Rome was going to collapse in upon itself and eventually turn to a single leader to reign over it with a firm hand. The republic would sink like the sun, and it wouldn't rise again. For one heartbreaking moment, Quintus was glad Vitus was gone.

It was while Quintus was struggling with these miserable thoughts that the body of Vitus began to stir inside its grave. The fingers curled in the dirt, shifting it. Then the hands crept upward, pushing, clawing, digging. A slow, arduous, mindless upward thrust. A body acting on feral instinct. Swimming in dirt. Forcing the earth to churn, to give way to this foreign thing inside it. At last, the hands broke through to the surface and could begin to pull, to allow the legs to kick even harder, the torso to twist until the head was free, and the rest quickly followed.

He leaped to his feet and turned, searching for someone he was sure was supposed to be there. They weren't. Perhaps he was supposed to be somewhere else? Something was not what it ought to be.

His body surprised him by taking a breath. As he expelled the air, bewilderment blew away. He was exhilarated to be alone. It wasn't how it ought to be for others, possibly, but it was exactly right for him.

Strings of memory came flooding back into him as he surveyed himself. The same strong, capable hands, only now imbued with an untold power. He laid his hands on his head, the hair still thin and balding but not unattractive for it. His face, his shoulders, his arms, all were the same. And yet different. So very, very different. He chuckled and liked the sound.

His neck. He touched it gingerly. Nothing. Not even a scab. Then he remembered. He pushed aside the churned-up dirt and looked at Felicia's cold, white body. Ugly black holes gaped in her neck. He half expected to be sorry, then realized he didn't care. There was no love left in him, no beating heart in this creature he'd become. What pulsed instead was something else, something bigger, something that threatened to burst from his skin. A demon, vibrant and alive. It embraced him. And it was hungry. So, so hungry. It filled him with a blazing energy that felt like a battle cry. It was time for food. It was time for fun.

The legion was awash in bitterness and disorder, with the officers unable to gain control. It was all a storm of pure chaos.

Hands on his hips, the new vampire appraised the scene. What Vitus would have found appalling was now delightful. This demon, so giant, so powerful, so completely in control, gave him new eyes, eyes that saw the humans as nothing but food and playthings. If there was a human memory of the love once borne them, it was as buried as his body had been some hours before. A memory that stayed underground. The demon was in charge now.

He skipped down the hill, seized the soldier nearest him, and pulled him just out of sight. The man began to scream and was silenced with a gentle pinch of the demon's newly strong fingers. There was time enough for screams.

What a wonderful sensation it was, these fangs sliding out from what had been human teeth. The face shifting and changing, becoming something so wholly else. When he sank those splendid fangs into the man's neck and drank, he knew bliss. Vitus had been right. Good Roman blood was something special.

Sated, he pitched the body aside and descended into the melee. He had been able to break a man's neck with his bare hands as a human, but now it took much less exertion. He had claws now, he discovered to his joy, and when they extended, they were like ten delightful daggers that obeyed him even more perfectly than a sword.

"How handy," he murmured, laughing.

He jerked his face back to its human self and smiled, interested to see what would happen as men took notice of his presence.

"The general!"

"Is it the general?"

"He's survived; he's come back!"

"General!"

Their hope was a sweet, funny little thing. And so he laughed again.

Quintus heard the laugh and approached with trepidation. He wanted it to be true, wanted to trick himself into believing the best, although he knew the worst.

"Oh, my gods and my ancestors, let me be dreaming. Let this all have been a strange and horrible dream," he whispered, even as he reached for a slim stick in the pile of firewood. He hardly knew why he did so. In fact, he hardly knew he did it.

The specter of Vitus continued to laugh, and the soldiers around him laughed, too, laughed at themselves, at the stupid joke they had let themselves become, all because they thought the world they knew was ending.

And then it did.

He did not yet know how to slow the change, tease it out, but this hardly mattered. They were so unwilling to believe it, it was only when men started falling around them that they had to acknowledge it was so: The man they loved so well was gone, and a grotesque discharged from Hades had been allowed to occupy his shell. It was an insult, it was an outrage, it was an impossibility—and yet, it was.

Some of them leaped on him in a vain attempt to quell the monster, and when the others saw what became of these brave men, they ran. What officers had hoped to achieve through the whole of the day was realized at last: The men were leaving. Or trying to. In the intensity of the chaos, the new vampire shed more and more blood.

"Vitus!" Quintus's cry was much more bold than anything the vampire might have supposed. He could only hear it because his hearing, too, had expanded in capacity and selectiveness. He did not yet know that the refined hearing he had had to nurture as a soldier, so as to hear his own men above the cries of the enemy, now made his vampiric hearing far more sensitive than that of vampires several centuries older than himself. He turned and smiled to see the saddened, grizzled, determined man running toward him.

"What are you fighting for, Quintus?" he inquired. "What reason do you have for life now?"

The man did not answer. He was preserving his energy. He wielded a sword, and the vampire was impressed with the aide-de-camp's prowess. He fought him casually, the gentle swats of a cat nowhere near ready to kill the mouse.

Quintus was snaking backward—an odd dance that intrigued his adversary, as it was so different from that the general had taught his men. It was only when the cries behind him dimmed that he saw what Quintus had intended—the creation of a berth to let the remaining men escape.

The vampire roared with laughter, acknowledging himself impressed.

"What a marvelous trick, you old beggar! Well done, indeed. But mark me, I won't be tricked twice."

"No," Quintus grunted. "You'll be ended."

He lunged with all his might, brandishing the stick rather than the sword and aiming for the heart, as his vague memory of his grandmother's story dictated. But the shell of his former friend was too quick for him, catching the stick and crumbling it to dust.

"What on earth did you think that would do?" he asked in naked wonder. Quintus didn't answer. He wasn't surprised that Vitus, who paid so little heed to the legend of vampires, had forgotten this detail of how to kill them. Even as a child, Vitus thought like a soldier. When he was old enough to put aside wooden swords, he had done so without looking back. Blades were all that interested him when it came to dealing death.

"I am sorry, Vitus," Quintus said, swinging his sword, which was readily ducked.

"No need," came the reply as Quintus's wrist was caught and squeezed just enough so that the sword dropped. "But I don't believe that is my name any longer."

Quintus was nothing to him, and this demon was devoid of mercy. However, something in the vampire still retained respect for a good fighter. It was this respect that made him painlessly snap Quintus's neck before the man even realized the hand had been laid on him. His body was hoisted over the vampire's shoulder and carried back to the grave where Felicia lay. Her father was tossed in on top of her and the dirt kicked over them, a cold laugh their last prayer.

The vampire smiled into the sky, giving the fading moon a wink. Once again, he ran his hands over his head. Then he flicked out his talons, using them as razors to shave his head until it gleamed white and silky as the moon itself.

"What a lovely night," the vampire proclaimed.

It was only then that he became aware of something hot in his chest. *That can't be right.*

He grinned, realizing what it was, and reached down for the green head of Hecate that lay against his tunic, ready to commune with her more closely than ever before. To his shock, the head scorched his palm, and he yelped, dropping it. He stared at the red and oozing blisters, perplexed and even fascinated, despite the pain. He hadn't noticed the head had burned a hole in his tunic and blackened the skin beneath. He plucked the head from the ground by its leather string and studied it. It was now gangrene-black, and the benign smile of the goddess had morphed into a forbidding scowl. The vampire laughed and skipped to the creek, into which he consigned the head.

"Then fare thee well, Hecate. But don't think you can keep me from my path, my dear."

As the ripples from the sinking head subsided, the vampire found himself an empty cave, perfect for bedding down. He tucked his knees under his chin and looked out from his safe spot at the predawn land.

"Enjoy the day, world. I'll be back tomorrow night. And for my name, well, whatever Hecate may think, I am plainly possessed of the powers of a god. And what other god could I be but the god of death? Who am I, if not Mors?"

He hugged himself in delight and settled down to sleep.

Chapter Six

Berlin. Late spring 1941.

Saint Hedwig's Cathedral was a beautiful building, neoclassical and topped with a dome. Mors liked this. What he didn't like was that it was a church.

"Can't millennials go inside churches?" Rembrandt asked. Mors had brought him along to point out Bishop Oster, their enemy, and the curate, a possible ally. One whom Mors thought Rembrandt could safely tail to discover a safe place where Mors might meet him.

"I believe so, but it's not pleasant. Or so I may have heard," Mors answered, studying the church.

"But you can! Really? What happens?"

Mors had no answer. Churches and crosses were mysteries, and whereas Otonia adored mysteries, Mors scorned them, except when they worked in his favor, like his special rapport with dogs. Whenever he had come upon the other vampires discussing churches, he found something else to do. It was enough to know they were places he had no business. He respected the faith of the humans, when it was true, and saw no reason to disrupt it.

"I would think as a pre-Christian vampire, it wouldn't affect you at all," Rembrandt pressed.

Otonia's favorite mystery. There seemed no reason why a cross or church should repel a pre-Christian vampire, since they had no effect upon those who had been Jewish. But repel they did.

"Yes," Mors grumbled. "That's a bit more—" He broke off. The curate had come out of the church, chatting to another young priest. Both carried a stack of books.

"That's the curate," Mors said, pointing.

A chill swept through him, and he smiled. Both vampires turned at the sound of a roaring laugh.

"And that's the bishop," Rembrandt said in a low voice.

Mors nodded to him, and Rembrandt slipped away after the curate while Mors tagged after Oster, who was walking with two men in crisp suits.

"Yes, yes, I do see your point. I shall be sure to take it up with Herr Himmler when next we meet," Oster assured the men with honey-toned condescension.

So, you're friends with Himmler, are you?

Mors had caught only a few chance words from Oster's conversations since their meeting. He wanted to glean more of the man before confronting him again. Thus far, he had learned that Oster never walked anywhere alone and commanded a great deal of respect. A friendship with Himmler would explain some of that. There would be those who assumed that if they couldn't petition the government themselves, perhaps they could at least gain the ear of their churchman, whose job it was to listen to them. And although Mors had not yet proved it, he suspected that they thought they had a good chance with Oster, less because of his friends than that he was happy to take any variety of incentives they might be willing to offer. It was no wonder the more honorable men of the church despised him.

Such business drew Mors's scorn, but it was not his concern. Although he had not caught the scent of Cleland in more than a week, he was still certain that Oster had something to do with his friend.

And I had damn well better find out what that is soon.

Oster bade his companions good-bye and sailed inside the church. The square was quiet. Mors strode toward the church as though he were approaching prey, exuding the whole of his charm. Only now, he was being sincere.

He brushed the door with the backs of his fingers. A tingle ran up his arm. He set his whole hand on the door. The same tingle, what he supposed it felt like when your hand had gone to sleep and was now awakening. Nothing he couldn't manage. Emboldened, Mors prepared to enter.

To his great surprise, the door opened from under his hand and Oster himself poked his head out, as though searching for someone. A smile overspread his face on seeing Mors.

"Sir! What a pleasure, what a pleasure. Were you coming in at last? Do, please, please. Is it absolution you need, or were you just interested in seeing the nave?"

"Yes," said Mors. "I'd very much like to see the nave. In fact, I was wondering if it was possible to get a tour? I have read the cathedral offers many charms."

"Ah, and you are a man who appreciates architecture, I remember. May I ask your name?"

"Von Mohren," Mors answered, knowing the honorific would curry even more favor.

He was not wrong. Oster's face turned pinker yet and he pumped Mors's hand several times, the massive pectoral cross on his chest bouncing up and down. Mors instinctively leaned back.

"Well, Herr von Mohren, do come inside," Oster invited, standing aside to let Mors go in first.

"Please, Your Grace, after you," Mors insisted. He didn't know what it would be like to walk on those pins and needles and didn't want Oster to see his body making the necessary adjustments.

Oster laughed again and started inside with a shrug. Mors took two steps after him, hardly aware of what he was feeling, when he heard a shout from outside.

"Do hold the door, please!"

Mors automatically caught the door and politely stepped back to allow the supplicant in. Their eyes met. It was Traugott.

Although Mors was not easily shocked, he felt himself close to reeling.

He started to look for Deirdre but controlled the impulse. He had no scent of her. The mad thought struck him that Traugott was coming to confess his sins with Deirdre. Mors bit the inside of his cheek to keep from laughing.

Oster clapped his hands together and rubbed them in delight as he bustled up to Traugott.

"There you are, Traugott, there you are. I had thought for a moment you had forgotten we were meeting here."

"No, no, only I was delayed," Traugott apologized, then looked at Mors, who nodded to him.

"Herr von Mohren, will you forgive me?" Oster begged in treacly tones. "Now that my guest is here I cannot give you a proper tour of the cathedral, but you should feel free to examine the nave on your own."

What Mors wanted to do was listen in on the meeting between Oster and Traugott, but he knew he couldn't. He knew, because in standing aside to let Traugott in, he had ended up straddling the threshold. The foot that was inside was aching and almost frozen. It was all he could do not to stamp on it. He had no sense that Traugott knew what he was— unsurprising, from a man who didn't recognize Deirdre as a vampire— but he could not betray physical awkwardness inside a church. Not in front of a Nachtspeere, however poor that Nachtspeere was.

"Another time, I think." Mors smiled at Oster. "I should be getting on."

"Oh, and I was so looking forward to getting to know you." Oster sighed, his face falling.

"Let us meet again very soon," Mors suggested, hoping Oster would not reach for an appointment book. He was longing to get away.

"A capital idea!" Oster cried, clapping his hands. "I am always available."

Mors tipped his hat to the men and stepped out, deliberately shutting the door behind him so that they could not see he was limping.

His foot recovered quickly, and he sped for the lair, his mind in a whirl. Of course Oster and Traugott were working together! He could not begin to comprehend it, but that hardly mattered. He wondered which of them was the master of the other, and how deep their mutual trust went.

Rembrandt was in the lair, sitting at a table laden with tools and machinery, his face shining.

"What a brilliant night I've had! The curate is called Father Ambros and is often found in the central library. And look! I've got us a recording machine! I'll have to do some tinkering so we can use it from distances, but—"

"Oster and Traugott are in league together."

Rembrandt dropped his screwdriver. Mors nodded and sat across from him.

"Do you think Deirdre knows?" Rembrandt asked at last.

"I'll have to warn her," Mors answered, ignoring the accusing tone in Rembrandt's voice. It was easy for Rembrandt to continue mistrusting Deirdre, who was never friendly to him, but Mors was concerned. It was already dangerous enough to be in Berlin. Mors felt a pang of guilt as he looked at Rembrandt, whom the Nachtspeere must still be hunting. He ought to be giving this vampire more protection, even though Rembrandt didn't want it.

We'll put the pieces together, rescue Cleland, and get the hell out of here. All of us. Alive.

When Deirdre came in, she reeked of a meal. Mors casually asked if she'd seen Traugott that night, and she said no, he'd had work to do.

"Did he say what?"

"No, but I'm sure he'll soon trust me enough with those details."

She was blithely confident and even giddy. It was the effect of having recently fed. It made her cheeks pink. There was still blood on her slightly parted lips. Mors pulled her into his bedroom and licked it off.

It was raining the day Mors visited the library, but he took no chances and entered it from the subbasement. Mors and Rembrandt had combined their exertions to find out as much as they could about the place and Father Ambros's work there. So Mors was prepared for the chill. The librarians wore heavy cardigans under their jackets.

He walked briskly to the floor where scholars did their research and inquired after the priest. He was directed to room seven.

The hall where the private study rooms were was even colder than the rest of the library, and Mors wondered how anyone got any work done. He rapped on the door. Presently, the priest answered. He was wearing a thick muffler over his vestments. His interrogative frown at being interrupted promptly paled when he saw the face of his interloper.

"Dreadfully sorry to trouble you, Father Ambros. May I come in?" Mors whispered.

The priest nodded politely enough, though his face was unhappy.

"There is no more coffee," he told Mors, and the regret in his tone was obviously more for himself than his unwanted guest.

"That is a shame, but perhaps you will have a sip of brandy?" Mors offered, pulling a flask from his coat. The priest's eyes lit up, and Mors poured him a generous serving. After a few sips, the priest smiled and his color improved.

"Very nice, I thank you, Herr . . . ?"

"Von Mohren, but you needn't use the 'von'."

Ambros nodded, waiting for his visitor to begin.

"Father, you are not surprised to see me. I think you already know we have a natural alliance. We both have, shall we say, a distaste for Bishop Oster."

The priest's eyes raked Mors's face for a long moment.

"I think perhaps I should have to thank you for the brandy and ask—"

"I know you know I am honest," Mors told him gently. "It's plain the bishop is not a man to be trusted, any more than any other member of this damnable Reich. I have unique abilities to work against him, but I must have more information."

Ambros licked his lips. He reached into his coat and withdrew a tiny Bible, beautifully bound and embossed. He held it before Mors.

"Swear on this that you are as honest as you claim."

All the skin on the back of Mors's neck crinkled. He had no idea if this was something he could do. The strength of the priest's faith was formidable and true. Mors respected it.

"I suppose even this is no real test," Ambros acknowledged, misreading Mors's hesitation. "Those who do not fear for their immortal souls can make any oath they wish. But at least I will have the satisfaction later of knowing those souls are truly damned."

Mors was grateful he had not removed his gloves. He trusted that whatever it was that might imbue the book with the power to repel him knew that he came in peace. With great solemnity, he laid his hand on the Bible.

The heat that ran up his arm was much less than he expected. His expression did not change as he kept his eyes drilled on those of the priest.

"I swear, by all that we both hold dearest and deem holy, that I am a true enemy of this Reich and have devoted the whole of my power to defeat it."

Ambros nodded and kissed the book, then tucked it back in his pocket. Wisps of smoke were rising from Mors's glove. He crammed his hand under his coat and leaned toward the priest.

"Father, I know the bishop is closely bound with the party, and I have reason to suspect he may have business yet more untoward, but I need your help if I'm to proceed against him. What can you tell me?"

Ambros took a sip of brandy. Mors continued.

"I know the church was forced to enter an agreement with the Nazis, that it would not be political," he told him. "I also know there is trouble for those who disobey."

"That's not stopping some of us," Ambros snapped, his eyes bright with sudden fury. "It might not have come to this if—"

His voice caught. He could not have been more than twenty-seven, but there were lines around his eyes and a hint of gray under his skin. Mors finished the sentence.

". . . if some in the church did not adhere to elements of this new ideology."

"They are not true Christians," Ambros insisted.

"No," Mors agreed. "It is no great secret that the Nazis have little love for the church. It seems more than likely that, should they quell all their enemies in battle, they will then remake the church in their own name."

Ambros's jaw dropped.

"So you know of that plan?" he gasped.

I do now.

"There is yet more to it, isn't there?" Mors pressed. "Something even less Christian?"

"What do you mean?" The priest looked confused.

"Oster has strange friends. They are working together in some capacity."

Ambros's brow darkened.

"We know he is good friends with Himmler, and we think—"

"'We?'" Mors interrupted.

"A large number of us hold fast to the true church and are attempting to fight its desecration, along with that of the spirit of humanity," Ambros announced with angry pride. "*We* suspect Oster is to be leader of this new . . . well, I suppose they will call it some sort of church. But we have no proof. And we must move with great care, as you surely understand."

Mors did.

"Father, I have reason to believe that Oster and his friends think there is another weapon they could use that would help them not only take over the church, but . . ."

He paused. He still had no idea what the plans were for Cleland.

"My point is that I can give you very valuable assistance, if perhaps you can let me into the bishop's house," Mors finished, thinking it unwise to give more detail.

Ambros frowned and rolled his silver pen back and forth across the table.

"I'm not sure how that's possible. I'm never asked there myself. And if it's a criminal act you are planning to commit, I certainly cannot—"

"Father, please do not mistake me. I have powerful contacts, friends among the Allies. Were I to obtain proof of the extent of the evil being undertaken here, it would be used well."

Mors almost wished he could tell this kind man the truth. He looked so troubled.

"Perhaps, Father, you can tell me what sort of work Oster does at the cathedral? He has an office?"

"Only Father Lichtenberg has a private office. Oster has pointed out that as bishop, it should be his, but he has also insisted no one need rush to accommodate him. So we haven't."

Mors grinned, then searched for the words to pose a delicate question.

"And there is no possibility he could conduct further business anywhere else in the church?"

"What on earth do you mean?" Ambros asked sharply. Mors hesitated, then decided to backtrack. He had to suggest something the priest would not like.

"Father Ambros, I am sure this has already occurred to you, but you must try to watch Oster when he is in Saint Hedwig's and when he thinks you are not."

The priest's mouth dropped open, but Mors was not done.

"Furthermore, any papers or books he has there must be examined."

Ambros leaped to his feet.

"I am sorry, but I must ask you to leave."

"Father, please. I know I sound like an enemy agent, but I swear, I am not. I am not asking you to sin; I am saying that this is what we must do in order to trap him. I will give you information as I receive it as well."

Ambros sat down and took another long drink of brandy. Mors grasped the man's hand and looked into his eyes. He was not trying to hypnotize him. He was sure that Ambros would see the honesty there and at least consider the suggestions.

After a long moment, Ambros looked away, his eyes full of misery.

"The party gave Father Lichtenberg a warning after he prayed openly for the Jews. That was when Oster was sent to be part of Saint Hedwig's. It could not have been clearer. He is keeping a sharp eye upon us all as he does . . . whatever he does." Ambros's expression slowly morphed to one of grim determination. "So perhaps it is only right we begin to keep an eye on him."

"Which, of course, he would never suspect," Mors pointed out. Their eyes met again and they both smiled. "More the fool, he."

As Mors devised strategies and he and Rembrandt threw themselves into plans for discovering the truth of Oster's business, Deirdre began to complain of her situation.

"I'd rather spend more time with you than Traugott. Can't we do things, go out on the town, have some fun?"

"This is war, Deirdre, there is no time for fun. Do you know how much time I've lost already?"

"How can you even be so sure Traugott has something to do with Cleland?" She crossed her arms and glowered at him. Mors swallowed the temptation to smack her.

"Deirdre, I'm sure, and that's all you need to know. You have done very well, and I believe we are on the verge of success. It only takes a bit more finesse, so you mustn't lose heart now." He felt as though he were speaking to a child.

"Can't I help the two of you, at least for a few nights? I'm longing for a change!"

Rembrandt glared at her.

"If you need a change, why don't you go on a holiday?" he snapped. "Get some sun."

Deirdre charged at him, and Mors caught her.

"Stop that! We're all a bit tired and on edge, and since I have the most reason to be upset and yet am managing to control myself, I'd thank you both to do the same. Now, Deirdre . . ." She squirmed in his grip and he took a firmer hold of her and forced her to look in his eyes. "I meant what I said. You have done well. All I am asking is that you continue with it as I undertake my own operation. Which is a two-vampire job only. Is that understood?"

Her eyes bore into him . . . and changed. The change was nothing like the pink haze before the red that all their eyes underwent upon shifting from human to vampiric faces as the demon rose—"the rose of the rise," Mors had once dubbed it. This was more like a kaleidoscope, as though her irises had broken into pieces and danced around the pupil in a game of musical chairs before settling into new stations. Mors blinked and it was gone, an illusion. Except that he knew it wasn't. He felt slightly ill.

She looked remorseful and pressed up against him with a placating smile.

"I'm sorry," she said in her sweetest purr. "Will you forgive me?"

She wasn't performing; this act was just who she was. Strange creature. He patted her cheek.

"When the war's won, we will all have a holiday," he promised.

He knew exactly where Cleland would want to go first.

When they next met, Father Ambros told Mors where Bishop Oster lived and confirmed that a man answering Traugott's description had been seen with him more than once. He had never seen a woman with them.

Mors told the priest that Traugott was part of a special cadre of the SS and, although Mors did not know the details, believed himself to be on the brink of immense power.

"It is something to do with the occult," Mors ventured. He was thrilled at Ambros's nod.

"Some of the Nazis are interested in that sort of thing," the priest conceded. "They took the Holy Lance from Vienna, you know, after the Anschluss. It's rumored that he who possesses it will rule the world."

"If that's true, wouldn't the whole world be eating Wiener schnitzel?"

Ambros laughed, and Mors went on.

"You haven't seen or heard anything of that nature from Oster, though?" Mors asked.

"I haven't, no. But a deep trespass like that would see him defrocked," Ambros said, his eyes bright. "I have been spying as you suggested, Herr Mohren, but the bishop is careful. In fact, he has been spending less time at the church of late, which everyone prefers."

"Hm. Well, I shall see what more I can discover. I hardly need tell you that if you see that Traugott again, you should avoid attracting his notice."

"Of course. Do please take care, good brother."

"You never need to worry for me," Mors promised.

It did not take long for Mors to discover when Oster was planning to have a meeting at his house, one that Traugott was due to attend. He and Rembrandt undertook a few reconnaissance missions to the house. This meeting was going to be recorded.

"They may talk in code anyway," Mors told Rembrandt. "I learned that back when I had access to military meetings. Most provoking. Still, we should be able to decipher it."

"You don't suppose Cleland is in his house?" Rembrandt wondered.

"No, Oster wouldn't have such compromising evidence under his own roof."

Neither of them mentioned that such evidence could quickly be destroyed, leaving only dust. Mors continued, speaking as much to himself as to Rembrandt.

"And he can't undertake such business at the church, although I suspect he's tried. Father Lichtenberg is too present, and keeps the others present, too. Unless Oster succeeds in supplanting him, he must tread with some care at Saint Hedwig's. At this point, my guess is that he's holding Cleland in an underground bank vault, something even a millennial could not escape. Oster is friends with the new owners of several banks. We'll find the right one and break in. That would be a heist to make Dillinger look like a schoolboy shoplifter."

Rembrandt grinned, his eyes ablaze with anticipation. Mors smiled back. Such an activity would allow Rembrandt to use all his immense tinkering skills as he likely never had before.

I should be careful—don't want him trying to lift the Crown Jewels as a lark.

The problem, of course, was getting inside Oster's house. Otonia would have been impressed with the research Mors had undertaken. The bishop did not own the house; he was only allowed residence there by the diocese. This pushed it close to being a public building.

But is it close enough?

Mors suddenly burst out laughing.

"Of course! I've been able to get in this whole time. That fool said I was always welcome to come and call upon him. That invitation could not be more clear if it was engraved."

Rembrandt laughed, too, and shook his head.

"What a silly idiot that man is."

They were ready and wended their way to the bishop's house at dusk. Mors lay near the cellar door, waiting for the right moment to attempt entering.

Rembrandt's low whistle, exactly like a nightingale's, sounded. A cluster of guests was arriving, creating a great deal of noise. Mors jimmied open the cellar doors and slithered inside.

The only light was that coming in from the doors, which would last until Rembrandt closed them and took his place by the rubbish bins, at which point he would turn on the recorder. Mors blinked, allowing his eyes to adjust to the darkness. His other senses reached out and into the house, feeling the rooms, finding the inhabitants.

They were in the sitting room, engaging in the typical mindless chat that only lasted till the first drinks settled before the business of the evening began. The kitchen above Mors was silent.

The door to the kitchen swung open without complaint. This room, too, was dark, except for a friendly light from the old-fashioned range. Suddenly, the smell of Cleland hit Mors hard, and he doubled over. The thought that he'd been wrong and that Cleland *was* in this house filled him with a wild joy. But then his senses sifted through the odor, and he realized it was not complete. Some small remnant, or shadow, but not the vampire himself. Something that made Mors recoil. He forced it from his consciousness—he could not have such ruses disturbing him now—and crept into the dining room.

Mors could not envision a room less pleasant for enjoying a meal, short of a dungeon. Three massive mahogany sideboards rested against all but the wall with the curtained windows. Between each one hung a portrait of a stern religious personage glaring at the diners. Wooden sliding doors were all that stood between Mors and his quarry.

He silently hefted himself onto the sideboard nearest the doors and laid a finger on one door's edge, sliding it open several inches. The men's voices flooded straight into the microphone Rembrandt had given him.

"There are several possibilities, of course, and it's crucial we not get ahead of ourselves." Traugott spoke in a placating tone that intrigued Mors. However powerful he was in his own sphere, he was the underling in this milieu. Mors could count at least three other strong Nachtspeere with him, along with five other men, including Oster.

"You're so amusing, with your caution." Oster chuckled, scolding him. "Sometimes I suspect you of having a tiny conspiracy of your own, my friend."

Everyone laughed, and several similar jokes followed in turn. From Mors's odd angle, he could see just a sliver of Oster's face through the crack made by the sliding door. It was pinker and more smiling than ever before. In his red cassock, belly resting on his thighs, he needed only a white beard to be Father Christmas.

The sort who promises gifts and whips you instead. Smiling all the while.

"In all seriousness, Your Grace," Traugott interjected at last, "we won't make further progress without some qualified help. A man of science. Someone with brains, skill, and a flair for invention."

"Are you implying that we have not done well thus far?" The smile was still there, but the ice was unmistakable.

"Not at all, Your Grace! Immense strides have been made. I only meant that insofar as the larger project is concerned, we will need a genuine practitioner."

"Hm. I suppose I see what you mean, although there is much to be done in the immediate, as yet. A shame that Schultze was killed. That was a very eager doctor indeed, and so learned! I think he knew the business better than you!" An obligatory chuckle followed this statement, and Oster went on. "We should consult with our Irish friends. I've also been thinking we need to improve our workspace, but there is much to consider in this—"

A cat's piercing, accusatory yowl pierced Mors's eardrums. He had not felt the cat enter the room, and it was now glaring up at him, back rounded and all its fur on end. Mors slipped a hand into his pocket, searching for something to toss that might distract the animal. His affinity with dogs was considered a remarkable thing in the world of vampires, but other animals knew he was something to be avoided or feared. This cat was brave enough to challenge him.

"It must be mice again, Your Grace," came the apologetic voice of a servant. "This house is overrun with vermin."

The men fell into a discussion of rodents while they refilled drinks, and Mors heard the servant padding toward the dining room. He flung the sliding doors all the way open, switched on the light, and swooped down upon the hissing cat.

"Yes, puss, that's very well done, but you mustn't interrupt His Grace during a meeting. I'm afraid I shall have to shut you in the cellar till the guests leave. But here, it's time for a saucer of milk, now isn't that nice?"

The man seemed oblivious to the struggles of the cat, who was still hissing and spitting up at Mors. For his own part, Mors had flattened himself to the top of the sideboard as much as possible, willing the fussy frontispiece to keep him hidden, willing the servant not to look up.

"Shall I prepare supper, Your Grace?"

"Why not? Herr Himmler should be along quite soon now," Oster's merry voice sang out, and the servant whisked into the kitchen with the cat, neglecting to turn off the lights.

Mors considered his options. He could not remain here; he was too visible. He would love to kill them all, but he had gotten too little information. It was not yet time to show his hand, much less his face.

With the servant in the kitchen and the men in the next room, he would have to leave via the window. He whispered into the microphone.

"Come to the dining-room window and open it for me."

Then he secured the microphone and waited. A few seconds later, he heard Rembrandt at the window through the brown damask curtains. As Mors had hoped, the window boasted only a simple lock that Rembrandt's skilled fingers broke easily, even from the outside. He raised the window and opened the curtains, gazing at Mors with eyes wide in worship and worry.

Mors slithered off the sideboard and pressed himself against it, eyes tight on the group in the next room. He nodded to Rembrandt to move aside. When he saw Oster turn to a man on his left, he took his chance, diving straight across the room, out the window, and somersaulting onto the street. Rembrandt drew the drapes and shut the window.

They waited until they were in the tunnels to talk.

"I heard someone exclaim, I think it was Traugott, but I couldn't be sure," Rembrandt told Mors. "Someone at least felt you leave."

"I probably created a draft," Mors acknowledged. "And they will discover the broken window latch sooner than later. But at least we've confirmed it's a conspiracy. Father Ambros can do something with that, I'm sure."

He was quiet, troubled, pondering what the "larger project" might be and why they wanted a skilled doctor.

At least I know there is no doctor skilled enough to put a man back together once he's been turned inside out.

Father Ambros admitted Mors into his cottage and took a copy of the tape with pleasure.

"I'll send it to the Vatican. Oster's bragged about his powerful friends there, but from what I've learned, it's just a relation at the museum. We have much better friends than that."

"Don't send it just yet," Mors advised. "I must get you something of more substance. I intend on finding him tonight."

"I'm sure he intends on finding this." Ambros handed Mors a heavy, leather-bound book. "He left Saint Hedwig's in a hurry today, and this was under a pile of papers. Very odd. It looks like a book of horrid fairy tales."

Mors took it. He could not read the ancient Irish writing, but he knew a vampire legend book when he saw one. There were engravings of Cleland inside. Mors's heart burned.

"Thank you, Father. I can't tell you how much I look forward to returning this."

"Oster left because he got a call from a Herr Konigsberg. That may be the one who recently took over the Bavaria Bank. Why are you laughing?"

"Nothing," Mors said, trying not to hug the priest. He knew in his bones that the Bavaria Bank would have a very deep vault. "I just love being right."

Mors stopped at the lair long enough to leave the book and order Rembrandt to grab his tools and join him. It was time for a battle.

He caught Oster's scent with almost absurd ease and trailed after him. Oster was accompanied by Traugott, two Nachtspeere, and two Irish hunters. Once again, there was that shadow scent of Cleland. Mors almost felt a beat inside his otherwise still chest. He knew he was near.

What he didn't know was why they were heading for the Chancellery rather than the bank. Then he realized they must be picking up Himmler. His joy expanded.

A half hour later, they had not reemerged.

"Do you think they went out the back entrance?" Rembrandt asked.

"Or via the underground one," Mors growled, cursing himself for not having thought of that sooner. He had used it himself, several times. Then he realized he hadn't thought of it because it would not take them to the bank—nor were they the sort to travel on foot and underground for so long. They had something else in mind.

Mors and Rembrandt hurried to the spot that Mors knew would take them into the Chancellery's tunnel. He took hold of the handle—and screamed.

He fell back against Rembrandt and stared at his hand. It was covered with large oozing blisters.

"That's not possible. It's not possible."

He ran to a side door and held his hand near it. He could feel the heat pulsing from the building. A public building. One he had entered. Sealed with a force he'd never felt. Mors and Rembrandt ran from building to building, and they were all the same.

"What are we going to do? How can we get in?" Rembrandt asked, bewildered.

"I will just have to get Oster to finesse that invitation," Mors said.

But although Mors pounded on the bank's heavy doors with Rembrandt's hammer for fifteen minutes, he could tell no one was inside.

In despair, they tried Saint Hedwig's. It was ablaze with light. A sign outside welcomed all souls to a special midnight mass. Even if the vampires could get in, there were far too many people. They would never be able to search without being seen. Mors went so far as to ask another curate if Father Ambros happened to be there, but the man said no, he had been called away.

A chill swept through Mors as they ran for Ambros's cottage. No one answered the door.

"We'd better find Deirdre," Mors said at last. "Traugott may have told her something, and if he hasn't, we need to warn her."

He felt the cry coming before he heard it.

"Mohren!"

Far down the street, Ambros was being led away by two SS officers. They were struggling to contain him as he lurched in their arms, seeing his ally run to help him.

"Mohren, you were right! Oster, he's—"

His captors landed a blow on his head that was not hard, but perfectly placed. Ambros slumped in their arms. A priest. They had killed a priest on the street. Mors supposed that any onlookers must think they had only quelled him, but Mors knew better. They shoved him into the waiting car and sped off.

The fire under Mors's feet was melting the pavement. He had taken only two steps toward the car when he spun, catching the stake that had been launched at him. It was a stake that could kill a millennial, and it quivered in his hand. He caught two more aimed at Rembrandt.

"Run, now!" He ordered, and Rembrandt obeyed, Mors giving him cover as he ran from a fusillade that could kill him so easily.

A number of Nachtspeere emerged from the shadows, and Mors smiled, pleased for the chance of a fight. He was prepared to rip the entire street to shreds. A chorus of "ooh"s stopped him. A group of orphans was being shepherded down the street, presumably for the mass, and had stopped, staring at the strange man surrounded by so many officers.

Mors heard Oster's delighted giggle.

"Perhaps it's best you simply come along with us rather than upset these children?"

It was an unexpected ploy on Nachtspeere's part to assume that he would not wreak the sort of havoc necessary to battle them all with children in the midst—that he would not risk innocent life. They themselves were not above such carnage. He could smell the oil they carried, knew they were prepared to use fire, to use whatever was necessary to bring him to his knees, and if a child was injured in the process, well, so it went.

They knew something of Mors, but not everything. Not all that he could do. Mors turned to meet Oster's eyes. He wanted the man to see his own burning red eyes and was happy when the fat face was wiped clean of its triumphant smile.

"Don't sleep too soundly," Mors warned.

He swirled with a burst of speed and charged toward the children, leaping straight over them and onto the house behind. Ignoring their screams—and the Nachtspeere's shocking barrage of language utterly unfit for children's ears—he barreled over a series of roofs toward the nearest station.

Mors caught up to Rembrandt within a few yards of the lair, and they tumbled inside. Deirdre was there, pacing wildly. She cried out as they entered and clutched at her chest.

She looked awful. Her hair was in disarray, her eyes were puffy, as though she'd been crying for hours, and her lips were completely white.

"Deirdre, what—"

Another little scream broke from her and she dropped to her knees. Mors knelt and took her hand. She began to sob.

"Oh Mors, oh Mors," she wailed, unable to say more. At last, she reached into her sleeve and pulled out a piece of paper with a trembling hand. Mors took it, ice subsuming his entire body, already telling him what it was. The sheet, in its neat, familiar folds, was covered in a heavy gray dust. He opened it. The picture of Cleland's beloved Padraic smiled up at him.

Mors shook his head, over and over and over.

"I'm so, so sorry," Deirdre croaked, putting her arms around his neck. "Cleland is dead."

Chapter Seven

Berlin. Early summer 1941.

Dead.

The word resounded in Mors's head like a heartbeat, but it made no sense. Cleland, dead. He wondered if Padraic could tell, could feel it from all those miles away. He hoped not. He wanted to believe Deirdre was wrong, but he knew she was right. Those phantom scents had told him so for weeks, and he hadn't wanted to believe them.

That he was going to avenge his friend—his brother—was of no doubt. The only question was how. Mors took a deep breath, blowing the debris from his mind and clearing a space for new thoughts to bloom. Action. He needed real action. There was London, under attack. He should be there, trying to help, to defend his home however he could. But he knew he was not yet equal to the task of facing his friends to tell them about Cleland. Soon, but not now. Not yet. Not when there was so little of anything else to tell them.

"How did Traugott know to give you this?" he demanded of Deirdre so suddenly she jumped. Padraic's portrait shook in his hand.

"He told me it was a souvenir, a symbol of greater things to come. But I'm sure he was lying, he looked so upset. I don't think they meant to kill him. I think he just didn't want to look at it, not right now."

"That's not the whole story, is it?"

Deirdre hung her head.

"I can't tell you; please don't make me," she whispered.

"I need to know."

"He brought me there," she squeaked. "He made me wear a blindfold until we got inside, so I wouldn't know where we were. I could barely see Cleland through the . . . doctors, I suppose. Traugott told me it was a grand experiment, the grandest. And he wanted me to see their moment of success. Well, I guess something went wrong, because there was a yell and a cloud of dust and then a lot of shouting, and it got very nasty. They certainly didn't mean to kill him, they were far too upset. Anyway, he found Cleland's coat and gave me the paper. He told me to keep it safe and tell no one I had it. That was all."

Mors still didn't want to believe it, but inside him he knew it was true. He could see it just as Deirdre described. Once again, his mind tended toward a tank. A tank and an army to go with it. An army trained by him. The general took the place of the vampire, unfurling a map of the war zone in his mind. Africa. The Western Desert. A place the Italians and Germans had governed in centuries past, but it was now the British who knew it best. However effective the German fighting machine, the sands were ultimately the Allies' to win. Possibly the people whose land it was by birth would help; possibly they would just hope whoever won would govern well. Perhaps they had found it easier to stop caring. Experience had proved no interloper would leave their land of his own inclination. The sand was always willing to accept more blood.

Mors forged that trail of blood farther, staging hard offensives in Libya and Algeria, circling and trapping the Germans in Tunisia. There they were vanquished, with Mors himself driving a bayonet right between the eyes of Germany's prized General Rommel. Amid the cheers, he cast his eyes north, at the land just across the Mediterranean: Italy. A sun-kissed woman sprawling upon the sea, smiling, just begging to be ravished.

A hot, mirthless smile stretched across Mors's face. Of course, the British would follow up such a triumph with an invasion of one of the Axis countries! Subdue the bases in Sicily and fight on toward Rome.

Here Mors's thoughts focused even harder, sharpening into an arrow that shot all the way up the boot to the French border. The Italians were not impressive in the field; such was obvious even through the propaganda. But on their home territory? That was something else again. They would not readily yield to such an invading force. No, to conquer Italy, one must know Italy. Whatever the people now were, they had the blood of the ancients in them. It would take the blood of an ancient to destroy them.

Rome's greatest general still lives. And he is stronger than ever before. He can conquer his own country, from the inside.

The brown uniforms of the British morphed into the tunics and breastplates of the Roman army, Mors at their head, sword aloft.

"Yes," he whispered. It was so clear. He would go to Italy and raise an underground army in the place where he once commanded one. He would create a resistance force strong enough to clear the way and meet the Allies when they arrived.

Then, with that tank and that army, he could blast through every sealed building in Berlin. Cleland's assassins would truly rue the day they had thought to touch him. Mors would give all the Nazis an education tattooed in blood. And he would give the world a new axis upon which to spin.

"We will all cry peace, freedom, and liberty. And the world will know a true soldier."

"Sorry?" said Rembrandt.

"Pack your things," Mors ordered. "We're leaving."

Rembrandt ran to obey, but Deirdre looked scandalized.

"What? Aren't you going to avenge Cleland's death?"

"Are you telling me how to do my business?" He blazed at her. "Because believe you me, they are going to pay. I'm going to blow a hole in Germany's side so big it will bleed to death. And I'll do it from the last place they expect. Rome is going to rise again, in the form of me."

"Do you . . . do you mean . . . go to Italy?" Deirdre ventured.

"That would be where Rome is located, yes."

She inexplicably blanched and shuddered, shaking her head.

"What the hell is wrong with you?" Mors demanded.

"It makes no sense. Berlin is the heart of the operation."

"Personally, I'd assign it a different organ." Mors tucked the portrait in his breast pocket, then hurriedly gathered his few things. "You may stay if you like; you have free will," he told her. "But I warn you, it's getting dangerous here. They've sealed the public buildings to us."

"If it's getting so dangerous, I'll just go back to Paris. The Nachtspeere will have left, now that it's clean of other vampires," Deirdre sniffed. "I'll rejoin the Folies. I'm sure they miss me."

Mors supposed she wanted him to beg, to say that he would miss her more, but he was in no mood for such nonsense. She hung her head and gathered her things, muttering words he couldn't be bothered to discern.

Five minutes later, they left the lair and headed down the tunnel. Mors took the first turn and was bounced back against Rembrandt.

"What on earth . . . ?"

He and Rembrandt exchanged a glance, then extended their hands toward the threshold. Somehow, the Nachtspeere had found a way to seal the tunnel to vampires.

"What's the matter?" Deirdre asked.

"The Nachtspeere have closed this door. They know where we are. Which means they have no intention of letting us leave."

"No!" she cried. "We'll have to go up. What choice is there?"

"We thwart them," Mors replied, leading them back through the tunnel, running a map of it in his mind. The Nachtspeere were coming, he could feel it. Even if he were to fight and kill the attackers and help Rembrandt and Deirdre survive, their options were shrinking. With tunnels being sealed and dawn coming, a net was falling. He was certain that descriptions of Rembrandt and himself were even now being printed on posters, warning people not to invite them into homes or shops. He had been too right. Now was the time to get out. Later would be time for a glorious, triumphant revenge.

The next available turning was also sealed. Mors knew Rembrandt wanted to ask how they could have done it and how the vampires hadn't sensed a human presence, but he, like Mors, was more worried about how to escape.

"Could we try to just talk to them, negotiate?" Deirdre asked. "Maybe—"

Mors's look quelled her, and she gulped and looked down.

For his own part, Mors looked up—and smiled. He had found what he was looking for. He handed his satchel to Rembrandt and leaped to the grate, catching it and then whirling his body to kick it through and somersault into the tunnel above. He released the rusted bars, and Rembrandt tossed him all their bags, over Deirdre's protests.

"I can't! I can't!"

"Yes you can, so shut up and do it," Rembrandt snapped. Mors held out his hands. She jumped and he caught her. Rembrandt jumped easily, and Mors grinned at him.

They continued wending their way through the tunnels. Even here, they found sealed entrances, but Mors was undaunted. The enemy would not get the last laugh—or any laugh at all.

It was nearly dawn. Mors could not hear their pursuers, but he could feel them. The Nachtspeere might think he couldn't get tired, but they must know that the others could, and that Mors would not abandon them. They had to find safety, immediately.

The rumble of a U-Bahn below decided him, and he reached down and pulled up another grate. Deirdre understood and shrieked.

"No, we'll be crushed, mangled! We can't! I won't!"

"We're all getting out of here alive," Mors promised.

The train tore below them.

"Now!" Mors cried, dropping onto a car. He could hear Deirdre's screaming, although it might have been the rush of the speed. He felt hands clutching his thighs while he himself gripped the front edge of the car. Deirdre was right: If one of the thresholds here was sealed, the force of the impact would tear them to pieces as the train roared on underneath, and the passengers would have no idea what was happening just over their heads, nor why clouds of dust were coating the windows. Mors dug in more tightly.

The train came to a stop, and Mors heard the doors open to let people in and out. He counted the seconds till it started up again. It would be enough.

"At the next stop," he shouted, staring straight ahead, "we're getting off beside the wall."

A grunt told him he'd been heard as the train gained speed.

The moment the train was still again, Mors slid down the car's roof and eased himself over the edge and between the windows till his feet found the tiny ledge of the carved arch in the concrete wall. There was barely an inch of clearance between himself and the train. Rembrandt slithered beside him, and Mors caught his arm, gripping him tightly as they both waited, trusting that the sleepiness of the early morning passengers would keep them from noticing anyone outside the car. He felt sorry for Deirdre, having to manage on her own, but it would all be over in a few seconds.

The line hummed and the train inched away. Mors instinctively sucked in his stomach. As the train picked up speed, the draft created an enormous pull. His fingers gouged into the wall to keep them steady. The last car tore past, and the draft dragged Rembrandt off with a scream, but Mors was still holding him and kept him from hitting the live rail.

"Hurry," Mors ordered. They hopped across the tracks and up the wall to the platform before any new passengers descended from the station above. They were both covered in black soot but otherwise unharmed.

"Where's Deirdre?"

They glanced at each other, then scoured the track. No trace of her.

"Did she jump onto the train?" Mors asked.

"I don't know. I jumped right after you."

Mors scanned the track again. He had no wish to leave a soldier behind; however, he had Rembrandt to consider as well. There were some risks a general did not take. If she had escaped, he had no doubt she'd find him when it suited her. They wiped their hands and faces, cleaning themselves up enough so that they could board a train without drawing too many eyes. Once on, Mors casually studied a map of the route. They were lucky, they could change at the next station and be within access of a freight yard. From there, they could make their way safely out of Berlin.

A young woman was staring at Rembrandt. Mors was pleased for his friend until he saw the sheet in her hand. Once again, he had been more right than he wished. A very detailed drawing of Rembrandt glared out from the page.

As the train roared into the station, Mors and Rembrandt inched toward the door. The young woman screamed, "Stop them! They're wanted men!"

The passengers looked around, confused. Mors took hold of Rembrandt and bore him swiftly through the crowds. As he had on the battlefields, he found the open pockets of space where none seemed to exist and melted in and out of them before anyone could notice someone had been there.

They swept upstairs. On the way, Mors snatched a hat off a man's head. The man shouted, but again, no one was seen. The vampires boarded the next train, Rembrandt wearing a round straw hat that hid much of his face.

"I like it better than my old hat," he noted, which had been a victim of that first harrowing train ride.

When they disembarked, Mors found his own hat, squashed in his satchel. The freight yard was not far, and the path to reach it was shaded.

"It's not direct sunlight," he told Rembrandt. "Will you be all right?"

Rembrandt nodded. Mors could see he was getting tired and hungry. He glanced around. No one noticed them. He turned his back to Rembrandt and squatted.

"Jump on."

"Mors—" Rembrandt began.

"I'm in a hurry. Jump."

Rembrandt jumped on Mors's back and took hold of his shoulders.

"Hang on to your hat," Mors ordered. Then he ran.

A few minutes later, the pink and slightly smoking vampires were ensconced amid pickle barrels in the last car of a freight train.

"Well," Mors remarked. "That was stimulating."

Rembrandt reached into his bag and pulled out two reels of tape.

"Good, they survived."

Mors raised an eyebrow.

"I know one is the recording of Oster's meeting. What's the other?"

"The copy." Rembrandt's grin exploded at Mors's quizzical look. "When you got me out of the way in that firefight, I remembered this and thought if Ambros hadn't sent it, they would surely find it. Well, he was dead, so the lock his soul had on the house was broken. I went in and found it. Bit lucky, really."

"More than luck, my friend." Mors congratulated him. "Much, much more than luck."

Chapter Eight

Being Mors was a glorious thing. Those on the receiving end of his happiness were inclined to disagree, but this never lasted long. Humans were fun. To tease, toy with, and torment them was a boundless delight. The longer his vampire life went on, the more ambitious he became. With his brains, skill, and power, what might he accomplish?

Before I'm done, the Trojan War will look like a drunken slap fight.

As Vitus had predicted, the republic, where senators ruled as a strong legislative body, gave way to an empire. The Senate remained but was little more than a declawed lion. The emperor had absolute power, and woe betide Rome if the man who was emperor was neither wise nor just. Or even sane.

Mors didn't care. The empire bred corruption, and the demon adored it. His still heart swelled with malicious joy. His only regret was that he was not a witness to the assassination of Caesar. It would have pleased him so much had the so-called Divine Julius seen his smiling face and polite applause through the wash of hot blood. He would have enjoyed teasing the assassins, too, for thinking they were ending empire in its infancy. He knew that when men saw the chance of such power, they would seize it. Thus did Octavian become Augustus Caesar; thus the stage was set, and a new show began. Mors was elated to be the audience but would have to be an actor, too. There was so much glory upon which to feed.

He loved his food. It wasn't the death of the humans that thrilled him but the life, the life that flowed into him with the force of lava. It sang through his body, tumbling through his cool flesh, warming him from core to skin. It was an erotic charge. On his hunting nights, he had the sensation of tearing into the world, long before he finally tore into a neck. As wonderful as that final moment was, when fangs pierced flesh, it was the chase that made all his organs dance a new sort of dance to a fast, flowing melody with a pulsing beat.

Roman nights were lively. There were always people about, engaged in business respectable or nefarious. Mors made no judgment. They all screamed when they saw the face of his demon, and each scream was its own song. Perhaps it would not be given a grand reception in the amphitheater, but this was, Mors was sure, a mere oversight. It was also just as well. He had become greedy, no longer willing to share his pleasures.

Which was why he eschewed acquaintanceship, much less friendship, with the other Roman vampires, of whom there were several. That there was more to be known about vampire life not only did not interest him, it did not even occur to him. He hunted, he killed, he created discord, and entertained himself. What else did he need?

"Companionship," the vampire Pompey the Greater explained, trying to ignore Mors's smirk.

Pompey had deliberately sought out Mors, which the brash young vampire found charming. He was growing a reputation.

"Ah, you wish me to be your companion?" Mors asked with a merry grin.

"No," Pompey told him, gritting his teeth. "I wanted to see what sort of vampire you were. They say you seem unschooled. That you have caused more than your fair share of chaos. That something about you is, well, unusual."

"I should hope so," Mors agreed.

"They say you always range alone. It's rude of me to ask, but I must know: What vampire made you?"

"Made me? What on earth do you mean?"

"You came to be somehow."

"Yes, the gods of the underworld willed it. They knew I was a waste down there."

When Pompey realized Mors was not joking, he was flabbergasted. Quickly, he explained how a vampire was made, how the maker bit the human, drank their blood, then offered some of their own blood for the human to drink before dying. Despite the spreading grin on Mors's face, Pompey went on: "Ideally, a vampire is chosen, is made with love and hope. . . ."

Mors doubled over, laughing hard enough to crack the pavement.

"Sorry! No, sorry, that's wonderful. My goodness. I was certainly not chosen. I suppose I am my own maker, since I drank some of Xenon's blood after humiliating him. As for love, well, I have always loved myself. Does that count?"

"Xenon!" Pompey was stunned.

"I see from your nauseated expression that you've met him," Mors said with polite sympathy.

"You are an aberration. An abnormality!" Pompey sputtered.

"Well, I always knew I was special."

Pompey's eyes glowed red. He whirled, his toga brushing Mors's face, and stormed off.

"Marvelous chat, thank you!" Mors called after him.

Well, look at me. A stealer of the dark gift. Magnificent. I do hope they all start calling me the thief of undeath.

As for Pompey's assertion that companionship was important, Mors dismissed that as foolishly human. He preferred to indulge himself as the god he knew he was. Let others have love. His interest was sex, fun and frequent. Mors's partners were very, very willing.

If he was no more truly handsome than he had been as a man, his appearance was far more overtly sexual. He kept his head completely razed, the skin as smooth as a honey melon and far more sweet to stroke. Let other men be ashamed of baldness and wear wigs; he knew his clean pate had a definite appeal. He wore the white tunic that told all who met him he was a man of power and substance. He accessorized it with vestiges of his proud military roots, wearing a soldier's cloak and the hobnailed boots that had been his life's footwear. He painted them black, which gave him extra distinction. And if he wore more rings than was considered tasteful, they were rings he had designed himself and all the more attractive for it.

There were always women to be found, and not all of them prostitutes. It took very little to bring a woman under his cloak. A half smile, a wink, a raise of the eyebrow. A gesture that said "Come and get a taste of the Elysian fields." No one ever declined.

Nor did they ever protest. Once Mors began to kiss them, his fingers teasing through their hair, down their necks, all speech was lost. Mors always took them to quiet, secluded places, such as the banks of the Tiber. And there, engaging in the most private of acts in a public place, a woman could experience a release beyond her imagining. Mors's hands and mouth were something undreamed of. He unpinned broaches and clasps with such deftness, it wasn't even felt. The women never even realized they were naked until he had stirred them to ecstasy. And it was then, as her heat reached its highest, that Mors bit. The blood was its richest, hottest, sweetest—a wine to savor and remember. The women, so swept up in their roiling sensations, never even felt the bite. Mors imbibed their rapture as well as their blood, and was a stronger, if stranger, creature for it.

As the empire grew, the emperors were able to rule as tyrants, a taint that created a cesspool wherein Mors could swim with cheerful abandon. Whether it was child slaves being auctioned off in a bathhouse, or a forced orgy, or a simple drunken brawl, he insisted on being a part of the fun, often changing the show so that it became his own star turn. When he wasn't actively in the mix of things or hunting, he was finding himself in music. The songs he felt in moments of drama and excitement became melodies he refined, and he would walk the hills in the darkest hours of the night, singing his harsh, horrible songs, frightening even the stoutest of men in their beds. He enjoyed the music of the humans, but it was his own hard-edged music that truly thrilled him.

Mors did not know how much his legend was growing until Pompey came in search of him again, this time with two other vampires. That he was meant to be alarmed by the deputation was plain. Even beyond the hardness in their eyes and the set of their jaws, the swords hidden under their togas told Mors all he needed to know. He wanted to laugh; they didn't know how well he could smell a blade on a man. So, they hoped to intimidate him. He wished them joy of it.

"Vampire Mors," Pompey began, with an amusing dollop of pomp. "It is not for us to try to correct the accident of your birth. That is Xenon's cause, and we take no sides. However, we are more than concerned about your effect upon the humans of Rome."

Mors raised an eyebrow but was otherwise silent, and Pompey continued.

"Although we have existed since Rome's nativity, and Greece's, and every place known, we relish our position as stories, myths, something in which the belief is slight at best. The Greeks grew the Legion of Artemis, now Diana—"

"The what?" Mors interrupted, but Pompey barreled on.

"But their number is small and their effect, minimal. However, your uncouth behavior and general terrorism is rousing an excess of fear and suspicion of evil. In short, you are too wild. You are a barbarous thing, fit perhaps to run among the blue-painted Britons, but unworthy to carry on in Rome. There are only so many people, and good food must be shared among us all or we will all be jeopardized."

"I heartily agree," Mors said, to general surprise. "So it seems what we need are fewer vampires."

With that, he set upon the smallest of the three vampires and skillfully liberated the sword he was not meant to know existed. One light, almost lazy stroke took off the vampire's head. To Mors's shock, both head and body dissolved in a cloud of dust. The moment of hesitation gave the other two a chance, and they launched themselves on him.

Mors was laid out flat, one vampire pinning his arms while Pompey slammed a hand into his throat and raised a wooden stake over his heart—reminding him of the long-forgotten Quintus. Mors flung his legs forward, catching Pompey's neck between his ankles, pulling him back. The other vampire's grip was loosened, which was all the advantage Mors needed to relieve that one of his head. Mors spit out the dust and released

Pompey, but that vampire had no chance to attack again. Mors plunged the sword straight in and up—a blow that never failed to kill instantly. However, although Pompey moaned and bled, he did not die. Puzzled, Mors withdrew the sword and examined it.

Pompey laughed then, a weak, garbled laugh, but a laugh nonetheless. He pulled himself to his feet, pressing his tunic to his wounds.

"Shouldn't that have killed you?" Mors demanded.

"You are a fool, Mors. Lucky, perhaps, but a fool. You won't last long."

"Longer than you, anyway." Mors told him, lopping off his head.

Mors replayed the cut and thrust in his head, baffled that it hadn't killed Pompey. It surely must have at least scraped the heart. But Mors was not one to be troubled long. He was elated to prove just how powerful he was, and to possess a sword again.

"What a jolly life it is."

But times were changing. Caligula had been murdered in an echo of Caesar's assassination, although in this case, it was hardly the stuff of tragedy. Caligula was a blot on humanity, and it was right he be slaughtered like a wild beast.

The reign of Claudius, however, restored a sheen to the empire that, though respectable, was dull. So it was that Mors took some of the words of Pompey to heart and followed the legions as they traveled to Britannia, intent upon conquest. He had tarried in Rome long enough. It was time to see more of the world.

From his safe spot deep in the *Augusta*'s hold, Mors could hear the commander Vespasian shouting orders to his men. The Britons were not going to be conquered without a fight. Mors crept as close to the surface as he dared so that he might observe.

Rain! Excellent!

The sky was almost black with heavy clouds and mist, providing fine cover for an intrepid vampire. The British tribes, indeed painted blue, were determined to keep the Romans from landing. Each fought with the vigor and valor of ten men, even though the skill of the Romans was vastly superior. Mors was gleeful. He slipped behind a Roman and snatched the soldier's sword, cutting off his head with it. Then he leaped into the battle.

Back and forth between groups he went, fighting for each side without rhyme or reason, simply at whim. The splash of blood on his face, the shouts, the sheer joy of the chaos he was at once a part of and creating filled him with an unimaginable bliss. He bellowed his music against the darling clouds that had given him the chance at such glory. None of the fighters identified the sound, yet all were inflamed by it, surprising themselves as they surpassed themselves.

The second day of battle was even more vicious. But strong and proud though the British were, it was heartbreakingly obvious that they were meant to fall before these foreign invaders. Back and back they were pushed, till they were on the edge of a great river, and there the war was won.

"Don't feel bad, blue Britons," Mors informed the subdued fighters from an observational perch. "There's no land Rome invades that does not end up the better for it."

The emperor was en route, and the men were exhausted, so celebrations had to be kept orderly. It was a Roman's sacred duty to set an example to those he had conquered. There was no true conquest without taming.

Mors knew there were always renegades—soldiers who would bend rules to their pleasure and trust that they wouldn't be caught.

Mors allowed his senses to wander down the river, feeling for a drop of chaos. They led him to a dwelling near a bridge.

Some decades previous, he had discovered that a vampire could not enter a house at will, even if a door was opened at his knock. An invitation must be issued by the inhabitants. A curious courtesy he found enchanting, and rarely troublesome. It added interest, because it meant a quarry was not a certain thing. A challenge. He liked challenges.

He rapped smartly at the door, which was answered by a Roman who had removed his armor and was happily drunk. A second Roman roared with laughter at the sight of the newcomer, for no other reason than that he seemed to be one of them, and as there were three parentless young British girls in this house, generosity could be afforded.

"Come on in, then," the second Roman cried heartily. "Plenty of nibbles for all."

But it was one of the girls who needed to invite him. Mors twirled his sword with some meaning as he caught the eye of the oldest girl. He winked and gestured lightly toward the Roman, who was now stroking himself in a manner the old goat Tiberius might have appreciated. His whole life, Mors had only ever spoken Latin, although he had learned some Greek as a student. But having spent many hours ensconced among British fighters, his powerful vampire mind had picked up some of the peculiar tongue—a musical language, even when shouted in fits and bursts. To the girl, he whispered one of the phrases heard in the battle: "Clear me a way, and I will kill them."

"Please!" she cried. "Come in!"

Before the soldiers had a chance to ask his pleasure, he had helped himself to their swords and thrown them outside.

"What are you playing at?" one man cried, bewildered.

"My own personal game," Mors answered.

If the girls thought he was their savior, they were sorely mistaken. Or rather, the eldest was, as she smelled delicious. The other two were children, with no smell at all. He would enjoy the female audience, though, as he played with these soldiers.

The men ran and Mors laughed, skipping after them. He soon caught each one and tied one of their own tunics around them, binding them together.

"The emperor is on his way, you know," Mors informed them. "You were supposed to spend the evening assisting with preparations. Doesn't 'duty' mean anything to you?"

"Look, you haven't got any right—" one man began, but the tip of the sword in his neck silenced him.

"My right is to my pleasure, and I'm not one to be talked out of it. And you know, I think I'd laugh rather hard to see one of these girls cut your fingers off."

"And they say you aren't generous," a voice spoke from the shadows. A voice Mors knew he recognized but could not immediately place.

Bracken crunched underneath feet as the voice's owner came closer. Fangs glinted in the moonlight.

Xenon.

The Roman nearest Xenon started to scream.

"Vampire! Vampire!"

"I am," Xenon answered, breaking the man's neck and glaring at Mors. "And so, it seems, are you."

"Well, good evening, Xenon. This is a surprise," Mors greeted him.

"Is it?" Xenon asked. "You must have known I would come to find you."

"It seems they all do. I'm delighted to be so popular."

"You won't have much longer to enjoy it."

"Oh, now Xenon, really. I have three swords and I'm a vampire. You can't think you'll kill me."

Xenon laughed and drove his fangs into the second soldier, sucking his blood so fast Mors wondered he didn't make himself sick. Then he launched his head into Mors's chest, sending him flying.

"I'll tell you what I think, 'Mors.' I think it's high time you pay for having stolen my blood!"

Xenon leaped on Mors in a white fury. He had grown stronger in the intervening years, and Mors could see he'd spent some time studying swordplay. He liberated a sword from Mors, and the sound of the blades clashing sang through the trees.

Mors danced backward, never missing a beat as he taunted his opponent.

"Do you know what I think, Xenon? I think the only reason you came to confront me in this place is because it is strange to me, and you thought you would have me at a disadvantage. Because you know full well that the skills I had as a human are a thousand times magnified now, and you did not want to risk being bested where other vampires might see and all would speak of it. I'm already an embarrassment to you, aren't I, and you don't want that compounded."

"You're a usurping, illegitimate spawn, is what you are, and if you think I'm going to die at your hands, you are sadly mistaken," Xenon bellowed.

He stabbed Mors through the thigh, and Mors staggered. Xenon thrust again; Mors knocked the sword away and swung. Xenon recoiled, but Mors was still able to cut an inch across his torso. He kicked Xenon's wrist, making him drop the sword.

Mors readied his own sword to cut off Xenon's head, but Xenon landed a kick of his own under Mors's chin, sending him reeling.

Xenon ran back toward the little hut by the river. Mors followed as soon as he had recovered.

"Running away are you? Where's the sport in that?"

Something heavy thrown in his face stopped him. The force made him lurch back, and he fell. Xenon laughed.

"Before long, I will have a power you cannot fathom," said Xenon. "Don't ever get too comfortable, my false spawn, and don't ever sleep too soundly. I will correct you yet. I promise."

He was gone. Mors bent to see what had hit him. It was the body of the youngest girl. Mors was surprised at his own revulsion. He picked it up and carried it back to the hut, knowing he would find the other two girls dead as well. The eldest had been Xenon's meal, the youngest merely sport to kill lest they scream and attract attention.

Dawn was coming. Mors decided he may as well sleep in the hut. There were a few drops of blood left in the eldest girl, which he sipped with relish. She was very tasty.

"Waste not, want not."

He fastened the shutters and bolted the door against any comers by piling up the girls in front of it. Then he sprawled on the bales of straw and rags that made a crude bed.

"Hm. I must say, I am quite, quite comfortable."

He closed his eyes and slept very soundly indeed.

Chapter Nine

Rome. Summer 1941.

The vampires zigzagged their way to Italy, so as to shake any Nacht-speere who might be tailing them. They trusted that Deirdre would eventually find them, should she so wish. The journey took weeks, as they were careful to let no one who wasn't a meal see their faces. They made their way by creep and stealth and luck. Even if they had wanted to board a train, it had become impossible. From what they read and over-heard, getting a ticket now required enough papers to fill a new Domesday Book. Mors thought about the scores, oceans perhaps, of people—mostly Jews—who must be trying desperately to get somewhere, anywhere else. Then he thought of what must have entered Brigit's mind more than once these last few years—Eamon and the Jews of York, back in 1190. Jews trying to escape the swollen hatred of their supposed countrymen and being mowed under, ground into dust.

What a piece of work is man, indeed.

Mors was concerned that posters of himself and Rembrandt might be plastered around the occupied countries and even Italy. The war, how-ever, was on the vampires' side. With so much news, so many new con-cerns every day, even if there were such warnings about two strange men, they would soon be forgotten. Once they heard that the Germans had invaded Russia, at last making true the lie Mors had told Brigit the year before, he knew they were safe. The Wehrmacht did not have enough resources to maintain a two-front war for long, and since the war on the humans took precedence over that on the vampires, the Nachtspeere would be forced into the daylight, at least for a while. Mors trusted that by the time they were at leisure to come and find him, he would be more than ready.

They were hiking like mountaineers, with packs on their backs and sticks to assist them. Mors suddenly felt a shot of sensation run up his leg, as he had when he put a foot over the threshold of Saint Hedwig's. Only this was warm and welcoming, as though he were wading into the sea. He thrilled to the unfamiliar feel, tasting it in his skin. Smells he hadn't known in centuries wafted through his nose, his eyes, his pores. His scalp tingled. He felt so present—so alive. Grounded yet floating. They were in Italy.

Italy. The land of his birth as both man and vampire. Italy, where so much of the glory of the human world had begun. Beautiful, sonorous, magnificent, and complex. Home.

Mors loved and was very proud of Britain. He remembered the song that ran through him the night he and Otonia had landed there. He had known, as soon as he felt that wild grass under his feet and looked around at the hills, trees, and sky—so full of color, even at night—that this was the place where he would live forever and, should it happen, die. It was the home of his heart.

But Italy reached inside and touched something deeper yet. This was the place where people who shared his blood had lived, died, been buried. Where he had grown, thrived, and so much more. As the demon stretched inside him, feeling the strength of tucked-away memories, he himself felt the pull of this magical world.

It was blazing daylight, that incomparable Adriatic sky roaring over him. The Via Claudia Augusta was packed with people waving, shouting, tossing flowers and kisses, bestowing on him all their love. He waved, his helmet's red feathers ruffling in the breeze as he returned their love. The people were his, and he, most assuredly, was theirs.

The sunshine was eclipsed. The people vanished in a plume of smoke, the flowers swept from under Mors's feet. This was not his Italy anymore.

This was a land engulfed in fear and wonder and a crisp obedience. They wore black shirts, Mussolini's men, a color that was a reflection of the new heart of Italy. A country glorying in a sham of glory. Industry hummed, so the papers said, and trains ran according to schedule. Children belted out Fascist songs with proud little voices, and the future glowed like the marble Augustus had loved so much.

But the soul, the soul . . .

Britain had disappointed Mors over the centuries, there was no denying it. A world dominated by humans would always give over to fallibility and sometimes dwell there long. And yet that green and pleasant land had always retained its soul. There was a truth in that island, down to its core, and a promise to its people that it would always right itself in the end, that inherent goodness, beauty, and love would prevail. Not for nothing had a new and powerful empire been built from that fortunate spot. Whatever happened as this war raged on, Britain would still be a place in which to believe.

Italy, though, had sold itself for less than thirty pieces of silver. Romulus and Remus had been overthrown by men with the power to destroy the land, even as they defended it from enemies they themselves had created.

Italy had made art, music, literature, impacted all Europe with its culture. Now, like Germany, it was foisting something else upon itself and all around it, conveniently forgetting that weeds choked fertile soil.

The land should return to the classroom. It needs to remember its past.

"Are you all right, Mors?" Rembrandt touched his arm, worried.

"I will be. Welcome to Italy. Let's get to work."

Three nights later, they each had new papers with decent-enough fake photos, Italian suits, and pockets full of lire. They boarded an Italian train that indeed ran on time, and it was not long before they disembarked at the Roma Ostiense station.

The melody ringing through Mors's skin was palpable. He could not stop smiling.

"We really ought to find a lodging," Rembrandt said at last, cutting across Mors's reverie.

"It's waiting for us," Mors answered. With that, he turned and strode through the streets with the familiarity of one who had lived there all his life.

The Temple of Minerva on Aventine Hill was long gone. Sorry though Mors was, he could not be surprised. There was now a pretty church to Santa Prisca, and Mors liked it because to the left of the vineyard opposite lay the ruins of an aqueduct. He ran his hand along the old stones until he found one with a groove that no one would think to investigate, because why should it move? It took a bit of persuading, but the stone had lain still for too long. It wanted to open, to reveal the secret that lay behind it.

Slim stone steps led the way into a miraculously well-preserved apartment. It needed linens and light, but it still bore comforts. Even the smell imparted a certain warmth. Mors greeted it with a smile.

"Well, old friend. What a pleasure to see the archaeologists haven't found you. I wonder what they would have called you?"

He touched the ancient table, chairs, and shelves. Each of the two chambers had a large bed, although they would have to acquire bedding. Mors smiled.

"Who would have thought I would ever be here again?"

Rembrandt smiled back.

"It's perfect."

The first order of business the following night was food. Rembrandt needed to study the map they had purchased, but Mors still traversed the streets like a Roman born. They had changed, of course, the Romans and the buildings and the city. But Rome was in his blood. He knew it with the intimacy of an old lover.

He reveled in the thrill that ran up his spine at being here, treading on such formerly precious earth. He still saw it through the haze of his memory—a city that glowed in the dark, its luminous buildings appearing so silky smooth you could slide naked skin over them. Statues of gods, goddesses, and nobles, painted with such loving worship, their eyes seeming to follow you wherever you went. A city that bustled even at night, with dinner parties, gaming halls, baths, and brothels. Even a few theaters. A beacon under the glittering black sky.

If it was no such shining light now, Mors could still feel a powerful beauty enriching the fibers of the city. Or perhaps . . . perhaps that was just the smell onto which his senses had latched. The most intoxicating woman he'd found in centuries. A virile, spirited mind and soul encased in succulent flesh. A woman reeking of defiance and purpose. A woman with a real knowledge of history and the desire to use it for real good. A woman whose determination to see genuine liberty flow through the Tiber and sweeten the palates of all the people was greater than her very reasonable fear. She had tucked her fear in an old wooden trunk, screwed her courage to a sticking place, and was now hurrying someplace vital, where work could be done.

He tracked the scent with ease and fascination as she padded down back alleys. At last, he spotted her. She was wearing a dark coat and thick-soled boots that made almost no noise. Her hair was hidden under a black scarf. She moved well—quickly but not so much so as to attract attention. She had a practiced stealth that was a lovely thing to behold. She was art.

Mors followed, turning over a host of possibilities in his mind. Not food, most assuredly, not food. Not this woman. She was something special. Something of which to know more. And, oh, he was going to learn more. His skin was singing, his fingers vibrating. Those live senses of his wanted to break free of their tether and wind their way deep inside her. Yes. He was going to know more.

But now, now he needed a meal. This woman would be found again. Her scent was inside him. He struck off down a separate path, searching.

A noxious human odor lassoed him from behind, pulling him back. Two men, full of a malicious, triumphant glee that made his fingers twitch, the talons eager to pop out. Mussolini's thuggish Blackshirts. Chasing his new interest.

Oh, no, no, no. No, little men. Poor choice of prey.

Hungry though he was, he and the demon swelled with adrenaline. He assessed the situation, following as closely as he dared. Now was not the time to announce himself, not to any of these three humans—even this wonderful woman. He wanted to meet her on more equal terms.

The men had caught up to her. They may not be Gestapo, but they were still dangerous. They were men with orders, and a world order to protect. Mors had known these sorts of men for two thousand years. In his experience, the only way to defeat them—once they were past a point of education—was to destroy them.

The woman's voice wafted over to Mors.

"I'm on my way to visit my grandmother. She's been very ill."

"I know you, Giulia Merlino," the fatter Blackshirt answered scornfully. "I know who and what you are. I remember you before you decided you were too good for us and went to England for education. I know that both your grandmothers are long dead, probably from broken hearts."

"You know nothing of the sort," she replied, indignant.

Her voice. It had a music all its own. A song he knew at once and needed to hear again. And her name—Giulia. Giulia. A name that danced over the tongue, flowed like water. An ancient name, and one that he had always liked.

They were arresting her, taking her to someone else for interrogation. At which point these two would be richly rewarded.

Hm. Over my dead body.

Mors saw her slip her hand into her pocket. She had a weapon in there, he was certain, and she was going to try to use it. They weren't going to get her without a fight. Mors's heart swelled. Although he was nearly always right, it still gave him pleasure. And he was so right about this woman.

He was just determining how best to assist her when the fat man was ordered by his superior to go alert the main office. Mors knew the only reason for this would be that the superior thought he could take some pleasure from Giulia before her imminent torture. How could she possibly say anything against him? A woman arrested by the Blackshirts was not someone whose complaints of rape would be given much heed.

As the plump Blackshirt passed, Mors reached out and sank all five talons into the man's face, taking care to plunge his thumb under the chin, sealing the mouth closed. He dove into the fleshy neck, needing the quick burst of energy that blood would bring. The taste was not awful; not so stomach-churning as Nazis, but no feast, either. Mors hoisted the agonized, half-dead Blackshirt above his shoulders and, with an almighty heave, tossed him to the roof of the nearest building, clambering up afterward with the speed of a lynx.

He hardly needed the grunts from below to urge him on. He could hear the fight, and hoped that Giulia had drawn some blood. The hard landing on the roof had finished off the fat Blackshirt; his dead face was frozen in terrified shock. Once again, Mors hoisted him and scanned the street. Giulia and the other Blackshirt were battling hard.

"Move aside, Giulia," Mors whispered, certain she would hear the warning. And down the dead man went.

Giulia did indeed move aside, and the Blackshirt who so stupidly thought he could have his way with her was crushed by his own companion. He didn't even have a chance to cry out.

Mors watched, pleased, as Giulia contemplated finishing the dying man off and changed her mind. He could see that the marks of an unnatural death in the fat man made her uneasy, but not so much that, after a scan of the building from which he so obviously was thrown, she wasn't able to replace her knife in her pocket and continue on her way. He was sorry not to hear her voice again, but it was resounding through all his deepest, grayest matter, and something deeper yet. It touched a time before the demon. It spun into his humanity and many happy years as a young married man. It was the voice of the wife he had loved so much. The voice of Valeria.

Mors tucked the voice in an inside pocket, the bodies in an incinerator, and went back to his search for proper food. He found and swiftly ate a prostitute who tasted of sausage and ricotta cheese, but that was the beginning and end of his contemplation of the meal. He wanted his energy focused on Giulia. Cleland, he thought, would be pleased. Pleased he had found someone to speak to his heart, quite unlike Deirdre. Someone who wasn't Brigit.

Brigit. Back in England. With Eamon. In the bed and the life they shared. But that didn't matter, not anymore. He didn't have the time for it to matter. He had his work and now this delicious question mark. The two were by no means separate, as Giulia was very obviously a key. Why else were Blackshirts mauling her? An organizer, an activist, an ally—she was certainly something, and he was going to cultivate that.

That, and perhaps a touch more.

The following evening, Mors's head was still full of Giulia, even as he and Rembrandt discussed plans. Mors drew a detailed map of the city, with government buildings. He intended to be able to fill in details, such as where factories and weapons storage were located, very soon. Rembrandt was hard at work building a shortwave wireless. They had not been able to hear the BBC in weeks and didn't trust the Italian press to tell them the truth.

"We need a lay of the land—garrisons and armories, all of it," Mors announced, stepping back to admire his handiwork. "Not just Rome but the outlying area and then all the way down to Sicily. And, of course, the whole of Sicily."

"So you need to get inside the Ministry of War," Rembrandt said.

"That would do as a start," Mors murmured, tapping a finger against his lips. The vision rose again of the Allies invading Sicily and finding a friendly force to greet them. The Axis would be encircled. It was beautiful.

"So, how will we do it, exactly—fight this battle?" Rembrandt was both excited and apprehensive.

"We create a complete dossier of the enemy, taking care they discover nothing of us, of course, then we start to weaken them. We know there are partisans here, so we'll find the best of them—humans dissatisfied enough to get organized and stand against the tide. They'll help us gather more followers. And so it grows."

"Humans!" Rembrandt wrinkled his nose as though Mors had suggested they sift through rotting entrails.

"I believe I've found a perfect one with whom to start," Mors went on in an even voice, frowning at Rembrandt.

"I only meant . . ." Rembrandt hesitated, looking mortified. Were he human, he would have been bright red. "I just thought it was going to be the two of us, you know. . . ."

"A vampire army of two?" Mors spoke kindly. There was deep disappointment in Rembrandt's face. Mors had forgotten that, vampire or no, Rembrandt was very young. Of course he would be enchanted by the idea of the two of them as lone underground heroes. There might be a tangential human, like Father Ambros, but he would not be admitted to the inner circle. Only the vampires would join the fray, and once triumphant, Rembrandt would then fight by Mors's side all the way back to a falling Berlin, so as to exact revenge on Oster and Traugott.

"That vampires could do it all on their own is the sort of thinking that got the millennials where we are," Mors told him. A truth he despised admitting.

Rembrandt nodded and turned back to the wireless, which was nearly finished. He oozed displeasure and even disapproval. Mors was surprised and hoped the mood would pass quickly. His least favorite part of being a general had always been disciplinary action.

A snippet of a music-hall song chirped from the wireless, then was overcome by static.

"Damn," Rembrandt muttered. "I almost had that."

A few minutes later, he found the local home news. They listened a moment. Mussolini was to make a speech in the next hour before the debut of a new piece at the Royal Opera House.

"Il Duce himself, hm?" Mors smiled. "I think I'll go and hear what he has to say. Care for a stroll?"

"No, thank you." Rembrandt grinned, his petulance abided. "I am determined to get the BBC."

"Fair enough; we can exchange full reports later." Mors waved and bounded up the stairs.

The crowd outside the Royal Opera House was huge, and Mors could tell by the clothes that many were not going to the opera itself but were just there to hear their leader.

Mussolini had never made as much of an impression on the world as Hitler, a fact that Mors suspected rankled deeply. The dictator was short, bald, and squat, but he plainly loved his people, and they him.

He loves his power more, though.

The opera, apparently, was yet another example of Italian superiority, another jewel in the crown of the new empire. Mors smirked. Everyone always wanted an empire.

He could feel someone else recoil as well, and knew just who it was. He snaked his way through the crowd until he was standing right next to Giulia.

It was several minutes before she sensed anyone beside her, minutes Mors enjoyed very much as he drank her in. Under the scarf that presumably kept her from being too easily recognized, she radiated a hot fury. Even if he didn't know she was a partisan, the blaze in her eyes would have told him as much.

Her eyes. When they finally turned and met his, he wanted to dive straight into them. They were big, black, and sparkling. Tendrils of frizzy black hair escaped from under her scarf. If her voice was that of the woman Vitus had married, her eyes and hair were those of the woman he had almost married—Felicia. It was all he could do not to stroke her cheek.

At first, her expression was one of distaste for this man staring at her so inappropriately, distracting her from Mussolini's speech. But as she looked into his warm green eyes and saw the half upturn of his lips, her whole manner changed. She flushed a deep red, and those black eyes warmed. Mors felt her fingers twitch and knew she'd had the impulse to reach for him. Everyone else might as well have been paintings on a fresco: They didn't notice Mors and Giulia, and Mors and Giulia certainly did not notice them.

She was, he guessed, in her late twenties. The absence of vanity about her appearance suggested she had believed what she had no doubt been told—that she was no beauty. But if her face was a touch thin and her nose too classically Roman, to Mors they only made her eyes that much more prominent. He didn't trust himself even to think about her figure.

Thunderous applause burst around them, and they jumped, not having realized the speech was completed. There was an immense jostling as some headed indoors and others off to cafés or supper. Mors took Giulia's elbow to keep her from being knocked into and guided her to a quieter spot. Once there, he had to fight himself to release her.

"How do you do," he said, wanting to say so much more. "I'm Marcus." He knew he should add a surname, but his mind was too busy elsewhere.

"And I'm Giulia. Merlino," she added, as an afterthought. They shook hands, longer than was considered proper.

"A pleasure to meet you, Signorina Merlino. Giulia."

She smiled then, and Mors knew he was completely gone. It was impossible, but that smile was the smile of the third in his trifecta of beloveds—Brigit. Giulia's soul, though, was uniquely her own, and it radiated beauty. Mors wanted to kiss her right then and there.

Giulia must have felt the same, because she blushed again and put a hand to her throat, wiping away a sudden drop of sweat.

"What . . . ah . . . what did you think of the speech?" She was struggling for neutrality.

"This is not the place where I can tell you the truth," he answered.

Her eyebrows shot up.

"Well, if that is a hint that you would like to buy me a coffee, I might suggest you would do better to simply come out and ask me if I am available and willing. Slyness is, I think, beneath a gentleman."

Mors didn't know what he loved more—the directness of her speech or the fact that something about it, despite being in Italian, made him certain she not only knew English but had been educated in Britain. Mors responded in his most refined, plummiest English: "You are only too correct, madam, and it is my hope you forgive me."

"How on earth did you know I could understand English?" Giulia laughed.

No doubt. She was a born-and-bred Roman but had spent many years in England.

"You're quite obviously an educated woman. I guessed that English was part of the curriculum."

"As a matter of fact, I took a degree at Oxford." She could not keep the pride from her voice, and why should she? Both women and foreigners were rare at Oxford.

"A first-class degree, I should think," he guessed.

The black eyes were boring into him. He could feel her turning question after question over in her mind. He was almost sure she was looking for an answer that made him a friend.

"You are wondering about me, of course," he conceded. "I have always had an affinity for language and accents. I've spent much of my life in England, but I was born in Italy. I do still love the land. And the food."

Giulia grinned.

"You will perhaps think me contrary, but I grew to rather like English food."

"Not at all," Mors assured her. "I have eaten in many places, and English food is my avowed favorite."

This is wonderful. I've yet to tell a direct lie.

"If that is so, Marcus, then what brings you back to Rome?"

You, he wanted to tell her.

"The same thing that brought you back," he said instead.

Her eyebrow arched. He had not spoken wholly true this time. She, he knew, had come back to fight the yoke of Fascism, to free all her countrypeople and help create a new government—a republic even better than what had once been. He wanted to overthrow the government so that he could use the military for his own ends—and that of Britain, of course. Still . . .

"Perhaps we ought to try working together," he suggested.

"I'm sure I don't know what you mean," she retorted. She had no reason to trust him, and he could indeed be a very good government spy.

Several Blackshirts marched past them, helping clear the crowd. Giulia sucked in her breath and ducked her head. Mors moved so that she was more hidden.

"They are exactly what I mean," Mors whispered. "They need to be given marching orders—straight into the sea."

Her eyes widened. She opened her mouth to answer him when cries of "There you are!" and the sound of running feet made them both turn.

Three girls were hurrying toward Giulia, their relieved faces suggesting they had been searching for her. Beyond them, Mors could see a tall man with iron gray hair in an officer's uniform, staring hard at Giulia and himself. Something about him made Mors think Giulia would be safer if left to the company of the girls.

He touched her arm and whispered, "I will see you again soon." When the girls met and surrounded their friend, he was gone.

It had occurred to Mors that, with so many officials going to the opera, this would be an ideal moment to pay a call on some of the government buildings.

The Palazzo degli Uffici, where Mussolini spent much of his days, was empty but for guards. It was a crisp modern building, cold and repellent, with columns clearly meant to evoke ancient Rome. More provoking were the mosaics and bas-reliefs that adorned it. Mors sneered at the image of Mussolini, riding without holding the reins, a hand in the air, victorious over nothing.

Mors circled the place slowly, assessing its permeability. So many ways to bring down a false empire, so many possibilities.

Empire. Even his beloved Britain had built an elaborate one. And now, here was Mussolini, wishing to emulate Augustus, raising a new Roman Empire in the modern era.

Modern is good. I doubt he's got the legs to pull off a toga.

Mors wondered if Mussolini really believed Hitler would let him have and hold his own beloved chunks of Europe and Africa. Besides, the world of empire was, must be, coming to an end. Even for Britain. But a republic. A real republic. One helmed by someone who knew what such things were meant to be . . . that would work.

A squeaking laugh shot up his esophagus and escaped through his mouth. He clamped his hand over his lips and bent over, hugging himself in wild joy. Of course. Once he helped the Allies overrun Italy and Germany, the next logical step would be installing a proper government. A republic. Exactly what Giulia was fighting for. Italy obviously needed a leader who understood how such things really worked. Who had seen it in action. Mors decided his being a vampire was of little consequence. He had been a general first and in his heart; that's what he still was. Successful generals were always the first heads of a new state. That was the way of history.

He was still chuckling to himself as he approached the building from the back, well out of sight of the guard. His practiced eye spotted a window ajar on the second floor. As soon as he scampered up the marble wall, however, he had a sense of what was to come. He attempted to reach through the open window, but a steady, strong vibration kept him from entering. This was not the vicious sealing of the Reich buildings. The palazzo was simply closed to anyone who was not a member of the government. He would have to secure an invitation.

When Mors reentered the apartment, he flung his hat across the room and swore fluently for three full minutes before taking notice of Rembrandt, who was surrounded by maps, papers, and train timetables.

Rembrandt was bemused at the verbal fusillade.

"I agree that the building being closed is irksome, but why do you have to embarrass a sailor talking about it?"

Mors laughed and asked what Rembrandt was doing. The vampire was alight with joy.

"I got the BBC! I've been listening to news, summations, analyses, projections. Mors, the British have been occupying Syria for weeks and are giving the Afrika Korps a hell of a battle in the Western Desert! They think Hitler's opening the Eastern Front is the end of him and that he's going to lose North Africa. That might be in just a matter of weeks, if that. There's a massive onslaught beginning now!"

"Rembrandt, you genius!" Mors pored through the scribbled notes, putting it all together.

"I've been making an itinerary for us to get to Sicily." Rembrandt showed him. "It's a bit convoluted, I'm afraid, but it looks like the safest route to avoid daylight."

"Nonsense, we'll just book a private compartment and keep the blinds down."

"But there's still a change, then getting on the ferry," Rembrandt pointed out.

"True, and if the invasion begins, that will affect the schedule." Mors was sure it wouldn't; he had not come all this way to have an invasion begin without him. He was cross not to have secured a map of the Axis bases on Sicily, but that did not matter. He knew he would be able to smell a battalion once on the island.

"Well, my friend," Mors said with his most wicked smile, "it seems as though tomorrow evening we set out to help the Allies win the war."

Before the vampires left the next evening, Mors wanted to find Giulia. He wanted to alert her to what was happening, but he also wanted to see her again.

It wasn't until they'd reached the city center that Rembrandt saw how deeply Mors was concentrating.

"Are you looking for a meal?" Rembrandt asked.

Mors shot him a baleful look.

"I would hardly do that with you here, and just before leaving. No, I'm looking for a woman."

"Oh no, not another female!" Rembrandt cried. Mors glared at him.

"No, a woman. Be polite."

"You mean, a human?" Once again, he wrinkled his nose in revulsion.

"Rembrandt, I do believe you're prejudiced."

Rembrandt started to argue, but Mors caught the scent of her. "Come on," he beckoned. "You'll see how wonderful she is."

He ignored the soft grumbling behind him as he ran to the source of the scent.

To Mors's disappointment, by the time they came upon Giulia, she was tapping her fingers idly on the window of a tumbledown house, a gesture that, to Mors's skilled assessment, was obviously code. Then she went to the front door, which was open and shut with a practiced speed, the vestibule dark so that the neighbors could see nothing—could hardly even see that someone had approached.

Rembrandt shrugged, but Mors drew him to the window. It was not open, but it was old, with cracks in the casement that could make winter nights drafty for the inhabitants. A human would only be able to catch the odd word, but the vampires, ears pressed firmly against the glass, could hear it all. Giulia was speaking, and once again, Mors was enthralled by her voice. It slipped under his clothes and rippled over his skin, running wherever it pleased. Even the demon was aroused, and Mors had to pulverize a stone between his hands to master himself.

"We should move more quickly," Giulia said. "If this continues, our path will be that much harder."

"But we can't go very far without more of everything. We would be crushed instantly, like that Blackshirt who tried to arrest you," another, younger woman pointed out.

"Yes, thank you for reminding me," Giulia said, and Mors could hear the smile in her voice.

"Sorry."

"And I know we need more, of course I do. Didn't I begin this revolution as good as alone, not knowing if anyone would join me? But look at how many of us now know that Fascism is a noose that can only grow tighter. Look at how many are already helping us find places to hide, making ready for the fight to come. We've blown up a bridge, for heaven's sake! And if the Blackshirts search for us, it means they consider us a threat. They know others want to find us, to join us. That in every household must be at least one who wishes to see Italy under a proper government. If we are all together, we will be invincible."

A worried girl spoke up then.

"But how, how do we truly end the reign of Mussolini? He is so powerful."

Giulia was reassuring.

"Leaders are only as powerful as those they command. When shopkeepers and clerks begin to question the laws openly, then teachers and students, then police chiefs and mayors, then some in the army, he will have to give way. That or kill us all."

"You say that very lightly."

"Trust me. When he has no one left to command, the only one he can kill is himself."

Mors was growing almost warm with desire, listening to her assuredness, her easy command of the facts. He would like to trace her family line, sure she went back to the noblest families of ancient Rome.

He especially liked her tone when the crushed Blackshirt had been mentioned. The words had been few, but he was a master of hearing what wasn't said. She harbored a suspicion of something untoward, even unnatural, but delicacy or superstition would not let this be spoken out loud. Perhaps Rome had not known vampires of late, but the fact remained that a man who had been walking down a street was suddenly dropped from a roof mere minutes later, bearing strange wounds. True, the Mafia had its ways and was no friend to Fascism, but then again, Fascism had broken up much of the Mafia—and in any case, they weren't much seen in Rome. No, Giulia knew there was something different at work here, something and someone unique who had saved her, and she was intrigued. And quite free of fear.

The cluster of women was interrupted by the matron of the house bringing in food. Rembrandt plucked Mors's sleeve. The train was leaving in ten minutes. He would just have to wait until they came back from Sicily to speak to her again. The thought of that conversation kept him smiling all the way to the station.

While Mors could not understand Rembrandt's quibbles with humans, he sympathized with the vampire's obvious expectation that, their work done in Sicily, the whole question of a human alliance would be moot.

Which was only part of why they were so disappointed, after an uneventful journey, to arrive and find that there was not a breath of concern throughout the island. As they traversed it, mapping the divisions and assessing battalions, all they felt was an armed force utterly at peace.

The Italian papers told them only that nothing had changed in the western campaign but that Leningrad was under a nasty siege. The vampires were not satisfied. They needed news they could trust.

They broke into a garage full of parked tanks, and Rembrandt went to work on the squat wireless. He had little trouble finding the BBC, but what they heard did not hearten them. There was nothing to suggest North Africa was on the brink of collapse. The news had been wrong.

"The analysts were probably just exaggerating to cheer up the civilians." Mors comforted him. "Besides, it is dangerous to get too specific.

In fact, it seems just as likely they were asked to say something to throw the enemy off. I suppose I ought to have thought of that. Look, it hardly matters; we can at least make our own map of Sicily now."

"Perhaps even engage in some sabotage?" Rembrandt suggested.

"Exactly what I was going to propose."

They had to take care, though, because Mors did not want the locals to suffer reprisals. Unlike when the millennials disabled the Luftwaffe planes, it was far more difficult for presumed gangs of foreign human partisans to infiltrate here, so the Sicilians would fall under hard suspicion. Mors would not have innocent humans enduring punishment for his actions. He much preferred to have a plain and open battle.

He touched a tank, impressed with the make of it. The temptation to hop in and drive away was eating at him.

"It would be a fun thing, wouldn't it, to power one of these?" Rembrandt marveled. "Do you suppose it's difficult?"

Mors went to a set of shelves. A few moments later, he held up a manual.

"Not if you learn how."

"Will we do it now?" Rembrandt asked, excited.

"Don't be ridiculous. No matter how good I am, they'd send dozens of tanks and planes to stop me. If I ever die, it will be spectacular, but I want a fight that I stand a damn good chance of winning." He scanned the shelves again, finding a Messerschmitt manual. "Right, now we'll have to get some information on the Italian forces, too, be ready for anything. The next time we come here it won't be . . . Rembrandt! Is it possible to tap into their phones or radios, from Rome, if you have the codes?"

Rembrandt produced his tools.

"A human can't, but I bet I can."

Mors grinned. Rembrandt's technological wizardry could almost rival Cleland's.

As Rembrandt busied himself deciphering the makings of the various bits of gadgetry, Mors studied the tank manual. He knew that if he came to Sicily on the eve of battle with a well-trained army, they could quickly disable some tanks while appropriating others. They would need British flags or something similar, to alert the Allies, but it was otherwise perfect. An army under his command, small and fleet, attacking just at the moment when the enemy was being attacked from the other side. Beautiful.

Mors heard footsteps.

"Someone's coming," he hissed.

"I haven't got it yet!" Rembrandt was anguished.

"I'll take care of it," Mors promised.

Two German captains entered, men far too important to be easily disposed of without an investigation. Unusual deaths, especially among Germans, would create trouble throughout the whole country. Mors preferred to keep things running smoothly for now. He glared at the men.

"Well, there you are at last."

They exchanged baffled glances.

"Who are you? What are you doing here?" they demanded, refusing to be easily cowed.

"The question you ought to be asking is how I got here," Mors barked. They had not yet noticed Rembrandt. "Do you want to know how? It's a most amusing story. A whole side of fencing has fallen down on the western perimeter! Anyone can just waltz on in, nice as you like. And before you try to pass the blame on saboteurs, Captains, I'll have you know that I inspected that fence very carefully, and would you like to know what I discovered? The pieces hadn't been fitted together properly! I have spent many years overseeing construction, and I have never seen anything so pathetically built in my life. I am not surprised it has fallen over; I only wonder how it stood for longer than five minutes!"

The men were so stunned by Mors's rage, they could not even speak. He continued to berate them for several minutes, thoroughly enjoying himself, until Rembrandt joined him.

"I've finished that report, sir."

"Well done, Lieutenant, thank you. Now then," he turned to the officers. "Our surprise inspection is complete. If when we observe the fence in twenty-four hours' time and see that it is under repair, we might consider not filing the report."

The captains thanked them, and Mors and Rembrandt started away. The brighter of the two men shouted after them.

"Wait! Why are you in civilian clothes?"

Mors gave the man a look of withering disdain.

"How would *you* conduct a surprise investigation?"

There was no answer.

As they left the base, the vampires yanked thirty feet of the fence straight to the ground. They were not at all surprised to find the floodlights trained on the fence the next night, and upward of twenty men busily repairing it.

Three weeks later, they satisfied themselves that they knew the entirety of Sicily and much of the south. They were happy to return to Rome, and although Rembrandt still did not warm to the idea of a human army, he at least seemed to appreciate how it would be of use.

For his own part, Mors was full to the brim of Giulia. He was almost bouncing as they pulled into the station. He knew he should drop off his bag and change clothes, but he didn't want to wait another moment to start searching for her.

A small festival was under way, marking the beginning of autumn. Mors imagined they were bigger when it wasn't wartime, but the people were still out in force, enjoying themselves. Rembrandt looked hungry. People in the midst of such large parties were always so luscious.

Children and adults alike had cheap sparklers that seemed in danger of setting someone or something alight at any moment. Mors grinned, liking the cheerful chaos of it all.

One such sparkler caught his eye; it was bigger and burned brighter than the others. His grin faded.

No. It can't be. Not now.

It came nearer and nearer. With a happy cry of "There you are, at last!" Deirdre flung herself into his arms.

Chapter Ten

A HISTORY OF MORS, PART FOUR
"You Have Potential, Mors. . . ."

As much as Mors liked to travel the empire, especially if there were more battles in which he could participate, he always loved coming home to Rome. It shone brighter at night than anyplace else. The people walked in comfortable, happy pride. They were delectable.

The other vampires, having heard what happened to Pompey, gave Mors a wide berth. Every now and then, however, an intrepid young female couldn't resist presenting herself, hopeful he would take an interest. Which he did. He preferred that which he sought, but he was always welcoming of what came to him.

Vampire flesh was fascinating. So nearly human and yet so clearly not. Cool, silky, even vibrant, but if you paid proper attention, the skin and all underneath it was too still. The molecules that formed it had frozen on the host's death. They were meant to have broken down, disbanded, gone on like the soul inside. Instead, they hovered. They were held in stasis, waiting. They had infinite patience. As though they knew that someday, one way or another, they would fly free at last.

Not that Mors gave it that much thought.

The female who had come around several times in the last decade or so was a sharp-nosed creature named Agrippina. ("For Nero's mother; I'm older than I look," she explained on her first introduction.) She claimed to have been a Vestal Virgin, which made Mors laugh.

"You're no virgin anymore, my dear."

She was very fun to kiss. Her mouth was always wet and willing, and she had powerful fingers that slid their way around his back and head, massaging him, pulling him closer.

There they were, kissing happily, when he nearly fell over. Agrippina's body was solid, then it was gone. He was doubled over, choking, sputtering, blinded from dust, and someone was laughing. Laughing at him. He looked up, but he didn't need to see the face through the dust cloud to know it was Xenon.

He had a sword strapped around him and was holding a long wooden stake, which he twirled idly as he continued to laugh, dancing away from Mors like an acrobat.

"Oh, Mors, you did look very comfortable right then. And didn't I warn you not to get too comfortable? You're really not one for listening, are you?"

Mors bided his time, recovering himself and considering what to do. He had no weapon, beyond his talons. He had no wish to run from Xenon, but if they were to fight again, he wanted the match to be more even. Or rather, he wanted it on his own terms.

Then again, he didn't really want it at all. The truth was, he liked Xenon being alive. Mors's existence was a plague on Xenon, and the older vampire must spend much of his time fixated on his accidental spawn, plotting how to kill him. This was hugely gratifying. Xenon wanted Mors to be afraid, on the run, but instead, it was Xenon who was, perhaps, a tiny bit afraid of the thief who was so obstinate in his hold on the life he should never have possessed. Although Mors rarely thought of Xenon, he reveled in the older vampire's obsession with him.

Xenon inched closer, his expression and manner goading, provocative. Hopeful.

"Well? I have just killed another of your ladyloves. What are you going to do about it?"

"I am sorry; I don't know what you mean." Mors was supremely casual, and Xenon prickled.

"Your vampire companion is destroyed at my hand! I warned you; didn't I warn you? There is nothing I won't do."

"Yes, of course. I was only confused by the words *love* and *companion*. Minor error on my part." Mors punctuated the concession with a polite nod.

Just as Xenon was realizing that Mors really couldn't care less about the death of Agrippina, an arrow sang out from an opposite hill. Xenon barely had a moment to flinch, so that, though it sank deep into his flesh, it missed his heart.

Xenon's scream was long and piercing. He pulled the arrow from his body and scanned the spot from whence it had been launched. Mors saw a shadow of a female form, a form that made Xenon guffaw. Another arrow whizzed toward him. He caught it and crumbled it in one hand, muttering, "Vindictive bitch."

But a third arrow came, shot with even more force. Xenon swore mightily. Without another glance at Mors, he dashed off through the fields, putting Mercury to shame with his speed.

Mors was cross. He preferred it when Xenon ran away because of *him,* not because of some random female. Who did she think she was? He certainly hoped she didn't think she was saving his life.

The female approached him, utterly unhurried. He wondered if she was deliberately allowing his impatience to build. An arrow was still nocked in the bow, which was a thing of exquisite craftsmanship. Her face remained shadowed, but he could feel her assessing him.

"That Xenon," she remarked nonchalantly, as though they had already been conversing. "He's always been tricky to kill." She raised an eyebrow at Mors. "Not that it is proper for us to try to kill one another."

"Propriety hardly seems Xenon's concern."

Her eyes glittered with interest.

"Yes, he does want to kill you. I have heard something of the reason why."

"Only something? Here I was hoping everyone knew the story. I stole my life from him."

"Yes, that is the story. He unintentionally gave you the power to make yourself. Very singular, that."

Something about her tone rattled him, and he wanted to change the subject.

"You're hardly very proper yourself, trying to kill him."

"Not at all. He did something unforgivable to me . . . and someone else. He needs to be killed."

"Perhaps it requires someone who's up to the task," Mors remarked with a sneer.

"Perhaps." The vampire—and of course she was a vampire—was not one to be swayed by contentiousness.

She replaced the arrow in her quiver, slung the bow over her shoulder, and stepped forward to introduce herself.

"I am Otonia." She spoke with simple authority. Her voice was more beautiful than her face, although she was far from unattractive. There was a confidence and quiet calm in her expression and manner, as well as a fierce intelligence that gave her a striking sensuality. She seemed to have been molded from clay, rather than the union of two humans. She had high cheekbones, a strong, almost masculine jaw, and a long nose. Glossy thick eyebrows framed wide, dark eyes, and black curls swooped over her high forehead. Despite her Roman clothes, hairstyle, and perfect Latin, she was plainly Greek, and if Mors had to guess, she traced her origins to Greece at its height. She exuded total nobility.

"And I'm Mors," he said at last, although of course she already knew who he was.

"Yes," she agreed, as if acknowledging he'd gotten it right. Her expression did not change: It was still that cool, calculating look that made him feel as if she were reading his history. Agitation began to grow in him, quite separate of the demon. He did not like this vampire. She didn't seem the sort to add any fun to life.

"I've been watching you," she informed him. He waited for her to say more, but she remained silent. It seemed condescending, and his fingers flexed, preparatory to the talons emerging.

"Lucky for you," he congratulated her. "I'm wonderful to watch."

She neither smiled nor scowled, which raised his hackles further. What was worse, he knew that she knew he was swelling with dislike and distemper, but she was entirely unconcerned and indifferent.

"You can be," she acknowledged at last, catching him off guard with the compliment. "You could be."

"I think you just contradicted yourself there."

She allowed the tiniest trace of a smile to shine in her black eyes. Although it gave her a marvelous glow, he felt his dislike only mounting.

"I'll tell you what," he offered. "You can explain yourself properly or you can go. Or just carry on playing games, but that is certain to result in me killing you, and you don't seem the sort to want that."

Even then, she did not seem upset. She did not even stop smiling.

"You have potential, Mors. You have enormous potential. I am quite impressed—and I do not impress easily."

She did not speak with congratulation for either him or herself. These were merely statements of fact. He supposed he was meant to feel gratified. Perhaps he was to fall at her feet—even though it was understood that he had no idea what she was talking about.

As though she had read his mind, she smiled again and leaned in closer. This time, her voice was low and even a touch conspiratorial.

"There is more, far more, to vampire life than you know."

Now she waited for a response. A question, a statement, or several of each, perhaps, all at once. But Mors did not care for assumptions to be made about him. He did not object to her having watched him—he adored an audience—but if she hoped to recruit him as an acolyte for some unimaginable purpose, she had the wrong vampire. He was more than three hundred years old and quite content with all he had discovered in vampire life. If there was more to be found, he was capable of finding it himself and didn't need this inscrutable, ponderous creature's assistance.

"Impressed with me, are you?" he half snarled. She inclined her head in polite confirmation.

"And you don't impress easily?"

Later, it occurred to him that he had seen a flicker of resigned comprehension in her eyes before he snatched up one of the fallen arrows and swiftly, brutally, carved an X into her bare upper arm, then backed away to admire his handiwork.

"No, Otonia, now I must contradict you. I would say you *impress* very easily indeed."

Otonia cast an indifferent glance at the bloody wound, then fixed her eyes on Mors with that same placid, observational expression he found so infuriating. She had not even flinched. He wanted her to shout, to denounce him, to fight. But the longer she looked at him, the less sure he was of what he wanted.

The shoulder where the blood was now beginning to congeal gave one halfhearted shrug.

"Oh, well," she remarked, without emotion. "As you like. I had simply been of the opinion that there was something more. Good night, Mors."

And she turned and walked away, back into the heart of the city. He watched her walk, admiring her steady, elegant gait and strong, straight back. Something about the swing of her arms and the way she held her head made him realize that she could have prevented his assault without the smallest exertion, and yet left him in great pain. She had chosen not to. What had happened had been a test, and he had failed it. He was not sorry, but he could not be wholly without care. Otonia was a vampire, and yet she was the opposite of chaos. That seemed singular.

Her figure was now only a dot on the cityscape, or perhaps he imagined it. Or, perhaps, he was following a light he had never yet seen. A glowing inner light, which radiated to those who knew how to look for it.

"What were you offering me?" he murmured. He would not be surprised if she could hear him.

Chapter Eleven

Rome. Autumn 1941.

While they were certainly stunned, neither Mors nor Rembrandt was particularly pleased to see Deirdre. She was far too giddy to notice. Her stream of conversation, though ear-bleedingly shrill, at least gave Mors a chance to give most of his mind over to the problem. He acknowledged that he was, at least, happy and relieved to see she was alive and well. He had not wished otherwise, though he had given her precious little thought since their Berlin escape. His heart and mind were full of Giulia now. Luscious and winning though Deirdre was, he had no desire to touch her.

Neither did he want her in their small apartment. He supposed he and Rembrandt could share the larger bedroom, but Mors knew Deirdre's mere presence would distract and distress Rembrandt. He would not have his friend so upset. Besides, they had far too much work to do. Work in which Deirdre would not want to engage, even if she were any good at it.

"I do hope you weren't grieved to find I didn't jump onto that train with you," Deirdre was saying. "I was just certain you were going to be cut to bits. I couldn't bear it. And wouldn't you know? There was a manhole just yards away, leading to the street! Well, so I begged a nice man to take me in, then I ate him and waited till nightfall and just hopped a train to Paris!"

"That is where you wanted to be, wasn't it?" Mors was unimpressed.

"I was going to come and look for you both right away, of course," she apologized in a light trill, "But then I met Gaston, and, well, would you believe it? I'm an artist's model!"

"What fun for you," Mors said, barely keeping the edge from his voice.

"Congratulations." Rembrandt's heavy sarcasm could drown rats.

"It has been quite a busy time. His family is very rich, so we have loads of fun even despite the occupation!"

"A wonder you could tear yourself away," Mors commented, wishing she hadn't.

"Well, I told him I needed to try to find some friends in Rome, and what do you think? He has business in Rome! He's been asked to teach an art class. So here we are, staying at the Hotel Clodio—oh, it is so chic—and he still needs to draw me, but I should have a number of nights free for other fun!" Here she broke off with a roguish giggle.

Mors was relieved. She had plenty to keep her busy and need not be involved in any of their business. Neither was she staying long. He was certain he could take her out a few times now and then, just to keep the peace. He could gently let her know he was no longer interested in her body. Hopefully this Gaston was exciting enough that she would not care.

"Marvelous, Deirdre, and I shall take you to the finest place in town. You deserve it after all your hard work in Berlin. We will see and be seen by all the most important people."

Suddenly, an idea struck him. An idea so absurdly beautiful it was all he could do not to shout. He cupped Deirdre's face and smiled at her.

"Deirdre! Dear little Deirdre! Can you get a black wig and a smart cocktail dress?"

"Well, I suppose so." She looked a trifle disappointed.

"Wonderful! And can you meet me outside the Ristorante Bolivar tomorrow at nine?"

When she agreed, he kissed her on both cheeks, and he and Rembrandt snaked their way back to Aventine Hill. He had a great many preparations to make, and he forced himself to wait until tomorrow to look for Giulia. He had to make the most of this opportunity.

"What have you got in mind?" Rembrandt asked when they were alone.

"A plan that might, if it works, gain us access to every public building in Rome."

Deirdre had made an exemplary effort. In a black wig and green dress, she looked like a very pretty human, and they made a fine couple. They were given a central table and gazed upon with admiration. Deirdre basked in the glow of it all.

They did not, however, get the opportunity to meet anyone. Mors hid his disappointment. Deirdre took his arm as he was walking her back to the hotel, chattering on and on in the breathy voice he hadn't missed. The doors to a lecture hall opened, and a huge crowd of people poured out. Just as he caught the scent that could make his heart beat, there Giulia was, staring at him. With a woman on his arm.

"Deirdre, I'm sorry, would you wait here a moment, please?"

Deirdre protested, but Mors hurried after Giulia, who had turned away. When he caught her, it was all he could do not to kiss her, despite her stiff face and hurt eyes.

"Giulia, at last, I can't tell you how much I've missed you. Please, please listen to me."

"I'm sorry, what was your name?" Her voice might have spent a week in a morgue, but it still delighted him.

"I know, I deserve that, but I promise . . ." He forced her close to him and bent to whisper in her ear. "Giulia, I'm a British spy, here to find out how readily Italy can be invaded. That woman is one of my co-agents. I'm Italian by birth, and I know there are partisan movements here, and I'm determined to use all my military expertise to turn them into serious fighting machines. I've been away on a reconnaissance mission and only just returned. Please, please believe me, let me prove it to you."

"What makes you think I'm not loyal to Il Duce?" she asked in a moderately warmer tone.

"Because neither of us are fools."

Her lips twitched, but her eyes were still calculating.

"All right then. Sunday, meet me by the Temple of Vesta. No one ever goes there. Six o'clock."

"Can we make it seven?"

She raised an eyebrow but agreed. He forced himself back to Deirdre, rather than watch Giulia go.

"That was quite rude of you, Mors. I'm appalled." Deirdre sniffed.

"A thousand apologies, my pet. Are you free again tomorrow, or the night after?"

She, too, raised her eyebrow. The effect was not the same. But she agreed to meet him, which was all that mattered.

Although he and Deirdre were once again unsuccessful, Mors was counting the minutes till he could meet Giulia. Cleland would approve. He had wanted Mors to think about someone who was not Brigit. Mors certainly found it easier not to think of Brigit in Italy than anywhere else in the last thousand years. During the Berlin mission, he could occasionally pretend Eamon did not and had never existed, and that once the mission was done a new victory could be won. Of course, this was only idle rubbish, the stuff of the most nonsensical dreams. He knew better. He had always known better even in the time before Eamon. The time before Eamon. Those were some times, indeed. Memories better left unsifted, unsorted, untouched.

The passions filling Mors now were something else altogether. Something new and something far, far older. He was overflowing with happiness.

Rembrandt was happy, too. He was building a field telephone and a radio that, he was certain, he could make tap into the army bases, using his own skills and the stolen codes. The table and every shelf in the apartment were packed with machinery and notes.

Despite not having access to the military information he wanted, Mors did have one piece of luck in coming upon two officers discussing munitions. Three bottles of grappa later, Mors knew where a small weapons storage facility was located and paid it a call, liberating a few guns and altering the records so that they had never been part of the stock. As soon as he had made some modifications and found a likely spot, he, Rembrandt, and Giulia would begin training.

And there will soon be more.

The Temple of Vesta no longer had much to recommend it, and Mors was not surprised that it was little visited, except in that it had once represented the domestic hearth of the city, which seemed something Mussolini would want to re-create. Then again, it was one thing to style himself as a new Augustus, to seem to venerate symbols of paganism would go too far. Both Germany and Italy wanted to rebuild their nations in the classical design, but with very different gods on the mount.

The Vestals. In their way, they had been the most powerful women of ancient Rome. It tickled Mors that Giulia wanted to meet him here. He fancied he could still smell strong women all around him, those long gone and their descendants.

"Marcus?" came that rich, thrilling voice. He wanted to hear her call him "Mors."

"Ah, Giulia. You are very punctual. I admire that."

"Thank you."

She stood a little apart from him, and he could feel how each of her muscles was tensed. He wondered how she expected to get away, if this was a trap. Most certainly, she had something planned.

"We can talk freely here," she said, though her stance and position belied the assertion. "Tell me again what you hope to do."

"Whatever it takes to bring down the current government."

The clicks were not in unison, but they were impressive nonetheless. Mors grinned, only in part because Giulia looked surprised that he did not jump or turn pale or even flinch. There were three young women staged strategically amid the ruins, all now pointing sawed-off rifles at him, and Giulia herself had drawn a pistol. It made too much sense to be startling. Giulia, whatever her attraction to him, was indeed no fool. She would not trust a man so blindly.

"Who says we need training?" the girl nearest him demanded accusatorily.

Almost without seeming to have moved, he was behind her. He gripped her waist and held the gun in his hands, pointed at the sky.

"That would be me, Marcus," he answered.

The others didn't dare shoot, lest they hit their friend.

"You see, ladies, this is a tricky situation." Mors went on, "You need to disable me in some capacity, but without harming—sorry, dear, what is your name?"

The girl he held so easily was putting up a valiant struggle.

"Patrizia!" she spat at him.

"Patrizia, a pleasure. Now then, a lesson. Giulia, were she sure of her aim, could quite readily put a bullet through my brain, but as Patrizia is thrashing about, it's not a risk she wants to take, and rightly so. It takes a lot of practice to trust yourself with such a shot. For example . . ."

He lowered the gun and fired into the darkness, just over Giulia's shoulder. The women could see nothing but heard the squeak and plop of a rat falling dead. Mors was impressed as well: They had either stolen or devised silencers for the guns, so that the sound was muffled.

"Of course, should Patrizia happen to stumble, like this"—he lightly pushed her forward but kept an arm around her waist so that she wasn't hurt—"one of you could fire easily."

Another woman did just that. Mors ducked the bullet adroitly, and it sank into a statue.

"Very good indeed . . . ?"

"Franca Orselli," the woman answered, in a tone that suggested she was astounded at what her voice was doing.

"Signorina Orselli, marvelous. But you see, a well-trained man might be adept at dodging bullets. Of course, you have noticed I am not holding this rifle in a manner that suggests I'm ready to do any of you any harm. That could indicate I am the friend I say I am. If you want further proof, well"—he released Patrizia and expertly opened the rifle, allowing the bullets to drop to the ground. He bent and picked them up, juggling them in one hand—"you need only ask."

Franca and the third armed woman glanced at Giulia, who nodded. They holstered their weapons and descended to join the group. The four stared at Mors—although Patrizia glowered.

"I'm Silvia, Franca's sister," the last one piped up, her voice sweet and shy.

"How do you do?" Mors was polite and she smiled. "May I ask how you ladies were able to transport the weapons unseen?"

Now it was Giulia's turn to grin. She produced a large shopping bag filled with sewing and knitting supplies and set the gun inside. Being sawed, it fit perfectly. So long as no one looked too closely, they were average, busy, honorable Romans.

"Impressive," Mors complimented the women. Giulia shrugged.

"Well, Mussolini wanted us all to do more home sewing."

Patrizia chortled, and Mors marked the worship in her eyes when she looked at Giulia.

"Let it not be said you disobeyed him. So. Are we partners?"

Giulia arched a brow.

"We blew up a bridge all on our own, you know. One of the nasty modern things."

"Very nice. But only just the one?"

"Do you think you could do better?" Patrizia goaded him.

He looked at her and realized that it was more than the intensity of Giulia that had kept him from sensing any of them before the ambush. Patrizia was only about fourteen, the others little more. They would not have a distinct smell for at least a year or two. Patrizia's soft face and body were still more that of a child than a woman, but her eyes burned with suspicion and dislike. She would take some effort to befriend.

"Let me work with you, Patrizia, and we will all do better," he promised. She sniffed.

Giulia broke in then.

"I shall speak to Marcus further and then meet you all at Franca and Silvia's house in an hour. We'll talk more then."

Patrizia very deliberately looked at her watch before giving Mors one final glare.

When the girls had gone, Giulia and Mors struck off in another direction.

"I am sorry, but I had to be sure." Giulia smiled.

"Don't be sorry; I'm delighted."

"And you mustn't mind Patrizia; she doesn't trust men. Her father abandoned them, and her own brother informed on her for distributing anti-Fascist pamphlets. She was only thirteen, so they kept her in prison just long enough to teach her a lesson, then told her mother that if she was ever seen with a piece of paper again, she'd be hanged. Then she was expelled from school. Her brother died in Greece and she celebrated. She's an impassioned fighter, but slow to trust."

"I cannot blame her. She's impressive. And she adores you, so she is certainly bright. How do you know them?"

"I taught school briefly; they were some of my best students."

Mors took her hand.

"You, too, are impressive."

She smiled at him, and he put his hands on her cheeks and kissed her. Every molecule on his skin began to dance. Her mouth was so alive, her hands reaching up to touch him so full of potent energy. When he kissed prey, it was a pleasant interlude in anticipation of food. When he had kissed Brigit in that Berlin tunnel, it was a stolen moment. Deirdre had been a jolly diversion. But this—this was kissing a woman who wanted to be kissed and to kiss him. A woman with whom he was falling in love.

When they broke away, she was panting, and Mors had to remember to appear to breathe. The air hurt his head. The glow in Giulia's eyes was almost ethereal, and that created its own, far more exquisite pain. He reached for her, winding her hair in his fingers. Her eyes lowered.

"My hair isn't pretty," she muttered, embarrassed.

"It's lovely," he assured her. "It's yours, isn't it? It's thick and wild and runs free. Definitely yours."

She shook her head, overwhelmed. Mors could tell from her smell, the move of her body, and the zing in her lips that she was not a virgin, but that it had been a long time. He did not want to embarrass her further, but he did want to tell her what she deserved to hear.

"You're lovely, Giulia."

She looked straight into his eyes. "I . . . I'm . . . twenty-nine," she admitted, the blush running all the way down her neck. She knew he was older but that most Italian men would consider her a spinster.

"Yes, you're a woman of knowledge and experience. Be proud of that. You carry it wonderfully well. And anyway, I am a bit older than you."

"It's different for a man," she muttered, not quite able to meet his gaze.

He took her chin and looked into those black, black eyes.

"I'm different for a man," he told her. They kissed again until it was time for her to leave.

"And again!" Mors called, setting the small group through its paces. The targets were readied and the guns shouldered, aimed, and fired.

They were training in the ruins of Palatine Hill, a place no one went at night. Mors had developed silencers of his own for the additions to their little weapons stash, so they could operate in relative quiet. They had to use lanterns to have enough light. It wasn't perfect, but it worked.

Giulia had not only convinced the Orselli sisters and Patrizia to join what Mors was now calling a legion, but had brought eight other women of her small partisan group.

"I'm sure we can recruit more soon," she told him. "Men as well, of course."

Mors was not troubled. If anything, he was all the more satisfied. He knew the potential of women. They had remained at home, suffering war's consequences. Even before the war, they chafed at the binds of Fascism. Many of them had grown up with it, but that did not make them loyal. They knew there was more freedom to be had. So here they were.

As soon as the women saw the sort of battle tactics Mors could teach them, they were ready adherents. Patrizia, however, though the quickest study after Giulia, still refused to meet Mors's eye or speak to him. Whenever he spoke, he felt her sharp glare. He thought it best to ignore her and let her gradually come to see he was worthy of confidence.

Rembrandt's reluctance was far more vexatious.

"Marvelous. Not just humans, but all women," he grumbled, looking at the troops.

"Don't underestimate the strength of women, my friend," Mors advised.

"They're still human," Rembrandt pointed out.

"Perhaps you'd like me to recruit Deirdre, then?"

Rembrandt shuddered. He was poised to continue the argument, then thought better of it and went off to practice shooting on his own.

The training finished at nine. Rembrandt headed toward Aventine Hill, but Mors accompanied Giulia, Franca, and Silvia part of the way home. Patrizia tagged after them. She lived only two streets away from Franca and Silvia but was determined not to be part of the group while Mors was there. Half of Mors wanted to make a concession and leave, but he didn't want to lose a moment with Giulia.

They were halfway across the Piazza Navona when Mors sensed Deirdre nearby. He turned around. She was talking to Patrizia. Horrified, Mors started toward them. Patrizia snapped something at Deirdre and ran to catch up with the others.

"Are you all right?" Silvia asked the flushed, scowling Patrizia, who nodded. The others exchanged glances and shrugs. They were used to Patrizia.

"I'll just see what that woman was saying to her," Mors murmured to Giulia.

"You should tell her Mussolini has banned Carnevale," Giulia advised, eyeing Deirdre's bright ringlets.

"Well, this is lucky," Deirdre crowed as he approached. "Our next engagement was days away."

"What were you saying to that girl?" he demanded.

"I saw that poor wretch stumping along there, all slouched and dumpy, and thought I would be helpful, tell her she should at least wear a corset. She was not exactly grateful. I can't imagine where she learned such language."

"Can you blame her? Why would you behave so appallingly?"

"I was trying to be kind," Deirdre insisted. "A silly waste of time. Anyway, I should be getting back to Gaston. Good night." She flounced away down the square and disappeared.

Only Giulia was still waiting for him; she had sent the others on.

"I thought, perhaps, you would walk me home?" she asked. He took her hand.

"I know you're a very capable woman, but I do worry about you being alone," Mors told her. He did not want to mention her near arrest, but it had been on his mind. She shrugged.

"Trouble is always to be expected. I try to be careful. Even if they arrest me, though, they can't hold me. They have no proof of any wrongdoing."

"Let's be sure to keep them getting any for a good long while, shall we?"

"Of course. But please don't worry. I know what I'm doing. I never expected it to be easy."

Just another reason why he loved her so much.

At home, Rembrandt was listening to the news and working on the field telephone, which was nearly complete. The news was grim. There was no movement in the desert, and the Germans had taken a number of Soviet cities.

"Russian winter can't come soon enough," Mors said, settling down to clean the guns. They hadn't yet used the machine gun, but Mors liked having it.

"Beretta, Carcano, and Breda." He smiled, looking at the array of weaponry. "They sound like they ought to be traveling players instead of firearms."

Rembrandt glanced at the guns with distaste.

"Trust humans to keep finding more ways to kill more of each other. It's enough to make one wish there was no such thing as evolution."

Mors shrugged.

"If we will have Gauguin and Gaudí, we must also have guns."

Rembrandt had other interests. He whipped a cloth off the radio.

"I still have some fine-tuning to do, but this little devil should tap into every Axis radio in Sicily. Between this and the field phone, we'll never run off on a false alarm again."

"It's like I keep saying, Rembrandt, you're a genius. The legion's guerrilla skills are getting— Must you pull that face whenever I mention them?" Mors remonstrated when Rembrandt scowled. "If it's just because it's all women, I'm sure we can recruit some men. Is that what the trouble is?"

Rembrandt jutted out his chin.

"I meant nothing of the sort. I have much more on my mind than sordid pleasures," he announced haughtily. "I just think it's dangerous to work so closely with humans. They are bound to find us out."

"Not if we're careful. You really are prejudiced. Why? Most humans are quite all right, you know. And you did name yourself for one."

"Yes, and I used to *be* one, till I got better," Rembrandt rejoined with a smirk. "Look here. Obviously, I want to run the Nazis into the ground. I appreciate that Europe needs to be free for humans as well as us. I'm in this fight. I just don't want to fight alongside weak humans, or call a mortal a friend."

Mors was unimpressed, but remembered that he had felt the same way himself once and had outgrown it. He could forgive Rembrandt this.

"I do understand. I don't ask that you befriend anyone, just that you be cordial. And fight your best, of course. War demands odd alliances sometimes."

"Like you and Giulia?" Rembrandt gave him an appraising look. "I saw the way you two kept looking at each other."

"Yes," Mors murmured, smiling. "We see all the great things that are ahead. This might be beginning as an underground movement, my friend, but it won't stay that way. I have my sights set much higher than that."

"What?" Rembrandt was alarmed.

But Mors had opened his tank handbook and was lost in the world of a firefight. After a moment, Rembrandt returned to the field telephone.

When they met outside the Ristorante Bolivar the next night, Deirdre was wearing a crimson dress with matching flowers in her black wig. Mors had a mind to tell her it made her far more beautiful than her usual hair, but resisted. She winked and handed him an envelope.

"A present, from Gaston. Only he doesn't know he's giving it to you." Mors slipped it in his breast pocket.

"I shall save it for dessert. After you." He waved her inside. The maître d', who knew them now, gave them a central table and called for a bottle of Mors's favorite wine.

The sommelier had only just poured the glasses when suddenly the entire restaurant was on its feet. Someone cried, "Beloved Il Duce!" and every arm shot up in the salute.

Mussolini. At last.

To his disgust, Deirdre's eyes were snapping with excitement, and she saluted eagerly.

Mors's arm, however, did not wish to obey him. That arm had offered that salute to men who deserved it. Mors knew he must play the part of a loyal, loving Italian, but in his heart, he *was* that loyal, loving Italian, and that kept his arm at his side. It was only the sudden flash of what Cleland or Brigit would say, the attention he was about to draw to himself, that made the arm inch upward.

"Per favore, per favore!" The dictator laughed. "Please, everyone, sit down. Enjoy yourselves."

The maître d' bustled up to the vampires, his face bright red with shame.

"So sorry, so sorry! This is Il Duce's favorite table. Please, if you would . . . ?"

"Of course, of course!" Mors was only too willing to accommodate and shift to a much less fine table. Mussolini, two men, and a beautiful woman whom Mors knew must be Clara Petacci, the dictator's mistress, approached the table. Mussolini took stock of Mors, and smiled politely.

"I hope you are enjoying your evening."

"Far more, now that you have honored us with your presence."

The squat man smiled again, although the expression did not suit him. He had sharp eyes that wanted to glare. Like Mors, he was bald, and like Mors, he radiated a kind of seductiveness; but in his case, it was the allure of authority. He was a commander to the core, an absolute ruler, and many found that irresistible. This Clara, nearly thirty years his junior, was a dark beauty who obviously adored and would do anything for him. Perhaps he was a fine general. But Mors could feel through to the man's core and knew him to be ruthless and, at heart, weak. Weak because he had no mercy, no flexibility, no love.

"I see you are drinking a Barolo '29," Mussolini complimented him. "An excellent choice."

"Thank you, sir. Whatever our enemies may be trying to take from us, they cannot deprive us of our wine."

The dictator laughed and his party joined in. He appraised Mors with care, admiring the cultured, perhaps aristocratic man. Mors could see him wondering why a man such as this was not known to him, not a member of the government in some capacity.

"I have spent quite a number of years away from Italy," Mors said smoothly, "and whatever anyone wishes to say about Rieslings, or even Bordeaux, there is no doubt but that ours are the finest grapes. I could expound on their superiority for hours. And indeed, I have. This did not make me popular in Berlin."

Deirdre was hovering at his elbow, excited. She wanted to meet the man who ruled Italy.

But Mussolini was fixated on Mors.

"And what did you think of Berlin?" Mussolini wanted to know.

"Quite cold. In every sense." Mors answered with a smirk.

The man and his coterie chuckled appreciatively.

"Yes," Mors continued, warming to his theme, "I far prefer being back in Rome. The sights, the sounds, the smells—the fine new government buildings, for which you are to be congratulated. The Palazzo degli Uffici is far finer than that excrescence of Speer's. A shame it is not open to the public."

Mussolini threw back his shoulders, clearly wishing he were taller than the cultured gentleman.

"You may rest assured, my dear sir, that every true Roman of the greatest pedigree—such as yourself—is naturally invited into the buildings that house Rome's government. Such was the way of the old empire; such is the way of the new."

With that, Mussolini smiled again, and Mors saw his cue. He began to offer the salute, giving the dictator the opportunity to brush it away, casual and easy, an affable man.

"Do enjoy the rest of your meal, my friend," Mussolini said by way of farewell, and Mors hustled Deirdre to their new table, trusting that the business of sitting and ordering would make Mussolini forget that he didn't ask for a name.

"Drink that quickly and let's get out of here," Mors ordered Deirdre, his mind spinning.

"I cannot believe you did not present me to Mussolini!" Deirdre wailed when they were outside.

"I wouldn't have known what name to give you. But another time, I shall not be so remiss. Will you mind dreadfully, my dear, if I call our evening short? I'm feeling the need of a meal."

"Of course." She reached up for a kiss, which he deposited perfunctorily on her cheek. There was a flash of disappointment in her eyes, but she bade him good night sweetly enough.

Mors practically soared home. He could not wait to tell Rembrandt the news. Tomorrow night, he could enter the Palazzo degli Uffici and begin gathering military information. After all, he had received an invitation into the heart of the government offices from Mussolini himself.

At the main entrance to the Palazzo degli Uffici sat a lone guard reading a leather-bound book. The vampires stood at the back, making final preparations.

Rembrandt found a dark corner, perfect for viewing the whole of the area behind the building and within earshot of the front. His job was to whistle a warning that would sound like a cricket to nearby humans.

Mors scampered up the building, guessing his quarry lay on the top floor. It was a careful hand that reached out to nudge the window open, but no such care was necessary. The building welcomed him.

Mors was not surprised to find the place empty, and he padded down the shiny corridor at his ease, studying the identical doors.

"Now, let's see. What fairy-tale hero am I? Some damn fellow had to pick the right door out of a dozen to find the princess. Where is my princess?" he muttered to himself, testing up and down the corridor for an unlocked door. He didn't really expect any of them to be so easily accessible, just because they assumed they were immune to intruders did not mean they mustn't be cautious. Finally, he jimmied a door open using his tie clip.

The windows were covered by shutters as they were in the ancient days, giving him the confidence to turn on a lamp. It took only a few glances through the files to learn that there were great plans being made for the whole of North Africa, despite the difficulties the Allies were giving the Axis in the Western Desert. Reading between the lines, Mors quickly ascertained that these were predominately German plans with the Italians latching on and expecting some crumbs beyond those they already held.

Greedy, greedy boys. Were probably never given sweets as children.

It took six more offices before he found what he wanted. Italy had been caught unprepared with Germany's invasion of Poland, not having enough materiel in place for a proper war, and was desperately trying to compensate with stepped-up production.

Well, if Mussolini wants to know what Hitler thinks of him . . .

Nonetheless, there was weaponry at the ready, and well-trained garrisons. Mors jotted down all the information.

The smell came so quickly he snapped the pen in his hand. A volcano of ink spurted onto his face and the rug. Fresh warm blood at the front entrance.

Mors shoved his list and the broken pen in his pocket and replaced the files so that nothing looked disturbed. He forced himself to be efficient as he hurried, wondering where Rembrandt was. Then he heard shouts and a scuffle.

Swearing to make a pirate weep, Mors cleaned up the spilled ink with his handkerchief and finally had to trust to the busyness of the design to hide the rest. It was a small trick to lock the door again. The shouts were louder.

"Damn it to hell!" he growled, locking the door at last and tearing straight back out the window from which he'd come, only making sure it was closed before leaping down to the ground.

Rembrandt and Deirdre were engaged in a furious tussle just outside the door, from which blood spilled. Mors pulled them apart and held on to each.

"What the hell is going on here?"

"I saw Rembrandt lurking at the back, got the sense you were here, and wanted to surprise you," Deirdre explained, spitting hair out of her mouth. "So I got the guard to invite me in. It was fine until that idiot interrupted me." She jerked her head at Rembrandt, who lunged for her.

"Deirdre, you—" Mors began, but then heard a ragged whisper from inside: "Help, help me." The guard was still alive.

Rembrandt looked toward the door, and the guard begged, "Please, come, help me." It was an invitation. Mors nodded to Rembrandt.

"Go, deliver the coup de grâce. I'll finish this," he indicated Deirdre.

"'This'? 'This'?" Deirdre snapped. "Your rudeness has become appalling."

"What game are you playing? And how did you find me here?" Mors's voice was not much louder than the guard's.

"Oh, ho, my dear!" Deirdre laughed. "You are well in me now. I can find you anywhere. Or at least within a few miles. Perhaps I just got lucky. Wouldn't you like to get lucky?"

She brushed her fingers down his neck, and he gripped her hand, bending it in half so she whimpered.

"Listen here, my girl. . . ."

She reeked of fresh blood, but as he drew closer, so close his face was almost in her hair, he smelled something else. Cleland.

Mors slammed Deirdre into a pillar, hard enough to make it crack. White chips rained down, landing in her hair. His talons gripped her throat. Five rivulets of blood trickled down her neck.

"You lying bitch. You said he was dead!"

She laughed. A mirthless, mocking laugh.

"Oh, he is! Most of him, anyway. But that isn't to say one can't use his essence."

Mors drew his talons farther down her throat. She cackled through blood-soaked teeth.

"Come now, Mors, you didn't think you were the only one who could control your scent, did you?"

As they had in Berlin, Deirdre's irises detached and whirled in a sickening, kaleidoscope-like fashion. He felt a punch in the stomach, an urge to vomit.

"Where is he? Where is he? Why did you come here?" Mors bellowed, shaking her.

"I'm here because we need fresh supplies!"

Deirdre kicked with far more power than Mors would have thought possible. She caught him squarely in the flank and unbalanced him just enough to free herself and dance into the square.

Mors and Rembrandt both ran for her and were doused in floodlights. A blacksnake whip lashed out and lassoed Mors, making him stumble. Stakes were shot at Rembrandt, who dropped and rolled but was able to grasp Deirdre's foot. Mors tore free from the whip and took hold of her, whirling her around like a shield.

"Apolline, hold him!" came Traugott's voice.

"If this is meant to trap me, it's a bit pathetic!" Mors taunted.

"I don't think so," Traugott responded.

Deirdre whipped around and sank her fangs into Mors's breast—an attack that could release an immobilizing venom on a vampire, but Mors's age spared him. The pain, however, was blinding, as though he were burning from inside. Mors and Rembrandt both attempted to pull her jaws open as a man ran up to Rembrandt, holding a bottle. Mors realized what the man was about to do and flipped their bodies around. Some of the holy water still hit Rembrandt, but Deirdre took the brunt of it.

The howls of the two vampires were deafening, although Mors could still hear Traugott screaming, "Apolline!" Deirdre released Mors and ran. He sprang for her and caught her shin so that she fell flat on her face; he heard the crunch of shattering fangs. Then he saw another stake being shot at Rembrandt, who was still writhing in agony. Mors bolted his fastest, catching it an inch before it pierced his friend's back. He picked up Rembrandt, and they stumbled away, hearing the roar of sirens.

Mors had no idea where they stopped, only that it was quiet. Blood was still dripping from his chest, and the throbbing pain was excruciating. He pressed his coat against the wounds and felt something crinkle.

"What the hell?"

There was an envelope in his pocket—the one Deirdre had given him the night before. He tore it open. It was a drawing of Deirdre, naked, winking up at him. A scrawled caption read: "Love you!"

Mors ripped and ripped and ripped until the pieces were no bigger than dust particles, which he then released out into the air.

Chapter Twelve

It was Mors who had come to find Otonia when next they met, and many more times after that. He never asked forgiveness; neither did she offer it. What he did ask, now and then, were questions about the vampire life. Her answers proved what he already knew—just how different he was. His never-ending pursuit of madness, the abilities of a vampire far older, and his continual disdain of friendship or love. These were things he loved to hear, and he loved to hear her tell them. Her voice reminded him of a rippling fountain.

"At some time, I expect you will encounter a difficulty," Otonia told him one evening.

"Oh, dear, just the one?" he asked.

Otonia smiled.

"You may always want to be a part of human events."

"Well, of course. Don't you?"

"We're not human."

Mors sensed that she was going to start philosophizing on vampire life and interrupted.

"Let's carry on talking specifically about me."

She didn't laugh. Instead, she gave him a slow, appraising look.

"Most of us were quite young." She held up a hand to stop his complaint, and raised an eyebrow. "We were young, and we hadn't had a chance to do anything worthwhile in the world." The hint of a shadow flitted across her eyes and was gone. "We were ordinary, unmarked, unmissed. You, I suspect, were something else."

"I was extraordinary."

"I would not be surprised." She was sincere.

"A veritable earthshaker." He was determined to carry on until he saw at least a crinkle around her eyes.

"Perhaps known, beloved, though with no bloodline to continue. In that, you are the same as all the rest of us. But in all other respects, you are unique. It will make things different for you. You may not have the easiest time."

"That hasn't been my experience thus far. But whoever said I wanted an easy time?"

"Just so you're aware."

He didn't want to touch her, nor she him. Which only added to her intrigue. He began to enjoy hearing her talk of things other than himself. Human politics, scholarship, food. Of her own history, she said nearly nothing. He did not ask about her connection with Xenon, although he assumed that a spellbinding story lay there.

Otonia was Greek—"Athenian, if you please"—and nearly one thousand years old.

"One thousand?" Mors was impressed. "Should I start planning the party now?"

"Perhaps you should. We change when we become millennial. We become even more powerful. And much harder to kill. It takes a special stake to destroy us then."

She had told Mors that a wooden stake through the heart could kill them, which he found absurd. He liked the idea that it would be harder as the centuries passed. He liked that Otonia would soon have that power.

"How do you come to know so much?" he asked.

"I pay attention, I study, I read," she answered. "I live surrounded by books."

The idea of the books planted itself in Mors, like his demon. Written words were a memory, a human memory, and a sweet one. It wended its way from his heart to his head so that when Otonia casually asked if he would like to see her library, his eyes lit up.

Otonia lived on Aventine Hill, below the Temple of Minerva.

"I prefer to call her Athena, but I will allow for some differences," she said. Mors paused outside the temple. He could smell incense.

"Are we allowed to walk on consecrated ground?"

"We do not go inside, if that is what you are asking," Otonia told him. "But we may be near, so long as we remain respectful." With that, she retreated past the temple to a wall of the aqueduct. She gripped one of the wall's stones, and it swung open like a door. Behind it were steps leading down.

"How did you build it so as not to interfere with the water?" Mors wanted to know.

"With care," was the simple answer.

Otonia's apartment was lovely. The oil lamps cast a bright, friendly light. Lovingly carved chairs surrounded a polished table. A divan was covered by a woven rug. Shelves ran from the floor to the ceiling, and on these shelves were books. Some in scrolls, others codices. They were histories, plays, poems, and maps. Most from Greece, but some from Egypt and Rome, including the Roman republic. Mors picked up one of these and opened it. He had hardly read three words when his heart did something it hadn't done in centuries. It thumped.

He yelped, dropping the book and doubling over, a hand on his chest.

"Are you all right?" Otonia put an arm around him and backed him to the divan. "Here . . ." she crossed to a shelf full of bottles and goblets and selected one, pouring Mors a drink. "He's fresh."

Mors sipped slowly, allowing the blood to calm him. He looked into Otonia's eyes, awed by his own body.

"My heart beat."

She did not seem surprised.

"Our bodies can sometimes respond with the vestiges of human emotions. Well, you know that already. How else do you enjoy yourself with women so thoroughly?"

"How do you know about that!" Mors was offended. He could even feel the heat rising in his eyes.

"It's in your skin. It is one reason you continue to live, even as you're so wild. You enjoy them, they enjoy you, and you send them off in ecstasy." Otonia smiled. "And to think the humans say we are the foulest beasts."

"I eat the way I do because it tastes best." Mors knew he sounded obstinate, but he resented the implication that he was kind.

"It amounts to the same thing. There is thought behind it." She gave him a steady look, then went on. "Our bodies are complex. We are, after all, impossible. As we grow older, gain experience, aspects of humanity find their balance with the demon. Our brains are strong the moment we break ground and only get more powerful, but our hearts take a while to find themselves."

"Well, they are our weakness."

"That depends upon how you look at it. But the wider point is that, in moments of deep emotion, our hearts can briefly respond as though they were human. The body's memory is very long. We can control—"

"I didn't ask for an oration!" Mors snapped. "Why on earth should my heart beat on reading a book?"

"If you read more, you wouldn't need to ask," Otonia responded. She picked up the dropped book. "It is a history of the Roman legions under the republic. The page you were looking at speaks of one of the most eminent, led by General Vitus Vipsanius. There is a charming illustration. Unusual. These illustrations are usually of the man alone. Let's see, 'General Vitus Vipsanius, his wife, Valeria, and—'"

"Stop!"

The force of his shout made Otonia jump. It echoed around the room, the feel of it hanging in the air long after it had dissipated. Mors stared at the silver goblet in his hand, which now bore indentations from his fingers.

"I collect whenever I can," Otonia continued in a conversational tone, rolling up the scroll and tucking it inside her tunic. "The humans can be careless. It's not always their fault, of course. Fires will happen, as will regime change. Things get erased, written over, disvalued, discarded. But

I like a library, and think it ought to include everything. It all has its worth. The people die. Books live."

She ran a finger over the many volumes, her eyes glittering. Mors wondered what else she had ever loved so much as she loved these books.

"Doesn't it all belong in the human world, though? It's their history."

Otonia shrugged. "Perhaps, someday, when they are willing to give respect even to words they would rather not read and history they would rather not remember, I will see about returning them. Copies, anyway."

He laughed then. Otonia laughed, too, and impulsively clambered up a short ladder to the top shelf. She seized several boxes and dropped them down to him. Brimming with curiosity, he followed her to the table, where she opened the boxes and drew out reams of paper.

"It has been a very long time since I showed anyone these. Look." She handed him a page. "I have been recording everything I have learned about our kind, telling our stories." He scanned the pages then turned back to the shelf. Dozens of boxes sat in neat rows. He blinked at her and she shrugged. "I told you. Nearly one thousand years. But in point of fact, this is comparatively recent. Here, would you like to see a real prize?"

He was hardly going to say no. She grinned and produced a book written in a human hand. This, too, was festooned with illustrations of people, but next to them, vampiric faces.

Otonia was too excited to let Mors ask the question that was just forming on his lips.

"It was written by a vampire hunter. The year before Caligula's assassination. I killed him."

"You killed Caligula?"

"The hunter. It's not for us to assassinate leaders, however much they may deserve it. But look, see? It is a record of vampires! The hunters decided it was time to know something about us. They started in Greece, I suppose, but this is the only one I have been able to secure."

"The hunters. So the Legion of Diana is real?" he asked.

Otonia frowned.

"I've told you!"

"I may not have been listening." He had the grace to look a little abashed. Otonia groaned.

"Mors. It is an absolute miracle you have survived. The Legion of Diana are men trained to hunt and kill vampires. Their efficacy has waxed and waned, but they are always here." She selected another volume and practically threw it at him. "Bedtime reading. You can study them yourself. Now, look at this!"

Her voice was swollen with pride and pleasure. Mors looked at the hunters' book. The very first vampire written about was Otonia. There was a poor rendition of her human face, and nothing more. Mors read the sparse text out loud: "The oldest known vampire in Rome is Otonia, originally from Greece, presumed Hellenistic, not generally seen with companions. Too Greek to be considered attractive; seduces prey with conversation. Hunts intermittently, mostly choosing young women or men less likely to be missed. Often seen near places of importance when meetings known to be taking place at night. Very hard to find, harder to kill." Mors turned to Otonia, who was smiling serenely. "Impressive."

"It's an accomplishment."

"Where does it mention me?" Mors wanted to know.

"It doesn't. Incredible, considering what a menace you were. You always moved a bit too quickly for them, I think."

Mors was not assuaged. He pored through the book, suspecting it was a forgery.

"This is ridiculous. How can they learn anything about us? And why would they bother writing about it if they're supposed to be killing us?"

"We study them and they study us. In their way."

But Mors was tired of talk. His energy was rising. He had to run.

He registered the fleeting disappointment in her eyes but didn't much care. He liked that she didn't entirely trust him, as it kept things interesting. He skipped away into the night, cold in the hours just before dawn. He wanted to find hunters. Men who were arrogant enough to think they could kill him. He wanted to break them into bits small enough for a child's toy box.

Not wanting to work too hard, Mors simply summoned the demon, asking it to have some fun. The demon obliged. It liked when Mors gave way to it completely. It took hold, turning his face monstrous, his hands into claws. Thus on display, Mors went dashing through the darkest alleys in Rome, the places where women not in the Guild of Prostitutes offered their wares—women and some men, too. The places where humans lived on the edge and where some went to taste the edge. The places where vampires hunted with pleasure and ease.

At this hour, there were almost no humans out, and those Mors passed did not see his features: He ran too fast for them. Instinct told him that if a hunter was out, the blur would tell the man what it was.

Mors was right. It was not long before he heard the unmistakable cry of "Vampire!" and felt himself followed. He slowed down, just to be fair. Arrows whizzed by him. He listened harder, ignoring the feet and just hearing the arrows, so that he knew when they had been discharged and could duck and weave accordingly. When the quivers were empty, he turned and faced his pursuers head-on. One turned tail and ran, but the other stood still and faced the grinning vampire.

"Mors," he informed the hunter helpfully. "My name is Mors."

The hunter said nothing, simply reached for the wooden stake strapped to his thigh.

A tiny change in the air behind him made Mors spin just in time to raise his arm and stop the second hunter from plunging a stake into his back. He shot his talons toward the man's eyes, but the hunter adroitly ducked and kicked—a blow that would have broken the wrist of a human. Mors yelled in pain but also in delight. A real fight! He slammed his elbow into the man's neck just as the first hunter leaped on him. He spun, gripping the hunter's wrist. Even as he twisted, the man struggled, sweating, determined to drive the stake into Mors's heart. Mors kept his foot hard on the downed man's neck and at last succeeded in breaking the wrist of the man who held him. He laughed, pushing the man backward so he toppled over his fellow.

The telltale sound of swinging metal told him to duck. A third hunter had joined the group and aimed to lop off Mors's head. Mors jumped back up, laughing harder.

"Nicely done, but a soldier never forgets the sound of a sword coming at him. Or how to disarm an opponent."

He spun, kicking the man in the stomach and snatching the sword. The hunter recovered fast and yanked a stake from inside his boot. Then the hunter whose wrist was not broken stunned Mors by grabbing his arms from behind and attempting to immobilize him so the other could strike. He knew Mors could shake him off with ease but was hoping that the element of surprise would give his fellow the only advantage he needed. It almost worked: The stake came perilously close. Even as Mors twisted so that the stake plunged into the arm of the man gripping him, he had to acknowledge he was impressed; he liked that they emphasized training.

The third hunter still wielded the stake, but Mors with a sword was not to be toyed with.

"Yes, I do know how to disarm an opponent."

And with four swift, smooth, beautiful strokes, the man was spread-eagled on the street, his limbs cleanly separated from his torso.

"But I show respect to a good fighter. And mercy," he was quick to point out, slicing through the man's throat.

The unhurt hunter took hold of his comrade and backed away, but Mors was done with killing for now.

"You be sure to write me well," he warned, his laugh bouncing off the dark walls. He could feel the shudders of the sleepers inside.

He bent to the dead man and scooped up some of the warm blood in his palm to drink.

"Mmm. Not bad. Not bad at all."

The sky was turning navy. Mors skipped to his own little hovel hidden behind a wine cellar, propped up the sword beside his bed, and tossed the book Otonia had given him into a corner.

"Who needs bedtime reading when you can have bedtime killing?"

Very early the next evening, Mors was deep in a dream. He was dancing on the top of flames while chased by assassins. He taunted them, playing a child's game: "Can't catch me! Can't catch me! Can't catch me!" Then he turned and smiled, just as a sword went flying into his throat.

Mors's eyes flew open, and a yell choked around the sword whose tip was nestled in his throat. Otonia was standing over him, her face calm but her eyes burning. For the first time in his vampire life, Mors felt a flash of fear. He could feel blood tricking down either side of his neck, staining the bedclothes.

"You think arrogance and hubris will keep you alive, which only proves just how great a fool you are," Otonia said. "You've done well, for one so impulsive and imprudent, but that has been your luck. It will run out. If you want to thrive thanks to something more than luck, you need to learn."

"Otonia," Mors managed to gasp, but she dug the sword in another millimeter. Her eyes swelled, glowing.

"You already know you are different. It is unfathomable that you would not wish to truly explore that. Perhaps I was wrong, to think you were worth my effort."

"No," he choked.

"If you want to make a true and lasting mark upon history, you must first learn history."

She turned and flung the sword into the corner in a gesture that might have been careless, had the sword not pierced straight through the discarded book.

Mors sat up and pressed the edge of his tunic to his sore neck.

"Maybe tonight we—" he began.

"No," Otonia interrupted. "I don't trust you. I realize this may not be a scruple for you, but it is for me."

He did not argue, but he felt a tiny twinge of regret.

As she left, he couldn't help asking. "How did you know where to find me?"

She didn't bother to look back at him.

"I knew."

Otonia had been right. Mors did not much care if she trusted him or not. But she had dangled something before him, and he wanted it. With more ability to tap his own power, he could create more mayhem.

Some weeks later, he came upon her as she prowled the city. Not knowing what else to say, he asked, "Why did you leave Greece?"

"I like to be in the world's power centers," she replied. "Home is where the heart of civilization is. Which means I'll be leaving Rome soon."

"What?" Mors was aghast. "Why?"

"You can feel it if you pay attention."

He felt nothing. She rolled her eyes and crooked a finger at him. He followed her into the sewers, which she strolled through like other ladies did gardens—and got less dirty. She led him into the palace.

"I thought this was private!"

"Not anymore," Otonia announced, "the Imperial Palace belongs to Rome."

Otonia knew how not to be seen. Mors could not understand how she did it, but simply followed, trusting in the aura she cast to keep them from confrontation. At first, Mors found it awkward to cling to the corners where walls met ceilings, the better to listen to conversations. But if Otonia could do it while wearing a long flowing tunic, he was determined to manage.

"What if the humans look up?" he asked.

"They rarely do," Otonia replied.

They were able to stay hidden there the rest of that night and on into the next day, listening to all that took place. The humans were full of frantic conversation. Colonies were breaking free, shaking off the honor of being governed by Rome. The empire was being forced to divide. And the emperor bewailed the new weakness of the Roman army.

When the sun set, the vampires took to the streets again. This time, Mors understood Otonia. His powerful senses slipped through every important place in the city, and he felt how it was weakening, giving way. The center of the world would soon be someplace else.

"I am bound east, for Byzantium," Otonia told him. She said nothing else, but he sensed there was an implied invitation. Which he accepted. But he had no intention of leaving quietly. Rome had displeased him. It must be punished.

The night before they planned to leave, Mors went to the quarters of the Praetorian Guard, whom he had always despised. This was no honorable fighting legion. Instead, it existed solely to guard the emperor and his family. The emperors had absolute power but were more concerned with maintaining their personal security than using that power for the people's good. Strong swords, not good governance, kept them on the throne.

Mors had not even knocked when Otonia spun him around and slammed him against the wall. Her eyes were red and glittering.

"What the hell do you think you're about to do?"

"And what do you think *you're* about to do, little slut?"

Mors was so startled and Otonia so livid, neither had felt the guards behind them. The one who had spoken also reached around and grabbed Otonia's breast.

Mors's talons popped out, but there was no need: The men had fallen to their knees in terror. Mors looked at Otonia. In all the years he'd known her, he had yet to see her full vampiric form. She seemed taller because of the sheer force and swell of her. Her reddened eyes bulged and swirled in their sockets, and her entire skull pressed up tight against her skin, turning her distorted face pink. Her fangs were thicker, longer than any vampire's Mors had seen. Veins popped up in her neck, her chest, her arms, tracing mountains of fury along her body. Worst of all, in its way, was her hair. Every lock broke free of its bind and took on a life of its own, so that the shiny black waves writhed like snakes. Even through his shock, Mors fleetingly wondered if she were the model for Medusa. It was the sort of sight that could frighten a man to death.

"Get out," Otonia told the cowering men, her voice still its deep, beautiful lilt. "Run hard, run fast, and give thanks to whichever god you think watches over you that you have been allowed to go home to your own beds tonight."

The men were gone so quickly they might have been vampires themselves.

Mors grinned and turned to Otonia.

"That was incredible—"

But now the full fire of her rage was aimed at him.

"You idiot!" She blazed. "You were going to try to murder half the Praetorian Guard! That is interfering far too wantonly with the ways of humans! It is not our purpose."

"Those men are a symbol of all that is destroying this world! They are corrupt, they are—"

"Then it is for the humans to decide how to manage them."

Mors looked at her a long time.

"No," he said. "Sometimes we have the advantage of them; we know more. We know better. And we can act where they can't."

Otonia's demon subsided, and her hair, face, and body returned to their usual appearance. Mors was so happy to see that face again.

"You are not, perhaps, completely wrong," she conceded. "In extreme times, it may be for us to guide the humans toward their best interests, when they have lost their way. But it is a point on which we must also exercise extreme discretion. Infinite care. We must always remember what we are. And what we aren't."

"And if we don't?"

"Good night, Mors," she said by way of answer.

He watched her walk home, remembering the first time he'd watched her walk away. It made him think of Xenon, whom they had not heard of in years. Whom she wanted to kill, although she had never told Mors why. Xenon, who wanted to kill Mors. If Mors kept close to Otonia, Xenon would come back and Otonia would have her chance. With that accomplished, perhaps she would sleep more soundly; and he could earn her trust. It surprised him to realize how much he wanted it.

When Mors came to her apartment the next night, he knew apprehension for the first time in his life. Otonia gave him a long, appraising look, then bade him inside.

Wordlessly, Mors strapped her book collection to his back, while she arranged her own bags. When the little apartment was bare, Otonia cast a glace around, taking in the furniture, the shelves, the lamps. She sighed—a very human gesture that startled Mors.

"The body has a long memory," she said, not looking at him. She doused the lamps, leaving the apartment in total darkness, and padded up the stone steps, Mors at her heels.

As they reached the city's outskirts, nearing the open road, a whine attracted Mors's attention. An almost skeletal dog was sniffing hopelessly around the clean front yard of a butcher shop.

Mors stopped, watching the animal.

"You cannot help," Otonia advised. "Animals know other animals; they know with whom not to fraternize. Let the poor soul be."

But Mors could not move. Something in the lonely, miserable creature spoke to him. The dog looked up with scared eyes, and Mors's heart lurched. He set down his bundles and approached the dog, holding out his hand. The dog came to him and licked it. Mors stroked the matted fur, scratched the chipped, sunburned ears, and the dog's tail, which had nearly taken up permanent residence between his legs, gave a rusty wag.

The dog did not flinch as Mors stood and rapped on the shop's door. He knocked several more times until the door was at last opened. The butcher was cross, but Mors dropped coins into his hand and asked for some meat. When it arrived, Mors made a bowl with his hands and knelt so the dog could eat.

Somewhere at the back of Mors's mind, it occurred to him that this was a creature who would someday die, and for the first time in centuries, he wished that wasn't so.

As he stroked and murmured to the animal, it took on a new liveliness. There was no question of it joining them.

"What will you call him?" Otonia said at last, when she had gotten over her astonishment.

"I don't know," Mors replied, untroubled. "He'll tell me soon enough."

Otonia nodded and said nothing else. Mors could feel her looking at him and he began to whistle, leaving Rome a tune by which to remember him. Now he was a vampire who had a dog for a friend. There was no question: He was going to push every other vampire clean off the pages of all the legend books.

Chapter Thirteen

Rome. Spring 1942.

The blinding rage that had driven Mors in the initial weeks of combing the city for Deirdre and Traugott—as well as any further hint of Cleland—did not subside even when he and Rembrandt had reached Paris. He had been master of himself just enough to leave a scribbled note of apology and false explanation at Giulia's lodging, then they had left.

Neither vampire had given the news or the time passing more than a few minutes' notice. Rembrandt had burn marks from the holy water, which didn't fade until the middle of February. The gaping wounds in Mors's chest had healed earlier than that, but only physically. He knew it had been no accident that Deirdre had bitten him right around the heart.

Deirdre. That evil, evil creature. Other vampires had earned Mors's deep despising, but he had never endured such a complete betrayal. He had never even conceived of such a thing. That all of it, from the moment she had met Rembrandt in Berlin, was all part of some elaborate plan of Traugott, Bishop Oster, and the rest of the Nachtspeere, was so overwhelmingly ghastly he thought his head might explode.

A vampire working with humans to help destroy other vampires. Exploit them in some unknown, unspeakable way—hence the need for doctors, which Oster had mentioned—and then destroy them. That had been her game all along, and yet he had trusted her. He had touched her.

Mors had always prided himself on his intelligence, his ability to read others, his complete mastery of any situation and anyone he wished to control. He had, he could admit now, been callous toward her. She'd known he didn't love her, wasn't interested in anything beyond the immediacy of her body and keeping her content so that she would continue to help him. She'd played along because she was playing him. It was all her game, not his.

Or perhaps it was Traugott's game. Mors was sure theirs was a relationship of constant gamesmanship. Everything he knew about them fell together like pieces in a jigsaw puzzle, making much of the picture going back to Berlin so clear. Traugott had been stationed in Paris—he spoke fluent French—and had seen her perform in the Folies. He might have known from the first moment he saw her that she was a vampire, depending on how well trained and educated he was. But he didn't care. She captivated him. They fed each other's lust for power and glamour perfectly. She promised to work for him, do whatever he said was necessary to propel him upward, and he promised not to kill her and to share the glory, give her a place in the limelight she loved. Perhaps there was even a kind of love between them—who knew?

They had guessed Mors would spy on them to test Deirdre and had staged all their conversations with a skill Sarah Bernhardt would have envied. Traugott had recognized him in Saint Hedwig's, perhaps warned Oster to watch for anyone watching him, which would have led to Ambros's murder. Traugott and Deirdre together had planned Mors's final trap: She had urged him to avenge Cleland's death and was expecting to lead him to the same place.

"She sealed the tunnels," Mors said aloud one night. Rembrandt glanced at him.

"How could she?"

"There must be some incantation, something. Maybe someone helped. She thought I'd be ready to run straight to the murder site, and with the tunnels sealed she'd guide me there, but when I planned to leave instead, that threw her. She's a wonderful actress, but improvisation may not be her strongest suit."

Mors remembered the look of shock and horror on Deirdre's face when he'd said he was going to Rome. He wished he had lied, the way he had to Brigit.

"I must congratulate you, Rembrandt," he said in a flat voice. "You never trusted her at all. You were right, and I was quite wrong."

Rembrandt shrugged. It didn't much matter anymore.

It seemed reasonable that Traugott would have taken Deirdre to Paris to heal after the disaster at degli Uffici. Mors had not seen her, but he knew that she'd been hit by a huge wash of holy water. He knew that at least one of her fangs had been shattered, possibly both, which would mean she would need to be fed until it grew back. A millennial could regenerate a fang within a month or so, but Deirdre would have a long while to wait. Then there were the gouges in her throat he'd given her. Dealt by a millennial, they would take much longer than usual to vanish. She'd have a lot to remember him by for quite some time. At least in Paris, the place she loved so much, she'd feel safe, at home. Traugott would surely see it as having the greatest therapeutic powers.

But there was no trace of them. Wearily, Mors suggested to Rembrandt they try Berlin, but they only got as far as Frankfurt and had to turn back. Germany had become colder, harsher, more impenetrable. Mors felt like he was being weighted down with stones, and Rembrandt could barely move. They only began to recover when in Switzerland. Thinking about the whole debacle, Mors did some halfhearted snooping, wanting to know if Bishop Oster was still at Saint Hedwig's. He learned nothing of Oster, but he found to his utter dismay that Father Lichtenberg, the provost, had been imprisoned for continuing to speak out against the Nazi treatment of the Jews. The provost of Saint Hedwig's Cathedral. It was no longer incredible. It was typical.

That same night, Mors and Rembrandt found a newspaper, and what they saw there broke Mors's heart further: The Germans were bombing cathedral cities in Britain. Bath. Exeter. York.

"I have to go home."

He was done. He had fought and killed and sabotaged and seen friends die, and for what? Europe was being brutalized, the Western Desert was a game of chasing circles, and his own Britain was being blown to bits. He may as well have been lying on the street, being bombed himself. There was nothing left of him.

"Come now, Mors," Rembrandt chided. "Things are turning around with the Americans in the war, and Germany hasn't got the resources to keep fighting on two fronts for very long. If we just return to Rome and—"

"What's the point? What can I possibly do anymore? I need to see my family, all those I love. . . ."

Giulia. He needed to see Giulia. Rembrandt was right, there was one reason to go back to Rome.

"Mors, I do believe this is the first I've seen you smile in all of 1942."

"Well, it's only the end of April. Yes, we're going back to Rome. We'll leave tonight."

"Hurrah! That's the spirit."

"I'll ask Giulia to come back to England with me and hope she says yes."

Rembrandt's jaw dropped.

"Giulia? That . . . you can't still be thinking of . . . you can't be serious?"

"Serious is all I am these days. Come on, let's go."

They caught the last sleeper train bound for Italy.

They could feel the change in Rome as soon as they arrived. There were more armed Blackshirts policing the streets. The city felt colder, despite the southern warmth. Mors was right: It was time to go back to Britain.

"Well, at least Deirdre never knew about this apartment," commented Rembrandt as they lit the oil lamps. The machinery and papers were strewn exactly as they had left them. They had gathered only the barest essentials before setting off to Paris. It was as though all those months had never been.

Mors had not spoken a word the whole of the journey to Rome. He bathed, dressed, and sat by the stairs, waiting till it was safe to go out. Rembrandt sat down among his equipment, cleaning everything and running tests. He kept the sound low, but Mors wouldn't have heard it even at full volume.

Once Mors deemed it dark enough, he left. He knew he was being rude, but he didn't want to hear Rembrandt try to argue him out of his decision. Or say something disparaging about Giulia.

She was not in any of the places she had been wont to be, but Mors was not worried. He knew he would find her soon. Stars had only just come out when he saw her coming out a side gate to a large house, carrying a basket of vegetables. She paused and looked across the road. Mors took off his hat and let it drop. He couldn't move.

Giulia walked toward him slowly, a woman possessed. She stopped a foot away, staring. They reached for each other at the same time and kissed until Mors thought he could just happily melt away. When they finally broke apart, Giulia burst into tears and beat at his chest with her fists.

"Months and months!" She bawled. "You couldn't have even sent one line—something, anything?"

"I wanted to. I told you in my note—"

"Damn your note! That was months ago!" She threw her arms around him and sobbed. "I thought I would never see you again."

"I couldn't have borne that." He was teary-eyed himself. "Giulia, please forgive me."

He offered her his handkerchief. She wiped her eyes and gave him a watery smile.

"Yes, of course, I understand. It's just all been so difficult. . . ."

She raised the handkerchief to her eyes again, and Mors caught her hand.

"I'm sorry!" she cried, even before he spoke.

He stared at the plain gold ring on her third finger. A recent acquisition.

"It's completely meaningless," Giulia insisted. "I don't love him; I don't even like him. I had to do something, though. I was already under suspicion, and then it all got worse after that guard was murdered at the Palazzo degli Uffici. I needed real protection. He's wiped my record clean. People are embarrassed to have ever thought I was a partisan."

Deirdre. Deirdre's killing of that guard, that useless murder, had created this wrinkle.

"He's a family friend, of sorts, and has wanted to marry me for a while." Mors had a flash of the night he'd met Giulia outside the Royal Opera House, and the man who had been staring at her with such intent. "—or rather, he has needed to marry someone understanding, who will keep his secret. He's quite high up, but if he wants to move higher yet, he must have a wife. He pays me no attention so it, well, it works."

"What if he found out what you were really doing with your time?"

The answer hung between them, swaying from the end of a rope. A man who had secrets, wanted power, and needed a wife was in little position to attack. But he had given her respectability and expected rules to be obeyed. Break them, and be broken.

"He has his own pursuits," Giulia whispered. "Neither of us asks questions. He expects me to be in my room in the mornings and to do my little duties. Beyond that, I'm free."

The word had never sounded so ironic, but Mors understood. It was an arrangement. It could someday be rearranged.

"And anyway," Giulia continued glumly, "we haven't been able to do much partisan activity or training. It just got so dangerous. It wasn't because you weren't here. People were being stopped at random, even searched. We thought it best to play all our roles, be proper Italian women, just until no one was looking at us anymore."

"It's the world's biggest fool who stops looking at you," Mors told her.

She flung her arms around him, and they stood like that a long time.

"This may sound silly"—she smiled—"but I'm rather hungry. Romano—that's my . . . him—isn't expecting me tonight. Perhaps you'd like to buy me dinner?"

"Nothing would delight me more." He picked up her basket, put on his hat, and they strolled toward the center of town.

Now that he was with her, Mors did not know what to say or how to begin asking her to leave Italy and come to Britain with him. He was suddenly not at all sure what he wanted, except to be beside her, listening to that voice and looking at that smile. Dinner was a fine idea. Even for a vampire, many conversations were easier to begin after a glass of good wine.

They were soon ensconced in a warm, poky café, sharing a huge dish of risotto and bottle of Pinot Grigio. Mors wanted to laugh. His first date.

"Giulia, have you ever gotten weary of the fight?" Mors asked at last. She finished chewing and laid down her fork.

"Well, naturally. Otherwise I would hardly be human, would I?"

"That's a harder question to answer than you might think."

She smiled. "Marcus, be sensible. How could we not get weary, or wonder if we'll ever win the day? I can't imagine there's a single soldier in the entire Allied force who doesn't have a moment of thinking it might be easier to just pack it in. And they are right, it would be easier. So long as you were prepared to submit to a brutal new regime. But that would mean a life spent living on your knees, wouldn't it?"

It was just the sort of thing he might have said, were he himself. He reached for her hand and kissed it.

Giulia looked at him with loving eyes, which, seeing something beyond Mors's head, promptly clouded. Mors turned, and every one of his organs stiffened when he saw what was happening. Three Blackshirts were standing over two older gentlemen, one of who still held a trembling soupspoon.

"Don't you know this is a Jew-free establishment?" One of the Blackshirts was glaring down at the men in triumph.

"Please, sir, there . . . there was no sign," the man pointed out, his voice soft and polite.

"Why should a nice frontispiece like that be ruined by a sign telling Jews to piss off?" The second Blackshirt was pleased with his logic. "You're lucky. In Germany, they won't even let you walk on the path."

"In Germany," the third man added, "they won't let you live."

The second Jewish man dabbed his lips with a napkin, folded it, and stood, his back ramrod straight. He looked down his nose at the second Blackshirt.

"Aren't you ashamed of yourself, Carlo Capelli? Harassing respectable older citizens in this way?"

"I know you!" Capelli exclaimed, grinning. "You were my mathematics teacher before they said Jews couldn't teach proper Italians anymore. Ha!"

"You were a very rotten student. I am not surprised you ended up in a job where a man doesn't need brains." The teacher was calm and matter-of-fact.

Capelli and his fellows were at first astounded, then roused. Capelli made to pummel the teacher, but a hand was gripping his forearm. It felt like a vise, and he almost cried out, only the man holding him smiled, and he no longer felt the pain.

"I think this can be handled without disturbing other patrons, don't you?" Mors asked politely. "Especially ladies. Now, the gentlemen are leaving, and so long as they do so peaceably, there's no reason to trouble them or anyone else further."

"They're not leaving without paying!" The proprietor, a rotund man who had given Mors and Giulia such a paternal smile when they entered, was now red-faced and indignant.

"Of course, of course," Mors cut across the protests of the uneaten food, most of which had not yet begun to be cooked. "Allow me to escort them out, and I shall bring the money in to you."

To Giulia's shock, the proprietor accepted this and went back to his station behind the counter, rather than enjoy the sight of Jews being thrown out of his café. Mors put his arms around each Jewish man and gently guided them out. Giulia could almost swear she saw him slip money into each of their pockets. She hurried to the door to watch the remainder of the scene.

The Blackshirts had recovered from their confusion and were now confronting Mors.

"See here, this is our job!" they protested.

"Yes," Mors agreed. "Intimidating and assaulting respectable gentlemen who are only trying to enjoy a meal and support a local establishment. Your mothers must be so proud."

The Blackshirts rounded on him, and Giulia trembled, although she could not help noticing that in drawing all the hostility toward himself, Mors had given the Jewish men ample opportunity to hurry away. The teacher, at least, seemed disposed to stay and not let Mors fight his battles for him, but a nearly imperceptible gesture indicated that Mors would prefer they leave and let him handle the Blackshirts. Better they not be drawn into an incident. Better they allow themselves to be forgotten.

"Who are you?" Capelli demanded of Mors. "Let's see your identification."

"I am wholly myself," Mors responded pleasantly. "You'll do well not to forget it."

Giulia did not blink but still was uncertain of what she'd seen. It was like a Commedia dell'Arte sketch: The three men lunged for Mors at once, and Mors sank into a squat so that the men instead pummeled one another. Mors threw his hands into the melee, and then all three men were unconscious on the street.

"Drunk!" Mors cried in disgust. "These men are drunk while on duty!"

He gave Capelli's body a kick before returning to the café and smiling at the proprietor.

"The lady and I would like to have the food those men ordered. And another bottle of your best Pinot Grigio."

The man scurried to fill the order, and Mors gave an appalled Giulia the tiniest of winks.

"Trust me," he whispered. "That worm is going to be very sorry he allowed such treatment of those gentlemen."

Once Mors was sure the food was being cooked and the proprietor's back turned to open the wine, he seized Giulia and barreled her out of the café. They were nowhere in sight when the proprietor, having lost profits for nearly a week, shouted into the street for justice. He thought his luck might be turning when two fat, prosperous men came in and ordered lavishly, but one chanced to sit on the chair Mors had vacated and was sent tumbling to the floor amid shouts and threats of lawsuits. On later inspection, it was found that the legs of the chair had been hacked through, although how this was possible, the proprietor had no idea.

"You gave them money," Giulia stated when they were far out of earshot. She was looking at Mors with a mixture of admiration and uncertainty.

"They'll need help to get out of Italy. Which I hope they do. I didn't quite realize—"

"No. It's not as bad as Germany or the occupied countries, but the racial laws—"

"Racial laws?"

"Mussolini appeases in his own way," Giulia said, her voice flat. "Besides, Jews tend to be anti-Fascist. The racial laws were passed in 1938. They are not supposed to extend to shops and things, but it's fluid. After all, look at the law enforcers."

They were on the riverbank. It was so dark and deserted, Mors thought that but for their modern clothing, it might have been the last millennium.

Racial laws, passed in 1938. He and the others had gone to Berlin in 1938. They thought they knew all that was happening in Europe, but they knew nothing of racial laws in Italy. He had been only too right: Italy was crying for rebirth. He looked at Giulia. Something released in both vampire and woman—something both dark and illuminating.

He took off his jacket and spread it on the ground; Giulia laid hers on top of his. She pulled him to her and they were kissing again, hands digging deeply into each other's flesh, as though determined to touch marrow. He had lain on the banks of the Tiber many times, but it was never like this.

To his horror, the demon responded to the Tiber, and to the woman, and took over. Mors tried to swallow it, to will it out of his skin, but Giulia saw. She gripped his neck and turned him back to face her. Even by moonlight, she could see the red eyes. The bulging bones and flesh, the popping veins, and the fangs—long, white, gleaming. The face of a nightmare that ended in eternal sleep.

Giulia didn't budge. She hardly even blinked. Almost as though she didn't realize she was doing it, she reached up and laid a finger on Mors's forehead, where the veins were like ridges on a globe. She traced a vein down, around his nose, to his cheek. The finger continued to explore him and Mors remained quite still, sprawled over her. He could feel her heartbeat under him and noticed it had not changed. It was pounding, but no harder than it had been. She continued to run her fingers over his distorted features, and her body rose involuntarily. Far from being alarmed, she was yet more aroused.

"I knew there was something more to know," she murmured at last. "I admit, this was not my first guess."

She tapped the tip of his fang gently, testing its sharpness. As though her finger were a trigger, the fangs slid back up into his gums and the rest of his vampire features followed. Green eyes looked down at Giulia, silently begging her not to think of him as evil. Her sweaty hand stroked the smooth skin of his cheek.

"No," she whispered. "You are not evil. Whatever you are, you're not evil."

Mors nodded, both in agreement and gratitude, and sat up, pulling Giulia into his lap.

"This puts a different complexion on things," he told her.

"I don't want to be a vampire, if that is what you were thinking."

"I don't want you to be. I wasn't going to bite. I . . . that was an accident. But I was going to tell you. I thought you had a right to know. You needed to know it was something more and less than a man who loves you."

Her eyes grew damp. Mors went on.

"I do, Giulia. I love you. For the woman you are, not anything I might make you."

She struggled for breath, tears slipping down her cheeks.

"Oh, Mar—"

"Mors. My name is Mors. In public, yes, you must call me Marcus, but between us, from now on, whatever we will be, please . . . call me Mors."

"Mors." The name rolled over her tongue like a caramel. "I know that, I remember that name. Mythology, he was one of the less-discussed gods. The god of death."

"In retrospect, it seems a somewhat prosaic choice on my part, but it fit."

Giulia shrugged, twirling her fingers over his.

"What is death but a definitive part of life? Nothing to fear. It just is, and it must be."

He felt himself fall just that much more in love with her.

At last, she leaned toward him, so close their lashes nearly touched, and said what he needed to hear: "I love you, Mors."

Words he had longed for, spoken in truth. Words that, if he were forced to admit, he despaired of ever hearing from someone with whom the sentiment was shared. Words he had waited to hear for centuries.

All in all, I would say it was worth the wait.

They sat there, foreheads leaning against each other, for a long time. They leaned in to start kissing again in the same moment. Slowly, very slowly, they began to remove each other's clothes. Mors realized it was the first time since his humanity that he was truly making love, and he wanted to commit every second to his memory. Build a trunk of its own in which to store it, deep inside him. His hands swept over her skin, thrilling to its vibrancy, its warmth, its utter aliveness.

"Do you trust me?" he asked, his tongue encircling her ear, his hand wrapped around her breast.

"With my life," she breathed.

And so he proceeded to taste the whole of her skin—a savory sweet confection that no chef could ever emulate. The demon stayed deep within him, quiet, happy. But not as happy as Mors himself. If perhaps it was he who physically entered her, it was she who pierced him far more deeply. With one hand on the back of his head and another on his back, she seemed to encourage him to melt into her. One of his own hands was entwined in her hair, at her neck, the other still on her breast. Only part of him was cognizant of what his hands could also feel—a pulse and a heartbeat.

They lay beside the river a long time, listening to the water. When Giulia next looked at Mors, her eyes were curious.

"So, you really are—were—Italian at some point?"

"I was a general in the republic."

She gaped at him. Her hand, resting on his chest, felt it as though to be sure it was real.

"That's not . . . is that possible?"

"Apparently." He chuckled.

"The republic." She sounded out the word like she was tasting every syllable and found it delicious. "The republic. Of course, it still excluded women, and almost everyone else. But it was a republic." Giulia's smile became rueful. "Until it compromised itself. Then the people lost confidence, the republic collapsed, and a dictator took over." She shook her head. "At least Julius Caesar wanted to do something more for the people."

"That's mostly just Imperial propaganda." Mors sniffed.

Giulia laughed. "You really did come here to fight to restore Rome, didn't you?"

"Well, how I ended up here is part of a much longer story. But yes." He hesitated, then spoke in ringing tones. "Yes, no question. I am here to assist the fight to restore Rome and bring freedom to the whole of Europe and the world."

"You could even help build a new republic," Giulia said, her eyes snapping. "You saw the original, after all."

"I could. Especially with you as my partner. You know this fight is going to get quite a bit nastier before it's finished, don't you?"

"I look forward to it," she insisted. "Rome was once the shining light of the world, and I would have it be so again. But better, better than anything you or the world has yet seen. It's possible, I know it, and I'll stop at nothing to make it happen."

"Yes," he agreed. "Liberty and love. Those are two things in this world well worth a fight."

Chapter Fourteen

Some years after Mors and Otonia had settled in Byzantium's capital, they learned that Constantine had done what no emperor had been able or willing to do since Julius Caesar—disband the Praetorian Guard. Otonia had been right: The humans had not needed interference.

Constantinople was a stunning, vibrant place, but Mors was restless. His dog, whom he'd named Jupiter, died a few years after they arrived, and Otonia had stayed far away while he performed the burial rites. He had felt a kind of love for the animal, though of course nothing like the love he bore himself. Still, he missed the dog dreadfully.

His hobby now was chasing war. He listened for where they were brewing and inserted himself in the midst of battles as best he could. Men did not do much fighting at night, which Mors found inconvenient.

When he returned to the city, he told Otonia about wherever he had been. One night, he asked if she'd come with him the next time.

"We don't have to fight, we can just explore."

"I thought you liked traveling alone," she said.

"I adore it, but sometimes I want someone to talk to. Besides myself, of course."

"Well, perhaps someday you'll have just that."

Mors glared at her. She was intelligent, fascinating, and sometimes, great fun. But she refused to really let him into her mind. A desire suddenly popped into his psyche. They shared an apartment now, had been companions for decades, but he knew there was still something about him she did not trust. He had gone from wanting to needing that faith.

"What am I to you, anyway?" he asked.

"What do you mean?"

"An acolyte? A trainee? A lapdog?" Mors glanced at Scylla, his newest canine companion, who was sprawled contentedly before the fire. "I don't seem to be a friend, and I've never sought to be a lover."

At that word, Otonia's eyes constricted at the edges and her pupils shifted away.

"Of course you're a friend, Mors," she said, although she still wasn't looking at him.

"But you don't trust me."

"Well, why should I?" she suddenly blazed at him. "You go away for years at a time and play in human wars, and I never know if you'll come back, so why should I rely upon you?"

"I'll always come back."

"Perhaps," she conceded. They both knew he wasn't the type to die easily, in an untold story. "Truth be told, Mors, I wasn't sure you wanted a real friend. That is very positive. It may mean you can someday fall in love."

"Why would I waste my time in such a ridiculous manner?" Mors snorted.

"Possibly it's the one thing you can't do, the mark of your wrong making. A shame, because without love, you'll always be only half of what you could be."

"That's quite rich, coming from you."

Otonia's eyes were fierce and all the more intimidating for remaining clear and human. Mors held his ground. She spoke in a low, almost guttural voice.

"I have loved."

"Have you? Well, now we're getting somewhere. Tell me about it."

She turned and picked up her pen. Mors seized her ink pot and flung it against the wall, smashing it into dust. Scylla yelped and ran under the nearest bench.

"You prefer not to talk. Very well. You stay there, then, and don't talk. I'm going out for some fun."

He whistled to Scylla and barreled up the steps and out into the night. A night he made much, much hotter. He did not return.

A few years later, the Arabs attempted to lay siege to Constantinople. Mors scaled the walls and fought now with the Arabs, now with the Byzantines, as he liked. He preferred to lend a hand to whichever side was losing, just to keep the battle going.

Unfortunately, it was soon an unfair fight. The Arabs could not make headway, and their supplies were cut off. Mors almost felt sorry for them, except that they were so pathetic. He found their leader, Maslama, and asked the man if he'd ever heard of Troy.

"The Trojan Horse—come on now, surely you know of it! Why not try something along those lines and see if you can't get in that way?"

But Mors had not learned enough Arabic, and the man did not understand him.

Mors had had enough. It was time to find Otonia again and see if she was willing to travel. Life under siege was unpleasant, and the world outside was growing.

But Otonia was not in the little apartment under the library. Mors settled himself to wait. She didn't come back at dawn. At nightfall, she was still not back.

"Stay here," he ordered Scylla. He scribbled a note and ran out.

All night, he combed the city. The entrances to the palace, the houses where great men congregated to talk, the seedy streets where the best hunting was to be had. She was nowhere.

Forced back to the lair at dawn, where only Scylla greeted him with a wagging tail, Mors felt a twist in his stomach. Panic. A foreign, ghastly feeling. His insides were being clawed, choking him. The demon. But no, no, the demon didn't care. This was something older.

The pain grew stronger; now his head was pounding. And then, almost inadvertently, he took a huge breath. The oxygen rushed into his head and lungs and paused, seeing it was not truly needed and wondering where to go next. But it seemed to open his mind and give space to his constricting organs. He closed his eyes.

Where is she?

Mors had always been respectful of Otonia's papers. Her work was private. So it was with something like guilt that he scanned the papers on the table in the hopes that they might guide him. She had been writing about vampire physiology, love, and churches—nothing to give him a lead.

As soon as the sun was down, Mors took to the streets. He did something he had never done before—approach humans and ask if they had seen a woman of Otonia's description. From private houses to public, the wealthy and cultured, to the proprietors of places only whispered about, Mors asked and asked. And learned nothing.

By the third night, he was frantic. He went straight to the heart of the slums to find Karas, one of the leaders of the criminal underworld.

"I'm looking for a woman," Mors began by way of introduction.

The man and his guards looked up at Mors and laughed.

"And what do I look like to you, a procurer?" Karas sneered.

"You're a man who sees and hears things. I'm willing to pay plenty for the information."

One of the guards stood, his dagger already drawn, and prepared to search Mors. Almost before the others blinked, the guard was curled on the floor, moaning in agony. Mors held the man's dagger and dropped five gold solidi on the table before Karas.

"That can be tripled. Or more. I want to talk to you. Alone."

Two minutes later, Mors and Karas were tucked in a tiny room off the main salon.

"I haven't seen you before," Karas began.

"Which makes you lucky. The woman I'm seeking disappeared at least three nights ago. She's Greek, about twenty-five, quite striking. . . . What?" Karas was shaking his head.

"I have seen no such woman. I apologize and wish you luck."

Mors hesitated just a moment, then plunged further.

"What do you know of vampires?"

"I . . . what?" Karas was perplexed.

"Vampires, man, vampires. Creatures who look human until they sprout fangs and suck all the blood out of your body. Have you heard of them? Have you heard of the men who hunt them?"

The man turned deathly pale. He took in Mors's fierce eyes, the slight twitching in his jaw, the steady tap of one finger on the table.

"I can see you have. I must find those men." Mors was ablaze with confused elation. He had never seen hunters in Constantinople, but most of his chaos had been performed elsewhere. Any decent hunter must know of Otonia, though. Perhaps, somehow, he could cajole them into helping him.

But now Karas was gaping at him in horror.

"Vampire? Vampire!" he began to scream.

"Oh, calm yourself and answer my question, I'm not planning on hurting you."

The terrified man whipped out a small gold cross from under his cloak and brandished it. Mors cringed. For reasons Otonia had yet to fathom, such symbols of Christianity could burn even their pre-Christian selves.

"Yes, all right, but will you please just—"

A stake shot from a crossbow pierced Mors in the shoulder. He ducked as another stake whizzed at him. Two hunters barreled in. Mors tried to ask them to stop, to let him speak, when a dagger plunged into his shoulder blade, snapping it in half. The injury gave the hunters a real chance, and they slashed at him, knocking him to the ground. Mors was bleeding from several wounds and couldn't remember ever being in so much pain or fury. He howled, sure he heard the men's eardrums rupture. But they did not stop. One slammed the hilt of a dagger into his nose, breaking it, while the other aimed a stake straight for his heart. Mors rolled; the stake barely missed. He managed to free himself and had just enough strength to jump out the window.

He landed hard on the cobbled street, his weakened body bruising. It was all he could do to stagger to his feet, and he was lucky to have that reprieve. The hunters were coming for him.

Although Mors could not run with his usual speed, he could still keep ahead of the men. He snaked his way through the streets, knowing they were following the trail of his blood in the hopes of catching him before it congealed. As he ran, Mors considered his options. These men were his one chance of learning something. He just needed an advantage.

On seeing a pile of wood next to a half-completed building, he dove in, wriggling down so he was completely hidden. The hunters passed him a few minutes later, panting.

"I can't believe we had a chance for Mors and lost him. Mors!"

"Never mind. We'll get him soon enough. He's good, but he's not invincible."

Mors crept out of the pile and followed them. Dawn was coming and they were trudging, exhausted. Mors was exhausted, too, and worried. He knew he had only about twenty minutes before he was in real danger. And yet he could not stop following them.

Otonia would kill me for this, he thought with a rueful smile.

The sun inched upward. Servants were emerging from houses, fetching water and firewood. Deep inside him, Mors felt the demon scratch at his tissues. He ducked under balconies, crept in tiny spots of shade, cursed the brightening day, but couldn't stop.

His luck changed when the tired hunters flagged down a man driving a cart and asked if they might hop on for the rest of their journey. The driver agreed and halted. Mors took his chance. He flipped his cloak over his head and summoned his full speed, tearing into the street and slithering under the cart. Those few seconds were excruciating. There was not a bit of it he didn't feel through to the bones.

He knew he would have to repeat the action when the cart stopped to let the hunters disembark, and tried not to think of it. His cloak remained wrapped around his head, and he pressed his stomach tight against the slats, gripping them so as not to let his back scrape the street. He trusted in the breadth of the cart to keep him hidden and hoped no dogs or children would happen to spot him.

Ten minutes later, the driver halted the donkeys and the hunters hopped down, thanking the man and giving him what Mors assumed from his grunt were the smallest bronze coins they had. He tugged at his cloak just enough to create a peephole and marked the house the hunters entered.

Mors moaned in relief when soon after, the cart pulled up to a stable.

He shimmied out and crawled inside, pausing in a dark corner to gain his bearing.

He had no sooner tucked himself where he thought he would be least seen than a horse reared and whinnied in alarm. Whether it was because of the appearance of a stranger or the nature of that stranger, Mors could not be sure, but he murmured the most soothing, seductive melody he had in him. The horse's eyes continued to roll, and it pawed the ground.

The stablemen came to investigate. Mors inched toward the back door, which lay ajar. He didn't know where it led, but the lack of sun pouring through it assured him that it must be safer than this spot. He didn't want to take any more risks. Not in daylight.

The door opened out into a sheltered alley that was the repository for a lot of local animal waste. Mors shot down it. He ducked and wove his way back to the hunters' house, finally taking refuge in their chicken coop. The hens squawked on his immediate arrival, but a hasty distribution of feed silenced them, even as he could feel their suspicion. Mors tucked himself into a ball near the door and squinted outside, considering his next move. Which was getting inside.

It occurred to him that he was behaving like a madman. What did he think would happen, that they would all sit down to tea? But he was sure these men had an answer for him. Perhaps, if he promised to clear out of Constantinople, they would see their way to not killing him.

A servant wearing a battered straw hat came in through the back gate and began to potter about the small garden, grumbling. Mors inched farther into the coop.

"Can't be arsed to do any of their own work and don't want to pay a person properly for doing it for them," the servant groused, snatching figs from the lone tree and tossing them in a basket. Some of the best went straight into his mouth. "Bunch of layabouts, is what they is, wandering the streets at night, doing nothing, causing trouble, I'll warrant. And for what?"

The servant knelt to muck for ready eggplants, continuing to bemoan his lot in life.

A stray dog put its head around the open gate. The servant, hacking at weeds with a hoe, didn't see the animal. Mors willed it away, but it trotted to him as readily as if he had whistled. Keeping his eyes on both dog and man, Mors slid his hand into the nearest nest, securing two eggs. The hen pecked him but otherwise kept quiet. The dog gobbled the eggs and wagged his tail in gratitude.

"Go on now, friend," Mors hissed. "Out the way you came."

"Here—what! Keep off them chickens, you cur!" the servant had seen the dog and come running, the hoe above his head.

The dog yelped and ran, but the servant was surprisingly fast. The iron hoe came down upon the dog's head once, twice, three times. Mors closed his eyes, their redness burning the insides of his lids.

When the servant burst into the coop to count the chickens, Mors clamped a hand over the man's mouth and dragged him into the straw.

"What's your name, you wormy little murderer? Tell me or I'll pull it out of you, inch by inch."

He circled a taunting talon over the man's abdomen.

"I . . . I . . . Ionnes!" the servant gasped.

"That had better be the truth," Mors warned.

The servant nodded and Mors smiled. "Good. Now, may I trouble you for the loan of your hat and cloak?" He spoke with utmost politeness, and the relieved servant complied. Mors shook out the filthy items with distaste.

"Thank you," he said, snapping the servant's neck and shoving him back down into the straw. Then he caught up a basket and began to gather the eggs.

A few minutes later, one of the hunters threw open the door to the house in answer to the insistent raps and glared at what he could see of the servant under his hat.

"All right, all right, Ionnes, get on in with you then. Try to leave the dirt outside, will you?"

The servant shuffled inside, a trail of dirt following him. The hunter sighed.

"You'll be cleaning that up without extra pay, I hope you know. Take that hat off; how dare you keep it on before your betters?"

"Charming manners, you have." Mors critiqued the man, taking off the hat.

"Symeon!" the hunter screamed. "It's Mors!"

Mors held up his hands, boring his eyes into that of the startled hunter.

"I promise, I only want to talk. I need your help if you can give it."

The other hunter ran into the room.

"What are you on about, Bardas," he began, but stopped on seeing Mors.

"You know who I am, and I know you know who Otonia is," Mors said, looking from one to the other. "If she is alive, I need to know. I need her. Can you help me?"

A glance passed between the hunters.

"I swear, she and I will leave Constantinople tonight. You'll never see us again."

"Exactly," Bardas agreed, as Symeon smashed a wooden chair, seizing a sharp sliver. Bardas ran at Mors with an ax. Each man jumped him, and in the scuffle, Bardas ended up with the ax embedded in his chest.

"This was not my intent," Mors told a panting Symeon. "I only want help. Will you help me?"

"Certainly, Mors, I will help you," Symeon answered. "Help you go back to the hell you came from."

He flung aside the table and leaped on Mors, but he misjudged the strength of his opponent. Mors gripped him from behind, twisting his wrist until the weapon was dropped.

"Don't be a fool, man. Just tell me what you know."

Symeon drove an elbow into Mors's bruised ribs and Mors yelped. The hunter expertly wrapped his legs around Mors's and threw him to the ground. But the advantage was short-lived. Their legs still entwined, Mors gripped the hunter and swung him over his head, smashing the man's head against the stone floor.

Wiping bits of brain and blood from his eyes, Mors got up and found a clean goblet. He poured himself some blood from Symeon's dripping wounds, dropped Ionnes's cloak over the smashed head, and wandered into the large main room.

The table was strewn with papers and legend books. Mors tossed back the blood in one gulp and began to read. Unlike Otonia's work, these were in no order. He skimmed them until his own name caught his eye: "'Mors, of the early Roman Empire, or perhaps earlier'—yes, a bit earlier than that, you sods—'not millennial, but many millennial powers. Tends to travel alone. Not known to have made any new vampires . . .' Can't they write my history better than this?"

He found a note, dated the night before he had hopped the wall back into the city.

"Caught glimpse of Xenon tonight. Tracked, but got away. Will set traps at favorite spots," the paper read.

Xenon. Of course. The hunters didn't know what Mors now knew in his bones, that Xenon had somehow captured Otonia. The plague of him would be ended tonight.

Mors slept fitfully, then packed all the books and papers into a leather case and gathered every weapon he could find. He helped himself to an ornamented cloak that was fitted with pouches in the lining, all designed to carry more weaponry.

The door slammed shut behind him the second the sun dropped below the horizon. A neighbor, heading into his own house, was startled and peered at the strange man.

"If you want chickens, you may take them all from our coop," Mors called. "This house will be empty for quite some while."

He fled into the night, feeling the neighbor's eyes deep in his vanishing back.

Despite the hopelessness of the Arab besiegers, the walls were still heavily manned. Mors didn't care, as the attention was focused outside, not in. He scampered straight up the limestone surface to the nearest tower and hopped onto a battlement. A soldier saw him and started to shout, but Mors held out a mosaic-handled dagger.

"You can stow this *on* your person or *in* your person, as you like."

The man shut his mouth, trembling.

Then Mors sent out the sort of cry normally heard only by dogs. He knew it would be heard by his intended listener.

"You killed me once, but you still haven't got the best of me. Not even close."

Soon, sooner than he might have hoped, there was a returning cry from a nearby roof.

"Haven't I told you not to get too comfortable?"

Mors tossed the dagger to the guard and leaped to the roof, landing with catlike grace. But Xenon had disappeared.

"Running away again?" Mors cried.

"Follow the trail," Xenon responded in a taunt, already well ahead.

The guard gaped at the man soaring from roof to roof. He began to scream.

"Vampires! Vampires are loose in the city. Vampires!"

The soldiers and the people came to attention.

The bloody trail smelled both like Otonia and a human woman. Mors ran faster, although he knew now that speed didn't matter. Xenon would be waiting for him whenever he arrived.

At the entranceway to a small house in a quiet street, an **X** was painted in blood. Mors snorted, disgusted by the vampire's cheap theatrics. It was a human home, but Xenon had gained entry, probably with his boyish charm. The bodies of a widow and four children were strewn through the living space. Children, again. Mors had paid little mind to the vampire laws of which Otonia spoke, considering himself above such things, but for all the careless mayhem he had ever caused or reveled in, he had never, and would never, kill children.

Mors descended into the cellar, where Otonia was bound in heavy chains. She could have fought her way out, but Xenon had done his work well. An ax was buried in her neck, and he had turned her so that she bled with torturous slowness. He had also sliced artful circles around her ankles and wrists. These were now nearly healed, but the ax kept her immobilized and barely conscious. Barely alive.

Her eyes gave a feeble spark on seeing Mors, and he felt a flutter of emotion.

"How the hell . . ." he began in a whisper, but stopped himself. The crusts of blood on Otonia's lips told him what had happened. Xenon had overpowered Otonia in one of the only ways possible. He had cowardly attacked her while she was buried in a meal.

Xenon leaned against the wall, juggling stakes. He grinned at Mors.

"It's rather sweet that you'd come to rescue her when she could care two straws for you."

He drew the edge of a knife over Otonia's arm, leaving a trickle of blood.

"Continuing to hunt me took her from her studies," Xenon went on "Keeping you nearby meant I'd come back eventually. Save her trouble."

"If that's true, Xenon, I respect her that much more."

"Ironic, really," Xenon sneered. "I wonder if it ever occurred to her that I might use her to get to you."

Mors stared at him. The hatred in his mouth tasted like iron.

There was a rumble in the streets. It might have been a strong wind. Xenon smiled.

"Well done, Mors. You attracted the humans."

"They will want to kill you, too."

"Undoubtedly, but I'll be long gone."

Mors had forgotten that Xenon was now a millennial. The speed with which he snatched the ax from Otonia's neck and swung back-handed at Mors was a formidable thing. An eye might blink more slowly. Ever the old soldier, Mors dodged the blow, but it struck his fighting arm, singing out as it hit the bone. Through his shriek of pain, Mors realized that was how Xenon planned it. He did not want too quick a fight. Just so long as it was dirty.

The ax came down again and Mors caught it with his other hand, delivering a scissor kick to Xenon's groin and head. Xenon spun and landed on his back, and Mors whipped off half of Otonia's chains to weigh him down, then plunged one of his purloined stakes straight into the vampire's heart with a sure, clean blow. He smiled.

To his horror, Xenon only gasped, fell, then returned the smile. He stirred feebly, but stirred nonetheless.

"Oh, Mors, all these years with a scholar and you still have so much to learn."

Then Mors remembered—it took a special stake to kill a millennial. He would have to aim for the head. He wished he couldn't hear more human rumbling.

"You're right, Xenon," he agreed. "There is a great deal I don't know. I don't know how you can kill children, for example, or be such a single-minded coward. I don't know how you can be over one thousand years old and yet still be such a whelp. But maybe it's like I said once before: You're the runt of the litter. Is that why your maker deserted you?"

The icy fury with which Xenon then attacked Mors was such that Mors wondered for years after if he had touched a nerve. Xenon fought like a thing possessed, screaming a high, endless scream, determined to beat the life out of Mors with fists and claws and teeth. It was all Mors could do to keep whole, let alone fight back. Somewhere in the midst of the whir of claws and blood and screams, Mors registered a different scream. Otonia.

"His head, grab his head! Hold it still!"

The force of the shock stunned Mors into obedience, and he focused. It was just another battlefield, after all. Just a mass of swinging blades. He did what he always did—reached through the empty space. There was always an empty space. It changed by the millisecond, but that only meant a small adjustment. Mors reached, and seized, and held.

The blade swung in a blur. One moment, Mors was gripping a sweaty mass of hair, then dust was spilling from his fingers, covering his stained tunic. The ax fell next to him with a clatter, and Otonia staggered back, collapsing onto the bench. The gash in her neck was nearly closed over.

Mors dragged himself to his knees and shook the dust off him. Then he spat into it and looked at Otonia. She was paper-white with sunken cheeks, but a contentment oozed from her.

"Always so rash, Xenon. If he'd kept that ax in me, he could have had us both."

Mors hated knowing that Xenon could have bested and ended him.

"I think you cheated me, old girl," Mors couldn't help chiding.

Otonia shook her head.

"No. That was my kill. I have waited far, far longer than you. That was mine."

She leaned over and spat into the dust as well. Mors caught her as she nearly toppled off the bench. He held her a moment, memorizing her solidity. But now was not the time to talk, or think.

"We can't hide here; he's marked the door. We have to run, Otonia. Can you run?"

With immense effort, she pulled herself back up so she could look him in the eye.

"Yes. If you help me."

He carried her up the stairs and outside. They hovered by the edge of the house as they listened to the cries of the growing mob.

"Which way, do you think?" Mors asked.

Otonia took his hand.

"Do you trust me?" she asked.

"Implicitly."

"Home. We must first go home."

He thought the lack of blood had driven her mad, but he did indeed trust her. However, she was too weak to go so far. Mors glanced around.

"Otonia, do you trust me?"

Once again, the big black eyes fixed on his—and grew warm.

"With my life."

"Then stay here a minute, and don't move."

Mors tucked her into a quiet corner and tore into the night. An interminably long three minutes later, he was back, carrying a not-quite-dead vagrant. He propped up the body so that Otonia didn't have to make the smallest exertion, just pop out her fangs, tilt her neck, and eat. Mors swore he could see her skin grow plumper and smoother as she sucked down the blood. The wounds on her wrists sealed, and her complexion regained some of its usual olive hue. The jagged, bloody gash in her throat congealed further. Inside him, Mors was begging, *Hurry, hurry, oh, please, hurry.*

Mors didn't know if there were other hunters in the city. But a mob was a creature—a hunter—all unto itself. If not a single individual in it knew how to bring him or Otonia down, it might count as nothing when there were many hundreds, all with their blood up, all wielding weapons. He had been right. This was the time to run.

They sped back to the lair, where Scylla barked happily on seeing Mors at last. Scylla! Mors felt another blow like a stake to the heart.

"You'll have to turn her loose, Mors; she can't possibly keep up with us."

He didn't answer. Swiftly, silently, they swept the books and papers into cases and draped them about their bodies. Lastly, Otonia reached for the bow and arrows she had used to hunt Xenon and set them on her back.

"Souvenirs," she told him. "And we might need them."

Mors privately thought it might take more than that, but he said nothing. The cries and rumbles were getting closer.

When the vampires emerged, it became clear that, though it was a mob, there was yet some organization about it. The people had fanned out into groups, searching, shouting. That the city had been under siege so long only made the bloodlust worse. Mors did not need to hear the words to know the people believed that killing the vampires would drive the Arabs from the gates. Find the vampires, free the city.

Why do humans always think their wars can be ended so simply?

They headed west, where it seemed quietest. Scylla trotted beside them, and Mors couldn't bear it. If the mob caught her . . . No. Better she die at his own hand than that. Which he also couldn't bear. He shouted an order.

"Scylla! Run! Run far away from me and don't come back. Don't argue, just run!"

Otonia's astonishment as the dog obediently spun around and fled was a palpable thing, but Mors closed his mind to it. Every dog he had kept as a companion had lived an unusually long, strong life. A life that, when it ended, ended in Mors's arms and with a blessing and a burial. Not . . .

She'll find me, that's all. She'll find me.

The mob, like a clever hunter, was swelling on all sides, teeming toward the nearest gate. Mors saw that crowds had been organized at every entrance, that all the soldiers had taken to all the battlements, that the vampires were not escaping without a fight.

"Our choice is to try to hide a few days, and hope they cool down. . . ." Otonia began.

". . . or go now," Mors finished.

They knew the Arabs outside would be distracted by the noise and the panic. Such chaos always created fine vampire cover.

Otonia broke the window of a hookah bar and snatched a torch, thrusting it into Mors's hand.

"Keep your head down," she hissed.

And she dragged him straight into the mob.

Mors knew a brief thrill of abject horror, but as he and Otonia became part of the masses baying for vampire blood, no one looked at them twice. Even their bundles, which at least marked them as travelers, garnered no notice. It was exhilarating. He and Otonia were smiling, shouting, cursing the walking dead spat out from hell. All around them were friends, siblings, bonded in this moment of bloodlust.

Until a cloak swirled and a finger was in Mors's face. Karas.

"Vampire! This is him! Vampire!"

Otonia dragged Mors at top speed up an outer stairway all the way to a roof. They worked their way to the building nearest the western wall, ignoring the confused screams below. Otonia shot two arrows, killing the two soldiers at the battlements. The bodies dropped on the crowd, which was thrown into further confusion while the vampires leaped to the wall and scrambled down the outside. Then they put on all their speed and ran for the sea.

It was nearly dawn, and sailors were sleepily heading out to prepare a ship for sail. The vampires ran for the water. Holding the cases full of paper above their heads, they walked underwater to the side of the ship. They took their chance and tossed the bundles aboard, clambering up after them. Their luck held: It was still too dark for anyone to be about. They crept down into the hold and tucked themselves into straw.

Otonia took Mors's hand and smiled. She was about to say something, but Mors suddenly shot back out.

Scylla had already run past sailors who didn't even notice the little shadow swarming around their feet. Mors caught her and pressed his face into her damp fur, then brought her down into the hold where Otonia's mouth fell open on seeing them.

"But how—"

"They're smart, my dogs."

"And she won't draw attention to us?"

"No."

Otonia smiled, shaking her head.

"I do wish we could be on the deck. I would love to see where we're going."

"As would I," Mors answered. "But on the whole, I would say it doesn't much matter."

Chapter Fifteen

Rome. Summer 1942.

The house owned by Franca and Silvia's mother had a large main room that included the kitchen. Every inch of space was filled with young female partisans, all proud to call themselves members of this new legion, determined to free Italy from Fascism and alliance with Germany.

Even despite the close quarters, Patrizia managed to be off to the side, as far away from Mors as possible. She was tucked in the window, half wrapped in the heavy curtains and smoking a cigarette. With her ankle socks riding down into the heels of her shoes, her plump face, and intense glower, she looked more like a bad-tempered child of five than fifteen—the cigarette notwithstanding. She was, however, listening as intently as the others.

Rembrandt had, not without some protest, helped Mors construct model grenades and other small explosive devices, which the women examined with great interest.

"We cannot yet know what sort of battle is coming to us or to which we are going," Mors explained. "We must be prepared for a number of possibilities, of which guerilla warfare is only one. We will build forts in the mountains, some underground, where we can store supplies and readily stage attacks."

He did not mention Sicily, as such plans were only to be revealed when troops prepared to move. Giulia saw it, that much he could tell. By the way she was flexing her fingers, he knew she was more than eager for the fight they would have down there.

"We can really learn to throw these at tanks?" Franca asked, holding up a grenade.

"Precision will be necessary," Mors warned. "They are improving the tanks all the time, and the only way we can take advantage of the surprise is if we explode a tank on the first try."

Rembrandt nodded. He made his distaste for being in this group all too clear, and the admiring glances of a number of the young women did not improve his temper. He was, however, enthralled with the battle plans and preparations. He was overjoyed by Mors's renewed vigor for the fight, and only crushed that it was Giulia who had done the renewing. If she saw his occasional scowls in her direction, she made no signal.

"I have read of sticky bombs," Silvia said. "Do those work? Can we try them?"

"They can work very well," Mors answered, "but as they involve running straight up to a tank to affix it, they are yet more dangerous. I can teach you tactics for such running and retreating, if you are willing to undertake that risk."

Franca and Silvia glanced at their mother. Signora Orselli crossed herself but nodded.

"Here's a thought," Patrizia shot out. "Why don't we sneak into wherever the tanks are kept and sabotage them before they go into use?"

"A good thought," Mors complimented her. "But they are regularly maintained and tested. The sabotage would be discovered. True, it would be a great expense, but when the tanks are replaced, the security will be heightened. Suspicion would remain high. Far better to wait until much nearer a point of battle and attack when they least expect it."

"So really, your plan is to kill us all," Patrizia commented. The others, Signora Orselli included, scolded her soundly, but she was unruffled. Giulia raised a steely voice above the hubbub.

"From the day you began partisan activity, Patrizia, you knew death was a possibility. If you no longer have the stomach for fighting, you may leave."

For answer, Patrizia concentrated on finishing her cigarette.

"The beauty of a light guerrilla force, Patrizia," Mors said, "is that we can strike and retreat before they even see us. We can break them down a great deal, and they won't know what hit them."

The girl's eyes flickered, but she remained silent.

"Should we wear trousers, do you think?" Silvia asked, breaking the heavy silence. "When we attack, I mean?"

"No, it's better, on the chance that you are seen, to look like women," Mors answered after a short consideration. "Even the most hardened soldier will think twice before shooting a woman, although, of course, I intend to have you so well trained that you won't even be seen. You will, however, need the most comfortable and sturdy skirts you can get."

Without a word, Signora Orselli bustled to a sewing machine in the corner, and all the others fell into a deep discussion about how to obtain the right fabrics. Mors basked in the warm glow of the room. The legion was only thirty strong thus far, but each woman had the heart of a lion—Patrizia the heart of two. And as for Giulia, the contemplation of her heart made him smile even more. She caught his eye and smiled back. Thirty of them, with more to come soon.

As the summer progressed, the legion threw itself into training with the kind of gusto Mors remembered vividly from his previous life. They moved around various ruins so as to have quiet and attract no notice. The old energy of the broken buildings nourished them all, not just Mors. The walls might not understand the weaponry, but they recognized the emotion.

The vampires, so long as they avoided discussing the human element, had other joys. Rembrandt's field telephone and radio were fully operational, and he had all the codes necessary to regularly overhear the German and Italian forces stationed throughout much of Italy.

"Is it possible," Mors asked, "to use that phone or radio to signal them from here and not be traced?"

Rembrandt was thoughtful.

"It must be, but I don't know how."

"Do you think you can manage it? I'd rather like to give them some orders and alerts of my own devising."

Rembrandt chortled like a child and snatched up his tools.

When the BBC announced that General Eisenhower had been made the American commander of the European Theater, Mors was sure it was only a matter of time before he was leading the charge in North Africa. He nodded his approval.

"He's very good, that Eisenhower. Very, very good."

"How can you possibly know that?" Rembrandt insisted.

"I remain a general. We know our own," Mors answered.

Giulia had been right about her marriage: It gave her a protection that extended far beyond her husband's presence. As Signora Romano, she traversed the city unmolested, so long as she was mindful of her path. Mors still didn't like the idea of her being married, but he did like knowing she was safe. And that she and Romano didn't share a bed.

Which was something he and Giulia very much wanted to share but had to content themselves with the riverbank. Rembrandt continued in his steadfast dislike of her, and Mors would not upset the waters so much as to bring her up to Aventine Hill. He did, however, try to broaden Rembrandt's mind on the subject of humans.

"After all, you know what they say about us."

The vampires had just stolen a supply of petrol and long matches, for making more explosive devices, and were wending their way home. The entire legion had turned into sneak thieves, stashing materials for grenades, grenade launchers, and tinned food. Despite the massive shortages, they all found that once they were prepared to work outside the rules, obtaining supplies was comparatively easy. Giulia, on the pretense of going on picnics in the mountains, had scouted several likely spots to build good forts. Mors wanted Rembrandt to see the value of this.

"I can see how it's fine enough for the humans," Rembrandt conceded. "But really, Mors, why should we be involved? Anyway, it's ridiculous. Sooner or later, they're bound to discover what you and I are. How can it be otherwise?"

Mors had known this was coming.

"We're operating at night; they know that's safer. They know I have my hand in a lot of pies and that I cannot always be with them. Giulia is their leader as much as I, and the Orselli sisters are good lieutenants. This is war, Rembrandt; it is mad by its nature. Adding a vampire general in the mix hardly makes a difference."

"Yes, and what about Giulia? What do you think will happen when—"

"She already knows."

Mors caught the petrol can that had slipped from Rembrandt's hands.

"You told her you're a vampire?" Rembrandt was aghast.

"Well, not 'told,' exactly, but yes, she knows. After all, she's married." Mors smiled faintly. "We all have crosses to bear."

Rembrandt shook his head.

"I do not understand you, Mors, I really don't. If you were at least going to turn her—"

Mors turned flaming eyes on him so quickly, Rembrandt inadvertently ducked.

"Don't you ever say such a thing like that to me again—not ever!"

The two stood there a moment, staring at each other—Mors in blazing fury, Rembrandt in utter astonishment. At last, Mors's eyes reverted to green and he resumed walking. After a moment, Rembrandt rejoined him.

"I . . . all right. I'm sorry. I only meant . . . I mean . . . that is how we—"

Mors clapped a hand over Rembrandt's mouth and dragged him back down a side street. Rembrandt had started to fight him when he saw that Mors was pointing. He followed the path of the finger to a group of men who had just exited a restaurant, some in uniforms, others in cassocks. And one of them was the pink-faced, laughing Bishop Oster.

"What can it mean? What can it mean? What the hell is he doing here?"

Well into the next day, Mors was still pacing the apartment feverishly. The bishop! He knew there was something to it, and was determined to discover what.

"He'll have to be killed, of course, no question there, but I must first find out what he's up to. Now, how best to do that?"

"Mors." Rembrandt broke in quietly. "Do you really think we have to?"

"What do you mean?"

"Well, you've given up looking for Deirdre, and Cleland's already dead—"

"I have *not* 'given up,' I've postponed looking for that monster while I've been focusing my attention on those more deserving. And anyway, don't you see? Oster connects to Traugott connects to Deirdre! And more, there must be more. Don't you remember what she said that night? They'd come to find us in Rome because they needed fresh supplies! Me, specifically. Or any millennial, I suppose, but we're thin on the ground these days. I won't ever have it said my brother died in vain. It's not just about avenging Cleland; it's about preventing these bastards from taking one more step down whatever blood-and-dust-soaked path they are walking."

"Well, I don't want to go anywhere near him," Rembrandt insisted. "That's moving in far too much light for me. I've nearly been killed enough times already. He's not worth it."

"That's absolutely fair enough, and no need to be sorry for it," Mors replied. "You've been truly marvelous. You really have. It was one of the luckiest turns of the war, the day I met you."

He put a hand on Rembrandt's shoulder. Instead of being pleased, Rembrandt folded his arms and scowled, looking like a miserable little boy.

"Don't be like that, Rembrandt, please. You're my right-hand man! Of course you needn't go near Oster. I'll just ask Giulia—"

"Exactly! Giulia! Always Giulia. You'll go straight to that adulterous little trollop and—"

Mors slammed Rembrandt against the wall. Rembrandt didn't dare struggle, but his eyes glowed red and his fangs slid out.

"You take that back," Mors demanded.

"I won't. I don't like her. I don't like any of them, except maybe that Patrizia. We could do this whole thing on our own, if we put our minds to it, and I hate that you've dragged a bunch of worthless humans—"

Mors roared, his features bulging. The terrified Rembrandt yelped and squirmed out of Mors's hold, racing out into the early evening light.

Mors was frozen in shock and grief. Something had broken between them, and he had no idea how to repair it.

He followed Rembrandt out.

Rembrandt had crossed the Tiber at the Ponte Sublicio and clambered to the top of the hill in Gianicolo Park.

"If a vampire's on a hill, it's hard to hide him well," came Mors's voice behind him.

Rembrandt swirled around. Mors had reverted to his human self, but the younger vampire was in his full monstrous glow.

"I don't want to fight you, Mors," Rembrandt began.

"That's because you are not a fool. I've always said quite the opposite," Mors reminded him.

"Are you trying to humor me?"

"You can't possibly think that."

"I just don't understand why you need those humans."

"They are women, Rembrandt, and you agreed back when we returned from Sicily that it would make more sense to have a larger army when we join the Allies there."

"That was a long time ago. I changed my mind, now that we have all this equipment. Dragging in humans to help us fight our battles is just ridiculous."

"Actually, it is us helping them to fight their war and reclaim Europe. Isn't that the fight you said you were in?"

"Yes, of course, but this is different now . . . now that—"

"Now that I am with Giulia. You can't really be so childish as to be bothered by that, can you?"

Rembrandt threw himself on Mors, attempting to punch him.

"Don't you call me childish!"

"I wouldn't, but that's how you're behaving!" Mors snapped. "I spent centuries being uninterested in love, too, but I hope to Jove I was nowhere near such a miserable moaning pest about it. I can tell you this, I didn't give anyone a moment's grief about their relationships."

Rembrandt backed away then, shaking his head.

"I wanted to fight by your side, I really did, but not like this. And I know you think you can lead the whole army, and then—what? Become emperor?"

"Rembrandt—"

"No! No. I would die for a cause, if I have to, but I will not die for you."

This time, Mors let him go.

When Mors reentered the apartment, he was saddened, but not wholly surprised, to see that Rembrandt had taken his clothes and gone. He had left his tools but no note. Mors wished him a safe and pleasant journey, wherever he was going, and hoped that someday, in happier times, they might meet again.

Devastated though Mors was by Rembrandt's desertion, he forced himself to remain focused. He told Giulia very little of why Rembrandt was no longer there, and she asked no questions. He also told her that a German bishop had arrived in Rome, which he was quite sure did not bode well for anyone. Especially himself.

"I'll find out all I can about him," Giulia promised.

They were in the tiled bath in the ancient apartment. Mors had felt odd, inviting her here, and she had felt odd accepting, but now they were comfortable. Both were grateful there was enough oxygen. The bath was a marvel. Giulia knew the old Romans were serious about their baths but had not expected such a thing as a luxurious underground bath built by vampires.

She scooped water in her palms and poured it over Mors's head. He caught some with his tongue and then licked her ear, her neck, her breast. She laughed as he pulled her on top of him again. They both did. It was all so unreal. The world had gone mad. Dictators, people enslaved and destroyed, a vampire and a married woman leading an underground fighting force and making love for the third time that day.

Mad hatters and March hares are bastions of sanity by comparison.

The legion next met on a stretch of quiet ground by the Tiber, where they practiced throwing fake grenades, with some of the girls carrying targets and others throwing. Patrizia and Silvia were by far the best shots.

As the drill was under way, Franca approached Mors, looking worried.

"Sir, Silvia and I, we both thought we felt someone following us tonight."

"What did you do?"

"Just as you instructed—zigzagged a new route. I think we lost them, but I wanted to tell you."

"Thank you. You lost them, that's the main thing. Well done."

She nodded and returned to the drill, still looking worried.

Mors wondered. They all looked so innocent, it was hard to imagine anyone associating them with underground activity. Of which, lately, there had officially been none, per Mors's careful plan. On the face of it, the fist with which Mussolini gripped the country remained powerful. Very little could slip through his fingers.

He's a tyrant who safely governs home, thanks to purchasing great alliance abroad. And so is Hitler. Enjoy it while you may, little men. Goodness will check thee soon.

No sooner had the thought finished, however, than Mors felt the enemy coming, long before he heard anything.

"Draw your weapons!" he ordered the legion. "The battle has come to us!"

The legion was momentarily baffled. But Mors had drawn both a pistol and a sword and had his eyes fixed at a spot through the trees. The sound of men's triumphant laughter, accompanied by shots ringing through the air, sent them scurrying for their guns.

"Lie low and let them come to you!" Mors cried in a voice designed only for his fighters to hear. In the excitement, no one except Giulia registered the manipulation of that voice. "They don't want to kill; they want to arrest. They won't expect a fight."

The general knew his enemy well. What came upon them was a throng of Blackshirts and what seemed to be hired mercenaries. As they neared, they shouted at the legion to get up, they were being arrested. But the legion waited until Mors let out a bellow like cannon shot.

"NOW!"

The legion opened fire, and the silencers on their guns only added to the confusion as the attackers were hit but had no idea what had befallen them. The darkness made aim difficult, however, and the mercenaries, who seemed to know their stuff, quickly assessed the situation and leaped into the fray, forcing closer combat.

Now Mors was in his element. The others fought valiantly, but Mors flew fast and furious with his sword, cutting down men before anyone could see him coming. Only Giulia really saw what was happening. And only Giulia heard the word Mors heard, the word one of the attacking men cried: *"Blutsauger!"*

"Bloodsucker." Shouted in German.

Mors could just make out the man. One of Traugott's closest cohorts. He drew a small crossbow from within his jacket and aimed at Mors.

"A stake, Mors! He has a stake!" Giulia's scream rang out over the crowd. Mors seized the arm of the Blackshirt nearest him and twisted it so that the man's pistol might shoot his attacker. The Nachtspeere released the stake, and Silvia, seeing the attack, leaped on him so that Mors had to pivot the gun away to avoid hitting her. The Blackshirt attempted to kick and even bite him, and Mors impatiently ripped off his whole arm. The Nachtspeere called to his fellows to retreat, but didn't realize how thoroughly Mors had decimated their numbers: Very few followed him away. Some of the legion aimed and fired. Mors was convinced none of them escaped.

The battle was won. The legion cheered, all except Giulia, who was examining the body of a Nachtspeere.

"Gather the weapons, everyone, and leave, quickly and quietly," Mors ordered. "I will take care of everything else." Something in the way he spoke made them all forget that there were bodies to dispose of. Instead, they all floated home, awash in the glow of their own abilities—abilities they could hardly believe they had.

Only Giulia was left. She helped Mors pull jackets off the bodies and tie bunches of them together. He was going to drag them to the Tiber.

"You don't think any of them heard what he called you, do you?" Giulia fretted. "Or . . . what I called you?"

"You have to know how to hear things in a battle, darling. Even if they did, I don't think they would register any of it."

Giulia nodded. She looked exhausted. Mors kissed her several times.

"You were wonderful, simply wonderful. Go home, sweet, and get some rest. I can manage this."

She did not argue and was soon gone. Mors wrapped all the identifying papers and badges into a bundle, trusting they could be useful sometime. Then he weighted the bodies and tossed them into the water with satisfying splashes.

Although one does feel badly about giving the fish such inedible food.

So, the Nachtspeere were in Rome, along with Oster. No question—a two-front war was opening up. Mors knew he could make a far better show of it than the Wehrmacht.

The water of the Tiber lapped at his boots. He bent and trailed his fingers through it. Then he stood, folded his hands behind his head, and smiled out at the night.

A smell possessing a vibrant, heavy sweetness wafted over him, so sudden and unanticipated that had he been anyone else, he would have started. Started and whirled, needing to see the source before he was ready to believe it. But Mors didn't even lower his hands. Only his eyes crinkled slightly into a smile as he said, "Welcome to Rome, Brigit."

Chapter Sixteen

The ship from Constantinople had traveled up the Black Sea to Constanta, in Romania. Mors and Otonia traveled a long way after that, searching for the place that spoke to them, the place to call home. Mors remembered Britain. As soon as he had set foot on her pebbly shore the cool night they landed, Mors knew this was his land. They had come to the capital of the northern kingdom, a city surrounded by Roman walls, though the Vikings now held sway. Once called Eboracum, it was now Jorvik, a beautiful place, steeped in learning. Otonia loved it.

Neither vampire wanted to live within a guarded walled city again, so they searched the woods outside until they found a welter of caves.

"A bit like being animals, but it's hard for humans to find," Otonia declared. "And we can expand them as needed. Besides, the cool air is better for the books."

"Expand?" Mors asked. "How many books do you plan on collecting?"

"All of them," was her answer. "But vampires will come, too. We will be stronger as a community."

"A community?" Mors's voice was scaling upward. "Of vampires?"

"A tribunal." Otonia's voice had a dreamy edge, as though she were envisioning something vast and celebrated.

"'Tribunal' sounds like a place for magistrates. What vampire wants to acknowledge a governing body?"

"Well, not you, of course," Otonia conceded. "But we are both wild and civilized. I saw something similar in Greece and now, here, I know I can see it live again."

"And I believe you. But I'm just saying that 'tribunal'—"

"It allows for possibilities!" Otonia snapped. Then she smiled, a sly, slightly mischievous smile. "Besides, I like the word."

And the word spread. Otonia knew how to find other vampires. Some did indeed want to be a part of something bigger. So the tribunal grew, becoming the nexus of vampire law, learning, and culture. It filled the gaps while they waited for the human world to take hold of its best self again.

Mors still loved to run wild through the land, but there was no denying the odd thrill of words, of learning. It wasn't screams and blood, but it was its own strong pleasure. He and Otonia had experienced art, music, theater, literature, the flowering of philosophy and medicine and democracy. They'd lived in a blaze of light in the darkness. Until the humans gave them light again, they must find it in themselves. Mors spent more and more time within the world of the tribunal.

A world that brought him new friends, the first and best being the deeply bonded couple Cleland and Raleigh. Mors had not imagined that such love could exist between vampires. Raleigh, a high-spirited and fun-loving sort, had been made by a female who misread him. He had found Cleland in Ireland.

"And that, my friends, was quite a night! The next few hundred nights, too," Raleigh said with a roguish chuckle.

Mors thought this was why Cleland was inclined to be more circumspect and cautious. But he had a dry wit, sharp intelligence, and expansive warmth. They were soon a merry band of brothers.

"I hope the humans have a war soon," Mors confided to his friends. "I can teach you all kinds of fun tricks. Don't you just love heavy fog?"

"Just what Raleigh needs—a bad influence." Cleland laughed. "After I've spent all these centuries taming him."

Mors, like all the vampires, did not question romantic love between two males or females. None of them understood why the human world quarreled with it. What Mors did find tedious was the way that love kept Cleland and Raleigh more focused on each other as a couple rather than with him, as a group.

"Stop bellyaching," Cleland ordered him, when Mors joked acidly about their devotion. "At least we're not Swefred and Meaghan."

Swefred and Meaghan had come from the Highlands. They never seemed to be farther than a foot away from each other, and they rarely spoke to anyone else. Both were studious, but Meaghan was given to a fretfulness that, when displayed, made one miss the quiet.

"No, then I wouldn't speak to you," Mors agreed. "Why do you think they are even here?"

"You can still value community, even if you're only tangentially a part of it." Cleland shrugged. "We were tribal as humans. Who's to say we still aren't, somewhere inside us?"

"Where? The spleen?"

Mors was not the only one who roamed. Individuals or couples could be gone for weeks at a time. It was all to the good—far better not to feed solely in Jorvik. Also, as Otonia had prophesied, hunters had returned. It was crucial not to attract an excess of attention.

Sometimes, vampires roamed and never came back, or only as stories. Mors hated it. As much as it panged him when his dogs died, at least that was definitive. He was there; the body was there. He mourned, he buried, he mourned further. But he still hated it.

"Is that why you don't have a companion?" Cleland asked with a shrewd frown. "You're afraid they'll die?"

"You don't know me very well," Mors retorted. "I'm afraid of exactly nothing."

They didn't speak again for several days.

Scylla died a few years after Mors and Otonia had come to Jorvik. When Mors returned from her burial, feeling like he had swallowed an icehouse, he found Otonia hanging her ancient bow and arrows in the main room.

"He killed someone you loved," Mors observed, not needing to use Xenon's name.

"My maker," Otonia answered, adjusting the arrows. "Xenon wanted me and I wouldn't have him."

"And you've never loved again."

"Not like that, no."

Mors knew she would say it was quite different from his own situation, but he felt vindicated nonetheless.

When Cleland next approached him, it was to share a sacred story. As a human, he had been a minor noble, until it was discovered that he and another man were in love. He had been forced to watch his lover tortured for hours before he was finally killed. He was then imprisoned to await his own execution at dawn. Raleigh had found him there.

"I would have given something to have seen the people's faces when they entered the cell and found it empty," Cleland remarked. Raleigh saved him and helped him get his vengeance with interest the following night, but that was not when or why he fell in love with him.

"That came soon enough, just because he's Raleigh."

"And we are happy for you," Mors answered, without sarcasm. "But I am happy as I am. It's far better not to try to change me."

Otonia had a few strict rules governing the tribunal, one of which was that any vampire who came and asked for a home there would not be turned away. The members all agreed, until Aelric descended on them. He was brash, hotheaded, and foolish. He was not even sure of his own age. But Otonia took pity on him. He was a discard. Made because he was handsome and virile, left either through death or abandonment. He was lonely. Of course he could have a home.

"He simply won't be brought into the innermost circle, that's all," Otonia said firmly. "Besides, he's hardly the type to last long."

Mors would not question Otonia in public but sought her out later.

"Are you sure about him? He seems the type who could get himself chased and lead hunters right to the door."

"Which we'd hear. And we'd take care of it."

Mors grunted. He didn't like Aelric. He entertained a vision of an accident wherein the young vampire fell off a cliff.

"How does someone so hapless survive?" Mors asked. "Seems like he would die fresh out of the grave."

Otonia shrugged.

"Fate walks its own path," she responded. "Life is strange, and sometimes unjust. But not boring."

"No. I wouldn't tolerate that."

One night, Mors and his new dog, Jove, were scouting the wilds south of the city. To his surprise, he could hear someone mucking about amid the undergrowth. A human. A girl. A child still, because she had no smell, but he knew it was a girl. A girl who reminded him of the Roman fire. A girl whose smoke swirled inside him.

Every night for months, he sought her out, and she gradually acquired a unique scent. The most intoxicating thing he had ever known. So all-encompassing, he would lie down for it. For her. He told no one. This was his own journey.

Cleland, however, was a keen observer.

"Do you know you have been smiling at nothing and no one lately?"

"I've been making up many new jokes," Mors answered.

"It's not the smile of the amused," Cleland said, smiling such a smile himself. "It's the smile of the besotted."

"Since when are you a connoisseur of smiles?"

"Oh, Mors, admit it. You have smelled a woman out there who suits you." He held up a hand to still Mors's protest. "It is obvious. So, why are you waiting? You never know what can happen with a human."

"The time isn't right." Mors was definitive.

"Don't be asinine. This is not the sort of thing for which one waits."

Mors could not explain even to himself what was roiling inside him, or why.

"Yes, soon. Soon," he promised, more to himself than Cleland.

He knew Cleland was desperate to remonstrate with him, to urge him on. But the younger vampire held his tongue. Mors had to do as he would, so Cleland could only hope for the best.

Inner turmoil worked up an appetite, and Mors was digging into a prostitute who tasted of Asian spices. He drew out the meal, feeling himself in a distant palace, under rippling fabric, the sounds of water lapping at marble steps, the sounds of a woman's laugh approaching. The laugh hesitated, then changed. It became something almost sinister. He lifted his head to listen, and the prostitute's head drooped to her shoulder.

The sound, and the shiver it had sent down his spine, stayed with Mors as he ran and ran and ran. The closer he got to the place he knew he ought to have been only an hour ago, the more dread he felt. He could smell the lingering scent of chaos . . . and he could smell death.

The Vikings were still carousing amid the ruins of the tiny village. Mors scoured the environs but found nothing. Not a trace of the girl who had drawn him there for so long.

Dawn forced him home. Once on his bed, Mors curled around Jove and inhaled the dog's strong, mangy scent. He closed his eyes, but that sinister laugh just grew louder.

The next twenty-four hours he remained in a stupor, unable to move. The next night, Aelric had a presentation for the tribunal. There was no formal way of introducing new vampires, but some ceremony was always appreciated. That it was Aelric's was a novelty that raised some eyebrows.

"Maybe he's leaving!" Benedict, a recently arrived Jewish vampire from France, hoped.

"No," his partner, the dark and lovely Leonora, shook her head. "He's made a vampire. I can feel it."

"Who wants to lay a bet that no good will come of this?" asked Raleigh. Cleland shushed him.

Aelric was not a vampire for speech. His words were straight to the point.

"I have a new partner. This is Brigantia."

The vampire stepped forward and brushed past Aelric, glancing around at her new community with interest. As her eyes locked briefly on

Mors's, he knew what it was to be staked, and only wished he would dissolve into dust. To sit there, that stake in his heart, every organ bleeding, and not have the relief of death was a torture the humans could never emulate. It was her. His wonderful girl. She had been found, and she had been made, by Aelric.

The ignominy of it was nothing compared to the sheer pain. He would have found her beautiful regardless of what she looked like. That she was exquisite, a striking creature of about seventeen, who would have been revered in Rome, almost didn't touch Mors. It was what lay underneath that pale silky skin that beckoned to him more tantalizingly than any siren.

Brigantia, naturally. One of the local goddesses. Associated with fire and battle. It was too perfect.

She walked up to Otonia and stood before her, knowing without being told that this was the community's leader. She smiled suddenly, and now Mors gasped in pain. Next to him, Cleland jumped. The look on his friend's face turned Cleland's insides icy. He went to take Mors's hand and gasped in his turn. Mors looked down. Inside his own fist, two of his fingers had popped out their talons, which now protruded through his palm. He looked into Cleland's eyes; his own eyes were wet.

Mors's first instinct was to rip Aelric to shreds and then run far, far away, joining in whatever wars were being fought and decimating all the fighters. But he stayed. He couldn't leave her. Brigantia was such a life-loving creature, full of laughter and venom, so fiery and bold. Fiery. What Mors had felt in the human girl was still there, with interest. The smoke lodged inside him and would not leave. Perhaps she felt it, because her eyes were often on him, wanting to look closer. Which he couldn't allow. He would need her to look closer yet, and that would break one rule he knew wasn't for him to touch.

Cleland argued vehemently.

"She hates Aelric! She hates him, she can't bear his touch, she can't even stand him looking at her. It would be unethical were you *not* to make her your partner instead."

"No," Mors answered in a hollow voice. "She has to break from him first."

"Since when do you obey rules?"

"Since now. Since her."

The two vampires stared at each other, shocked. Cleland tried to put the best face on it.

"Well, she'll certainly break with him. Once she knows that's allowed."

"Yes." Mors sighed involuntarily. "And then she has to choose. She must choose me, not the other way around."

"Well, then it's as good as done! She adores you," Cleland insisted.

"I represent fun to her," Mors said, tossing a stick for Jove.

"For the love of Fate, Mors, you look like a sad whelp out of a bad Greek poem! Brigantia is exactly the partner for you. How much love do you think there is in the world that you can let it go when it presents itself to you? Are you really going to keep yourself from her because you didn't make her? The world takes its own turns; even you can't stop it."

"Can't I?" Mors rolled his eyes toward his friend. Despite his best efforts, he still looked wretched, and Cleland dropped the subject.

Love. Something in which he had never believed. But there was Cleland and Raleigh, Leonora and Benedict, Swefred and Meaghan. Love not confined to books, but walking under the stars. He could feel what the smoke of Brigantia had done. It had burned a hole in buried memories, setting them free. He knew what it was to love, and it ached.

A raucous, wicked, gorgeous laugh bounced over the wind. Brigantia was running, perhaps chasing Vikings. Mors thought he could see her long golden curls cascading behind her. He wanted to catch them, roll himself up in them, and stay.

Some time later, after a literally fiery confrontation, Brigantia broke with Aelric. Mors could feel her tending toward himself and did all he could to encourage the feelings. Until one night when Aelric's stupidity resulted in he and Brigantia's running for their lives from hunters. Aelric was caught and killed. Brigantia, though near enough to help, had been frozen in fear and disbelief. The guilt overwhelmed her, and she was inconsolable.

Cleland kept his counsel until a few weeks after Aelric's death. Mors was just the one to bring Brigantia back to happiness, and claim some for himself as well. It was Raleigh who reminded him of the other, crucial point—that Brigantia must still be the one to choose him.

Midsummer night. That atmospheric confection that tickled every sense in a vampire, sending reason flying out to sea. The danger of the short, hot night, full of the heavy summer flora scents, plus the lust of humans everywhere, was the only sort of elixir that could make a vampire drunk. If their favorite night was the winter solstice, when they could roam longest, this night was the one when they were least themselves and could embrace it.

Mors unleashed his most wild self and went dashing around the nearest moor, arms outspread, singing. His music was a volatile thing, perfectly suited to the night. It could stir souls, even as it unsettled them. Could humans hear it, they would move like they didn't know possible. Mors thought perhaps some of them did hear it, but it existed outside a place they understood and so they stayed away.

Someday, someday you'll sing my songs. Or not—I could give a damn.

He threw himself deep into the heather and rolled, exulting in this rush of joy. He had no dog at present, Jove having died the year before, and Cleland and Raleigh had chosen their own way this night, but he felt too full of life to be lonely. The demon was big inside him, making him not vampiric but a different sort of beast altogether. Mors sang and the demon danced.

And as he sang, he sang of Brigantia. The name rolled out long and sweet over his tongue: "Bri-gan-ti-a." Four delicious syllables. One for each perfect limb. A song without end.

He somersaulted down a hill, and suddenly she was there. She had come running to find him. Possessed of her own demonic madness and joy and hunger. She had heard his cry, and her own demon danced as it overtook her and drew her to this spot, this place outside herself, outside anything but this raging, desperate need to be inside Mors's song. As though to enter that music would mean to exit the guilt that had marked her: To leave her mind would mean to come back to it cleansed. Because she was plainly not in her mind, any more than Mors was sure he was in his, but each was too swollen with the night and the demon to care.

He kissed her and thought he might melt into her body right then. It seemed impossible that they were able to remain kissing and yet tear off each other's clothes, but they embraced the impossible. As her hair and limbs enveloped him, he realized it had been centuries since he had been completely naked with a woman. It was wonderful. Her body rippled under him, her blood rising so that her skin was as warm as the sand on the Amalfi Coast. And her eyes were bluer than the Mediterranean. There was no longer any demarcation between one body and another. If there were no words, there was no shortage of sound. Even the smallest touch on each other's skin resonated for miles around, and their cries bounced and volleyed all throughout the countryside. Animals scurried as though from a wildfire.

They continued this way for hours, Mors unable to get enough of her breasts and those hips that moved with a rhythm many belly dancers would envy. And the way she touched him! Rough, inexpert, careless, and yet thrilling. He was far past thought and never wanted to return.

Before the moment darkness began to fade, she swept on her clothes in a single fluid movement and went running into the west, her hair streaking behind her. She was like a bolt of lightning. Mors ran in a different direction, to a small cave. He knew neither of them was going home that dawn.

The enchantment lasted the next three nights, encircling them like a cloud. They never spoke, they never stayed together in the day, and yet they knew exactly how to find each other when the sun dropped. Their bodies moved separate of themselves, finding unknown roads to ecstasy, and their screams haunted the nightmares of humans for miles around.

Mors wanted it to go on and on forever, but as with the best of dreams, it was over almost as soon as it had begun. The fourth evening, he went looking for Brigantia, but she was gone. He went back to the caves, to his own bed. He slept for three days straight, and when he woke, he went and lay at the bottom of a bath for many hours. On emerging, he wondered if he hadn't just dreamed the whole thing. He thought he must have, because it was too unreal. He was nearly faint from hunger.

He hunted and ate quickly, determined to find his way back into his full mind. He walked a long time, surprised and yet not at all when he was back on the hill on the moor—the scene of that first night. The moon was just rising and there it was—the patch at the foot of the hill where the heather had been burned away.

Mors pressed a hand into the dirt. It was still warm. He closed his eyes, memorizing the feel of the place where he had finally, after so many centuries, made love to someone he loved with his whole heart. He tucked the memory deep inside himself, where not even the demon could touch it. Because he knew, with cold certainty, that it would never happen again.

When he next encountered Brigantia, she seemed her usual self, except without the shadow of guilt. She had a bounce and spark, a new vim and hunger. Brigantia kept a garden, a vestige of her human passion, and a peculiar, unnecessary thing for a vampire, but lovely all the same. Every plant she touched now began to smell different. There wasn't a vampire in the tribunal who didn't notice.

Yet she had forgotten. Or rather, she seemed not to know. Mors caught her eye many times, but the look and smile she returned were no different from any she had ever given him before those three dark nights.

"I thought vampires never forgot anything?" Mors was sitting with Otonia, watching her weave a tapestry.

"A vampire's memory, as I understand, is as long and strong as his or her life. Of course, it can be a touch more complex than that."

"You astonish me."

She smiled and unwound some red thread before continuing.

"Memory is its own creature, a living thing. Look at it like a river—it moves in a solid direction, retains a recognizable shape, but has its fluidity and capriciousness. It rises, it falls, it branches. You can follow its path a long, long way and then suddenly lose it and have to shift direction to find it again."

Mors watched the hypnotic movements of her fingers for a while, thinking.

"I do love talking with you, Otonia. My brain always aches afterward."

She cast him a quick glance and returned to her work. He wondered if she knew. She had bonded with Brigantia much like a mother and daughter.

And her bond with him remained closer than with any other vampire. He wanted to open his heart to her, but it was easier to stay silent.

"Just tell her you love her!" Cleland insisted, barely holding back a punch.

But Cleland couldn't know what Mors now saw only too clearly. Brigantia needed a partner to balance her inner fire. With him, they would each be their most wild selves. Something bigger than the both of them, but too big for her. At least, for now. She would try to eat the world with him, try to live like a millennial with him, but only he could have had that luck. Nature was a bigger creature yet, and it knew. Vampires existed in uneasy tolerance with nature, as part of it and yet wholly against its laws. Nature had given Mors a pass because of who he was, but Brigantia was just the sort of sacrifice it would demand. And he would not see the death of anyone he loved, not when they were meant to be immortal. Better he love her from across this divide, better she be a best friend, a sister. Better she live. He might die a little without her touch, but better she live.

Which was not to say he didn't hope. He wanted her to share his deepest passions. He was restless, waiting for the human world to give him more outlets for his many energies. He wanted to wake up civilization, stage a one-vampire campaign to arouse artists and poets out of the day-to-day workers. He fashioned a six-string instrument not unlike a lute and played the sort of music that could get a vampire's blood pumping. He stood on hills, playing and singing, hoping his voice might reach into the mud and pull out the beginnings of a cultural awakening. Instead, it only grew his own legend. He was a different sort of chaos magnet now, with a song that both lured and repelled, and an endless appetite.

Sometimes, at the edges of a city or a village, Brigantia came to him, wanting to talk.

"Are we like shadows? Is that why we cannot cast them off our bodies?" She looked at him with clear, fascinated eyes.

"Is that what you think?" Mors asked.

"I don't know. What else can we be? Replacements of things that were. Still are, but only as an imprint. Those things themselves, they aren't anything, not anymore."

"No. We're bigger. Darker. We're something meant to be, and no prayers or hopes or hunters can ever erase our kind."

"So what do you mean, that the world needs us? I don't believe it." Brigantia laughed.

"But we belong, just the same. We're nightmares of children and their parents. It's those in between on whom we thrive. The young, who are no longer children and not yet married. They dream of us, of our cool touch and its burn. They dream of the heat we would raise in them and what they imagine to be the eternal, sweet heat they would enjoy if we chose one of them to join us. Their mothers no longer sing to them, so it's our song they hear as they drift off to sleep, hands between their legs, longing and guilt swelling their hearts. For those in whom it grows too big, they seek us, and so goes all our cycles."

They paused, listening to the wind tearing through the rushes. Mors heard it as its own song. He whistled, answering the tune, and the notes seemed to take shape and flight, soaring into villages, where they hopefully caught. He and Brigantia smiled at each other in delight, and she took his hand.

"The dead are awake."

That was where the point turned. Mors thought her memory unlocked, that she was coming to be with him. Instead, she found Eamon.

At first, he was Jacob, and at first, he rejected Brigantia, sending her into a spiraling sadness that made Mors long to kill the dark-haired creature. A vampire so bound by the peculiar partial soul that was the mark of an observant Jew who was turned, he could not let go of the family that was murdered in the castle tower while he himself had been plucked to a sort of safety. A vampire who could not see the wonder that was Brigantia because all he could see was the ashes of his little brother and sister. Those years were a new sort of torture, with Brigantia and this Jacob in one dance and Mors in quite another. Cleland and Raleigh could only give cold, quiet comfort. The dance would go as it would.

Eventually, Jacob became Eamon and danced to Brigantia, who herself became Brigit, and they formed an unbreakable bond. Brigit. It was many more years before Mors could call her by that name. He missed what she had let go of to become it.

He also missed the part of himself that flew away with that name. Three hundred years had passed since he had sensed her as a human, till now, till this moment when she had found someone she could love and who would love her exactly as was meant. If he could not be happy for himself, he could find in himself some happiness for her. And it was this that made him feel what he no longer was. After so many centuries, the truly bestial vampire was gone. Real love had found him, had played a game with him, had run a teasing finger through him that not even the demon could overcome. Mors most truly controlled his demon now. He had been broken, and this made him bigger and stronger than ever before.

He traveled down to Penzance and gazed over the waters. No one could stop him from going farther.

Except that I have an older love, don't I?

Britain. Home. His truest love. He would hug it, cherish it, defend it always.

"Well. Well then. All right. Only make me a promise, my dear Britannia. Promise you won't let me make the same mistake twice."

Some years later, it would occur to him that he ought to have been more specific.

Chapter Seventeen

Rome. Autumn 1942.

When Mors finally turned and looked at Brigit, she was not smiling. Even so, he could tell she was pleased to see him, happy and relieved that he was alive and well. Not that there had been any doubt in her mind. He was Mors. He would always be alive and well.

However far his heart may finally have shifted from her, there was no denying Brigit's immense beauty. Her silky blond curls bounced lightly on her shoulders, and her blue eyes sparkled under well-groomed eyebrows. She was dressed in a navy traveling suit, trimmed in cream and made of a good silk-wool blend that the Italians would appreciate.

"Well," said Mors, when it seemed plain she was not going to open the preliminaries. "It really is you. How did this come to pass? You fancied a Roman holiday?"

A slightly arched eyebrow was his only answer. Mors skipped up the bank to join her. Looking closely, he could see something was different. The memory of their last shared moment wormed its way into his head and sat there, smirking at him. Him telling her he was leaving, sending her home to England and Eamon. Telling her he loved her. Kissing her with the kiss he wasn't sure he could give, the one that gave her some of his own power and life force. And then he left her, left her sobbing and begging him not to leave her. Walked away without looking back. Whistling.

He readied himself for the slap he deserved, hoping that, once delivered, the alien chill would thaw. But she didn't slap him. The longer he looked at her, the angrier he became. What the hell was she doing back here, when he had sent her home to be safe?

As though she knew what he was thinking, she averted her eyes and began to walk.

"You didn't go to Russia," she observed, a slight edge in her voice.

"Not yet," he rejoined. "I didn't specify when I was going."

She snorted. He could not understand why she was this cross with him, any more than he could begin to comprehend why she was here. Or even that she was here.

"You went to search for Cleland." An accusation. Headway.

"Among other things."

"You might have told me the truth." The edge in her voice would have sliced his hair, if he had any.

"You might have not left."

Brigit closed her eyes. Mors knew this was only the preliminary round.

"He's dead, isn't he?"

He hesitated.

"I believe so, yes," he whispered.

Brigit looked away for a long time.

"But I know who killed him, and they're . . . Brigit, this is the last place you should be."

"Because they want millennials? If you think I'm going to let you work out what's going on here and avenge Cleland alone, you have sadly mistaken my character."

"How in hell . . . ?"

At last, she filled him in. "A refugee named Rembrandt came to England—"

"Rembrandt! He's safe? He got to you? Oh, thank Jove. Well done, Rembrandt."

"We like him very much. Ulrika and Wolfgang were delighted to know it was he who shuttled out so many refugees. There will be European vampires to return the culture to their respective countries when this war is won."

There was no doubt in either of their minds as to who would win the war. That was settled. It was just a question of when.

"Anyway," Brigit went on, her voice hardening again. "He told us about the Nachtspeere and a bishop. But he was also under the impression you had a grand scheme to take over the army and topple the government."

"Well, I wouldn't put it quite like—"

"Mors, what the bloody hell are you playing at?"

"Mind your language, my girl."

"Actually, she's my girl." Eamon's helpful voice chimed in.

That made Mors start. He had not expected to see Eamon. The vampire was as well dressed as Brigit, a fedora tipped jauntily over his thick black hair, calfskin shoes gleaming. He carried two small leather cases strapped together, slung casually over his shoulder. He took Brigit's hand and smiled.

Mors looked from one to the other, thoroughly flummoxed.

"I was hardly going to travel alone," Brigit told him by way of explanation.

"And I wasn't letting her go without me again," Eamon finished.

"But what—" Mors began.

"We're here to keep you from losing your head," Brigit announced in a tone that suggested there was no argument. "You sent me away once, and as it happened, you were quite right to do it, but you need us, and don't say otherwise."

"I don't think I was going to," Mors answered, delighted.

"And we'll keep you focused," Eamon put in.

Mors was insulted.

"Who says I am without focus?"

Brigit put a hand on both their arms.

"It's been a long journey. Can we go indoors, please?"

"Of course. This way. I'll have to change the sheets," he added, as they headed toward Aventine Hill. They would talk more there.

Brigit and Eamon were delighted with the ancient apartment. They were still holding hands. Not long ago, it would have pained Mors to see it, but now he could be generous. They were entitled to their happiness.

Mors flung himself into his favorite chair as the other two settled themselves, allowing an uncomfortable silence to descend before he spoke.

"Eamon, the Nachtspeere, you should know—"

"I know." Eamon was curt. "I may not be a millennial, but I can more than manage in a fight, believe me."

Mors studied the younger vampire. He'd always thought there was a softness about Eamon, but now his eyes glinted with steel.

"If Otonia allowed you to come, why not Padraic?" Mors demanded.

Brigit and Eamon looked troubled and took hands again. Mors could not imagine what Padraic must be experiencing, stuck in London. Eamon began.

"There was no question of me coming, not when Brigit was. As for Padraic, well, ultimately Otonia had to agree that if she stayed, he did."

"That was quite the fracas," Brigit said, smiling faintly. "And we thought the Blitz was something."

Mors did not want to think about the Blitz. London was still there; that was what mattered.

"Otonia wanted to come?"

"Of course she did, silly idiot," Brigit told him with a real smile. "But it's best she stays in London, directing everyone. There's still a lot of work to be done there."

Eamon cleared his throat.

"Mors, about your military plans—"

"Which are immutable. You see, with a new regime in place—"

"Headed by whom?" Brigit was glacial.

"Those who know their stuff, now listen—"

"No, Mors, you listen!" Eamon ordered. "I know you've been keeping up, so I know you know Italy is weak in the field and Germany is having to run round and put out all its fires. We haven't got many advantages, but that's one. If you turned Italy on Germany, then the advantage would be to Germany. Don't you see?"

"You're forgetting that I would have some real influence then. That would change everything."

Brigit leaped to her feet and thrust a finger almost into Mors's nose.

"And you're forgetting that you're a vampire! *That* changes everything!"

"Exactly! It makes me wiser and more powerful."

"You must be touched by the sun!" she shrieked.

Eamon laid a hand over Brigit's and sat her back down.

"Mors, think reasonably," Eamon implored. "Otonia thought we could bend rules, stop something before it started or in its early days. But the course of war is set now, and we have to adhere to our own means of fighting."

"We tried, and look where it got us. What we needed was—"

"Human allies, I know." Brigit's voice was tinged with regret. "Rembrandt told us that's what you have here."

"Did he, now? What did he say about them?"

Brigit spoke like one choosing her words with care.

"He said there was a woman who seemed to be making you think that you were . . . a man."

Mors smiled. He couldn't help it.

"You always did have a way with words, Brigit."

Her eyes softened then, and she stood up.

"We are here to help." She spoke in a ringing tone. "But we also came to make sure you do not forget who and what you are. There are still boundaries, and they cannot be overstepped. Move beyond the shadows, and you die. I will not lose you again."

She turned on her heel and marched out of the room, her head held high and straight.

Eamon coughed pointedly and rose to follow Brigit.

"For what it's worth, it's good to see you, Mors."

Mors glared, but Eamon grinned. He was no longer the easily intimidated, gently respectful young vampire. Things had evolved. He tipped his hat and sauntered down the hall.

I did say I wanted the help of other vampires, didn't I? That'll teach me.

The following dusk, Mors woke elated. However much the past colored his view on Eamon, he did not dislike the vampire, and he was always happy to have Brigit nearby. With their help, Oster and the Nachtspeere, and especially Traugott and Deirdre, would be dealt a blow to be heard around the shadow world. That accomplished, if Mors knew Brigit and Eamon like he thought he did, they would overcome their reservations about the rest and fight like a pride of lions.

"So, Otonia says Italian food has quite a nice zing to it." Brigit grinned.

"It was better before Fascism, but it runs rings around the Germans," Mors assured her. "I need to eat tonight, too, and then I was going to meet Giulia. I'd love for you both to meet her."

Eamon checked his watch. "I hope you both can be quick about eating. I want to get to work."

He trotted up the stairs and the others followed. Mors let Brigit go first so that she did not see his broad grin. Eamon had craved action. He was going to want to stay and fight.

Mors wandered into the city center. His thoughts were in such a bundle, he was too distracted to hunt. He circled the Colosseum, which he still thought of as the Flavian Amphitheater, his fingers brushing lightly over the travertine stone. He whistled a tune he knew the building remembered.

At first, he didn't register what sent the happy daze skittering away like a mouse. It was beyond comprehensible. But it was, without a doubt, the smell of Cleland.

It came from the East Entrance, and he was there like a shot, but he saw no one.

"Cleland!" he bellowed.

The only response was a light reverberation of his own voice.

He had never been inside the tunnels there but swiftly found a way down. As he ran through them, he heard the roar of a car's engine on the street above, speeding away. By the time he was back outside, it was long gone. The air smelled of nothing but Rome.

Oh, that was a very poor move, mine enemy, very poor. I have allies now like you cannot imagine. Together, we can light a curse upon the limbs of men and cumber all the parts of Italy. Woe betide anyone who thinks we can't.

* * *

Giulia was pretending to peruse the window at a milliner's with a lively display, playing the role of a woman who wished she had more daytime leisure to shop.

Mors came upon her so suddenly, she yelped.

"Wild things are afoot tonight, my darling. Has anyone else been by?"

"Anyone . . . What?"

Giulia gaped as a beautiful young couple came to join them.

"There you are!" Mors cried. "Giulia Merlino, or rather Romano, these are Brigit and Eamon, just arrived from London, and this is Giulia." His eyes were darting about wildly. The others barely took notice of one another, they were so busy staring at him.

He shepherded them all through the streets, instructing them to seem to be laughing and joking. At last they came to a square he deemed quiet enough and sat them all at the foot of a fountain, pulling wine and glasses from the basket Brigit had brought.

"There was a smell of Cleland, just half an hour ago!"

"What?" Brigit and Eamon were aghast.

"Who?" Giulia asked.

"Oh, my darling, I have so much to tell you still. My friend, my dead . . . they found a way to, I don't know, use his scent somehow. Bottle it and use it to attract me. They obviously still think that can work!"

"Mors—" Brigit began, but he cut her off.

"Laugh!" he ordered, and they all obeyed as an oblivious couple strolled near them. When they were far enough away, Giulia broke in on the others' questions.

"Mors! They call you 'Mors.' They're from London. . . . Who . . . are . . . ?"

Mors took her hand in a gesture the couple observed intently.

"Yes. They're vampires. Brigit and I have known each other over one thousand years."

Giulia's glass slipped from her hand, and Mors deftly caught it before it hit the pavement.

"I'm only seven hundred and fifty-two," Eamon put in.

Mors tipped more wine down Giulia's throat. "That makes you quite the infant of the group, my love," he told her.

Giulia didn't smile. She glanced nervously at the new vampires, who in their turn were scrutinizing her. Something in Eamon's expression suggested he was pondering a deep question. Brigit's look was even more unsettling. It was the face of a prospective mother-in-law, an incongruity in a face that was otherwise so young.

"But I . . . I don't . . ." Giulia struggled to command herself.

Mors could not contain himself.

"We can discuss this more later. For now, we've got to—"

Brigit cut in on him, touching Giulia gently on the wrist.

"You need not be afraid of us, any more than you are of Mors."

Giulia blushed. "I'm not afraid, I just—"

Mors's firm instruction came yet again: "Laugh!"

The three vampires laughed uproariously, covering Giulia's forced chuckle—a sound that rang increasingly false as their group was approached by two Blackshirts . . . and two blond men. Mors did not recognize either of them and wondered if his hat made him unidentifiable.

"You're all out quite late this evening!" the captain said in a falsely jovial tone. It was hard to gauge which couple garnered more disapprobation, the older or the younger.

"Well, it's such a glorious night!" Brigit cried in the elevated tones of the upper class, her Italian impeccable. Her color was high, her broad smile infectious. "Would you like some wine?"

"Darling, they're on duty!" Eamon chided her, his Italian just as perfect, his manner that of the careless layabout whose family money had spared him military duty.

"Oh, and what will one glass hurt?" She laughed back at her lover, leaning in to kiss his nose and then his mouth, forgetting their audience.

Mors smiled apologetically at the officers. "Of course, we'll be getting on home. Just enjoying the evening."

The Blackshirts seemed satisfied, but one of the blond men nudged the captain and whispered to him. Mors could hear it, the Italian in a German accent: "Ask to see their papers. Especially these dark things."

Mors's thumb tapped his index finger, trying to keep his talon contained.

"Papers, please," the captain snapped, although not without first casting a baleful glance at the German.

Mors and Giulia exchanged the smallest of glances. Being Signora Romano gave her protection and respectability, which Mors suspected did not extend so far as to be cavorting with another couple and a man who was not her husband.

Mors stood up. The Germans were taller than he, but they nonetheless looked uneasy.

"If there is a problem, gentlemen, you may discuss it with me." Mors smiled, and the four men shuddered. The captain attempted to soothe the aristocrat's ruffled feathers.

"No problem, sir," he said. "But we can't have any sort of drunken behavior in public; it's unseemly. There is a war on, you know."

"Merely practicing for the victory party," Brigit simpered. She stood and made a bit of a show of shaking out her skirts so that even the Germans' eyes swiveled to her curvy hips.

Eamon and Giulia packed the basket. The officers nodded and headed on their way. Mors saw the Germans looking over their shoulders at the group, but they kept on walking.

"Excuse me a minute," Mors muttered. Brigit cleared her throat.

"Too public. And the bodies . . ."

"I'll take care of it," Mors insisted, but Giulia clutched his coat.

"No, Mors, please. She's right. They already know you're here; don't make it worse."

He touched her cheek, then thrust some lire in her hand.

"Go home, please. It will be all right. We'll talk properly tomorrow," he promised. A distant train whistle, still many miles from the Termini Station, made him smile. "Think I'll go for a run."

"Mors!" Giulia shrieked, but it was too late. He went dashing after the officers, Brigit right behind him.

When Mors caught up to the officers, his face aglow in its full vampiric wonder, he promptly saw that the Germans, at least, were prepared for this possibility. They were most definitely Nachtspeere and better trained than any he had come across in Berlin. The terrified Italians shrieked and ran, but the Nachtspeere attempted to fight him. Mors laughed, a laugh that bounced off all the surrounding walls and skipped away from them.

"Can't catch me! Can't catch me!" he taunted happily.

And the chase was on. The Nachtspeere undoubtedly congratulated themselves on their good training and ability to keep up, never guessing that Mors, now turning cartwheels, was moving slowly enough to stay in their sights, leading them toward the train tracks.

Brigit, meanwhile, caught the fleeing Blackshirts and doubled back. She was well ahead of Mors and out of sight of the others, a firm hold on each man, a hand pressed tightly across mouth and nose, suffocating them.

"Which way?" she asked Mors.

"East, straight on!"

She was gone before anyone else knew she'd been there.

Mors continued to scamper just ahead of the panting, furious Nachtspeere. He leaped and whirled as though he were auditioning for the Royal Ballet. As he neared the tracks, he slowed. The train rounded the bend, and Mors made quite a show of pulling out his pocket watch and examining it.

"Marvelous how Mussolini's made the trains run on time, isn't it?"

The first Nachtspeere reached him and screeched in shock and pain as Mors's talons slashed his torso. As the train zoomed by, Mors deftly swung the man between the wheels of one car, so that he was sliced and crushed.

The second Nachtspeere yowled and turned tail to run, but Mors's arm seemed to grow longer and caught him. The man was consigned to the same fate as his fellow, under the mercifully empty observation car.

Brigit had disposed of the Blackshirts in the same way, although they were already dead on impact. Now she relieved Mors of the shredded clothes he was holding.

"I'll go burn these with the rest," she said, having started a small fire.

"I must say, I'm really enjoying Rome," Eamon remarked, grinning at Mors.

But Mors had gone glassy-eyed.

"Mors?" Eamon ventured. "Are you still with us?"

"It's him. It's the bishop!" Mors answered, not hearing the question.

Brigit and Eamon then had to move fast to keep up with him.

. . .

He hadn't gone far—only down the Via Cavour to hover in the shadows outside the Basilica di Santa Maria Maggiore. The massive church had the look of a palace, and indeed, the cluster of clergy leaving after a private dinner were ushered out with all the ceremony accorded crowned heads.

"It's him, that one," he said to Brigit and Eamon. "He's—"

"Oh yes. We can smell it, too," Brigit said, her face crinkled in concentration. Eamon nodded.

Bishop Oster busied himself in saying a lot of nothing to his friends, not even glancing at the waiting car. His Italian was not good, but that did not affect their obvious respect for him. Mors sensed something more than respect. Something more like envy. Or perhaps fear.

"He was working with the Nachtspeere," Mors murmured, his words slow and deliberate. "And I very much want to know what he is doing here—because I know damn well, it's something to do with Cleland."

The bishop spread his arms in a dramatic gesture and breathed deeply, smiling up at the stars. With every expansion of his chest, Mors moved closer, closer . . . he was almost at the place where he might be seen.

"Mors!" Brigit's hiss was anxious, urging.

The bishop and his underlings got in the car. Both the priests from the basilica and the vampires in the dark watched the car until it veered onto the Via Panisperna and disappeared, heading west.

Mors allowed his senses to follow it, although he hardly needed to. The dawning realization and shock radiating from Brigit and Eamon weren't necessary, either. He could see it all as clearly as if he were there, omniscient, riding along with the bishop all the way to the gates. Another piece of the puzzle fell firmly into place.

"He's alive. He's alive, and they have him." Mors spoke in a voice like a knife twisting slowly into intestines. "Here. That . . . man . . . has him here. Our Cleland. In the Vatican."

Chapter Eighteen

Rome. Winter 1942/1943.

The words still hung over their heads hours later, large icicles twirling in the air. Cleland, alive. In the Vatican.

Brigit and Eamon struggled hard to keep Mors from going after the car. This was no time for such recklessness. Like it or not, they had to plan. They were going to need help.

"I beg your pardon?" Giulia asked, sure Mors was making some outrageous joke.

"We need to break into the Vatican. Or at least be able to follow someone inside."

"Yes, that seems reasonable," she said, her mouth curled in incredulity.

Mors had used the field telephone to call and ask her to come to Aventine Hill at once; it was an emergency. Brigit and Eamon were enormously impressed at Rembrandt's skill in having built such a useful device. Giulia, alarmed by the call, had rushed over. Now she looked as though she wished she hadn't. Mors could not blame her. It could not be an easy thing, being asked to assist with what was a hanging offense.

"We have to, Giulia. That's where our friend is," Mors told her.

Her mouth dropped open.

"This must be where Bishop Oster fits in the picture, isn't it?" she exclaimed. "I was going to tell you last night what I've found out. It's odd."

"It would have to be," Mors observed.

"Officially, he's doing research in the archives, something about a great new path for the church in Germany. No one knows exactly what, and he has been granted absolute secrecy, but here's the part that is prompting whispers . . . it's said he's been granted that secrecy by Mussolini. They say the pope doesn't even know he's there. It's only someone else, someone liaising with the government, who said if it was a request from Germany, then it must be heeded and no questions asked. No one can imagine such a thing; it's completely unheard of, although since Mussolini agreed to let them create the city-state, he might have a right to ask such favors. Oster has a cousin who's head of the Vatican Museum and apparently made a lot of the arrangements."

"Yes!" Mors snapped his fingers. "Father Ambros mentioned a Vatican connection. So he wanted to get to the Vatican even then. I wonder why?"

"Isn't it obvious?" Brigit was astonished. Mors looked at her blankly. "Oh, Mors, don't say you don't know about the churches! Otonia's talked about this."

"You know it's not the sort of thing to which I've ever paid much attention. Tell me."

Brigit and Eamon exchanged a glance of exasperation and apprehension. In a firm, flat voice, she explained.

"A younger vampire can't go in at all, but if we do, we lose our millennial powers."

"Oh." Mors paused, digesting that. "But the Vatican in itself isn't a church, is it?"

"Well, no," Brigit conceded. "But look, even if the ground isn't sanctified, it's still the original epicenter of Christianity. Well, besides Bethlehem. The Holy See must radiate an incomparable power all the way to the city walls. Why else would Oster have wanted to take Cleland there?"

"I see your point." Mors nodded. "Although I think I'll be all right. I went inside Saint Hedwig's Cathedral in Berlin. It was a bit tingly, but I managed. Don't let's forget I'm a double millennial; I was probably just dropping down to your level." He winked at Brigit.

"Charming." Brigit smirked. She turned to Eamon. "And I'll be equal to you, my darling."

Eamon kissed her hand. Giulia pointed at him, her brows knit in concentration.

"But then, how can you go in?"

"Ah!" Eamon lit up. "I was Jewish. We come with a whole different set of complications. Not that I go inside churches. I respect that space. But neither they nor crosses can touch me. A Magen David, though, that's another story."

Giulia did not smile. She turned to Mors, utterly flummoxed.

"You said you were from the republic; you can't have been Christian, either. But crosses—"

"Oh, that." Brigit broke in. "Yes, that's one of those infuriating complexities we don't quite understand. Which isn't to say we don't guess." She gave a kind of laugh, although she didn't seem amused. "I think it's about faith."

Mors raised an eyebrow at her.

"Yes, faith," she insisted. "Crosses are supposed to ward off demons, and that's what we all have inside us, a demon."

Mors felt Giulia's hand turn to ice. He wrapped both of his around it. Brigit continued.

"And I think the reason they don't work on Eamon is not because his demon is so different, or because he has a partial soul—"

"A what?" Giulia cried shrilly.

"Complications," Eamon reminded her.

Brigit seemed to hear neither of them. She looked straight at Mors, her eyes sad. "I think it's because our religions died. People stopped believing in our gods, and so the trappings had no power over us. But nature still knows we're, well, unnatural, and so there must be something beyond the hunters to keep us at bay. So the religion that supplanted ours also now defends its adherents against us. A sort of symbiosis, I suppose."

Everyone sat silent for several minutes.

"You had quite the talk with Otonia about this," Mors said at last.

"No," Brigit told him. "This is my own thinking on the subject. I can think for myself, you know."

"My apologies," Mors said, and smiled. Then he turned to Giulia. "Well, there you have it. We need to get inside the Vatican. Will you help us?"

Giulia's wide eyes slowly focused.

"I suppose we should start with some maps," she said when she was able to speak.

The scale of activity over the next many weeks meant there was little time for anything else, including much thought. Mors had drawn a giant map that filled an entire wall. Another wall was covered with notes, including pictures and names of any Vatican resident or employee they could identify. This was an invasion. Strategy was required.

Giulia reported that there was a new rumor among her husband's colleagues—that although Oster was ostensibly there as a favor to the German church, it was the German government that had made the request, the one that Mussolini acceded to so readily.

"And it wasn't exactly a request," Giulia added. He had been allotted a laboratory below the museum, brought a large guard, and demanded utter privacy while explaining nothing.

"At least we know where to find him," said Mors, drawing a circle around the mapped museum.

Each vampire had gone to the Vatican and circled the walls, walking as closely as they dared to ascertain the place's strength. Mors felt a soft vibration, a snake's warning rattle, telling him that while the city-state was not sealed like a private home, it nonetheless did not want him there. Brigit reported the same, while Eamon confirmed that he would have no trouble.

"Beyond trying not to get caught, of course."

"But you don't think we need an invitation?" Brigit asked Mors.

"Good luck getting it," he answered. "Oster invited me into Saint Hedwig's, but that made no difference. No, we can enter the Vatican, just like we can enter churches—at our own peril."

"The real question, once we find Oster's workplace, of course, is whether he's prepared for the possibility of our arrival," said Eamon, tacking another note to the wall.

"He knows I'm here, of course," Mors responded, studying the map. "So I'd say there are two possibilities. One is that he's sealed the door to vampires and rescinded my invitation. The other is that he hasn't, in the hopes that I will walk in and find myself trapped somehow."

Giulia had arrived with a large bundle and heard this last exchange.

"If the door is sealed to vampires, but I go in first, can't I invite you in?"

Mors was only half listening as he was still contemplating the map.

"It needs to be the person who it—" He broke off, realizing what she had said. "If *you* go in?"

"Well, naturally I'm coming with you. What did you think?"

Mors took note of the defiant jut of her chin.

"I know you're not afraid of danger, my love, but this is different. It's not your cause."

Giulia gave him an exasperated smile, then came and put her arms around him.

"It's your cause, therefore, it's my cause." She kissed his nose, then his mouth. "Now then, let me show you what I've brought!"

As she was busy unpacking the bag, the three vampires exchanged smiles. Mors loved that his friends thought well of Giulia. He couldn't wait to have her meet Cleland.

The one thought that did occasionally intrude, as they studied their quarry, was that perhaps he had been wrong, that the smell at the Colosseum had been just another trick, or a phantom. That the one truth Deirdre had told would be the worst: Cleland was dead. Mors threw back his shoulders, pitching the thought off of him. If it was true, at least it would be confirmed—and he would have his vengeance.

Giulia had pulled four black cassocks from her bag.

"I always hated sewing, but I'm rather good at it," she observed, admiring her handiwork.

Mors had suggested they disguise themselves as priests, even Brigit.

"I'll just keep my hat on and my head down," Brigit said, and shrugged.

They thought it inappropriate to wear actual vestments, so Giulia volunteered to make some. She had outdone herself.

"You are a queen, my darling," said Mors. "But if we do meet any Nachtspeere, it might be best to pretend you're a vampire. Just in case." Mors kissed her, then rubbed his hands together in pleased anticipation. "Well! I suppose we're just about ready."

"No, not quite yet," said Giulia. "An invitation went around today. There is a special mass being said to give the priests more strength to guide their flocks. People have been asked from miles around. It's got to be easier, sneaking in with all those clergy."

"Too right. Well done!" Mors complimented her. "When is it?"

"Not till Twelfth Night, I'm afraid." She bit her lip. That was more than two weeks away.

"Twelfth Night," Mors echoed. "I suppose it gives us more time to find the tunnels?"

One of the many rumors about the city-state was that, besides the great Borgia tunnel, there were other tunnels by which one could escape, should it fall under siege. Mors had thus far found no trace of them.

Brigit set one of the priest's hats on her head.

"We'll make a willow cabin at the gate," she said.

"And thence to enact a decidedly improbable fiction," Eamon finished.

As soon as the sun set on Twelfth Night, they caught the bus that took them down the Viale Vaticano and within reach of the main entrance. There was a crush of similar black-clad men, eager to get inside.

"Pope Pius pulls quite a crowd," Eamon remarked. "Does he do impressions?"

"He has good food and wine," was Giulia's answer.

Just as they had hoped, the overwhelmed Swiss Guards were giving cursory glances at everyone's papers, a foolishness the battle-hardened vampires looked on with scorn. It hardly took a cynic to realize that such an event was ideal for insurgents; the cassock was a perfect hiding place for a weapon. In fact, they had all brought guns. This war was becoming more human. Any opportunity to surprise the enemy must be seized.

The plan was to drift toward the museum; the dim light and black throng would be disguise enough until they could get inside. Mors hoped the bishop would be working and they could meet. It seemed unlikely he would attend a mass meant to bolster the spirits of Italian priests.

The museum door was only yards away, but the tingle Mors had felt once they had cleared the entrance was now a shooting pain. There was a weight on his chest, then his head. His mouth opened as though to take a breath, and his knees buckled. A sharp exclamation made his head turn almost of its own accord to see Brigit nearly collapsed onto Eamon, who was propping her up and trying to keep her moving, just enough so that they could get behind the door, away from eyes. Mors made a move to reach for them, and Giulia, alarmed, gripped him.

"Try, please try," she implored. "We must get inside."

He shook his head, unable to speak. They had trusted that his skill with locks would get them into the museum, but when they reached the door, it was all he could do to remain upright. Eamon seized the door handle and broke it open, hustling them all into the darkened building.

"But someone might see the door; they'll know something!" Giulia protested.

"I don't care," Eamon answered, lowering Brigit to the floor.

Mors sank down and Brigit grasped his hand. The pain was dissipating, although the tingling persisted. He could begin to think. He turned his senses inward, searching, testing each bit of himself.

"Are you all right?" Giulia asked, her voice trembling.

"Mostly," Mors answered, staggering to his feet. "But I think I was wrong about one thing."

"Perish the thought," Eamon said before he could stop himself. Brigit gave a gasping laugh.

"Yes," Mors grimaced. "I was wrong, and Brigit was right. I'm not a millennial at all now, not in here."

Brigit nodded in grim agreement. Her skin had a green-gray cast, but she was otherwise regaining command of herself.

"But I'm still me," Mors said with finality. "And if you're all still yourselves, we're a firestorm. Let's find the entrance to the storage rooms. I hope there aren't too many crosses down there."

They padded down the dim corridor. Mors hardly knew what was around him. Every piece of him from skin to marrow to demon was struggling to adjust, as though his body had shrunk a foot and needed to rearrange to fit in the cramped space. It was spinning back in time, shedding years, chipping away like the elements at the architectural ruins he so loved. He thought he could see particles of his strength and skills floating in the still air. So many, many years since this time, this time of not being something so unique among vampires.

Except that I was always unique.

This was the thought he clung to, the remembrance of what he had possessed, even before his first millennium. That certainty of being special. And now that he had the benefit of his tempered self and his knowledge, these would compensate for his weakened body.

Ah, knowledge. The wing wherewith we fly to heaven. Bit of irony for all who like it.

"Here, this way!" Eamon hissed, pausing at a door. Mors and Brigit nodded. They opened the door and headed down.

The museum's storage rooms were vast, stretching on for what seemed like miles, perhaps encompassing the whole of Vatican City. The vampires and Giulia squeezed between two enormous wooden crates and took the risk of whispering.

"I don't smell anything, human or vampire," Brigit said. "Do either of you?"

"No," Eamon replied. They looked at Mors.

Mors was attempting to command his disordered senses to obey him, but they lay scattered like children's toys.

"The doors to the archives and special collections may be iron, for fireproofing," Giulia pointed out. "Would that impede your sense of smell?"

"It shouldn't, but who can say?" Mors grumbled.

Brigit suddenly—and to Mors's mind, inappropriately—lit up.

"We need to hunt!"

The others looked at her blankly.

"This place isn't just stripping us of millennial power, it's sending all our abilities into turmoil." She turned to Eamon. "And you're worried about us, which is distracting you. But our senses are always at their apex when we hunt. We must convince the demon it's on a hunt."

Giulia's lips had turned pale. "Hunt. You mean, for . . . food?"

Brigit curled her hand around Giulia's cold one. "I know. I'm sorry. But, come now, you knew there would be violence at the end of this search. We won't eat; we just need to let what's inside us turn toward that possibility. You understand, don't you?"

"I don't," Eamon interjected. "Sweetheart, Cleland is our brother, Oster is our enemy. The demon should be able to search for both."

"No, she's right," Mors said. "She's right. We can't know the whole of what's happening to us in here. We have to try it."

"Nothing's happened to me," Eamon insisted.

"Can you smell anything?" Mors snapped.

"Well, no. But how . . . ? We don't hunt in groups. And pairs only on special occasions."

"There is no more special occasion than this," Mors said, the argument won. He turned to Giulia. "Stay close behind us. And please, try not to worry. Save your strength. You'll need it."

Each vampire began his or her own time-honored formula for the hunt, closing off everything else so as to seek food, even in this singularly barren place. Brigit and Eamon each emitted almost soundless hums— Eamon's was musical, Brigit's a vibration—sounds that were living things, that could touch and be touched. They swirled over Mors, a veil of silk and water, and burrowed their way into the empty spaces in his own wandering senses. All the many filaments bound together, twisting into a rope, resisting the forces of the building surrounding them and extending out and out and out—an almost visible path.

The three vampires walked in measured steps, trancelike, letting the rope lead them. If the demons inside Mors and Brigit were each shrunken and confused, they could still do this. They knew this was no hunting ground, but they obeyed the order nonetheless.

The rope ended at a plain iron door with a curved handle. An ornate sign hung on the door: STRICTLY NO ADMITTANCE WITHOUT PERMISSION. A sign that was hardly necessary, since extra security was enabled in the form of a padlock.

Mors reached a finger toward the lock. Heat emanated from it. The door's actual handle, however, was cool.

"Yes, I see," he muttered. "The Nachtspeere have no jurisdiction here. They can't bypass all the laws and do what they need to do to seal this door, but they can bring their own locks. Genius. They just weren't counting on us having a human at hand."

He took Giulia's hand and positioned it on the lock. Then he, Brigit, and Eamon wrapped their hands around hers. With one colossal pull, the lock snapped off.

Mors nodded, and they all took out their guns. It took only a nudge from Mors to push the door open. The room was cave-black, but Mors soon found the light switch. None of them could register what they were seeing.

It didn't seem real. It couldn't be real. Even Giulia's muffled gagging couldn't make it more real. Mors drifted toward the table in a trance, barely cognizant of Brigit and Eamon beside him. He reached a hand toward the figure on the table, but it froze, unable to move another inch.

Cleland was emaciated, his cheekbones almost poking through his skin. His eyelids, bereft of lashes, were dark red and crusted shut. Only tufts of hair remained on his scabbed head. His wrists, where he was bound to the table, bore deep cuts and bruises, as did his right ankle. His left leg was bound at the thigh . . . his left foot was missing. The room was ice-cold, and he was wearing only tattered drawers. Mors thought he could perhaps bear all of this. But the drawers revealed more than they concealed: Cleland's entire body below his face was stripped of skin.

Brigit recovered first, taking note of the IV giving Cleland the occasional parsimonious drip of blood. She tossed aside her gun and jumped to the IV, adjusting the feed. Eamon scanned the room for more blood, finding a tiny bottle and a syringe.

"It's just animal blood, but better than nothing."

"Here, mine," Giulia offered, holding out her arm.

Brigit hesitated.

"No, better not. We need to move fast."

Brigit whispered an apology to Cleland and stuck the syringe into his vein.

"Cleland, can you hear us?" Mors asked in a croak. There was no answer.

"He's alive," Brigit assured him. "It's better he stay unconscious as long as possible. Don't just stand there, get those bindings off him!"

Mors still stared at his friend, the brother he had been searching for so many months. He felt even weaker—a human, a human child, something unknown. That all this had been happening all this time . . .

A brush on his cheek shook him out of his daze. He turned and looked into Giulia's eyes.

"You found him," she said. "Now we just need to get him home."

Home.

Galvanized, Mors seized a chain holding Cleland's good leg and snapped it in half. Eamon had already freed one of Cleland's arms, and Mors swiftly liberated the rest of him.

"A sheet, we need a sheet—something to protect his flesh," Brigit said, tearing open cabinets.

"This!" cried Eamon, spying a white lab coat hanging on a hook. As he snatched it, the wood panel on which it was hanging slammed open, knocking Eamon back. Two Nachtspeere stormed the room while another two blocked the door from which the rescuers had entered. A stake flew straight into Mors's arm. Mors and Giulia were each able to grab their guns and fire, but the bullets simply bounced off their targets. A Nachtspeere swung a sword at Mors, who abandoned the pistol and caught up a long knife from the operation table. Eamon and a Nachtspeere toppled into Giulia, sending her own pistol skittering across the floor.

"Halt!" rang out a harsh voice. The Nachtspeere whipped out large crosses and wielded them in front of even Giulia. For added measure, they produced swords, which were held to every neck. The cross was blinding: Mors felt as though he were surrounded by volcanic ash. He glanced at Giulia and Eamon, indicating that they should pretend to be in the pain he and Brigit were enduring. For anyone else, he would have seized the advantage, but Oster and Traugott were now bearing down on him, and he wanted to learn their secrets before killing them. He knew by now there must be others who would take up their mantles, if Mors could not cut out the heart of the operation.

The Nachtspeere reached over the crosses to pull off the priests' hats.

"Well, well, well!" Oster rubbed his hands together and laughed happily. "Uninvited guests! Uninvited, but hardly unwanted. Hardly unwanted at all. My dear, dear Herr von Mohren! Have you found religion so much that you've become a priest? No, no, that seems unlikely. Do you know what I think?"

He pushed aside the Nachtspeere's cross and leaned toward Mors until they were nose to nose. The pectoral cross he wore singed straight through Mors's clothes and charred his skin, but Mors did not blink.

"I think," Oster went on, his eyes bright with triumph, "that you are not a noble, nor are you a priest. Nor, if I had to guess, are you much of a man."

"I'm about as much of a priest as you are," Mors retorted. "And, if I had to guess, at least fifty times the man."

"Look closely, Oster," Brigit taunted. "We're the faces of death."

Oster turned to Brigit. His smile spanned the width of his round face, and his skin turned even pinker with pleasure.

"My goodness." He crowed. "When I said I wanted fresh supplies, I never dreamed of anything quite so delectable."

Eamon and Mors lurched, and the swords against their necks drew blood.

Traugott assessed Brigit with professional interest.

"I should have to confirm via the books, Your Grace, but I believe she is one of the British millennials. I am less sure of the dark ones."

Oster folded his hands behind his back and rocked on his heels, drinking Brigit in. His eyes never left her face as he addressed Traugott.

"You say vampires are especially delicious to sleep with?"

"A man hardly gets much sleep, I'll tell you that." Traugott laughed.

Mors could feel his friends' revulsion, but for himself he started to be pleased. The Nachtspeeres' attention was tilting as they contemplated illicit sex. He just needed to distract them a hair more, just to split their minds in two.

Divide and conquer.

"So, a real man of God, are you?" Eamon's sarcasm could draw blood.

Oster glanced at him with a condescending smirk.

"Enjoying the flesh of a vampire would hardly be breaking a vow. Human women are forbidden to us, but Jews, Gypsies, vampires . . . well, that's all fair game."

Eamon's hand reached for the cross looming over him, but Mors's voice cut in.

"You haven't been sleeping with our friend Cleland, though, have you? Perhaps a bit of buggery doesn't tickle your fancy?"

The Nachtspeere on him released the sword but smacked him full in the face with the cross. Mors sucked in his lips so as not to scream. The pain lashed his whole body. He could feel his face scalding, flesh peeling away. However, the advantage was won.

Eamon seized the cross before him. The Nachtspeere's mouth dropped open.

"This one is human! He's human!" the Nachtspeere shrieked.

The cross splintered in Eamon's hand. Mors and Brigit laughed.

Traugott stared at Eamon.

"No, he isn't. He's a Jew vampire."

"Damn right," Eamon agreed, kicking the sword-wielding Nachtspeere so that the man's testicles broke open.

Mors, Brigit, and Giulia launched into action, with Mors determined to protect Giulia before someone recognized she was only a human. Eamon snapped the neck of the agonized Nachtspeere and snatched the sword. He swung at Traugott, but the man ducked, seizing Eamon at the knees so that Eamon crashed hard into the floor.

Another Nachtspeere attempted to stake Giulia, and she sent a finger into his eye.

"Well done," Mors congratulated her, seizing a scalpel from the table and drawing it across the man's throat.

"Spare the blonde! Spare the blonde!" Oster was screaming, which further agitated Brigit. Her face was in its full vampiric glory, and this only seemed to delight Oster more. The Nachtspeere fighting her was too enraged to hear his master and was swinging his cross at Brigit. She caught his wrist and twisted, flipped him high over the table where Cleland still lay unconscious. The man landed on his head, snapping his neck. Oster scampered behind her and pressed his pectoral cross into her hair. She howled and whipped around, slashing at him with her talons. He jerked back, but four trails of blood still appeared on his face.

"Ungrateful bitch!" Traugott was horrified at her dismissal of his master. He leaped for an ax in the corner.

The Nachtspeere whom Brigit had been wrestling saw a chance to slam a stake into her back. Eamon plunged his talons between the man's shoulder blades, drawing them all the way down his spine.

Mors was struggling with a Nachtspeere who had mastered martial-arts techniques and was a shockingly good fighter. Ancient soldier though Mors was, this was a style of fighting with which he was unfamiliar. Worse, the man seized the bishop's iron crosier and was swinging it so that Mors had to continually duck to avoid both the little cross in the crook of the staff and the crook's sharpened edge. At last, he was able to grasp the staff and hold it, despite the fact that this, too, burned. He jerked the Nachtspeere closer—and then was splattered with blood. Giulia had regained her pistol and shot the man in the head.

As Mors was wiping blood and brains out of his eyes, he saw Traugott swing the ax at Brigit. Eamon was a hair too late: The ax sliced into her pelvis, and the vampires were deafened by the sickening sound of crunching bones and Brigit's elongated scream. In her fury, the fire in her rose: Smoke poured from her eyelids, and flames danced around her face. Traugott and Giulia stared, stunned. Eamon grabbed the lab coat to smother the flames as Mors ransacked the shelves for water. Giulia snatched up a flask and flung it, remembering too late what it might be.

The holy water sank into Brigit's flesh, pushing the flames higher. Brigit's scream was a terrible thing, but Eamon rolled her in the coat and tore the skirt off his cassock, tamping down the blaze.

Traugott, snapping out of his daze, pointed at Giulia, whose screams rivaled Brigit's in horror. She had backed against the operating table, her hand inadvertently lying on a discarded cross.

"Apolline was right: He's consorting with humans! Or is it another Jew vampire?"

Oster gripped Giulia around the neck and started to throttle her. Mors jumped on Oster and flattened him to the floor. Eamon turned on

Traugott, but the Nazi flung a chair in front of him, then whirled and ran, leaving the bishop to his fate.

"What have you been doing here? What have you been doing?" demanded Mors, talons digging into the bishop's flesh.

"I wasn't going to kill him. I wasn't!" the man screamed.

"Just doing God's work?" Mors sneered. He leaned closer. There was a whiff of Cleland coming from this man, more raw than that he'd smelled on Deirdre. Mors tore through the man's vestments to find a loose, clumsily stitched undershirt. Made of several layers of skin. Cleland's skin.

"And you call us monsters," Mors whispered, hardly believing what he was seeing. "What is this? What the hell have you been doing?"

Oster laughed—his highest-pitched giggle yet.

"It's merely the beginning of our plan: This is bulletproof armor. Why, you saw it yourself, when you tried to shoot us. Make it thick enough and it seems to work beautifully."

"Mors we have to get them out!" Eamon cried, attempting to tend Brigit.

Mors knew it, and he knew Traugott would soon return with reinforcements.

"I'll spare you three of your limbs if you tell me who your orders come from," Mors offered the bishop.

"The greatest men of the Third Reich will be invincible!" Oster taunted. "And if you think you can get back into Berlin now to try to stop them, you are a very silly vampire indeed."

He laughed again. Eamon slammed the bishop's own crosier into his open mouth with enough force to drive it through his skull and into the floor, holding him fast.

"Sorry, Mors, we've got to go."

Mors shredded the skin shirt on Oster's body and stood. The lab coat, though sooty, was still better than nothing for wrapping around Cleland. Mors could not bear to use any of the clothes from the dead men on the floor. He approached his friend gingerly, hoping the increased blood drip might have yielded some improvement. Cleland's eyes were still crusted shut with no movement. But when Mors wrapped the coat around him and hefted him into his arms, he swore he heard the tiniest groan.

Eamon was at some pains to carry Brigit because of her broken pelvis. At last she gasped through her agony, "Just get me the hell out of here!"

Giulia had said nothing, but now she jumped up in terror.

"Someone's coming!"

It was a rumble of feet, perhaps above them, but of course the men knew the Vatican better than the vampires and Giulia. Traugott was on his way.

"A tunnel—can we find one of the tunnels?" Giulia cried.

There was no space to concentrate, but Mors sent his senses flying through the corridors anyway. He had felt nothing aboveground, but down here he knew, knew that there was indeed an escape route. Somewhere.

Cleland was at once heavy and light in his arms. His body was so frail, Mors could feel every bone. And yet Mors's own weakened state made his friend harder to carry.

"Help me," Mors whispered, but only in his head. "Help me help you. Please."

The words sang over and over in his head like a mantra. He wanted to believe he could feel something—Cleland's own starved demon pressing against his—but now he could smell fire. Traugott and his cohorts were gaining on them and had brought torches.

Worse, Giulia was losing strength. She wasn't used to this amount of running. She said nothing, but Mors could hear her labored breathing, could feel the stitch forming in her side.

Help, help, help.

They passed a line of stacked wooden crates with rolled tapestries leaning against them. Suddenly, Mors stopped and doubled back. There, sticking out from behind a roll inches thick in dust, a division in the wall that was slightly out of alignment. He kicked the tapestries, sending up a fog of dust, and then kicked at the wall. It was a sliding door, covering the entrance to a tunnel.

"Jump onto me!" he ordered Giulia. She obeyed, leaping on his back, trying to avoid touching Cleland. He ran into the blackness, Eamon just behind them.

Whether the tunnel went straight or twisted, Mors could hardly tell, so focused was he on getting them out. He did think it was gradually getting lighter. At first, he took heart, thinking they were nearing the end, which would mean the return of his millennial strength. But then he realized the light was behind him. Their pursuers had found them.

Mors sprinted harder. A ball of flame flew by his head, just missing Giulia's hair, and Mors was oddly grateful for such a weapon: It lit the way ahead.

They were nearing a wooden door. Giulia jumped off Mors's back and tried the handle. It swung open. They all ran out and shut the door behind them but there was no way to secure it.

Luck was with them, however. The tunnel had ended in a makeshift garage, in which there were two Mercedes sedans.

"There aren't any keys," Giulia said, searching the walls.

Mors put his foot against the car door. Nothing. He kicked in the window.

"Mind the glass," he warned Giulia as she jumped in to open the back doors.

Eamon laid Brigit across the backseat, then reached for Cleland. Mors tucked him against Eamon and slammed the door, then slid into the front seat to wire the car to start.

The wooden door swung open just as Mors revved the engine, and he drove the car hard into the door, splintering it all over their pursuers. The larger doors leading outside were heavy, but Mors knew how a Mercedes was built and put his foot all the way to the car's floor, enjoying the satisfaction of bursting through the doors and into the open air.

They were well outside the Vatican now, and Mors didn't know this road, but he didn't care. Giulia navigated and he drove on, feeling his body tingle as his millennial self began its slow road to return.

Mors drove as close to the lair's entrance as the narrow road would allow. Giulia hurried ahead to open the door. Mors was sure every awkward twist as they carried Cleland down the steps must be torture, but knowing the pain was near an end kept him from fretting too much. They laid Cleland on the sofa, and Mors went to help Eamon with Brigit.

As soon as she was settled on Eamon and Brigit's bed, Mors tore off his cassock and grabbed his coat and hat.

"What are you doing?" Giulia asked.

"I have to get rid of that car," he answered. "And bring back food."

Giulia blanched but nodded.

"Should I go?" Eamon asked, although he obviously didn't want to leave Brigit. "You're still not at full strength."

"No," Mors answered, the words grating on him. "We'll manage."

Giulia had changed back into her own clothes, and they sped off together.

Mors was too exhausted to speak and was glad Giulia said nothing. He wished he could fling the car over the Tarpeian Rock, the ancient place where so many traitors had been tossed to their deaths. Instead, he drove it through the park to the Tiber, where they found a stone heavy enough to keep the accelerator down, and sent it into the river. Mors was pleased for the river's sake that the car would be fetched out soon and was confident that it would only lead to awkwardness between the visiting Germans and the Italians.

He grabbed Giulia into a quick hug. She squeezed him back and whispered, "Tomorrow?"

"Yes," he answered brusquely. "Bring what medical supplies you can. They'll need help."

Mors lost no time finding a vagrant and emptying his blood into two bottles. One would do for both, just for tonight.

Back in the lair, Eamon was sponging down Cleland as much as he dared, not wanting to hurt him further. He had laid clean linen over Brigit's face and she seemed to be asleep. Silently, Eamon took some of the fresh blood and went to feed her. Mors bent down beside Cleland and dabbed at his eyes with the sponge. One of them slowly, so slowly, cracked open.

"Mors?" came a whisper that might have belonged to a mouse.

Tears filled Mors's eyes.

"Hello, old chap," he greeted his friend. "You're halfway home."

Chapter Nineteen

"I am enjoying the Restoration. With this one exception."

"How do you know how ridiculous you look?" Cleland asked, attempting to stop laughing as Mors adjusted the waist-length curly mop of a wig on his head.

"Oh, I know," Mors assured him. He struck the practiced pose of a gentleman, then snorted and flicked his head, sending the wig flying into a corner. "I'll save it for state occasions. This is one era where I won't be at the height of fashion."

All the vampires were happy with the Restoration, even those who had mixed feelings about monarchies. The Puritans had been a misery. Mors now opined that a successful government must be either a monarchy or a true republic. Woeful in-betweens did not work.

Mors had defied Otonia and gone to join the Royalists at Worcester. He knew a final battle when he saw it, long before it happened. Hacking into Puritans was untold bliss, reminding him of days long gone. Unfortunately, the king was not a natural general. Mors tried to get to him, in the role of an adviser. By the time he got close enough, it was too late for fighting. Instead, Mors suggested to the king that he hide in the branches of an oak tree until the enemy was gone. He had the satisfaction of seeing the king escape, and hoped he would return soon.

And here he was. He had ruled nearly twenty-five years already. Britain was thriving again.

The vampires always thrived, but they were happiest when the human world was at its best. They had known plenty of their own tumult. Raleigh, the exuberant, boisterous, life-loving Raleigh, had been caught by hunters. Caught, tortured, and murdered. Cleland collapsed inside himself and Mors feared he would never see his best friend smile again. It was only the War of the Roses that roused him to action. Soon after, the vampires moved to London and he had begun to take interest in the world, and even men, again.

Now there was much for everyone in which to take interest again. The arts and sciences were blooming, the coffeehouses were full of exciting chat, and there were actresses.

As much as the vampires enjoyed theater, the bizarre insistence that women be played by boys rankled. It was nothing new—Mors and Otonia pointed out that in their day, many of the female roles were taken by eunuchs, so it could conceivably be worse—but no one liked it. The night—and it was blessedly nights now—when a woman first played Beatrice, and then Viola, Rosalind, Juliet, Lady Macbeth, and so on through the canon, Mors was filled with a new sort of satisfaction. It was a deeper truth, and he liked the truth.

Cleland was not much of a theatergoer—much preferring mathematics and science—but he adored the drama of his existence and the challenge of hunting prey. Sometime during the reign of William and Mary, he admitted to a different hunt. For a new partner.

"Why are you surprised?" Cleland demanded. "I want someone to love and be loved by in return. It's the best part of life, human or not. It's bigger than the whole universe."

"You talk a lot more about the universe since your friend Galileo came into it," Mors observed.

"Well, he showed us something like the whole of it, only there's so much more to see," Cleland answered. "Even we are small compared to the stars, Mors."

"Bite your tongue!"

Cleland grinned.

"I have no doubt that if we could turn a telescope on you, we'd see more than anyone ever wanted to know."

"Precisely."

Cleland admitted it was difficult to find a man in the demimonde who answered his idea of love. Not that there weren't homosexuals. They had to live carefully, with less freedom even than vampires. They kept to circles where a vampire could not readily gain entrance. It was frustrating.

"But at least I'm trying."

Mors took the criticism in stride. He knew Cleland's opinion of his persistent singleness.

"Honestly, Cleland, you act as though I don't ever enjoy the company of a woman."

"A few hours, with her dead afterward, is not quite the same thing."

"I send them off well," Mors argued, and Cleland wrinkled his nose. Mors did not just mean the ecstasy. He still left a coin in the women's mouths, a habit he could not, would not, break.

"My point is, you should have a vampire companion who is more than a friend, at least for novelty's sake," Cleland went on, clearly intending that this cavalier attitude might awake his friend's interest. Mors was known to be fond of novelty.

"Stick to your own interests, my friend. Just because you're on the prowl doesn't mean the rest of us want to work so hard."

Cleland was always surprising. One night, a few years later, he suggested they go to the theater.

"Aren't you feeling well?" Mors asked.

Cleland just smiled. Mors had already seen *The Way of the World*—"a rather all-encompassing title, I'd say"—but there was a new Mirabell.

"So?"

Allisoune and Althius, a Lancashire couple as lovely as their names, joined them, in a manner that suggested they'd been lurking.

"We saw her the other night, Mors, and she's really worth seeing," Althius told him.

"She has a peculiar sort of appeal," Allisoune added, although she seemed more reserved.

"I've already booked us a box," Cleland insisted. Mors laughed.

"Oh, all right. It is a good play."

He knew what they were doing. Their timing was superb. Brigit and Eamon were on a European tour, and he hadn't had a prized face to sneak glances at for some time.

The actress was called Mercy Hope, a name Mors suspected was contrived. Otherwise, his friends had chosen well. She was pretty, with snapping eyes and a small, curving mouth out of which shot Congreve's spiky language with zing and a pulsing kind of music. Music. Her voice was a visible thing, a mythical animal—dancer and dance. Mors closed his eyes, allowing her to wash over him. She had an undefined smell that he found captivating. She was nothing like Brigit, but a human woman hadn't caught his attention quite like this in centuries.

"I oughtn't pursue an actress, though," he murmured to the others. "People will miss her."

"You'll be giving her a chance of an eternal career," Althius said. "Besides, there are new young actresses every week."

Mors was very happy to go backstage after the play. He liked theaters. They were busy, dark, energetic places. And he didn't require an invitation.

The various protectors of the actresses were already out in force, watching their possessions strip off stage dresses and don street clothes that were scarcely more respectable. Mercy did not have a protector, so Mors thought this would be even easier. Until he met her.

"Mistress Hope," he began with great gallantry. "I must say, I enjoyed your performance very much. I am a longtime patron of the arts and I know brilliance when I see it. You, my dear young lady, are something to see."

"Thank you, sir," she responded, but her eyes were wary and didn't entirely meet his.

Undaunted, he continued. "You are unusual, I think, in not having a protector. It suggests you earned your place in this company on your talent alone, as it should be."

Now she looked straight at him. Her eyes were a pleasant soft brown that warmed under the force of his smile. He winked, and she blushed.

"I have not been looking for a protector, sir, although I do appreciate the offer," she told him with a sweet firmness that, he suspected, was less a rejection than an opening gambit toward negotiations.

"You mistake me, my dear," he told her. "I was making no offer, merely an observation."

Mercy's eyes narrowed and she flushed in a combination of embarrassment and calculation. She busied herself in trying to clasp on a silver charm bracelet, which was adorned with cavorting white bears. Mors took her wrist and fastened the bracelet for her, looking into her eyes. She turned bright red and smiled.

"Truth be told, I have been hoping for . . . someone. This stage life is a bit more difficult than I'd imagined."

"Perhaps you need a different stage," Mors advised.

Mercy scarcely needed persuading to come with him on a carriage ride and, from there, a walk that led up to Hampstead Heath. Mors was stroking her back and humming, contemplating the journey ahead.

It had occurred to Cleland that Mors might not know how to make a vampire and was certainly not one to ask, so he had found occasion to tell again the story of his own making by Raleigh—the seduction, the exchange of blood, the burial. Once again, Mors marveled at the luck of his own existence, the sheer accident that had made him and allowed him to thrive.

A light grunt greeted the bite but soon dissolved into a low moan. Mercy's fingers dug into his arms as he sucked out a good quarter of her blood. He popped out a talon to poke a hole in his finger, offering it for her to drink. She sucked on it placidly, like a sleepy baby. He finished her off, dug a grave, and set her inside. It was only later that he realized he was concentrating so hard on the ritual, he had forgotten to put a coin in her mouth. Her soul would not be able to pay the ferryman.

I suppose the Styx dried up long ago, since I'm the only one who still honors it.

Mors spoke to no one in the twenty-four hours that passed. He wanted to wait till it was completed before giving everyone a reason to nudge and smile over him. That was the sort of attention he knew he would find tedious.

About an hour before she was due to start digging her way out of the dirt, he was pacing around the grave. For the first time in his memory, he was doubtful, wondering if he had done the right thing. The thrill of anticipation danced through him. The demon was pleased, though Mors was anxious. He could hear it long before she reached the surface, the *scritch, scritch, scritch* of dirt being plunged through by strong fingers. Her hands burst through the top and clenched, scrabbling, until at last her head emerged and she pulled herself out, kicking violently.

She rested a moment on the ground. Then she smiled, stood, and shook the dirt from her hair to hem, wriggling like a wet dog, so that Mors started to laugh and couldn't stop. She reached out and slapped him full in the face. He caught her wrist and glared down at her.

"Mind yourself, little one. Manners are a valued thing in society."

She spit a wad of dirt onto the churned-up earth, then laughed. Scornful though the laugh was, it was still contagious and enticing.

"Manners!" she cried, her voice brimming over with the vim and music that had so attracted him. "Manners are well and good for lesser beings who must do as they can to survive with others. We are well above manners, I think."

"You think wrong, pet. And if you persist, I'll have to teach you proper behavior."

She pressed up against him and purred. "Promise?"

Mors laughed again. She would take some reining in, but this was already fun. She pinched him meaningfully, and he returned the gesture in kind.

"I'm hungry," she announced, trotting toward town. He followed, liking the way her bottom bounced up and down under her skirts. "Oh, and I must give notice at the theater. I shan't miss it. It is just as you said: The world will now be my stage."

By the time Mors realized she was only quoting Shakespeare by accident, it was the least of his disappointments.

Mors observed that first hunt and was dismayed to see her simply grab the first man she saw and smile at him with her terrifying new face. The man screamed a bloodcurdling scream that made even Mors jump and look around, hoping there was no one nearby that he would have to chase off. But the new vampire dug in and ate, then dumped the body on the street.

When she was finished, Mors reproached her.

"That's not quite how we do things—"

"It's how *I* do things." She corrected him in a dizzying singsong. "And who are you to tell me otherwise?"

"I'm Mors, my *dear,* and you don't have to ask too many to find out that mine is a name that means something."

"Pleased to meet you, Mors. I'm still Mercy," she said with a beautiful curtsy.

"Are you certain?"

"Why not? It suited me better than Mary ever did and suits me even more now. Mercy. The one thing no one can ever expect from me."

She laughed and it sang right through him. He was reminded of the wind on some of the harshest nights in Yorkshire, and he grabbed and kissed her hard, feeling again like he wanted to eat her. She must have felt the same way, as her talons poked out just a millimeter, just enough to make four little holes on either side of his neck. She ran her tongue over each line of blood, then smiled.

"You are delicious, Mors. Simply scrumptious. And that's just the blood."

Right there, against the rough plastered wall of the coffeehouse, he jerked up her skirts and entered her, his eyes boiling red, his fingers nearly indenting her head. The growls and grunts could be heard for miles around, but no one was intrepid enough to want to investigate. On discovering the woman-shaped indentation in his wall the next morning, the coffeehouse owner knew he should call an expert in witchcraft, but instead paid a plasterer over and above to take care of it.

They spent much of the next three days and nights in bed, shedding a fair bit of each other's blood and covering every inch of skin in bruises. Mercy loved that they both healed so quickly, especially Mors, and kept trying to hurt him harder. She shrieked with joy as his bruises faded so soon after they arose, hitting him again like a child playing a nasty game.

At first, Mors found it all hilarious. But then he noticed something unexpected in his demon. It laughed, but it also shrank. It wanted to pull Mors away. It didn't trust Mercy.

Mors ignored the demon. What did it know? He was Mors, the god of death. He had teased and outwitted death for centuries. Why should death or anyone think that this little squit of a vampire should be any sort of threat to him? She was only a thing he had made. He could tame her, and he would, once the sex stopped being so much fun.

The other members of the tribunal ranged from amused to appalled. Otonia quieted them. She could see that Mors had sensed something more vibrant and elastic in Mercy, something of promise. He was rarely wrong. True, Mercy was violent and hungry, but Brigit had not been much better. Mors was very capable of handling the little beast. She might yet be a remarkable thing and make him happy to boot.

Althius certainly thought so.

"Aren't you glad you took us up on our recommendation?" he asked with a mildly inappropriate wink.

"I'm keeping entertained," Mors answered, winking back.

"You wouldn't know it now," Althius confided, "but Allisoune was very much the strumpet in her early years. If that lass is a shrew, you'll tame her soon enough."

"Just not too much, though, yes?"

Cleland, on the other hand, was mortified. This was not what he had intended for his friend. Leonora saw him pacing, distraught, and asked what was the matter. When he told her that he had encouraged Mors to make Mercy, she stared at him for a full ten seconds before punching him in the nose, sending him tumbling all the way down the library's stone steps.

Mors knew that Cleland tailed him worriedly as he and Mercy took to the streets, looking for chaos in a way Mors had not done for years. To Cleland's credit, he was not trying to be seen or felt. He was simply trying to protect Mors from this unreliable bit of disaster. The idea boiled Mors's blood. He was enjoying himself! Although it was not what he had really looked for. Mercy didn't even want to go to the theater, although she did think it might be fun to kill her former cast mates.

"We don't do that sort of thing, Mercy," Mors explained.

"Don't you condescend to me! I am a vampire. I kill whom I please!"

"No. To kill just for the sake of killing, without food or—"

When Mercy's eyes changed, they turned into slits, like a cat's. And when she launched herself on him, screaming, talons at full extension, hair flying, she looked even more like a cat. With rabies.

"Stop telling me what to do!" she screeched, attempting to throttle him.

Mors turned her over in one swift movement and slammed her talons into the street. He set one foot on her neck, the other on the small of her back. His sang in a whisper intended to stroke her skin and tangle in her hair as it kissed her ears.

"See here, my Mercy. In a moment, I will release you. And when you get up, you will begin to obey me. You will become a vampire worthy of the British tribunal. Under my tutelage, you will learn what that means and what it demands of you. And if you choose to be anything less, well, then you will truly know the meaning of pain. I think you understand me."

Her talons had retracted of their own accord. Mors helped her up, and they regarded each other soberly. He raised her hand and pushed aside the bears bracelet so that he could kiss her wrist.

"Now, perhaps we can start again?"

She nodded, a glimmer of the human girl's shy smile playing around her lips.

"Charming. Only you'll have to catch me first," she shrieked, running off into the night.

He could have caught her in seconds but for Cleland jumping on him from behind and holding him fast.

"What the hell are you doing?" Mors demanded, struggling to shake himself free of his surprisingly strong friend.

"Let her go, Mors. For the love of the tribunal and yourself, let her go! We can deny her reentrance and let her find her own home. The hunters will find her easily. And then it will be done."

"Mors, come play with me," sang Mercy's voice from a distance. It encircled him. The demon smiled, and the old Roman woke, ready to dance. Mors gave Cleland a cold grin.

"Who says I want to be done?"

And off he ran to join his demon sweetheart. They broke into twenty stables that night, setting the livery horses free. Mors liked watching the horses run. Mercy would have run them into the Thames, but he guided them to the West Country road. Who knew where they would end up, but for a few hours at least, they could run without reins or blinders. He hoped it was something they would always remember.

Chaos reigned in the hours before dawn as the people discovered the outbreak. Mercy wanted to create yet more trouble, but Mors sensed hunters afoot and told her it was wisest they stay in the next few nights.

"After all," he pointed out, "we can keep ourselves well entertained all night long. We can take turns being rider and wild horse."

They spent many hours in games, shredding the bedclothes and dislodging most of the mattress filling. Later, sprawled on the rug by the fire, in that foggy state before sleep reigns supreme, Mors pulled a shiny twist of hair from her face and moved to kiss her. He paused, his mouth inches from her cheek. Her eyes slid sideways to study him.

"Well," she teased. "Aren't you coming closer?"

He wasn't. He didn't want to. His desire for her was a living thing but unfettered of affection. He nipped her jaw instead, then her shoulder, then breast. She pushed him off her with a chilly laugh. She stood and pulled on a thin chemise, then an equally filmy dressing gown, and trotted to the door.

"You're not wandering about like that!" Mors was aghast. Otonia preferred decorum in the castle corridors.

"And why not?" Mercy responded with a shrug. She swung her hips fetchingly on her way toward the baths.

He knew he must get up, dress, and go after her. Always, always going after her.

At least a dog eventually gets trained.

He sat for a moment instead, gazing into the flames. Fire. Life and death for humans and vampires alike. Light and heat, both within and out. One of his constants. As the world around him had changed and changed and changed again, the need for fire remained steady. Cleland, who studied science with such passion, was sure this, too, would change in time. As did all things.

Mors closed his eyes, the better to see his own body. That did not change. His head remained bald, as he preferred and as suited him so well. The shape of his nose, the breadth of his shoulders, the slim, hard, defined stomach, and the tautly muscled limbs. The body of a warrior, eternally. A body frozen in time but endlessly active. A body of still water, of hell's fire. Organs in stasis and a soul fled. But though his heart did not beat, it as yet had a life of its own. And a hunger. An appetite unfulfilled.

He reached his fingers toward the flames, appreciating the heat, testing his strength. He must get up; he must go and fetch Mercy, put a proper wrap over her, stop her from irritating and scandalizing the others. Mercy did indeed consider the world her stage. She wanted an audience, always. Mors could understand that. It was most of what made her so tempting.

But temptation is the fire that brings up the scum of the heart, isn't it? I am entertained, but I am not in love. And that, my friends, is the shame of it.

With a sigh, he got up to capture and corral the creature he had made.

Occasionally, Mors would get a premonition of something about to happen, most often a battle. It unfolded in his mind almost exactly as it eventually occurred. Now, as he was starting to dress, he saw—saw what had already happened and what would surely happen if he did not stop it. Mercy, lingering by the baths, and Althius looking up to see her as good as naked, leering at him.

"There's no harm just in looking," she teased.

"I'm not susceptible to silly games, Mercy. Go play elsewhere," Althius told her firmly.

She flung herself on him, her strength a shocking thing. He was centuries older but couldn't shake her.

"Get off of me!" Althius ordered, embarrassed by her grip on him.

"But you like me. I know you do. You suggested Mors turn me."

"A mistake I'll always regret," he promised, landing a fist in her face. She staggered but still held him.

"Say you're sorry, or I'll make you," she singsonged.

He got in a good kick and twisted away, not seeing her red eyes and extended fangs until it was too late. He ducked, but her speed was fierce and she caught him, sinking her fangs into his cheek and jaw, holding the side of his head steady with her talons, one gouging into his eye.

Allisoune, still wet from the bath, leaped on Mercy, digging all her talons into Mercy's back, just missing her own chance to bite as Mercy whirled to face her. The two rolled down the corridor as Althius collapsed, a howling mass of blood.

Mors moved as though in a nightmare, fast but slow, too slow. Otonia, Cleland, Leonora, Benedict all came running, too. It was Allisoune's fight, but they must help; they had to help. The flails of arms and hair and fangs were indecipherable. A hand ripped at a wall hanging, snapped the rod holding it, and plunged the makeshift stake.

The scream tore through Mors, layering his flesh in pure ice. The physical pain in which Althius was still swathed was nothing, nothing to seeing Allisoune, his beloved for five hundred years, collapse into dust at the hands of this bold young monster.

Mercy twirled the stake. "And here I thought that was just some silly story." She laughed. She dropped the stake and ran, trusting in the shock, horror, and confusion that she could get away. And she did.

No one said a word to Mors. His green eyes burned with a human fire more frightening than any vampiric face. As Otonia and Leonora bent over Althius, Cleland padded after Mors, who stalked through the castle to the meeting room, snatching an ax from the wall. Mors did not run but was gone with a violent swiftness just the same.

Hunters were fanned out through town; Mors could feel them. They knew it was something more than human that had broken through the stable locks so efficiently. Mors wanted only to be sure they didn't find Mercy before he did.

He could not determine at whom his fury was most directed—himself or Mercy or Cleland, for having talked him out of his instincts. He had known, he had always known, that there was something about him that should not make another vampire. The accident that had made him should be confined to him. If he had wanted a companion, he ought to have looked for a lone female vampire. Something in him had known all this but paid it no mind. This was his punishment.

He kept his eyes half closed, allowing his senses more freedom to roam. He could almost see them through his shuttered lids, wisps of sparkling smoke, white in the black night, swirling, darting. Searching. Whatever power Mercy had, his was more than a thousand times stronger. His senses would find her, would dive into her marrow. Would lead him to her as assuredly as a trail of white stones on the path. He closed his mind to everything else except that body. That body he had enjoyed with such sickening fervor and that he would soon collapse into a billion tiny bits.

Mercy is a devil. But the god of death is stronger.

She was lurking outside Westminster Abbey, searching for a likely place to set it on fire. When she saw Mors, she giggled.

"I can't get too close. It's a bit of a challenge. But there are people in there. They are praying. I think they want saving from the likes of us! Isn't that marvelous?"

"I haven't come to praise you, Mercy, but to bury you."

She threw back her head and laughed that tinkling sound that had lit him up so completely. Then she looked at him with a sweet, knowing smile.

"Oh Mors, don't you think I know what you really are?"

His blood ran cold. Her voice was an exact imitation of Brigit's. How could she possibly know the power that voice had over him? But she knew. She sauntered to him, her hips swaying.

"It's true. I know something of what you are. I could feel it inside you, those few minutes we ever actually slept. Oh yes. I know you're a hell-creature. A demon in more ways than one. You've controlled it for such a long time, but you want to let it out to play. You do! And see how I help you? You want to come and eat the whole world with me, I know you do. That was why you chose me. We can travel. To Paris, to Venice. We can do anything, everything. We can take the world by storm. You want that, don't you?"

He stared down at her glowing face. It was Brigit's. This—this is what Brigit would have turned into had she become his partner. An impossible blaze of light that would have burned itself out. Inside her, somewhere, she had known it. Perhaps it was her demon that told her so because it wanted her to live long. And he—he knew it, too. This was their desire, once, but also their fear. It was a gift of Fate he'd never pursued his love, because he could not have seen it destroyed.

He gave Mercy an icy smile.

"Take the world by storm. A lovely idea. But there's one problem. You haven't got a crucial aspect of what it takes to be a true ruler— mercy."

She cocked her head at him, confused. With the sure, easy swing of a great warrior, he lopped that head clean off.

As he was walking away, wiping the dust off his ax, a hunter came up behind him and swung a sword. Mors caught it without turning around.

"Already done, my friend. Already done."

He tossed the sword in the air. By the time it descended and the hunter retrieved it, Mors was nearly home.

The tribunal was gathered, anxious. They all turned to stare when Mors entered, and no one said a word.

Mors looked at no one but Otonia. He dropped the ax, then threw the bracelet of white bears, which landed with a soft rattle at Otonia's feet.

For one quick moment, he and Cleland locked eyes.

Then Mors turned on his heel and left the castle.

Chapter Twenty

Rome. Spring 1943.

The initial days after their escape from the Vatican went by in a blur, with only a few exceptions. Mors was shocked when he saw Brigit's face under light. The holy water had eaten chunks of her flesh. It was already starting to heal but still looked appalling.

"I'm sorry; I'm so sorry," Giulia said many times, till Brigit shushed her.

"It was good of you to try something," Mors muttered. "It was all so quick, you couldn't have thought about it."

"No," Giulia agreed. She eyed Brigit again and shivered. "I wouldn't have thought it could have such power."

"It's like I said, belief gives things power," Brigit groaned, shifting on the bed. Her bones were taking a long time to mend. Eamon assumed that the ax had either been dipped in holy water itself or the fact of its having been in the Vatican had made it more lethal.

"I'm just happy nothing came off," Brigit murmured, eyeing Cleland's missing foot. He still couldn't speak more than a few words, and no one wanted to press him.

"Now you know why you screamed when you were baptized," Mors joked to Giulia, but she could manage only a wan smile.

"We weren't exactly religious," she mumbled.

"That, and you're Jewish," Eamon finished. Both Mors and Giulia's mouths dropped open.

"How did you know?" she asked him in wonder.

Eamon shrugged. "I know my own."

"But . . . but your education, your marriage . . ." Mors didn't know why he was so stunned.

"We converted," Giulia explained. "Or said we did. It was the only way I could get the best education, and, well, it looked better. Where has it ever been better to be a Jew?"

Eamon's lips curled in displeased agreement.

"Well, so anyway," Giulia continued, a blush spreading to her ears, "we managed it. You can always find a priest who needs more money and is happy to arrange papers. The Jewish Merlinos became Catholic Merlinos. And like some other modern families, we didn't go to church. We hadn't been religious anyway, so it made no difference."

"Not then, not now," Mors agreed. He was surprised she hadn't told him, but he liked that there was yet more to discover in her.

Cleland woke then. For the first time, his eyes were clear. Mors turned his friend's head to see the unfolded portrait of Padraic propped up beside him. Cleland's cracked lips bled when he smiled.

"My treasure," he rasped.

Mors turned so no one could see his wet eyes. He couldn't wait to tell Cleland he now had a treasure of his own, at long last.

Mors and Eamon traded off tending the patients and hunting food, information, and Traugott. They had been cheered by the news of the German surrender at Stalingrad—the Wehrmacht's first major defeat—but were now far more concerned with their own war.

The official news, according to Giulia's husband, was that Oster had completed his research and he and his German coterie had left Rome. Mors snorted.

"Left it in a casket. No mention of that?"

"None," Giulia insisted.

Eamon was convinced Traugott and the Nachtspeere must have remained in Rome, as underground as the vampires themselves. Their plans had been thwarted and they could not be pleased.

"No, I think they are making new plans," said Mors, pacing the square where Traugott had tried to capture him. Brigit was hobbling around now, and they felt safe leaving her and Cleland alone for a few hours. Mors felt peculiar. He had never spent so much time alone with Eamon before.

"I suppose they want more 'armor'," Eamon acknowledged, shuddering. "Although how they think they'll be lucky enough to land one of you again, let alone more . . ." He trailed off, not wanting to imagine Brigit in Nachtspeere hands.

"I suspect he's consulting with whoever is overseeing this . . . project." Mors knew how battle plans worked. Traugott was a nimble thinker. Unable to bewilder and lure any of them with the scent of Cleland anymore, other tactics were needed. "And he's gone to retrieve Deirdre. She's probably strong enough now to be of use again. We've made it all far easier for them now, you know. They don't need to even try netting me or Cleland or Brigit. They know they can save themselves trouble and kidnap Giulia, or—"

"Me," Eamon finished with a resigned shrug. "I'd like to see them try. I've got centuries on that Deirdre thing."

Mors's toe scratched at the spot where he, Deirdre, and Rembrandt had battled so ferociously. In all the months since, a thought had taken root at the back of his mind, one that he had tried to ignore. It hadn't mattered, because she was going to be killed. But now he was certain she was on the verge of being a weapon again, and he had to confront a horrible possibility. Worse, he had to voice it.

He glanced at Eamon, the vampire of whom he had been jealous so long.

"Eamon, may I tell you something in complete confidence?"

Eamon looked mildly taken aback, but nodded.

Mors looked straight into Eamon's curious eyes.

"She might have gotten some of my blood."

"You don't—"

"She bit me, and held on for . . . I don't know, more seconds than I care to count. She went deep." Mors's stomach turned over, remembering. "It didn't immobilize me like she expected. . . . Perhaps it would have, if I couldn't get her off me. I don't know if she drank—maybe she couldn't— but her fangs went in up to the gums. At least one of those fangs was shattered." Here, Eamon couldn't suppress a cheer, and Mors had to smile. "Yes, but she might still have gotten enough. I don't know if it would strengthen her, but if it could, if it did . . ." He didn't want to finish.

Eamon put a hand on his shoulder.

"We'll tell the others she might be a bigger threat than warranted. And we had better wire Otonia, if nothing else to get her to keep a firmer hold on Padraic. No point putting him in danger, too. We don't have to tell anyone exactly why you think she's so dangerous if you'd rather not yet; it's enough that you think it."

"All right, good." Mors was satisfied. Eamon was a fine strategist. "Good. She certainly does need killing, though."

"Oh, yes!" Eamon nodded fervently. "And I hope I'm there to see it."

Cleland was regaining millennial powers and healing more rapidly. It was fascinating to watch new skin creep over his body, to see him regrow flesh. His voice was raspy, and he could speak only in short bursts before getting tired, but he was determined to tell them everything.

"I'd lost the whole leg in Meaghan's explosion," he told them, contemplating his missing foot. "But I do like to think that if I'd been conscious when they found me, they still wouldn't have stood a chance."

"Not bloody likely!" Mors insisted stoutly, and the others agreed.

"They drained me of a lot of blood, that's how they kept me. I think I was in a bank vault for a while, but they wanted to get me into Saint Hedwig's."

"Do you know how they extracted your scent for Deirdre?"

"I don't. But once we got to Rome, whenever that was, they took me out from time to time, when they needed me to regenerate more skin. From what I gather—they didn't tell me much, you know, but they talked when they didn't think I could hear—they'd been planning for some time to take me to the Vatican. I guess they thought it was a quieter workplace;

I don't know. Certainly it was a better prison for me. But when you left Berlin, that decided them. That was a long journey: They kept sneaking into churches to hold me a few days when they thought I might be getting stronger. It must have taken months.

"Well, so we got here, and I can tell you for certain that no one knew, not the pope, none of them," Cleland went on. "Oster and Traugott laughed about it all the time, the way the Italian clergy was so easily rolled over."

"So glad they had their fun," Eamon remarked, his voice dripping with acid.

"They were planning something else, though," Mors pressed. "Something bigger. Did you ever hear anything of that?"

"I did know it was more than skinning me for armor," Cleland said through gritted teeth. "They wanted to keep me alive a long time, and Traugott kept telling me stories about how all my friends would soon be there."

"German stories. Smashing," Mors drawled. "They did produce the Grimms, didn't they?"

Cleland fingered the ancient legend book that featured tales of his youthful days, the book Father Ambros had liberated from Bishop Oster back in Berlin. He pushed it aside and looked at Mors with large, sad eyes.

"They want an empire. And they think they can make theirs greater than any other. Immortal. Using us, in some capacity. I don't know how, but I did hear them talking about a scientist, or doctor— What?"

Mors had smacked his forehead and bounded to the shelves. After a quick search, he produced a tape.

"After Rembrandt left I put these out of my mind. We managed to record part of a meeting in Berlin. It only proved Oster was a nasty piece of work, but there was a bit more to it."

He set up the machine, and they all leaned around to listen.

"We won't make further progress without some qualified help," came Traugott's voice. *"A man of science. Someone with brains, skill, and a flair for invention."*

The vampires all exchanged glances, and Eamon took notes. Then came Oster's silky voice.

"Hm. I suppose I see what you mean, although there is much to be done

in the immediate, as yet. A shame that Schultze was killed. That was a very eager doctor indeed—"

"Play that again!" Brigit shrieked, launching herself across the table. Her eyes were round, and the scars from the holy water were vivid red in her white cheeks. She wrested the machine from Mors and replayed it.

"A shame that Schultze was killed. . . ." Brigit stopped the tape and stared as if it were an unexploded bomb. She looked up into Eamon's slowly comprehending eyes.

"Schultze," she said at last. "Doctor Schultze. Of course. What must they be playing at?"

"Would you care to—" Mors began. Brigit's hand clamped hard around his wrist.

"A doctor tried to . . . waylay me on the way back to England. I thought he was after the children—"

Both Mors and Cleland started to question her, but she ignored them.

"—then later he told me it was me he wanted, for experimenting."

Mors could hear a growl deep in Eamon's throat.

"I thought he was just a madman—you know, the sort who knows about us but hasn't got the chops to become a hunter, so becomes all the more obsessed. Unhinged. And most of these Nazis haven't got far to go down that road anyway. Well, I killed him—"

"I should hope so," Cleland put in.

"Yes, but don't you see? That must be the man Oster's talking about." She pointed to the tape. "Which means he was part of a larger operation. He made it seem he was ordered to retrieve the children, but he wasn't. He was after me, and the children were just extra prizes."

Her forehead puckered as she sifted through her memory.

"He told the Irish hunter I could be killed in Ireland, but that he needed to bring back results of his study. That was a lie, to placate the hunter. Of course. Why didn't I see it? When they realized they had millennials in their midst, they must have gone mad imagining our power."

For a few moments, they were all silent, each seeing more pieces of the puzzle before them and looking for where it all fit.

"I heard them say once it was a shame they couldn't do more with me," Cleland remembered, fingering the tape machine. "Maybe they meant they wanted more from me, more power, and didn't want to risk becoming tainted with homosexuality."

"Possibly." Brigit nodded, her nose wrinkled. "Or they just wanted me and Mors as well."

Eamon looked doubtful.

"But here, weren't they set to kill all of us in the Vatican?"

Mors and Brigit locked eyes, each going through every moment of that battle.

"No," Mors told Eamon. "They were happy to kill you and Giulia, but they only wanted to subdue Brigit and me. Perhaps they lost control when they saw it wasn't going to be easy—I don't know—but they had something else in mind for us."

Eamon moved closer to Brigit and wound his hand through her hair, making sure of her safety and solidity before continuing.

"Something's missing. If they want millennials, and you lose that in a church, then . . . ?"

They had run out of pieces, and the puzzle was not even half completed.

"Perhaps it's that we're still strong at all," Mors said at last. "Deirdre said they were extracting essence. She was a consummate liar, but we do know they've been plotting something, there in Berlin, and there is no chance they have given up."

"Well, we'll just have to pay them a call and inquire in person." Brigit smirked, popping out her talons and examining them. Eamon laid a hand over them till they retracted.

"No," he said quietly.

Brigit began to argue, but Mors broke in, his voice low.

"Eamon's right. Berlin is powerful. They even found a way to seal tunnels to us." He was too sober to enjoy the shock on their faces. "It's the heart of all the operations—the human war and this one. If we're going to really break that heart, we need the power of an army." He paused, thinking of the legion he had come to love so much. "The human war must be in some ascendance to soften up Germany. We continue our course, helping with that, and thus build ourselves a weapon powerful enough to penetrate where we must. We can help them; they cannot help us."

Cleland nodded slowly. "I bet they want us to come searching for them, walk straight into the cage."

"Perhaps." Mors was doubtful. Then the general took over. "We have two advantages. One—we know more than they think we do. And two—we'll make them wait. You get more exhausted waiting than fighting. You lose focus. They'll come to us again. And whatever weapons they may have, they will still be far from their place of power."

"Their weapons might be formidable," Eamon reminded Mors.

"Yes." Mors grimaced. "Whatever you do, don't let Deirdre bite you."

"What a horrid vision," Brigit said, shuddering.

"And as for Traugott"—Cleland's voice rang out with a deep chill—"unless it's self-defense, none of you are to touch him. That human is mine and mine alone."

There was no argument.

"Good," said Cleland, rubbing his hands together, his eyes glittering with anticipation. "Now hand over that radio and field phone, will you?"

Later, Mors met Giulia for a walk. It had been a long time since they'd been alone together. They strolled by the Tiber—the quietest, darkest spot.

"I think we should call the legion the Matteotti Brigade, after the socialist," Giulia said.

"I prefer the Moonlight Brigade, myself," Mors responded with a wink.

"Of course you do," she said, and laughed. Her eyes glistened. "We can do this, can't we? Free Italy, free France, free Belgium, free everyone! Freedom will always be the victor in the end."

"Exactly," he agreed. "Sometimes the end takes its time getting here, but not this time, I think. Not this time."

Mors slid his arms around Giulia's torso, raising her so that her legs wrapped around his hips, and from there he sank to his knees in the tall, soft grasses and laid both of them down.

"Quite the foe to tyrants, aren't you, darling?" Mors asked, his hand trailing up her skirts.

"And my country's friend. Yours, too, of course," she added, unbuttoning his shirt.

It was dangerous to lose so much sight of everything around them, but in a world raging mad, danger was practically a requirement. At least here, the wind and the river could absorb their moans.

The demon had not risen with hunger when making love to Giulia, not since that first time. It was not rising now, but Mors could feel it tapping away in him, sending a telegram, a question: "How long can this go on?" A question Mors did not want to hear, much less answer. The present was a whole life, with Giulia's blood coursing under his hand, hard and fast, a wicked song under his fingers. He kissed her breasts and fancied he could taste her heart, feel its beat on his tongue. And when he kissed each closed eye, he was sure he could taste her soul. Nothing else could be so delicious.

Mors drowsed, dreaming. He was in his plumed helmet and armor, smiling at the sun. Somewhere in a crush of excited voices, Giulia whispered, "What is to become of us when this war is won?"

But Mors kept his eyes on the sun.

The legion, all except Patrizia, were overjoyed to welcome Mors back into their midst. Brigit and Eamon were popular, too. A small cluster of young men had since joined the partisans and were impressed with the commander and his closest cohorts.

Deep in the Villa Ada, in the northeastern part of Rome, they had prepared a perfect fortress in the untouched woods.

"You see," Franca explained proudly, "if there is to be a battle in the city, we will not be taken unawares. From here, we can retreat to the mountains and then wage a much longer guerrilla war. But if the Germans and Blackshirts think Rome is theirs, well, they might be surprised."

For his part, Mors was pleasantly surprised to see just how many grenades they had built and bullets they had on hand. There were tins of food and water canteens. The legion was more than ready to fight.

Patrizia made a point of prodding him firmly in the arm.

"As you can see, we've not needed you at all," she informed him happily.

"My goal was only to help," he assured her, earning nothing but a sneer.

"Go on, Patrizia, it's your turn to be lookout," ordered Silvia, gesturing the girl along.

With a haughty toss of her uneven pigtails, Patrizia scampered off into the woods.

"She'll grow up someday," commented Giulia, attempting to stifle a giggle. Mors laughed as well and then proceeded to run the legion through drills they hardly needed, so ready were they for a fight.

Two hours later, as they were preparing to leave. Mors heard a distant shriek and shouts, then running.

"Defense, quickly!" Mors cried low. "Brigit, Eamon, take offense north; Franca, Silvia, south. Giulia, cover me from behind."

The legion was ready when a frightened, sweaty Patrizia burst into their midst.

"They were marching, they saw me! They're coming!" she wailed.

"They're coming because you led them right to us," Mors hissed. "A lookout is supposed to signal."

He turned away from Patrizia's burning face and prepared for the battle. Patrizia had, at least, been able to run much faster than the soldiers, and so Mors led the legion in a circular path to catch their pursuers off guard. It worked beautifully, as he knew it would. Brigit and Eamon came up behind the Blackshirt troop and fired in perfect symmetry, knocking two men into those whom they'd been following. In the dim moonlight, he could see Franca and Silvia meet the men in front and give them a similar greeting. He himself went to work on the frightened and muddled middle.

Blackshirts were retreating, and Mors whistled signals, sending pockets of the legion in pursuit. Then he heard a man screaming into a radio, calling for soldiers to quell a partisan uprising.

Mors leaped upon the man, who had crouched down to scream into the radio. He flipped him around and could hardly believe his eyes: It was the wormy Capelli, who had humiliated the nice Jewish gentlemen in the café so many months ago.

Capelli recognized him, as well, him and Giulia, who promptly shot his would-be rescuer. Mors saw what Capelli was about to do and broke his wrist, but he was only half successful in stopping him: Giulia was shot through the calf.

Mors popped out a talon and slashed Capelli's throat. Then he swooped up the groaning Giulia and bore her out of the woods to the Via Salaria.

He heard Eamon's shout and saw the uniforms through the corner of his eye, dropping just in time to shield Giulia and take a round of bullets in his own body.

"Stay down!" Eamon shouted. Mors played dead, keeping his eyes open so that he could see Brigit and Eamon—again in perfect symmetry—shoot the Blackshirts who were coming from two different directions to examine his body.

Brigit reached him first and helped him up, digging her fingers into his arm to yank out a bullet.

"Leave those, I've got to get Giulia to a doctor," said Mors, as Brigit bent to help him gather up Giulia.

"Behind you!" Brigit cried to Eamon, but he knew. He slung the gun around and shot the Blackshirt running at him from behind even as he kept his eyes on Mors.

"That's the last of them, but they've got soldiers coming. Street tanks, too. They'll be looking for anyone running."

"Right. Both of you, split up and get the legion home," Mors ordered. "No one else injured?"

"Not a one." Brigit gave him a quick smile.

"Good. I'll be back at Aventine Hill as soon as I can. Don't come looking for me," he warned. They nodded and bolted off in different directions— running while they could before the planes came. Mors picked up Giulia again.

"You're hurt," she said through heavy gasps.

"Shush. So are you."

Sirens were wailing throughout the city, and nervous heads peeked through curtains. Mors ducked into a dark alley and felt Giulia's leg. The bullet had sunk too deep for his fingers. He pressed his lips around the wound and sucked. It came out in one fluid motion, and Mors slammed his hand over Giulia's mouth to contain the cry she could not help emit.

He popped all the bullets out of himself with less finesse and tossed them in a rubbish bin. Then he tore a length of silk from his jacket lining to bind her leg.

"That'll do till I get you to a hospital."

"No," she grunted, clutching his tie. "Our neighbor, he's a doctor. I trust him. Safer."

It was farther away, but it made sense. It was better that Giulia get home. Mors could hear soldiers pouring into the streets, with more on the way. He wrapped Giulia's arms around his neck and climbed the wall to the roof.

From there, he ran and leaped their way into town. He wished it weren't quite so close to dawn.

They reached exactly what Mors had been hoping they could avoid—a wide chasm. He could descend to the street, but it was too well lit here. Mors whispered to Giulia to steel herself, even knowing he was buoying up his own self more. Then he jumped.

There was a millisecond of self-congratulation as he caught the edge of the opposite roof, before his right hand slipped and they swung precariously. Mors made a Herculean effort and flipped them both over onto their backs, dislocating Giulia's shoulder and snapping his left wrist.

"Bollocks!" he gasped, but there was no time to feel pain. The sun had started to rise. The old building boasted a large and glorious chimney. Mors scooped up Giulia again and scampered to it, peering down. A long, black abyss. Getting down would require full sensitivity. He yanked off his boots and tied them together. Then he gripped Giulia and snapped her shoulder back into place. She was too exhausted even to scream. He looked her full in the face for the first time since the ordeal had begun. Her skin was gray, her features pinched. He clutched her chin and forced her eyes into his.

"This is going to be harder yet, my love. You're going to have to stay on me, stay quiet, and trust me. Can you do all that?"

She nodded dumbly.

With that, Mors stood and pressed her to him, then tipped them both backward till his fingers caught the brick behind him. The pain in his wrist made even his toenails burn, but he used fingers and toes to catch the grooves between the bricks, thus beginning their slow descent into who knew what. At least most of the buildings here were offices. Mors had the vague sense this one was important, which was encouraging, but did not make the immediate task at hand any easier.

He would have preferred to drop to the bottom but couldn't risk further injury to Giulia—or himself: The andirons might have spiked edges. Better to feel the way down.

Giulia could not have helped even if she wasn't hurt. Her weight was not much to bear, but he wished she could better control her raspy breath and occasional grunts of pain. Suddenly his toes missed a groove and slipped, sending Giulia sliding down to his leg. She yelped before biting her lips shut and using her good hand to clutch at his waist, crawling back up his body. She laid her head on his chest, panting. The small noise echoed through the chimney.

Finally, after what felt like hours, he sensed dim light below them. His muscles ached, his wrist throbbed, and he longed for food and rest, but now was not the time to risk moving any faster.

He was just reaching an exploratory hand toward the andirons when the blare of a phone ringing nearly toppled him and Giulia into the grate. Heavy feet rushed to answer it.

"Is it you?" demanded a harassed man in the exhausted voice of one who had been called to the office at an absurd hour. "Have you got any better news? Well, what's the good of you, then? How do you expect to earn your money?"

Mors held tight, willing his sweat not to drip into the fireplace. His fingers and toes were damp, making them slippery. He shut his eyes, concentrating on cooling, drying thoughts. Vampire bodies were so curious, so changeable. Otonia had spent centuries studying them and still hadn't learned all there was to know. Why did vampires sweat? It went against all reason. Then again, as Otonia was always the first to point out, their very existence defied reason.

"So why do you bother trying to understand the incomprehensible?" Mors had once demanded.

"There is no good reason not to," Otonia replied with that sly smile he admired so much.

The man on the phone was now ranting so furiously, it was nearly impossible to make out any words. He sounded like he was having an apoplectic fit.

Mors redoubled his effort to control his sweat. Sweat was, after all, just a matter of the skin's memory. But his skin's memory was strong. His body was determined to sweat.

Giulia was sweating as well in the stifling chimney. She lay perfectly still, curled up on him, allowing herself the smallest of breaths, but their combined sweat was dripping into the fireplace. Sooner or later, the room would be quiet enough that someone would notice.

It could be worse. We could be outside.

"Partisans!" the man screeched into the phone. "Don't bother me with talk of partisans. They are the least of our concerns. If a ragtag group of malcontents think they can disrupt the plans of Il Duce and Hitler, they are even more deluded than we ever imagined. No, the trouble is the army and—"

The pause was a sickening thing, so very obviously not due to an interruption. The talker had heard something. They were both so damp, Giulia had started to slide off Mors, and he tensed, rolling her back into place, but it sent drops of sweat dripping onto the bricks, and it could not be missed. However, the conversation continued after a brief hesitation.

"—whomever had the training of them. I don't know how the Italian army ever came to such a sorry state. Yes, yes, I know I mustn't say such things, but that's the whole trouble, isn't it? No one is supposed to state the obvious."

He droned on, and Mors hoped the noise in the fireplace was being blamed on mice.

The phone was slammed down at last. Mors tensed, waiting for the man to leave the room. He could hear the slow, considered steps of someone trying to move silently.

"What's in there?" the man whispered to the wall.

The sweat was making his fingers slip, but Mors remained steady.

"You would do better to give yourself up, rather than have me come to you. I promise, I am not a man to be toyed with."

That's where you're wrong, my friend. To one like me, all men are toys.

But Mors was hardly in the most advantageous position, and he sensed some resolve under the man's brave talk. It made him admire his challenger. He pushed forward slightly, readjusting his balance, freeing his right hand, although it was agony on his left.

It was the sharp end of a fire poker that thrust up from the fireplace and into Mors's side, nearly piercing his appendix. He bit back a yell, seizing the poker and jerking, so that his astonished attacker was pulled half into the fireplace. Now Mors launched his claws down into the man's face, reaching up and squeezing, enjoying the satisfying sensation of the jelly brain running into his palm and onto the hearth's mosaic tiles.

It took a few tries to free his claws at that angle and to push the body far enough away that he could reach down and slide the pronged andirons aside.

"Keep your head low," he instructed Giulia, who needed little urging. With that, he lowered himself to the floor and wriggled both of them out, grateful for the largeness of the old-fashioned fireplace. Giulia couldn't help groaning at the sight of the body. The man did look rather unpleasant, with his eyes gouged out and a variety of emulsions dripping from orifices new and old. But he was the least of Mors's concerns. Giulia's shoulder needed binding, and her leg needed a new bandage; his wound needed to congeal and his wrist, mend. Then there was the issue of getting home. . . .

One thing at a time, old boy. One thing at a time.

He tore off his blood-soaked shirt and wrapped it into a sling for Giulia. He jerked the jacket and shirt from the dead man, making a bandage for her and a tourniquet for himself. Finally, he bound his wrist.

"You've done this sort of thing before," Giulia observed.

"You get a couple thousand years in you, and some experiences will repeat themselves, yes. But there's always something brand new to excite the mind and senses. Keeps me young."

He gingerly looked down his blood-soaked shirt. The blood had stopped flowing, so that was something. His appendix ached, and he could feel every rip in his flesh, but it was already starting to heal. Rest and food, that's what he needed. Rest and food.

A gold-plated carriage clock sang out the hour with a shrillness that startled them. Seven o'clock. They stared, astonished to have spent so long in the chimney and horrified that nightfall was still such a long way away.

"A shame leisurely mornings are a thing of the past," Mors remarked. "Where do you suppose we are?"

The room looked like a private office. Mors gave the desk a cursory search.

"Tesoro," Giulia said. She had pulled some papers from the man's pocket.

"Is that me you're calling 'treasure'?"

"It's who he is. Was."

"I gathered. An army secretary, wasn't he?"

"They shifted him to intelligence, something secret. So is this a government building?"

"That would explain why I got in so easily."

"I wouldn't call that easy."

"It's nothing compared to what would have happened if this had been a private house."

Mors sat down and drummed his fingers on the telephone. Rembrandt had rigged the vampires' field telephone so that it could make calls from an unmarked location, but there was no way to know if that worked when the number was dialed. Brigit, Eamon, and Cleland would have to worry a while longer. He decided to hide the body, just to make things more unpleasant for an investigator. He rolled it up in the Persian rug onto which it had bled profusely and shoved it up the chimney.

"That's nicer, isn't it?" he asked. Giulia nodded feebly, trying to smile. The circles under her eyes were deep purple and her face so drawn, she looked almost cadaverous. Her food and rest must be the first priorities now. Mors closed his eyes to concentrate, feeling the building. Much of it seemed to be unused. He only felt one other human presence . . . coming upstairs.

He laid a finger over his lips and indicated for Giulia to hide behind the largest armchair. At a light tap on the door he called pleasantly, "Come in!"

A uniformed maid entered with a tray set for coffee. She came in slowly, her eyes on the overfilled tray, careful not to spill anything. It was only when she had set the things down that she looked up and screamed.

Mors quickly had a hand over her mouth and never stopped smiling.

"Now that's no way to treat your new employer, is it my dear? Signor Tesoro has been called away, and I am filling in. It's only temporary, of course."

"How did you get in? Who are you?" the girl cried when Mors released her. "You're one of those dirty partisans, aren't you!"

"I am dirty, that's true, but only because I was out chasing the partisans," he assured her in a low purr. "Is there a bath, by any chance?"

He had backed her into the corridor and closed the door behind them.

"You're one of them!" she continued to shriek. "You hate Italy and Il Duce and deserve to be shot!"

"You'll be delighted to know that's already been taken care of."

When she was emptied of blood, he hefted her up to the attic and found a large trunk in which to deposit her. He tossed several more trunks on top.

It will take them ages to uncover the source of the smell.

On returning to Giulia, he found her fast asleep in the chair, the tray now spotless. He carried her into the drawing room and settled her onto the sofa. Despite the coffee, she never woke, but slept as soundly as a child. He folded her hands across her belly, taking a moment to notice in a way he never had just how small they were. Small, but full of strength. He kissed one and then the other, but she still didn't wake.

He knew he should scour every office, send confusing telegrams, make phone calls. But body and demon were united in exhaustion. He drew the drapes, barricaded the door with a chair, and sprawled out on the floor, dropping quickly into the sleep of the dead.

By evening, no one had discovered them and they could slip out of the windows and escape. Giulia could not walk, but Mors kept his arm around her and she hobbled well enough.

"Romano will be displeased," Giulia fretted. "I'll have to come up with a good story."

Mors flinched, hating the mention of the husband's name. It was so easy to pretend the man didn't exist. Which, as far as they were mostly concerned, he didn't. His invisible protection allowed Giulia to act as she would, so long as she wasn't caught. He was useful. But Mors still despised him. He wished she didn't have to go back to his house.

Once at the door, however, she threw herself into his arms and kissed his cheek.

"You were wonderful, Mors. I can't possibly say how much I love you."

Which made leaving her there somewhat easier to bear.

Brigit and Eamon fell upon him with relief when he returned, and Cleland squeezed his hand. Each group hurriedly told its story. The entire legion had gotten to safety and all the weapons had been stowed. Far from being frightened, the legion had expressed delight in this show of its strength. They knew they must lie low for a short time but were looking forward to the next battle, certain it was coming soon.

Two nights later, Mors took a risk and rang Giulia's house. A bored housekeeper told him that the master and mistress had gone to the country for a few weeks. Mors did not leave a message.

The next few weeks did little to abate Mors's restlessness and worry about Giulia. The only bright spots were that the Allies were on the brink of taking Tunisia, and Cleland's health was increasing. As good a tinkerer as Rembrandt was, Cleland was better, and he was having a very good time working on the radio.

Mors was studying his map of Sicily, drawing several different possible scenarios, while Brigit and Eamon were writing a fake radio script for Cleland to transmit to the Axis, once he had finished the necessary adjustments. An earsplitting screech rent the air when Cleland misjudged the strength of a signal, making Mors spill ink all over himself. He leaped to his feet, swearing violently.

"Oh, keep your hair on," Cleland scolded. Mors shot him a baleful look, but Cleland was grinning broadly, running a hand through chestnut hair that was once again thick and shiny. Brigit and Eamon were snickering behind their hands, and Mors shook his head.

"Nice to have you back in the land of the unliving, Cleland," he congratulated his friend.

"Yes, and in fighting form, too," came the rejoinder as he flung his leg upon the table. With a great flourish, he whipped off his blanket, revealing a fully regrown foot, complete with toes that could wiggle. Amid the applause, Cleland studied the appendage with pleasure.

"I should make a list of all the bottoms I look forward to kicking."

Feeling much happier, Mors went hunting. He didn't even have to make an effort—barely two hundred yards from the apartment, he found a drunken Blackshirt who had been preparing to shoot a stray dog. London's demimonde was more enjoyable, but this was war. The Axis needed to be aware that the Allies were already in their midst.

He drew out the meal, thinking of Sicily. At long last, he knew that battle was drawing nigh. He wished Rembrandt were here, and hoped Giulia would return soon.

"Well, isn't this a surprise," came a low, ecstatic voice, cutting across his reverie.

Mors's eyes flew open and his gaze rolled up—to face the gleaming, triumphant eyes of Patrizia.

Chapter Twenty-one

Rome. Early summer 1943.

Mors shot his face back to human form with record speed. Not that it mattered. He dropped the body and kicked it aside, then whipped out his handkerchief to wipe blood from his face. The whole time, Patrizia, perched on a plinth, watched with malicious interest.

She looked more like a child than ever before, clearly reveling in her lack of scent for a vampire. Her dirty socks still slid down into her shoes, one of which reached up to scratch the back of her calf. Her skirt was wrinkled and more hair was escaping her braids than was in place. But the cold delight of her expression was that of a capable, malevolent adult.

"I knew it, knew it for ages," she crowed. "From the very beginning, I knew there was something funny about you. I've followed you, and Giulia too, to find where you live and prove what I thought. And now I have!"

Mors searched for the words to speak to her, the words that would stop her from sowing doubt and fear into the hearts of the legion. The words that might make her realize he was the friend he had sought to be.

"Of course, Patrizia. I knew you didn't trust me—I was a stranger and a man. And now you see I am not a man, which makes me even less deserving of your trust, much though I have worked to earn it. But please,

please try to see past what you see. You're clever, we all know that. You must know that I'm an enemy to Fascism and Nazism, not humanity."

"I know that you're a filthy beast, that's what I know!" she snapped, hopping from the plinth and marching up to him. Mors couldn't help admiring her. She was a head shorter than he and bore no weapons, but with her hands on her hips and nose in the air, confronting danger head-on, she was most certainly a Roman.

"You're a predator and a murderer," she went on in a shrill voice. "You sneak around looking for people, and then you drink their blood."

"That's not entirely wrong, but it's rather more nuanced—"

"Hah! I know a monster when I see one. Just you wait until I tell Giulia!"

"Tell me what?" came a low voice from the shadows, accompanied by an ominous click.

Mors had smelled Giulia coming but had hardly dared believe it, nor had he wanted to take his focus from Patrizia. But here she was, brimming over with country air and controlled menace. Patrizia's jaw dropped as Giulia stepped closer, aiming her Beretta at Patrizia's head with a perfectly steady hand.

"You were going to tell me he's a vampire?" Giulia went on. "Sorry to disappoint you, my dear, but that is very old news indeed."

"You . . . you knew?" Patrizia seemed more shocked at Giulia's knowledge than that she was wielding a pistol. "And you let him come among all of us?"

"Patrizia, think of what you're saying!" Mors snapped. "Have I not been one of you all this time? You can't be so silly as to think I'm planning to harm any of you."

But Patrizia was still staring at Giulia, sorrow etching her face.

"Has he hypnotized you? Or . . . he hasn't made you a monster, has he?"

"Oh, for heaven's sake!" Giulia looked like she wanted to smack Patrizia very hard. "Come to my house for lunch tomorrow. We'll sit in the garden, in direct sunlight." She leaned in till her nose nearly touched Patrizia's. "And we'll talk."

Patrizia, who had been so fearless confronting Mors, now looked frightened. Mors cut in quietly.

"I don't ask that you like me, Patrizia. Not at all. Nor do you need to trust me, on a personal level. But I have military knowledge and experience to fill a hundred history books, and you have already seen how I have used it in your cause. A cause that is also my own. You have the makings of a fine fighter, once you learn total control, and from me, that is no small compliment. Within mere weeks, we will be engaged in the sort of battle for which we have planned. It will be hard, brutal, and in daylight. I will be far happier knowing you are one of the fighters in that battle. But if you wish to leave the legion, I certainly understand."

Patrizia gave him the sort of fierce scowl that must have made many teachers relieved when she was expelled.

"Surely it's you who should leave the legion, and not me."

"No." Giulia was firm. "Where he goes, I go. We're fighting for Italy together. There is no question."

"But . . . but he's . . . and you . . ." Patrizia struggled for words. "You're married!"

Giulia's smile was rueful.

"Come to lunch, as I said. Depending upon how our conversation goes, I may explain a few other things. Go home now, and don't give me any reason to have to come and find you later. Is that understood?"

Patrizia bit her lip and nodded. With one last look of deepest loathing at Mors, Patrizia turned and fled.

Giulia sighed, and she and Mors turned to face each other at last. They fell into each other's arms, and Mors thought he would need to be pried away from her. There was something indefinably different in her mien, besides that lingering country sweetness—as though a light melancholy had wrapped itself around her shoulders. She must have known this confrontation with Patrizia was coming, and now that it had, she had new worries to haunt her.

"We'll manage," he promised. "She must know I am the enemy of her enemy."

"She does. But whether she uses that knowledge is another question.

I will convince her. She despises you, but she loves the legion—us, and being one of us. She won't dare compromise that any further."

"No," Mors agreed. They walked in silence a short while before he couldn't resist making the observation that half amused, half awed him. "I honestly think she would have liked to kill me herself, only she doesn't know how. I think that's why she didn't call out the hounds."

"Don't ever talk about being killed!" cried Giulia, throwing her arms around his neck. "I would not want to live without you."

"Nor I you," he told her in a husky voice. "Nor I you."

The lock outside the Ara Pacis Augustae was easily opened. There, on the ancient Roman altar itself, Mors and Giulia lost themselves in miles of bare skin, warm eyes, eager tongues. They became a new animal, one smiled on more fully by both the human friezes and the gods. An animal old as man, and one of its best.

Much later, still naked, they walked slowly around the building, studying the façade.

"The Altar of Augustan Peace," Mors murmured. "Built after he'd brought an end to the civil war. And the republic along with it."

"And then Rome went forth to conquer the world, destroying people's lives so as to improve them," Giulia sighed. Her eyes were raking the walls hungrily, as though she longed to step inside them, to move back into another time and see the world in a different light, a different light that was all too familiar.

"You were really here," Giulia whispered, her voice full of sudden longing.

"I was," he said simply.

She reached for his hand, her eyes still on the carvings.

"And you're still here now."

"I am."

Unspoken was how he sustained his existence, how he continued to walk an unmarked realm, in a state unwritten in any dictionary. Undeath. The correct word, because it was less than death, not life. Life *plus ultra*. Giulia had said she did not want to step into the world hidden from the sun. Neither did Mors want her to, but his fears on that front were melting. He did not want ever to let her go. He was determined to find a way to convince her that even the world of shadows was in fact full of light.

"We can do this, can't we?" she whispered, her eyes dreamy. "Conquer Fascism, restore Italy."

The vision of himself at the helm of an army rose brighter than ever before—the easy step that from there led to a new and great government, Italy in the sun again at last.

"We're true Romans," Mors told her. "What can't we do?"

Giulia left at midnight, but Mors tarried a while. The altar filled him with immense peace. It was places like this where he had once come to pray.

He would not sully his former gods by attempting to pray now, but he could feel them appreciate his recognition of them and his respect. In turn, they told him that he must not hesitate. Giulia must be his and must be able to fight by his side with a strength more akin to his own. She must be with him always and never age, never change, but only grow stronger. She would not be like Mercy, or Deirdre. He loved her and she loved him, and that love would not die with her. It would be stronger when she rose. He knew it. They told him so. It was done.

Back on Aventine Hill, the others were in a state of high merriment. Otonia had sent them a telegram confirming what Mors already knew—that the Allies were planning an invasion of Sicily at last.

"She says she got it from the War Office. Can you believe it?"

Mors remembered Otonia flitting so easily and unseen through the Imperial Palace.

"I can, actually."

"And I got a telegram from Padraic," Cleland sighed, his face aglow with happiness. "Isn't it wonderful? We're alive. We're each alive."

Alive. Thousands were dying by the day throughout Europe and Asia, but these two who had loved each other so long were still alive. They may not be human, but it was something. Neither Mors nor Cleland had asked for details about the state of London, and Brigit and Eamon had offered none. Mors suspected this did not bode well, but he preferred not to know. Not yet.

"The thing of it is, Mors," Eamon pointed out, "This will be a dawn invasion. In the Mediterranean."

"We'll start before dawn. And we'll soon have tanks." Mors was firm. "And helmets. And infinite care. I have been waiting for this a long time. I'm not going to let a trifle like dawn stop me."

"You do recall Meaghan and Swefred?" Cleland asked.

"I have been to every base there, and I tell you, we can manage," Mors insisted. "There are plenty of places to take shelter. We can do this and we will. This is how we fight our way back to the heart of Berlin."

The heart of Berlin. What the humans wanted, the vampires wanted, but for very different reasons. Mors was right, and they all knew it. The more they could help the Allies to victory, the quicker they themselves could find their own enemies and destroy them, before at last going home.

Brigit was studying him with suspicion. Cleland had not been told of Mors's brief, mad ambition to step beyond their boundaries, but although Mors had kept it hidden, Brigit had by no means forgotten. It was plainly on her mind now. Mors was tempted to tell her that it was neither brief nor mad, that they had simply never imagined the scope of their capacity. There were those who had wanted him to rule in Rome centuries ago. He was still a true Roman. It was time.

"Now that Mors is back, shall we begin?" Cleland cut across their thoughts.

"Begin what?" Mors wanted to know.

Cleland's smile could break his face. He thrust the radio toward Mors.

"I've got it! We can tap in and pretend to be the British being careless, sending codes and making plans!"

Mors shouted happily.

"They ought to think the Allies are about to invade Greece or Sardinia; both of those are fine targets, ones the Axis should divert a lot of equipment to defend."

Eamon handed Mors a script. Brigit, although she still had a sharp eye on Mors, smiled.

"I'm calling it Operation Blood Pudding."

The vampires stayed awake all day, allowing plans to be heard at a number of German and Italian locations. They were still going strong at dusk, when there was a scratch at the stones outside: It was Giulia.

Mors, Cleland, and Eamon were delighted to show her their activity, but Brigit seemed oddly unnerved. She scrutinized Giulia, a thin line appearing between her brows. Giulia, however, did not notice.

"I wanted to tell you it's all sorted with Patrizia. She's not happy, but she'll keep her mouth shut and go along with the legion. She's a fighter first."

Mors hastily filled the others in on the previous night's adventure. They were appalled.

"Does she know we're vampires?" Brigit asked, indicating Eamon and herself.

"You didn't come up in conversation," replied Giulia. "It's Mors she hates and always has."

"I do like being singled out." Mors shrugged, winding a finger around a strand of Giulia's hair. "Gives me a bit of a distinction, don't you know."

"You're truly sure about her?" Cleland wanted to know. "We'll be going to Sicily soon, and we can't have trouble from within the ranks."

"The war really is coming to Italy at last, isn't it?" asked Giulia with shining eyes.

"It is," Mors answered. "Mussolini's days are drawing to a close."

They watched Giulia contemplating the end of the long reign. Mors thought she had never looked so beautiful.

"Yes, you may be absolutely sure of Patrizia," affirmed Giulia, throwing back her shoulders. "Her and all the rest of us as well."

Giulia could not stay, and Mors walked with her outside. They spent a long time saying good night.

He was still contemplating the path she had taken home when Brigit joined him.

"She can't really come with us, of course. You know that," Brigit told him in a voice full of regret.

"Because of her husband? I don't think that will be a concern for long," Mors replied with a shifty grin.

"She's getting divorced?"

"No. The hope is that he will be getting widowed, in the strictest sense of the word. I'll actually have to pop a question. Rather funny, that. Should I buy a ring, do you think?" Mors hadn't meant to say a word, but once he'd begun, he could not contain himself. He actually hugged Brigit, but she remained still . . . and stunned.

"You . . . you're not thinking of turning her?"

"I know what you're thinking. I've thought it, too. I swore never to turn anyone again. But it's a world of difference if I convince her, if she agrees. Even welcomes it. That will go a long ways toward guaranteeing she remains some of what she is. I love her, she loves me, we want to be together. Always. And how else is it possible?"

"Mors, you can't."

"Don't be like this, Brigit, please. I thought you'd be happy for me."

Brigit shook her head. Her face was actually flushing.

"Mors, no . . . you . . . she's—"

"Don't you want me to be happy?"

Tears dripped down her cheeks. She spoke, and her voice was very soft but quite clear.

"I thought perhaps you knew. You can't turn her, not anymore. She's pregnant."

Chapter Twenty-two

Rome. June 1943.

Pregnant. Giulia was pregnant. Of course she was. Mors did not know how he could have missed it. A recent phenomenon, to be sure, but most definite. He could see it so clearly now, that shift in all her molecules. The beginning of a beginning.

Brigit, Eamon, and Cleland discreetly found new lodging the night Mors brought Giulia up to Aventine Hill so that she might tell him what he already knew. It was a long and awkward silence between them before Mors at last said, "Congratulations."

"How did you know?" Giulia asked, her eyes filling with tears.

"I thought something was different. It was Brigit who told me what." Mors bit his lip. "I didn't realize that when you went to the country, it was for country matters."

"You mustn't joke like that, please," she begged. "After that night, when I was injured, he wanted to know if I'd been with the partisans. He knows I'd been one, but he thought I'd given it up. Such a fool. I had to placate him—he keeps me safe, you know—and he wants an heir. He didn't want to go through what it takes to make an heir, but he . . . well . . . he managed. I'm so sorry."

"Why?"

"Because I . . . he . . . we . . ."

Mors pulled her into his lap and stroked her hair. He was burning with jealousy. Jealous that this man who had only been a specter was now increasingly present, that a piece of him was in this very room, where he had not been invited. Jealous, too, that his body was capable of doing the one thing Mors's could most irrevocably not.

So much for being the most aberrant vampire that ever lived.

"Tell me, Giulia, do you still want to fight?"

Her wide dark eyes met his.

"More than ever."

"By my side?"

"Is that possible?"

"I am not supposed to be possible. But here I am."

He laid a hand on her belly. He fancied he could already feel warmth. Somewhere deep below his palm, molecules were moving, multiplying. Beginning that beginning.

"I think it will be a girl. A girl as bright and brilliant and beautiful as her mama."

Giulia stroked his smooth head. "She'll certainly start off as bald as the man I think of as her real papa."

Mors unbuttoned her blouse, raised her camisole, and set his cheek against her skin. It vibrated the way it always did, and yet completely differently. She wanted this, and so she should. So did he.

So he forgot all of the impossibilities. He forgot who he was, who they were, all of it. He forgot everything . . . because he remembered.

It was thought that when Vitus Vipsanius married, his wife, Valeria, would bear him many sons, all as powerful as he. The couple wanted a large family of hearty, rough-and-tumble children who would be an example to Rome. But it was many years before Valeria finally conceived. At first, she was frightened, lest Vitus put her aside for a more fruitful woman, as many Romans of his stature might. Vitus was quick to allay those fears and teach her that, though she might be sure of little else in the world, she could be sure of her husband's love for her. A child would come in time.

At long last, it was so. All throughout the months of her pregnancy, every man in the legion cheered to see her, and Vitus never stopped smiling. He pressed his green head of Hecate against her growing belly every night, asking the goddess to watch over and bless the child while they all slept. The day Valeria's labor pains began, the entire legion seemed to stop breathing for all the many hours of the birth.

Near dawn, the baby was born at last. A girl. A weak, gray, undersized girl that gasped for breath as though under water. The midwife and doctor struggled over her, and the parents hovered and hoped and prayed. It seemed impossible that such a thing could be so, and yet it was. Nine months the pregnancy, nine hours the labor, and yet only three hours could they call themselves a mother and father. The parents looked upon their little one's ravaged face, and each thought they saw a spark, a glimmer of the soul within, before the eyes that had yet to completely open shut for good.

Valeria wept in his arms for a long, long time, and it wasn't until he raised her chin to look into her eyes that he realized she was weeping from shame. She, the wife of a great soldier, finally gave her husband a child after so many years, and the child was a girl, a girl who promptly died. She was a failure as a wife, a Roman, a woman.

Vitus rocked her, saying nothing until she had cried herself silent and put her arms around him. Then he smiled at his beloved wife.

"I am the luckiest man in Rome. I have one thousand brilliant sons of whom I could not be more proud. And I have the strongest, bravest, most wonderful wife of any citizen. Truly, Valeria, I need nothing more. Would it not be testing the goodness of the gods, were I to ask?"

It was only the years of living with him, knowing he was an honest man, that made Valeria believe him. They buried their daughter and asked the gods to bear her well.

One year later, they had a son, but that infant too, turned its eyes inward and was spirited away. Valeria despaired, but once again, Vitus comforted her. He felt sure they would have a living child at last. He was not a man to worry.

At last she came, a squalling, robust little daughter born with a shock of golden hair and a gleam in her black eyes. Lucia—a burst of hot light on a February morning. She was instantly the pet of the entire legion. By the age of two, she was wielding a toy sword and demonstrating a prowess that made men swear they'd follow her into battle before long. They nicknamed her Minerva and swore she was watched over by that great goddess. Her mother, nurse, and tutors watched with a mixture of pride and astonishment when, overlooking a bloody battle from a safe distance, she waved her sword, cheered, and shouted orders that echoed those of her father, though he was well out of her hearing range.

Vitus resisted the urging of the augur to read her fortune. "My daughter will make her own future. This is a girl to defy even the stars."

It would never have occurred to him that such a strong, healthy child could give way to a powerful fever that swept through the legion the next winter. Some of his best men succumbed, but she, the girl touched by the goddess of war and learning, she must survive, he thought. His only blessing that awful week was that Valeria did not know; that when she was in her own feverish stupor, she kissed his hand many times, thanking all the gods that he had the gift of their daughter to carry him through the rest of his days.

"I am so glad, my beloved, that I was able to give you such a child. Your name and line must live forever."

"It is I who am glad, Valeria, to have had such a magnificent woman for my wife, my partner. You have been and always will be the guardian of my heart."

He hoped she heard him. Shortly after he slipped a coin into her mouth to pay the ferryman, he was summoned to Lucia's bed.

The girl's breath was raspy. Her body, which suddenly seemed so tiny, fluttered under his touch. He held her, staring into her eyes, reveling in each millisecond of their focus on him.

"Once upon a time," he told her, "there was an extraordinary little princess in a great and glorious land. All who knew her loved her, but not for the reasons princesses are usually loved. Not for her beauty, nor her sweetness, but rather for her brilliance and her bravery. She was skilled with a sword in a manner to make great men envious. And there was not one drop of fear inside her. One day, an evil sorcerer came to the kingdom. He stole all its best men and said he would kill them one by one unless the people bowed to his will and made him their ruler. The people were ready to do as they were bid, but the princess said no. She went to the cave where the sorcerer lived and demanded he face her. He laughed, for she was only a small girl with no magic, so what weapon did she have that could defeat him? But the princess held up her sword, and said, 'This sword was touched by Minerva herself, so that I might keep my people safe.' The sorcerer scoffed and threw his most powerful spells against the princess. But she ducked and weaved and dodged each one. At last, he took his own heavy sword and fought her like a man. He raised his sword as though to split her in two. But she ran beneath him and stabbed her sword into his belly. And he collapsed upon himself and died. The men were freed, and there was a great celebration. And the princess was visited by Jove, who declared that from then on, she was a daughter of Minerva and thus his own grandchild and would have a treasured place on Olympus from which to guard all those who looked to her for help."

In a corner of the tent, Lucia's nurse wept. The small girl was rapt, smiling, but Vitus knew a story was not enough to keep her with him. The light faded from her eyes at last, and they turned inward so that she could follow her next journey.

After the burials, he stood before his men and spoke:

"For many years, I have known I was the luckiest man in Rome. I have been the leader of the finest legion of fighters the world will ever know. We have been undefeated on the battlefield. We have been singularly blessed by the triumverate of Mars, Apollo, and Minerva. The gods have tested us many times, and we have always proven true. Now we have been tested another way. But my friends, although we are bloodied, we are not defeated. I look at you and see the greatest of Romans. It is we of whom the history books will write. We who will always defend the honor and glory of Rome until our last hour. And for as long as I am privileged to lead you, I will continue to proclaim myself the luckiest man in Rome."

His mourning was something that happened later, and alone.

Mors touched his lips to Giulia's belly, then her lips.

"What do you think of the name Lucia?" he asked.

Giulia kissed his palm and smiled.

"It's perfect."

Later, he knew it was only a fantasy, that the beginning of the beginning inside Giulia could only be the beginning of the end for them, because he could not be a part of that life. Those lives. That was wholly the human world and no place for him to tread. It was ground more truly consecrated than that on which stood any church.

But if I defy all rules, why not in this?

In a quiet moment, Brigit told him some of the harrowing journey she had undergone from Berlin to London, shepherding a brother and sister who the Nazis had decided would die, but who she determined would live.

"You are a heroine, Brigit," Mors congratulated her.

Brigit demurred. "Possibly I only know something of what it is to behave as a human."

"Are you sorry to have never known motherhood from the inside out?" It was a shockingly personal question, but they had been friends more than a thousand years. If she didn't want to answer, she wouldn't.

As it was, she smiled. "I've known the world. Women have endured much worse than I. That's life."

"Indeed. It's a shame, that all we can implant is a demon. It's so much nicer to implant a child."

He could feel her wanting to ask if he knew that from personal experience. He had lived a longer life as a human than most of them and she knew there must be more to his history than he had ever told. But she kept her question to herself, and he kept his memories where they safely belonged.

The more useful memories were of organizing troop movements. The legion would travel in separate groups, but openly—like girls and boys going on a summer holiday. The Orselli sisters had a wealthy Sicilian cousin who owned an olive orchard in Augusta, located almost ridiculously near the German division's barracks.

"He's quite happy to have us come and camp for a week or two," Franca crowed.

"What exactly did you tell him?" Mors wanted to know.

She grinned.

"Just that my church group wanted a holiday. He knows me well enough not to believe me, but also not to ask questions."

Not to be outdone, Silvia showed him what she and their mother had accomplished. The girls would all have flared, sturdy skirts, the color of sand. They would blend in well but also be seen as women, which would offer them some protection.

When the moment was right, they would mark themselves as Allies, made easier by Eamon's acquisition of a number of British flags for the legion to hoist at the appropriate juncture.

"All right, I'll bite," Mors grinned. "How?"

Eamon shrugged modestly. "The British embassy didn't take everything home when it left, and the Italians were slow on the mark to clear it all out."

"You ought to do this more frequently," Mors told him.

Eamon smiled. "I might just."

Everyone was going to Sicily in stages. Everything had been arranged; now it was only the getting there. Per Mors's instructions, the clever Orsellis had inserted false bottoms in everyone's suitcases. Summer clothes and swimsuits lay on top; ammunition, knives, and grenades, below.

The vampires and Giulia were traveling separately. They had connived their way into procuring cars to carry the boxed-up field telephone and radio, as well as trunks, which were filled with rifles. Their own things were crammed into the top shelves. They had to hope their obvious privilege was enough to wave them through checkpoints.

Cleland, Brigit, and Eamon were leery of Giulia's joining them, although she was perfectly well and, if anything, seemed stronger than ever before. Her husband was going on a northern tour and had ordered her to stay home and rest. Everyone except Mors thought this was not the worst idea. Brigit gently broached the subject, and Giulia tossed her head.

"If I had wanted to stay safe, I would have stayed in Britain. I have been fighting Fascism far longer than you and will continue to do so until I see it vanquished. And I take orders from no one. Not even a vampire."

"That's my girl!" Mors gloated.

He was bedazzled, drunk on love and the coming victory. The promise Giulia carried inside her changed her skin, her smell, her sheen, making her more beautiful. Only it made the other three vampires skittish. They were not meant to be so near to this. Mors did not seem to notice, and they didn't dare mention it.

"I'll see she stays out of harm's way," Mors assured them.

And there was nothing else to say.

Driving a car was nowhere near as much fun as driving horses. Mors appreciated industry and technology, but was not convinced that this was one of humanity's greater improvements. He had to admit, however, that the speed was impressive. And if he knew humans, they'd find a way to increase it.

For safety's sake, they slept one day in a pensione. No one remarked on their evening travels or even gave them a second glance until they reached the checkpoint in Reggio.

Here, the checkpoint was being run by both Italians and Germans. That meant a more thorough inspection was in store. Tricks would have to be employed.

Nazis respond to two things—charm and assertiveness. They like bullies. Makes them feel at home.

"Why are you visiting Sicily?" the German sergeant wanted to know as their papers were examined. Giulia sat with her hands folded in her lap. Mors had taken the precaution of acquiring new papers so that she was now a Palermo girl, a newlywed on her way to visit the family.

Mors spoke to the sergeant in Italian-accented German, knowing this would be appreciated. His tone was deeply condescending, so as to garner yet more respect.

"Is it not obvious? My bride wants to be with her family for the joyous event. It's a few months off yet, but I would much rather make the trip in summer than winter." Mors had an air about him that suggested a proud and loving family man, and one so rich that he could travel with three servants and do whatever his wife asked without any further care. It was a status to be envied but also marked. He was a man who knew the enemy was near but was not one to be worried about such things. Nothing could touch him.

Eamon had gotten out of his car as well and leaned against it with casual insouciance, barely stifling a yawn. He was a young man in Mors's casual employ, and his own pretty girlfriend was along in hopes of fun by the shore. She was enjoying the scene, having pulled herself up to sit on the car's door, her arms folded on the roof, grinning at the uniformed men. She might be the young man's girlfriend, but she was clearly always up for a good time should circumstances offer.

The sergeant nodded, handing Mors his papers. There were no orders to bar Italians, especially Sicilian natives, from entering the island, and the sergeant had no wish to tangle with the likes of such a wealthy and powerful man. The Italians might be their allies, and the army laughable, but there was also a Mafia in Sicily, and that was a different animal altogether.

"This all seems in order. I will have to inspect the trunks, however. You understand. Merely procedure."

Cleland leaped out of the backseat. Mors did not look at either him or Eamon. His mind was racing. The sergeant might look only at the top layer, but if he wanted to see anything more . . .

"I'm not having my mistress's trunk opened on a dirty road like this! You must be joking!" Brigit cried with deep indignation. "Besides which, it's dark and breezy. If any of her silks blow away, you may be damned certain we'll make the German army pay for them."

Mors glared at the sergeant with distaste.

"My wife spent nearly a week packing these trunks, and I'm not having them interfered with by the likes of you. Now, do be reasonable, man. It's quite late, and we have a good way to go yet before we reach our lodging."

"Standard procedure, sir," said a corporal, standing in the guardhouse door. He rested a hand on his pistol in a manner that could have been casual, even absentminded.

Well, all right—so they'll have to be killed. They need killing anyway.

"I'll open the trunks, sir," Cleland said in the clipped tones of a well-trained manservant.

Four men. The bodies would go in the Straits. But the Allies weren't coming for another week at least. It was going to create trouble.

"You'll hear quite the complaint for all this later and be rather sorry," Mors promised as Cleland unlocked and opened the first trunk. They were humming madly, trying to lull the sergeant into submission, into laziness. The man didn't really want to prod through the belongings of the wealthy. He wanted to play cards with his fellows until his shift was completed and then go enjoy the company of the sweet Italian girl he'd taken up with.

But the sergeant also knew his orders. His job was to inspect trunks; he was going to inspect them thoroughly. Mors's talons were just popping out when the sound of retching startled them all. Giulia had opened the door and was vomiting on the road.

"Darling!" Mors cried, hurrying to her. Brigit leaped out of the car and bent solicitously over Giulia, giving the sergeant a generous view of her curves from behind. Even the corporal stepped around to get a better look.

"Is the lady not well?" the sergeant asked, sounding foolish.

Mors frowned and spoke in a scathing whisper. "My wife has been having a bit of a difficult time. That's why she wants to be home. She needs her mama and sisters."

The sergeant nodded briskly and stepped away from the car.

"On your way then," he grunted, waving them toward the ferries.

When it was indeed safe, Mors turned to Giulia.

"Was that your first bout of illness with the baby? How do you feel now?"

"Oh, it wasn't the baby," she told him carelessly. "I simply put my fingers down my throat. Seemed to do the trick all right, don't you agree?"

Mors's laugh echoed all around the Mediterranean.

Chapter Twenty-three

"Hang on to your seats!" Cleland shouted up to his friends. "You've never seen a show like this before!"

The vampires were assembled on the apex of Tower Bridge. Cleland and Padraic had been busy for weeks, creating—as they said—something very special to ring in the new year. The new century.

"Which technically doesn't begin till 1901," said Otonia, ever the stickler. Not that she had let such details stop her from putting on her best dress and adding a new feather to her hat.

"It's a round-numbered world, my dear," Mors commented. "Couldn't change it if we tried."

Couldn't and wouldn't—he loved it too much. London was full of excitement, and he drank it in, so happy to be there. He hoped never to be anywhere else again.

After killing Mercy, Mors had gone to Bath for the healing waters and the Roman architecture. He stayed longer than intended; he just couldn't bear to face the others, especially Cleland.

One night, mingling around the Assembly Rooms, Mors saw a fashionable lady enter, one to whom every eye was drawn. An olive-skinned girl with strong features and sleek black curls, wearing a silk gown the others all envied. He smiled, as she knew he must, as he always did. How could anyone not smile on seeing Otonia?

"How did you know I was here?" he'd asked as they strolled along the pavement.

"I hope I always know how to find you," she answered. It was at once her usual enigmatic speech and one of the loveliest things anyone had ever said to him.

They went to the baths, staying for hours. Mors liked how the water failed to wrinkle their skin.

"Is it just me," Otonia said, "or does it seem as though the world has only gotten more fun as we've gone along?"

"Well, there's more to do at night. And more people around. Perhaps we just keep improving our ability to enjoy ourselves."

"Perhaps."

They fell silent again, each as deep in their thoughts as the water.

"When my maker was gone, my passions changed," Otonia told him. "One set died, the rest flourished and became demons all their own. I never minded. I still don't miss them."

There was a plainness to her honesty that made it impossible to want her to be anything other than who she was. Otonia was already whole.

He knew what she was trying to say. Whatever he had once been, his still heart was now strongest when surrounded by his friends, when part of his community. They had forged this world together, she and he, and were its most integral components. Which meant he must come home, forgive Cleland, forgive himself, and move on.

Althius had recovered from his physical wounds but left the tribunal and was never heard from again. Mors was relieved to see that Cleland was still very much there. He was tucked in the library, which had grown to massive proportions, reading Newton's *Opticks*.

"Am I disturbing you?" Mors asked politely.

Cleland started, and the book tumbled to the floor.

"Mors."

"Cleland. I behaved inexcusably. Your friendship is one of the greatest lights of my life. Please say that you forgive me."

They both knew he didn't have to say anything at all.

It wasn't so many years later that Mors and Cleland were wandering through Soho when Cleland paused. Mors followed his brightening eye to a doorway where a handsome young lad was hovering. He exuded loneliness and worry but also intelligence and good humor. He seemed to feel Cleland's gaze and looked up, a hopeful smile teasing around his features.

A few nights later, the tribunal welcomed Padraic, and Cleland, whose air of melancholy since the death of Raleigh some wondered if Shakespeare hadn't observed, fairly glistened with happiness. They were a good pair, each continually enhanced by the other. The inventions and discoveries they wrought in their lab could have taught human scientists a thing or two. But they weren't bothered. The world would soon catch up.

In a few hours, it would be 1900. Only one hundred years until the start of another millennium. And what a millennium this last had been.

The streets were so bright now, with the gas lamps outside and lights pouring from windows. There was more and more electricity wherever one looked, and it made everything even brighter. It was already difficult to remember how black the nights had once been.

Everyone spoke of the immense progress, the improvements, the putting aside of outdated conventions to embrace a particular sort of morality—that of the soul. Civilization. It was all about bringing more "civilization" to the world entire. If that meant the peoples of other continents were to be bent and broken, their gods whipped out of them, their homelands pillaged for jewels and gold—it was all about civilization. The Romans had been the same. Mors wondered if this was the sort of thing that could eventually change.

A new century. It was said with absolute authority that war was at an end, that civilized men no longer needed to lower themselves to such behavior. Mors wondered if such a thing were possible. No matter how stiff the collar or tight the waistcoat, there was still a beast within. A need to be leader of the pack. He had as yet seen nothing to indicate that men might stop waging war on one another anytime soon.

And what of the women? Always so corseted, in body and opportunity. Always called second. Lesser. Someday they would no longer stand for it. Much went on under those constrained skins, and someday it would all come out. Then the men might reconsider what was indeed the weaker sex.

Mors put an arm around Otonia. No one could ever call her weak, that was certain.

They smiled out at Westminster Palace and the marvelous clock tower, which was just beginning to chime in the new year.

Cleland and Padraic began their fireworks show. It was extraordinary—they had created rippling fountains and palaces and mythological creatures using the same chemistry used by humans, only far different.

Humans pointed and gasped. Mors prodded Otonia.

"Isn't this what you warned against, us influencing the human world?"

"Under certain circumstances, we can at least nudge things along." Otonia shrugged. "Help the humans help themselves. Though I think they'll take a while to catch up to Cleland and Padraic on this one."

A massive firework of Mount Olympus leaped into the air and hung there, glittering.

"The night world is so much lighter now," Otonia whispered, momentarily awed.

"Yes," Mors agreed. "On the whole, I like it."

Chapter Twenty-four

Sicily. July 1943.

They were ready. Within easy reach of the base Mors and Rembrandt had infiltrated so long ago, they had set up an innocent-looking camp, hidden the cars, readied the weapons. The others all thought it was wonderful luck that they had gotten there undetected and unsuspected. Mors said nothing. He knew it was more than luck. He was a soldier who had never lost a battle. He wasn't about to start now.

The bombing began in earnest at midnight, on the ninth of July. Mors watched, elated and fascinated. It was impressive, the varied ways humans came up with to destroy one another. Battle had never been a quiet thing, but the deafening quality of the bombs, both as they came down and as they made contact, was astounding. The shouts and cries of a thousand men were nothing to it. They were reduced to whispers as the targets were reduced to rubble.

The distraction made it almost disappointingly easy to steal helmets, gas masks, and more radios. The bombs created the ideal atmosphere for further sabotage. A matter of nothing to add fuel to a fire already burning. A gradual clearing of the path.

So here they were. At last. Mors looked around at what must have been the strangest group of fighters the world had ever known. Young girls, a handful of men, ancient vampires, and a pregnant woman who was planning to abandon her husband for her vampire lover. But they had the fire that had taken Agincourt. This was only the beginning. He smiled at the gathered group.

"My friends, I salute you. You are of an especial courage, for you have undertaken to fight for true liberty. Now is the time for boldness. Rome was once great, an example to the world that the strongest governments are those that embrace the human rights of their citizenry. A strong government will strip no liberties from that citizenry, even those who speak against it. Dissent is not treason; it is sometimes duty. This is not mutiny, this is a bid to restore true liberty and justice to all Europe. Oh, yes, all Europe! Because I shall not stop with Italy, and nor will you. Not a one of us here will rest easy until all the tyrants are vanquished. Today, it's we who awaken Aurora. Go well, and good luck, everyone."

The Axis, caught completely unawares, had taken to their battle stations. Mors went in first, as soon as there was an advantage, and set himself upon the guard at the gatehouse.

"Time for a changing of the guard," he told the man, slitting his throat.

Eamon, Brigit, Cleland, and Giulia took over the little station. They would be able to stay there through the day, they assumed, and if not, there was an armored truck parked outside that, as Mors put it, was just waiting to be stolen. The vampires wore helmets, gas masks, and gloves, none of which would be enough protection in the case of real disaster, but they could do only what they could.

"Right, now how do I get myself that tank already? To hell with the P40. I want a nasty German Panzer—to attack the bastards with their own bloody tank."

"Until either they or the Allies blow you up," Brigit reminded him, cutting across his fantasy. He hadn't realized he'd spoken out loud. Now that they were in the fight, Brigit was high and excited, but the reality of the coming sun intruded upon all of them. Even Mors.

While it was still dark enough, however, they would fight. The legion ran in controlled chaos. Their enemy had never seen such tactics and was baffled. They had no idea what was happening, only that soldiers were dropping.

Those who kept their heads retreated to the base's command center to send word for help. One attempted to ring headquarters, but the phone was answered by a woman with a warm British accent.

"Good morning," she said. "You have reached Buckingham Palace. To whom may I direct your call?"

Those radioing had no more luck. One was told to man planes and go bomb the Allied warships. As soon as the pilots attempted to start the planes, however, they all exploded. Another was told to drive two tanks to the north gate and get out to receive further instructions. Instructions that turned out to be "Play dead."

Mors practically sauntered into the command center and proceeded to lay waste to those inside.

"You wanted an empire?" he bellowed so the whole base would hear him. "An empire must be fought for! You want a powerful country? You want the respect, the admiration of the world? You must earn it!"

By dawn, the legion had cleared the way and retreated enough so that the British could claim the base. They then prepared for the real onslaught—a fresh wave of oncoming Panzers. Mors returned to the guardhouse, where Cleland was trying to find the code to signal the British. They needed to know they were surrounded by friends.

Mors radioed instructions to Franca and Silvia at ground command. Then he paused. The safest thing to do would be to stay where he was; a very bright day was dawning. But they were here, the Allies were here, and he had the tank. He belonged with his troops.

He turned to Giulia and kissed her. "Wish me luck."

She embraced him quickly and said nothing.

"We ought to stop you," Eamon grumbled.

"You couldn't possibly," Mors answered with a wink.

"Give them hell!" cried Brigit, caught up in the thrill of it all.

The tank's hatch gave way as though to a lover, and Mors clambered into the dark metal beast. Hulking monstrosity of a machine that it was, it was also just a weapon, like any other. He smiled around at the interior in approval. Just as he had known, as soon as he touched the controls, they sprang to obey him.

The Axis burst upon what had been their base with all their vaunted ferocity, but the British, high from their recent victories in North Africa and the ease with which they had gained ground here in true enemy territory, were more than ready for them, thanks in part to the unknown help they were receiving from the unlikeliest of forces.

Allies and Axis alike were astonished when a Panzer burst into the battle on the British side, festooned with British flags. It fired and fired and fired with incredible accuracy, setting its would-be fellows ablaze. An entire Axis division was going down at the hands of its own formidable weapon.

Every target hit felt like another year added to Mors's life. He shouted with wild glee. From nearby, he could hear Patrizia shout as well.

"You won't have Italy, you dirty Huns!" she cried. "Not our wine, our food, our sun, or our sea. I hope there's enough trees in the Black Forest for you all to hang yourselves!"

The enemy rallied, realizing that many shots and grenades were coming from foliage. Mors saw one tank turn and he radioed Silvia.

"Cease fire and retreat! Double back! Cease fire! They see you!"

The moment Mors's own fire hit the tank, a fireball engulfed several trees. Mors felt like he had swallowed nails.

Patrizia howled and sent fusillade after fusillade into the mass with a ferocity that stunned the Germans. Mors could see another woman throw grenades into the center of the Axis onslaught, attempting to scatter them. A German soldier screamed about the "Italian bitches" and began to fire mercilessly.

"Mors, there's another wave coming!" Cleland's voice burst through the radio. "We're going to—"

The radio died, and Mors's hear leaped so violently, he had a brief moment of thinking it had exploded, of thinking that he had been hit and was spiraling into death. His reflexes continued to work separate of his mind, and he saw the muzzle of an oncoming Panzer take aim. He aimed back and hit it first.

As the Panzer exploded, there was another burst of fire from a rocket launcher. It was coming straight for Mors's tank. To jump out was to burn in the sun; to stay inside was to burn in the tank. He was done.

There was a massive explosion. A grenade had been thrown into the rocket's path. It should not have saved Mors, but somehow it did. He heard a high, happy laugh. Patrizia.

The Allies were gaining ground, and Sicily's defenders were struggling. Mors could not see any of the legion. He negotiated the tank around, needing to go to the guardhouse to see why the radio there had stopped. He radioed again and again, but no one answered.

Patrizia screeched something unintelligible, and Mors heard Franca shout at her to fall back, to stop drawing attention to herself. He provided covering fire, but she had taken too big a risk. Two men fell before her rifle, before she fell in her turn.

Mors closed his eyes and took a breath. Inside the tank, inside an illusion of safety, he forced himself clear. The battle was not yet done. There would be time for burial and mourning. There always was.

He felt the bullets coming, the fusillade attacking his tank. His mind began to tick again: he could launch himself out, run, outrun the sun just long enough; he must be near some shade, he must—

"Get out now! We're on your left!" came the beautiful sound of Brigit's distorted voice through a barely working radio.

And the ancient general obeyed the order, launching himself out of the besieged tank and into the path of bullets and sun rays. But there was rescue beside him, and he needed only seconds. He needed only to move between the weapons, to find the empty spaces of safety through which he could slip, up and down and in—into the cab of the armored truck, into Brigit's lap on top of the radio, into the back, where Giulia crouched, both of them rolling sideways as Eamon made a hairpin turn and plunged the truck into retreat.

Giulia kept her arms tight around him. He inhaled her tangy scent, reveled in the heartbeat fluttering against his cheek, the rich warm bounty of her love.

"I love you, I love you, I love you," she whispered again and again, each word coating him, creating a new protective skin, an armor that could never be pierced.

There was a blockhouse under the armory, and there they all took cover to wait for evening. Everyone's words tumbled over one another as they told him what had happened.

"We were hit, but the fire started slowly. We tried to radio, but it fizzled. We were lucky: The smoke gave us cover as we ran for the truck. So good to have those gas masks; could never have managed otherwise; Giulia would have had the world's fastest driving lesson. A good thing we had more flags. Once we found you, we knew we'd get you out all right. No question."

Late in the afternoon, the Allies had a new front line. Everyone knew many of the Axis forces were evacuating, but that could not be helped. What mattered was that there were more of them dead or captured than Allies. That was all they needed.

Evening came at last, horrible evening, darkness in which to search for their dead.

Of the fifty-member legion, fifteen had been killed. It took hours to recover the bodies. Mors and Giulia found Patrizia. He picked her up and held her a long time, now wishing he had made them all retreat once the battle was joined. She should have seen a free Italy. He went to kiss her forehead but thought of how much she would have hated that. Instead, they dug a grave and he slipped a coin into her mouth. He fancied she had just begun to develop a scent.

A few hours before dawn, Mors heard a lone German fighter plane take off from within enemy lines, where the retreat was still under way. Cleland's head spun around to it as well, and Mors, without thinking, seized an improvised rocket launcher. It was a thoroughly pointless shot, far too far away. Mors wished he hadn't sabotaged all the base planes. He had driven a tank; now he wanted to fly. He wished he knew what it was that bothered him about this plane so much.

Franca and Silvia approached him. They were as exhausted as the others but still buoyant.

"Sir, our uncle has a very fast yacht. We were thinking it might be fun to return to Rome that way and prepare to meet the Germans again in our own city."

"That's an excellent idea, ladies. Can you take everyone?"

"It will be a very difficult fit," Silvia ventured.

"We five," he said, indicating the vampires and Giulia, "can drive back and meet you there."

While he helped transfer the weapons and see them off, Cleland,

Brigit, and Eamon paid a quick call to the spot where the British had rounded up the POWs. They didn't bother explaining how they had extricated four Germans from the holding pen without being noticed. For Giulia, they had slipped some bread and sausage from the kitchens before the British got to work on the evening mess.

"Some things are easy, anyway," Brigit observed.

They hunkered down in the armored truck and finally discussed the battle.

"It wasn't quite all I'd hoped," Mors admitted. "One misses rain."

"Partisans might do better remaining a guerrilla force," suggested Giulia, hating to say it out loud. "For a while longer, anyway."

"Perhaps," said Mors. "The Orselli sisters certainly have it under control. I'd lay money it's them who will end up ruling Italy."

"Do you still want to?" Brigit asked, looking hard at him and Giulia. Mors laid his hand on Giulia's belly.

"We have a lot to fight for," he answered.

He knew the other vampires were exchanging glances of frustration and dismay, but he didn't care. True, the fight had not been what he had dreamed of. He had not taken control of the army. But he had blown up tanks full of the enemy. He had commandeered a fighting force. He was by no means done. Berlin should be afraid, waiting for him.

That night, they stole a Nazi officer's car to take them to Messina. They were impressed with their progress—"These German cars are seriously built for speed, aren't they?"—and trusted in the rush of other evacuating Axis forces to cover them as they made their way back to the mainland. They hid in a barn the next day, and the next night found them wending their way back up the coast.

Outside Cosenza, they abandoned the car. It would be safer to take the train now, although they had missed the last one and would have to wait until the following evening. But they had found a lovely summer cottage that stood vacant. They decided to enjoy it.

Mors and Giulia went for a walk. The night was hot and still, the feel of fear heavy. Everyone knew more bombs were coming; they just didn't know when.

"Can you feel it?" Giulia asked Mors, her voice at once apprehensive and elated.

"Specifically?"

"The hatred. The tide is turning. We've begun to win. Mussolini couldn't stop this, and the people are turning against him at last. We're going to win!"

He cupped her face and smiled.

"Yes. We're going to win."

The feeling swelled up in him, and he began to sing. Giulia kept her arms around his neck, listening hard. Mors's music was an amazing thing. It tore through the earth's crust and ripped a hole in the sky. Ancient sounds, sounds of a violent, exciting world that rolled and tumbled through glory and lust and fury like an avalanche.

"I wish I could climb inside your music," she breathed.

They kissed a long time, and Mors closed his mind to everything else. Funny how easy that was to do with Giulia. With her, it was always just them, always just now.

The shot cut through the kiss, sang its own clear song straight through Giulia's lower back and out her abdomen, where Mors, far too late, caught the bullet. Giulia slumped in his arms, gasping and groaning, her blood pouring out all over him. He lowered her to the ground and pressed his hands to the wound, but the blood still came. He could hear the others running to help, as though they could. Then a high, happy laugh whipped through the air, flaying his skin.

"Bye-bye, baby!"

Deirdre. Mors remembered the enemy plane from the night before, the one he and Cleland had wanted to shoot. Now he knew why. He knew who had been on it.

Brigit and Eamon bent over Giulia, while Cleland, his face in full vampiric fury, raked the environs to find Traugott.

Mors slowly raised his head to look at Deirdre. He stood, blinking away a wetness in his eyes that was not tears. It was hotter, more viscous. It seemed to be overtaking him, like a glaze. Only when it dripped into his mouth did he realize he was sweating blood.

Deirdre snickered.

"Oh, dear, have I upset you?"

Mors waved his hand just enough to tell the others to remain where they were. He walked toward Deirdre, feeling the demon expand into every inch of his skin.

"This is very dramatic, but really, Mors, how on earth do you expect it to end?" She gave her shimmering curls a coquettish toss.

Mors jerked loose a stick from an olive tree, never breaking stride.

The revving of the engine startled him: He'd been too focused to sense a car nearby. Cleland's battle cry startled him even more. The car sprang out of the darkness and swerved, smacking Cleland and knocking him over the cliff. Deirdre hopped in, cackling, and the car circled Mors. Traugott was at the wheel, laughing uproariously.

Mors caught the car door and held it. Traugott slammed his foot to the floor, continuing to circle, grinding the car into the soil. The finest in German engineering struggled hard against one of the greatest vampires on earth, and was losing.

Mors dropped the stick so he could jerk Deirdre partially out the window, just enough to grasp her head—which had turned vampiric. Her fangs had grown back, longer and sharper than before. And those damn kaleidoscopes swirled in her eyes, making him feel ill.

"Hold them, Mors! Hold them!" Cleland screamed, running hard.

With more deftness than Mors could have dreamed, Traugott kept a hand on the wheel, pulled out a pistol, and fired, aiming right between Mors's eyes. He dodged, but the bullet hit his cheekbone. That and the nausea of Deirdre's whirling eyes were enough to make Mors release both Deirdre and the car. Another bullet caught Cleland in the neck, making him spin. They drove off, sending a spray of mud into Mors's face.

"*Au revoir, cherie!*" Deirdre trilled. "And by the way, I prefer to be called Apolline!"

"Mors!" Brigit screamed, high and frightened.

Giulia. Giulia!

Brigit and Eamon, their hands covered in the blood they'd tried to stanch with Eamon's torn shirt, backed away. The smell of Giulia's blood made Mors feel even sicker. He closed his eyes so Giulia would not see the devastation in them.

Giulia clutched at him. Her eyes were wide, wild—unseeing and unthinking.

"Mors. Don't . . . don't leave me," she begged in a croak. "Don't let me go on alone."

He clutched her hand, not knowing how to answer.

"Please. Keep me with you. No light without you."

It was the power he had, to turn the coil immortal. To wrap her in a different shroud altogether. To keep her, as he had wanted.

As if in a dream, he laid himself over her, closing his wet eyes and kissing her still warm, lightly pulsing neck, letting the demon do the business of the bite.

But seal it! The dark kiss must be sealed!

He couldn't quite bear for her to drink from him; it just all seemed so hopelessly wrong. But it must be completed. He could not deny her this, nor himself. He sank his fang into his lip and kissed her, letting the blood drip down her throat of its own accord.

She was fighting for breath now, her hand still on his face.

"We'll always be together?" she asked.

"Yes," he promised.

"And . . . and . . ." Her breath stopped and her eyes turned inward.

Mors didn't move, feeling the warmth and movement of the skin dissipate and slow, like an unwinding clock. Her heart had already stopped; now the rest of the organs were mechanically giving way, going still, the blood settling. Mors wondered if the soul slipped out from under her lashes and if it looked back. If so, was it punished, like Lot's wife? Or did it just go flying free, like Ariel released? Then he remembered that Giulia was Jewish, though nonobservant. Would she be like Eamon, with a bit of that soul still inside her?

Brigit and Eamon had left, and he was glad. He briefly buried his hands in his face. That was when he noticed one of Deirdre's silvery hairs caught on his ring. Three years ago, he had taken one of Brigit's blond hairs as a talisman. He found it now, a forgotten charm, and consigned it to the wind. In its place he coiled this poisonous thing. There would be no true rest, no whole pleasure, until all those hairs had turned to dust. He bent to the dirt and began to dig.

Chapter Twenty-five

Calabrian countryside. July 1943.

It gave Mors some harsh pleasure to dig that grave. This time, he was so careful, so grateful to the dirt that was going to act as a womb and thus be forever changed in its turn. He made sure that each scoop was dug out with hope and love.

He folded Giulia's hands over her heart, palms up, ready to dig. He put a coin in her mouth, just in case.

Mors kept his eyes closed as he shoveled the dirt back over her, concentrating only on his love—for her, for the two of them together, for the baby they had lost, for the freedom they would still claim for Italy. A true freedom. He wanted to secure it, but it was not his to govern. He saw what had happened when he'd allowed his passions to blind him.

Only when Mors was done did Cleland return. He put a hand on Mors's shoulder, and they sat, watching the clouds scud over the yellow half-moon.

"They managed to cover their scent, didn't they? Neither of us felt them coming."

"I suppose so." Mors didn't much care anymore.

"I wonder how they knew we left Rome."

A claw gripped Mors's stomach and twisted it, as bits and pieces of realization came to him.

"Patrizia might have sent them word."

Cleland was thunderstruck.

"Patrizia! You can't be serious."

"Deirdre found her once, spoke to her. She might have told her what to do if she ever met a vampire—told her how to contact Traugott. Patrizia wanted to keep Giulia safe from me, wanted that more than she wanted me in the fight. Poor confused kid."

"I can't believe it. You must be mistaken."

"I hope so. It hardly matters. What's done is done. Deirdre has had a very tasty revenge."

They fell quiet, thinking of how long that revenge might be enjoyed till it was returned in kind. Cleland squeezed Mors's shoulder.

"Giulia knew she might be a target, just like Eamon knows. It's not your fault."

Mors did not answer. He was disgusted with himself. He was one of the greatest vampires who had ever lived, and he had failed to recognize a traitor in his bed. He had failed to lay complete waste to the enemy. He had failed to protect the woman he loved.

"Why kill her?" he burst out suddenly. "Capturing her as bait, I understand, but coming back just to kill her and run away again?"

"They might have meant to injure her, and Deirdre's a lousy shot," Cleland mused. "But more likely it's just a show of power. She's well now, and they knew what we'd been doing and wanted to remind us they're still out there, that they can get us at any moment."

"They want to make sure we keep coming after them. As though we wouldn't."

"They want us. Very, very badly."

Mors nodded, wrinkling his nose hard to hold back tears. When he felt stronger, he looked at Cleland.

"Have I done the right thing?"

A question he could not remember ever asking before.

Cleland hesitated a long time. Then he turned and looked at the moon again.

"They showed me a film once. When they thought I might be getting stronger. Young men. Boys. All homosexuals. They took one, stripped him, put a bucket over his head and . . . set dogs on him. He must have been deafened by his own screams. And only because . . . He could not have been more than eighteen. And they laughed, they laughed at me because I wept. Said how much stronger they were than me, a silly poof vampire. I wanted to say that no, I was stronger still. Not because I wanted to kill them all, but because I could weep at inhumanity. They wouldn't have understood."

Mors closed his eyes, letting the demon absorb his hate.

"You haven't answered my question."

"Oh, Mors, who can ever say? This is our world. We do the best we can, like anyone else. But what can we control? We hope. We live. We love. But you can't let them claim Giulia; you can't let them have that victory. They'll dance on a lot of graves before they're done, but we'll find a way to dance, too. We'll continue to help, because we haven't got a choice. After that, well, we'll just have to see what Fate says."

Mors shook his head, unsatisfied.

"Do you know, Cleland, sometimes I hate death."

Cleland squeezed his shoulder again. They sat in silence a long time.

Brigit and Eamon came to fetch them as the sky turned purple. Inside, there was a warm drink waiting, and Mors sucked it down greedily. Only as he was collapsing into sleep did it occur to him that the drink was not blood. It was one of Brigit's ancient herbal concoctions. For sleep, perhaps, or healing. Whichever, it was potent. He remained asleep until the hour before Giulia was due to rise.

He sat beside the grave, arms wrapped around his knees, trying to think nothing, although thoughts would intrude. He pushed aside any that smacked of Deirdre and thought instead about the old way of war and how much he missed it. It was always a horrid business, but it had at least once demanded real skill. Guns allowed you to have distance. Planes more so. And more destruction. There was something so very cold about this new way of war, where you no longer needed to see a face or hear a cry before you killed.

For the first time, he understood why the Greeks had been so meticulous in their mythology. It was much easier to hope humanity was simply a plaything and that the gods ruled the chessboard. Otherwise, life was too maddening to comprehend. And what of vampires? Outside fate and faith and humanity, but subject to all. Perhaps this was one reason for Cleland's love of science. In science, there was still mystery, but also sense. The world writ clear. A light in the darkness.

He touched the grave, deciding it was warm. Love. If it didn't solve everything, it at least helped. It was a start.

The demon jerked back his hand, reminding him how dangerous it was for the maker to give any help in the birth. He must not touch her until she rose.

So he stayed hunched, his limbs folded under him, his brain feverish and heart seeming to twirl as if on an axis, all while she dug. Slow, steady, methodical . . . then faster and faster. The hunger and impatience rose like steam until, at last, the dirt-covered hand he would recognize anywhere burst through, and then the other. He didn't want to watch, but he couldn't blink. As she pulled herself up and out in one fluid movement, shaking the dirt from her tangled hair, he had a vision of Botticelli's Venus and almost wanted to laugh.

Giulia. Or not Giulia. She touched her face, her neck, her belly. She looked at the dirt-encrusted fingernails, then at the churned-up earth.

"Mors?" She blinked, as though not sure it was him.

"Yes."

She sank to her knees next to him.

"What did you . . . What happened?"

He hadn't expected this.

"What do you remember?"

She hesitated, then ripped at her clothes to lay bare her skin. It was perfect, not even a hint of blood remained.

"Oh, oh, no," she whispered, biting her lip.

He seized her hand.

"What is it?" He was suddenly terrified, the sickness returning.

"I . . . oh. I asked you not to let me go on alone. I asked you not to. And you didn't."

"It was the only way," Mors told her, hoping he didn't sound uncertain.

She nodded, not looking at him.

"Yes. Of course. Yes."

There seemed to be an impasse. Her head rose sharply, as though in response to some noise.

"I'm . . . hungry," she told him, her voice tinged with what might have been fear. Mors was at a loss. He knew, however, that these could be hard moments. They all felt better after a meal.

She jumped up with a force that almost knocked him over and marched toward the town, Mors tagging after her. As she walked, she straightened her jacket, tidied her hair, wiped dirt from her face. She might have been preparing for a business meeting.

A lost, drunken German soldier was trying to find his way back to town. He looked at Giulia and sniggered. "Good God, what man would even *take* money to truck with a filthy Eyetie like you?"

Giulia smiled. "At least I'm only filthy on the outside," she informed him before pulling him to her and biting, sucking with a hard ferocity that made Mors's spine tingle.

She dropped the body and turned to Mors, kicking the soldier so that he rolled facedown into the mud.

Mors reached out and wiped droplets of blood off her mouth. She took his hand, holding it tight between hers. The skin had that pleasingly cool feel that marked a vampire, but it was static now. He hoped the molecules remembered him.

"The baby," she said suddenly. "She's gone, too, isn't she?"

"Yes," he admitted.

"And then I . . . Do you still love me?" she demanded.

The truth was that he wasn't entirely sure who she was or what was happening inside her. But the black eyes still sparkled. There was still a world underneath them. The world of the dream she'd had, those many hours inside the earth. A world to explore. A new world. And like all the others, he had to trust it was welcoming, and promising. So he said what he knew he must, and trusted it was the truth.

"Yes," he answered. "I do."

She smiled, that bold, bright smile that made his heart bounce.

"And I love you," she told him. Her voice was strange, uncertain, as though she was surprised it still existed. "I would like to still be Giulia. I don't want to hear another name come out of your mouth."

"I don't want to call you anything else," he said, relief flowing through him.

He kissed her then. She still tasted—very faintly—of his blood.

The others greeted her with polite caution. Mors could see them trying to read her, wondering what sort of vampire she was, what she might become. Questions that could not be asked and would not be answered for a long time.

Planes roared overhead. Heading for Rome. Allied planes. Rome was going to be bombed. The reign of Mussolini was drawing to an end.

We helped. And we are not done yet.

Giulia laughed softly and took Mors's hand. They all went outside to watch the planes' progress, at once wishing they were in Rome and glad they weren't there to see what ancient beauty would fall victim to the ruthlessness of the Allied bombs.

"'*Quamdiu stabit Coliseus, stabit et Roma,*'" Mors said, his face solemn.

"As long as the Colosseum stands, so shall Rome," Brigit repeated. "Yes, and it will."

Through the corner of his eye, Mors thought he saw Giulia stroke and even prod her stomach. Brigit turned to her then, her eyes full of curiosity and concern.

"What?" Giulia snapped at Brigit, making them all jump.

"Are you all right, darling?" Mors asked Giulia.

"Of course I am." Giulia glowed. "I'm with you, aren't I?"

Brigit took Eamon's hand.

"We should press on. We have a great deal of fighting left ahead of us."

"There's work to be done," Eamon agreed.

"Blood to be shed." Cleland's eyes were fixed on the planes.

"Yes," Mors said at last. "We will have to meet the legion and tell them we are going on ahead. We can get help as we go, but for this next battle, we'll have to be our own army."

"We will need to help the humans, too." Eamon had a faraway look in his eyes. He seemed to be seeing something he would rather go blind than witness. "They need us."

Giulia turned to Mors, a sharp accusation in her eye.

"We were going to lead the army, rebuild Italy, and govern it together."

The mad dream. It was time to wake up.

"We will do what we can do," said Mors, stroking her cheek. "But we have to stay in the dark now. It's no good shedding tears about it. The fault is not in our stars, but in ourselves. There are other ways to create light. Now come." He took her hand and nodded to the others. "We've got a ways to go yet."

They followed the long, gray contrails back toward the falling Rome.

Acknowledgments

My fellow history geeks will note that I occasionally take liberties with absolute accuracy in favor of emotional honesty. But I do enjoy employing real actors of the era, where appropriate. I want to take a moment to pay tribute to one such man who appears in this book. Father Bernard Lichtenberg was provost of Saint Hedwig's Cathedral in Berlin and used his pulpit to protest the Nazi treatment of the Jews openly. The Nazis threatened him many times and finally arrested him in 1941. He died in 1942 as they were transporting him to Dachau. The inspiring nature of his bravery is such that I had to include him in this story.

For allowing me to continue playing with history in this mad fashion, thanks go to:

My stellar agent, Margaret O'Connor, who always goes above and beyond and whose energy never flags. I'm proud to call her a friend as well as an agent, and damn lucky to have her for both.

My amazing editor, Hilary Teeman, whose patience and guidance—and consistent belief in me—has been absolutely invaluable.

Two of my dearest friends and "siblings," and brilliant writers themselves, Stephen Smith and Allie Spencer, without whose input, support, and love I could have never started, much less finished this book.

The incomparable Melinda Klayman, my other "sister," can never be thanked enough for anything. Not to say that I won't try.

Detail-goddess extraordinaire Amanda Kirk was above and beyond heroic at a pivotal moment. And the lovely Peri Lyons is always inspiring without even trying.

Massive thanks to all the wonderful people at the Writers Room in New York, most especially to Sarah Canner, Greg Lichtenberg, Karol Nielsen, and Jerry Weinstein, all of whom are fantastic in about twenty different ways.

My lovely family, who are stuck with me, but it seems to be working out all right.

Additional accomplices include: Martin della Valle and Diana "the Enabler" Goodwin, as well as Paul Anderson, Nathan Dunbar, Andrew Furrer, Rob Intile, Mark Jeffrey, Tim Kirkman, Jessica Stuart, Raphael Sutton, and Eric Van Lustbader.

And, of course, William Shakespeare.